W9-AER-489

# SHADOW
## OF THE
# MOUNTAIN

## Also by Sylvia Wilkinson

MOSS ON THE NORTH SIDE

A KILLING FROST

CALE

THE STAINLESS STEEL CARROT:
AN AUTO RACING ODYSSEY

# SHADOW
# OF THE
# MOUNTAIN

a novel by

Sylvia Wilkinson

*Houghton Mifflin Company Boston*

*1977*

This novel was written with the aid of
a Creative Writing Grant from the
National Endowment for the Arts.


The author is grateful to the Society of Authors as the
literary representative of the Estate of Norman Douglas
for permission to reprint from *Some Limericks* by Norman Douglas.

*Library of Congress Cataloging in Publication Data*
Wilkinson, Sylvia, date
Shadow of the mountain.   I.Title.
PZ4.W688Sh  [PS3573.I4426]  813'.5'4    76-57742
ISBN 0-395-25170-2

Printed in the United States of America

C  10 9 8 7 6 5 4 3 2 1

for Shannon

# Part 1

* * *

Alice Faye Hutchins . . .

*I'm wondering who bought that wreath. I ain't paying for it, no siree. Funeral home maybe. I'll owe them a pretty penny before this is done just for the fixing and the box, or somebody will. Cost me three hundred dollars to put Papa under and him specifying in his note to lay him away with no fuss. And Jane mouthing off about how she thought we should give him the finest money could buy. She talked big till it come to doing the buying. That sorry good-for-nothing husband of hers. Never see him again, that much I'd wager my last quarter on. What anybody want to buy a wreath of hothouse flowers and lay them out here to wilt before the service is over and done. Look like a dirty Kleenex, already cold stung.*

*Cold stung her good. What's the sense of it? I caught myself today about to phone her up and ask if she knowed where Papa left that blue cup and saucer that was Grandma's. She's done a lot of things I didn't approve of, but to save my life if somebody said to me last week even, you know Jane is going to kill herself, I'd of told them Jane wouldn't hurt a hair on her pretty head. She was froze hard as a rock and they hold her up there at the coroner's office till she's unfroze so they can do their fixing and send me the bill. I don't want to think about it. Bury her froze up, sitting up for all I care. She makes me so mad. What made her do that? Could feed a family two weeks on what that wreath cost and feed those two she left on me not thinking twice about. I didn't let them put her under in that pink knit suit. Come spring nobody will recollect which one of us wore it before. I don't recall her taking it outa the box but onc't. I'll be in a fix if it ain't paid for neither. I got to git my mind off all this dollars and cent thinking. The Lord turned over the tables of the moneychangers. He's looking in on my thinking.*

Suffer little children . . . *That's all you can say, ain't it, Preacher Paulson. What about them little angels left behind? I ought leave them little angels on your doorstep, Preacher. Let you feel that little girl angel heave a piece of stovewood at your head. There's children and there's children. There is no sech thing as every child being heaven sent. They are what you raise them. And they are the black sin they come out of. That little girl could wear a red suit and carry a pitchfork and not surprise me none. How-de-do, Agnes Anne, so you're really the devil. Alice Hutchins wouldn't bat an eyelash at that. Give you a week, Preacher, them under your feet, and what you have to say about them little angels then? You say it out here over the grave because you can't think of a thing else that might be good about my sister. I don't know how you remember her, it was so long since she darkened the door of your church. Jane Bulock Boey, pu-too-ee. I'm wondering somebody did buy that wreath. Somebody bought it didn't want to stand here and freeze while they put her under. Somebody got more sense than I got. But I'm the only living blood kin she got.*

*Ain't no standing ones. One on the box must come from the funeral home. I'll git it in the bill, you can bet on that. I got to git my thoughts off it. That wind's cutting under my coat like a knife.*

. . . took her life by her own hand. *What's the meaning of that, Preacher? She didn't use her own hand any more than I did. My hand, your hand. She just give up. She couldn't have things like she was wanting them so she give up 'out a thought for the kind of trouble she was wishing on others. The Bible says she goes to hell. You know it too, Preacher Paulson, but you too scared to say it. You had sinners in Bryson City, but they died natural. To hell. The Bible says that the lost shall be cast into the lake of fire. God made the lake for the devil and the devil's angels, and all that serve the devil instead of the Lord Almighty. That's her lost angels. The devil's angels. If the Lord would lead me to that fiery lake and bid me toss them in, I would do His word. I wish*

*the Lord would tell me what to do. Oh, Lord, don't tell me to take
them in.*

*That frozen ground. They picked out that hole in it deep
enough to pass the inspection and I stand here freezing in my
good shoes stiff as a board from the cold and nylon stockings,
might as well be barelegged as for all the cover they offer. Because I got to look proper for no one but a preacher and that girl
and crazy Annie. I said to myself when they buried Papa that
Annie would be crying for the next one I buried like it was her
own. I declare I thought it would be me going before Jane.*

. . . gathered here together. *Three make a gathering. How
come she come? What business is it of hers how we do our burying, standing there in a coat cost more than my car I'd wager,
and wearing pants like a man to a funeral and me standing here
barelegged and freezing. Let that girl have them devil's angels.
She's got money. She bought that wreath. I can betcha she
bought that wreath and never knew* . . . the dearly departed,
*never knew Jane Boey for one second alive. The Lord is watch-
ing my thoughts but I can't hold them back.* I shall not want. *I
wish the buzzards had picked Jane Boey's bones and they had*
. . . He maketh me to lie down . . . *rolled down the mountainside
when the snow melted no one the worse off for it.* He restoreth
my soul. *Her only blood kin. Oh, Lord, tell me what to do with
them. Jane said I could wear her pink suit, any time she wont
wearing it, long as I wore my girdle and didn't git it rump-
sprung. Sometimes she makes me so mad. She just give up. Why
did she do that? Sometimes just as sweet as peaches and cream,
then she was so mean to me. I didn't feel it a sin to not like her
when she was taking what she had no intention of giving back.
Why I got to feel bad to not like her when she's dead? I'd rather
not know my sister is in that little short box* . . .

\* \* \*

I had settled in the bushes like a flea in the hair of a dog. I
looked up at the sky over Mount Le Conte, ice blue with clouds
moving so quickly they made me dizzy. My hair threaded out of
the single braid over my shoulder, tickling my face along with
the mucus that rolled onto my lips until I rubbed my face on my
sleeve. I could almost hear my mother's voice saying, Use your

handkerchief, Jean, and see her go through her purse until she found a Kleenex without a lipstick blot to slip to me. It had been a number of years since she tried to tell me anything — I was a college senior — but she still picked lint off my clothes and jabbed at my hair until I shook her off.

The wind rattled the myrtle bushes around me, but the cold did not blow through my clothes; it only seeped in slowly through spaces in my coat zipper, stabbing through the holes the needle had made seaming my jeans. The time was ever-green in the Appalachians, black-green above the hardwood timberline, as barren as the Smokies ever are. The hardwoods were stripped to spears, the balsam fir were slanted and broken, covered with the green wool of a blight. All of the trees leaned in the direction of the wind. There was little else that could be seen living there even in summer, a few bees in the myrtle bushes and moths floating like feathers and windseeds, eaten by small birds, rare as the bugs they ate. When a bird moved through the bushes in that silence, its noises were shocking, bear-sized.

The rock on the trail up was slick with black ice, its bulk bending and dumping down the mountainside like a frozen waterfall. One misstep, and I would have bounced and fallen until there was nothing left of me to hit the bottom, like a slate rock I had rolled over the side, hitting and being spit off into space until it disintegrated and showered on the trees below. A legend says that a soldier on horseback running from the Yankees rode over these cliffs and was lowered to safety at the bottom by the vines in the trees.

A hawk moved out over the valley. It spread out flat, drifting, holding the wind under its wings in the vacant space. Then it moved up and down over the treetops, as if the ground were lifting it with puffs of steam. A lazy bird using the air to propel it. A crow panted and flapped near the cliff edges, dropping often and rocking on its big feet. When the hawk turned, the sun flashed off its feathers; the shadow of its form on the rocks was like an airplane, like two hawks in formation. The bird continued to drift across the valley, the eyes I couldn't see looking down for the slightest movement of a small creature in the grass. Then it would dive, scooping the prey up and snapping the tiny bones in its hooked claws. I wished it would dive near me so I could see the angular detail of its head and wings, the colors in its feathers. If it came close, for a moment I would feel fear. If there had been someone to speak to, I don't think I could have made a sound. As I watched the bird I felt weighted, trapped. It made me jealous as I never am of people.

I got up and continued on up the mountain, the climb much steeper to the top. As I lifted my pack across my shoulders, the wind seemed to stop until the path curved and a blast hit my face. It was getting colder, so cold that even constant motion didn't keep me as warm as I liked to be. But I didn't want to put on long johns because they made walking up the steep sides much harder when they pulled tight around my knees and made me sweat in the joints. I told myself they would feel good to slip into when I stopped at the top.

When I finally reached the open-front shelter on top, I started to prepare for dinner without resting. I didn't want to stop moving. I took the path to the spring. The water there ran blue-clear over the ice into my plastic jug, freezing in strange shapes as it splashed down the hillside. On my way back to the shelter the water started to freeze and pieces of ice rattled inside the jug. The jug was almost a solid lump of ice as I forced a trickle into my drinking cup back at the shelter. I held the jug near my Primus stove until the water melted enough to cook with. Just like blood in the veins, it has to keep moving. After supper I washed my cook set with a soap pad in the last of my heated water and packed away my stove. Before it got dark, I spread out my insulated mattress to keep the ground cold from seeping into my sleeping bag.

The sun was starting to set, so I took my flashlight and began the short walk to the point where I would watch. Small trees hugged the mountain top, twisted down by the wind. To the touch they were stiff and unlifelike; not bending but bobbing. The path would be very dark on the way back. I pulled on my gloves when I stopped moving and sat on a rock on the edge of the cliff. The cold soon seeped through the seat of my pants. The winter red was spreading like a liquid across the hills. The evergreen shadows stretched to points as the sun dropped. The hawk was gone.

It moved rapidly, the sunset, catching the bottoms of every cloud and reaching to the end of the valley. I watched the orange circle until it halved. Soon only a sliver was there, but the sky around grew brighter, swollen with color. Then the moment, full red as the sun, vanished. The round form stayed in my eyes a second longer and bounced on the mountain top. It dissolved. It was black now and cold and silent.

I moved back to the shelter carefully, flashing the light on the rocks, looking for the ice shine. A strange orange-yellow flat moss clung to the winter rocks. I glanced down another trail.

Someone was there, a person sitting on a rock, still looking out at the sunset that was gone. I hadn't noticed another campsite. I walked towards the figure, clearing my throat and scraping my boots so whoever it was would not be startled when I walked up behind. It would be easy to fall out there. The figure did not move.

"Hello," I called. "If you need any help walking back to the shelter, I have a flashlight. I saw your car at the trail entrance and figured I wasn't the only crazy person hiking today. When the sun sets, the light really goes fast, doesn't it?" Still no movement. I could see now that it was a girl. She had long black hair and she sat at a slight tilt. I put the circle of my light on the girl's back; she wore only a light jacket. As I walked closer, my body started to shake. I couldn't control it, the shaking. A question. I had asked the figure a question and could still hear my own voice breaking the silence. I could hardly walk now on the uneven rocks; the ground seemed to bulge and heave beneath my thick soles. The cold air went in my lungs and hurt as if they were being beaten by something strong and flapping. Inside I was wet and broken, but the outside was too cold for me to cry and my eyes ached and wouldn't shut. In the thin light of the new moon I could see the color of the blue hand. Looking out where the sun had set, frozen with one knee slightly bent, holding up a blue, ringless hand, a dead girl.

\*   \*   \*

The girl with the blue hand . . .

*She walked the path to Le Conte in the fall when the leaves were turning, the hardwoods a pattern of orange and yellow and* red with dashes of purple. That is a favorite hiker spot, and in the fall people make reservations weeks ahead of time to stay in the lodge on the mountain. No.

She watched the sunset and never left, and no one watched it with her. She must have come recently. Someone else would have found her. She must have come in winter, this month, January, or she would have been found. Only a few days. She was wearing only a thin jacket when she started up the trail; she was dressed like the tourist hikers who come to see the leaves in the fall. The tourist hikers who leave before the sun sets and the temperature drops to go in the lodge to the fireplace. Could she have thought the lodge would be open? No. She knew it was boarded up. It is winter and deserted. She planned to die there. This is the story I tell myself. This is the story I have written here in my journal. This is the only way the story could be. And I found her.

The temperature on Le Conte was not above freezing for over a week. I know. I had checked before I left. She had been hard for days and the sun did not thaw her. Like something in the freezer. I wonder if the sun could have made her warm to the touch, softened her. Why did I have to be the one? What chance was there of finding her? Almost none this winter. Except that she went where everyone goes to watch the sunset. By spring almost anyone could have found her, even a tourist hiker. By spring she would have thawed and rotted and the buzzards would have come.

I wonder if the hawk saw her.

I've thought of it over and over, hearing me say: "Hello. The light goes really fast, doesn't it?" and she sat there like stone, ignoring me, as if some power within her kept her from turning around to speak to me.

I knew they would find out that she had been "despondent." They always say that. Almost anybody could be called despondent. Especially if they are soon dead. She worked a lot harder than most people would to die the way she did. Not a lazy, simple death to have to climb the face of a mountain before you are ready.

I've put it together now, talking to myself on this page. The girl with the blue hand took a long walk alone. Like me. She went up to the top of Le Conte. Like me. It was a stiff climb if she wasn't used to hiking, over five miles. I think she had on sneakers. The cold from the rocks would have come through canvas sneakers like paper. Her feet must have hurt from stone bruises. She went to the edge so she could look at the sunset. Maybe she had planned to jump. But instead she watched the red spread across the valley in front of her, the evergreens point, the same things I saw. The sun circle probably bobbed in her eyes; that's what bright light does to everybody's eyes. She may have been crying so the light had fuzzy edges. That was the last her eyes saw except for the stars if the night she died was clear. She might have lived a while into the night, but it would only have taken a part of one night to kill her; I don't know how many hours, but I don't think she saw the morning. The Le Conte morning is almost as famous as its sunset, the gold cutting the fog. It's a horizontal view, a flash of light inside a tunnel. I didn't go and see the morning come either, though I had planned to.

She sat and let the darkness completely surround her. She had no plans for a campsite. She made sure she had no choice. Once the sunset started she was committed to die. She let the night and cold come and take her, turn her blood to stone. Did she feel it turn her insides like my plastic water jug full of water, or is it that quick for blood that is warmed by organs like oil in a machine? When people quit fighting, does the cold make them like everything else, water, trees, rocks, does the weather do with them what it will? I wonder if at the last she thought of why she was dying or if she just wanted her mind to stay on the red sunset and to never go on anything else again. She watched the colors and changes and movement of the world. I wonder how long your mind stays alive when you are freezing. Does it turn to red stone like frozen hamburger?

\*   \*   \*

I lay in my bag awake all night listening to the wind, wondering if it would blow the frozen girl off the cliff so I would never be able to say I saw her. I thought of being back home, of slipping between the clean sheets of my own bed. I could have been there, or in a motel or the dorm if I hadn't taken that hike. Doing the same thing she did put me there with her. I almost never had been able to stay awake, even when I wanted to on Christmas Eve or high school graduation night, but that night my mind faded just a few times into half-awake, half-asleep dreams. I saw morning come slowly, only my face feeling the cold snap at dawn before the weak light started to spread.

But she was there in the morning; she hadn't blown off any more than the boulders around her had. I walked back to the place, not direct, but around old campsites and the deserted lodge so that my body would be warm when I saw her and I would be able to control the shaking. Maybe I was looking for someone to go with me. When I had first gotten up, I had been so shaky from the cold I had a vision of falling off the cliffside when I saw her. I took short steps.

Then I saw her shoulder. She *was* a person and I was not crazy. I went close enough to be absolutely certain. In a half dream I had seen bugs walking on her, a string of ants marching up her arm. But there were none. In the dream I had seen her bare arm like porcelain, but awake I saw she was just as she had been the night before, dressed in her light jacket. Her jacket was pale yellow; I hadn't known that the night before. She was there in her realness, a human form so recognizable that I wondered how I could ever have thought I was imagining. But I'd never seen death before. I saw a Band-Aid on her index finger. It was starting to come off and it moved a little too, lifting and settling, and her clothes trembled.

I left and got my things into my pack and went down the mountain as fast as I could without falling. It was so steep I was glad I hadn't given in to my impulse to get out the night before. Why do we run to tell people that someone is dead? I was going to warn other hikers, but there were none. I drove to the ranger station and told the forest ranger. He asked me why I had been up there in the winter. He didn't believe me, but they went after her. Maybe a law says they have to. I remember reading that an anonymous phone call caused the police to dig up a whole acre looking for a body that hadn't been there. I'm sorry I had to tell, but for my own sanity I had to; she must have thought she would be missing a long time before she was found. I always won the prize on Easter egg hunts; I'm a good finder.

\* \* \*

Half sisters . . .

*Alice Faye Hutchins is a different-looking woman from Jane Boey, although they were half sisters. She is heavy boned and rangy, and Jane was small but filled out on her light frame. I phoned Alice Faye from school and found that she had made the funeral arrangements. She seemed surprised that I would drive up to attend the funeral of someone I didn't know. Maybe that is strange, but I know I wouldn't miss it. Jane Boey is as much a part of my life now as a friend would be.*

\* \* \*

When I got to Bryson City, I asked Alice Faye about the car that Jane had borrowed the day she disappeared.

"I thought sure as you're standing there she stole it, if you want to know the truth," she told me. "Her mama, who was my daddy's second wife, used to act like Jane wasn't sorry, but I knowed how they talked about her in school." Alice Faye looked too old to have been in school with Jane. "They say she jumped off a radiator for an hour trying to miscarry with Agnes Anne. That's a mean little girl too. I was right irritated, I can tell you, when Jane took off acting like she was coming right on back and left me with these younguns and not even a change of clothes for them. She knows I never took to Agnes Anne. I never expected Jane, mind you, to offer me a penny for keeping them. She'd act like they wont worth keeping, like she was going to go off and leave them to fend for theirselves, knowing just as good that ever' time good old Alice Faye would give in and keep them. She'd pick fun at me then git sweet as sugar when she was wanting a good turn.

"I called up the sheriff and told him to pick her up if he saw her gallivanting around in my automobile. Was three days 'fore I knowed what happened to her or my Chevy, and they asked me to come down and tell them if the coroner had her. I never suspicioned for a second she might be dead. I didn't like doing that one bit, her feet sticking up under that cloth like they was made of wood. I couldn't hardly look at her. I didn't know she was crazy in the head too. I swear I didn't, but I guess that's the way them crazy people are, can't nobody tell it till they go hurt somebody or something. Lady come here inquiring 'bout the children and told me that she could just as easy have killed them babies, that's the kind of head sickness you have if you kill yourself. I don't know which is the worse, I tell you the truth. Them children dead with her in prison or her dead and not a soul wanting neither one of them. Maybe the baby, but the devil hisself wouldn't have the little girl. I got my own family and it's all we can do to make ends meet. I ain't got it in me to love them like my own. I'd be a liar to say I could. I'm not putting Jane's children on my Ed. He works like a dog now."

She wrinkled her face and looked at me from the green couch in her living room. "Who you think ought to take them children? What you know 'bout things like this?"

I don't know why she thought I should know anything. All I did was find out her name from the newspaper article on the suicide. I asked her if Jane had any other close relatives, a living parent, or a sister or brother, trying to be helpful. There were none. I said they would have to go to an orphanage if the father couldn't be located or wasn't a fit father.

"A fit father! He wont a fit father, all right," she snapped. "He wont fit to live if you ask me. How she got messed up with him. I for one didn't even think he was good-looking, but the girls back at school did, so that meant Jane had to have him. I don't think she had no intention of gitting caught having to marry him. She just wanted to go around latched on his arm for a while so people would look at her and be jealous, that's the way she would of thought. Made fun of my Ed when I married him, but he ain't ever left me for a day I didn't know where he was at. Jane should have quit that man 'fore she got farther than hanging on his arm. You can just kick a grown man out on the street and say good riddance. But them little children. A week-old puppy'd last longer than them little human babies.

Poor little babies. She's gone for good. I got to git it through my head that she's gone and ain't coming back."

I don't think there is any chance that they'll find Jane's husband since she was buried today and he didn't come. Only three people were there. The only flowers were on top of the casket. Alice Faye didn't cry, but the third person, an old lady, did. I wanted to talk to her and find out if she was a relative, but Alice Faye told me later she was a crazy woman who went to every funeral in Bryson City. "Crazy Annie Davis. She used to have enough sense to teach school. Taught us both in the fourth grade. Only looks like I end up with a sister who was crazier and it didn't show as good. Didn't show at all, if you ask me. I thought she was crazy like a fox. Musta got it from her mama. Never enter my mind to do sech a thing over that sorry husband and owing a bunch of bills. There's more husbands to be had and money for them half willing to earn it. But she wouldn't lift a finger to do the nearest nothing. I seen the day she stood there and let me wash up her dishes because I was tired of looking at them." Alice Faye looked down and shook her head. "I shouldn't be talking ill about the dead not here to defend theirselves." With that she stopped talking about Jane.

I couldn't spend any longer in Bryson City because I had already cut two days of classes. Also it looked like snow, so I wanted to get out of the mountains before dark. Alice Faye asked me about my finding Jane. "What in the world you doing atop Le Conte in the wintertime? I know they go up in the fall to see the leaves turn or some sech." I told her I was a hiker, that it was an endurance test. "You see what can happen to you now," she said, waving her finger at me. "You see how Jane endured. You learnt a lesson to stay outa them mountains when you ain't got no business there. What a girl want to go tromping up there for when you got money enough to take you down to Hawaii or Florida where it's warm. I had the money, that's where I'd be. You git older, you see. How old are you?"

We both sat silent when we found we were the same age: twenty-two.

I couldn't talk anymore. I looked at her. I must have stared because she looked away at the children whom she had been ignoring. Jane's children were playing with Alice Faye's in a side room. Jane's seemed different, more glum and distracted. I saw the little Boey girl, Agnes Anne, intentionally hit Alice Faye's boy with a toy truck. I didn't think they were long for that house. I didn't know what they had told the little girl. She did cry for her mother when Alice Faye slapped her. I was even more uneasy when Alice Faye asked me again what I thought should be done with them. Two women came to visit so I got up to leave.

Alice Faye wouldn't have flinched if I had driven off with the children in my car. In fact she would have breathed a sigh of relief. Her boy took the truck weapon away and sat on it. That made Agnes Anne start to cry and say she wanted her mother again. No one got up to comfort her. My mother would never have left me like that. But I don't know if it would have been for me or for herself. When our dog was hit by a car, she turned her back and cried while my father gathered him up. I held him on the way to the vet's and talked to him because I thought if I could keep his attention he wouldn't think of dying. She paid the vet to keep him long after he was able to come home because she wanted him perfect before she saw him. My father said she was tenderhearted. Maybe I was scared to comfort that little girl because she might respond and want to go with me. I was already closer to the whole thing than I should have been. I found it hard to see anything that no one loved. I even ate the refreshments at a party that weren't good because I knew no one else would. But those people were strangers. I had never been in a home that had pictures like a motel, cardboard landscapes with fake paint grooves. I wanted to get out.

When I was out the door, I saw that Agnes Anne had come outside alone. She was molding dirt mounds with a teacup beside the walk. She dug at the frozen dirt with a piece of wood until she broke away enough to fill a cup. She was angry with the hard ground. I passed her as if she were a deaf child. Her coat was much too large and covered her body like a tent when she squatted. She would be adopted or taken care of by the state. It would probably be no worse for her and the baby without Jane than it was with her. They had time ahead to make their own lives.

\* \* \*

James Talbert Boey . . .

*What did he look like? I am trying to make him real, see the color of his hair, his height. I thought he would be there by the grave and I would see the grief of a man who let something slip away through his carelessness. He would pick up a newspaper in a cafe in Asheville.* Suicide by freezing, Jane Bulock Boey, 19, a Bryson City housewife and mother . . . Neighbors of Mrs. Boey said she had appeared despondent for several weeks because of mounting debts and an apparent separation from her husband, James Talbert Boey, an unemployed construction worker. *James Talbert. Jim. Jimmy. J. T. Alice Faye never said what they called him. There were no pictures of him in the house, and no pictures to show the painful comparison of the half sisters, side by side.*

*J. T. would wring his hands, slam his fist on the wall in the men's room. He would be ashamed to tell the bartender who he was. He would wonder if the law was looking for him. Could they get him? Non-support, desertion? I am starting to be able to hear his voice. Jane would understand if she were there for him to explain. He intended to get work and send a check home. Now he had lost her for good. He would catch a bus home to see his children; in the face of the little girl he would see her like a fresh start. Agnes Anne would stare at him like he was a stranger. Jane thought she had him trapped now. She must have been nuts to go up there and let herself freeze.*

*J. T. would tiptoe out in the night, leave a note to good old Alice Faye and ten dollars. They would go to the orphanage and he would start again, this time to have a few good times, a woman to laugh with who liked a lot of sex, a woman who didn't just act like she knew what she was doing. He wouldn't think of the warm body he had gotten pregnant in his Chevy* credited to prolonged exposure to temperatures below freezing . . . as low as 17 degrees below zero with a chill factor of 30 below.

*J. T.'s voice has gone from my mind. What did Jane think would be done with the children when she was sitting on that mountainside before it got too cold to think? Alice Faye would look after them. Even if they had to go to another home. It would be better than she could give them, right? No need to worry. They wouldn't be alone. This is America. America takes care of little children. It just doesn't take care of Jane Boey. Only if she cooks and washes and gets a welfare check and goes to a lawyer for child support. Jane knew about welfare and child support. She didn't know about goose-down sleeping bags that cost a hundred dollars, or Vibram soles to keep her from slipping on mountain trails. America doesn't take care of her if she climbs up on a mountain. And that is what she wanted, to go so far up that America couldn't take care of her. And she could die. I don't think she thought about the body she left on the mountain if she died. She died and took it with her. She didn't think that Alice Faye would have to arrange for the burying. Maybe it's because two different people can't know each other.*

*Hello. What is your name?*
*Jane Boey.*
*Do you come here often?*
*No. I've never been before.*
*Did you see the hawk that went over the valley earlier?*
*No. I don't think so.*
*Most people would think we were crazy for being up here, especially this time of the year. The views are better now than in the summer when there is so much fog. There are times when there are more tourists up here than trees. The suburban set from Asheville comes up so they can talk all year at cocktail parties about their day mountain climbing. The women complain the whole way about being hot and having sore feet and about their husbands walking too fast and not caring whether they get left behind and eaten up by bears or not. Then comes the cocktail party and they just talk about the colors of the leaves, how breathtaking the sunset was. Really rubbing it in to the ones who stayed home around the pool. .*
*I don't know about the suburban set. I'm from Bryson City and I didn't graduate from high school. I had to git married and didn't mean to have Jimmy Ray either.*
*Well, don't feel bad. I don't know anything about people who*

aren't the suburban set. I've been trying to figure out lately about my life too, you know what I mean, my parents, my background. My grandfather was so rich they called him a philanthropist. That means he had enough money to give it away. But no one else in my family would know the first thing about surviving up here.

I don't remember my parents. They're dead. My sister is all I got.

I like the out-of-doors myself, doing things that are hard. I'm a graduate of a wilderness training school in Colorado. Sometimes I even do things that are ridiculous. It's hard to take a horse over a hedge so I did it sitting backwards. I was wondering why you came up here.

I came up here to die where I wouldn't have to explain it to anybody.

How? Are you going to jump off?

No. I'm going to starve to death.

I have food that you can have. I always carry extra.

I won't take it. You can't make me eat it. Besides I will probably freeze to death before I starve.

I have a sleeping bag and we can build a fire in the shelter. All isn't lost yet.

I won't go in there. You can't force me.

I can go down below and tell people what you are going to do.

You can't git to the bottom before dark, not without taking a chance of falling and gitting killed. And you didn't come up here to die. What I'm doing is none of your business. You have no right to even be asking me questions. You know nothing at all about what it's like to be me. You're a smart-ass rich kid.

But I'm going to learn. You're the first mountain woman I've ever met. I finish college this spring and I'm going to try to get a job working with mountain people.

And what do you know about mountain people? What did your fancy school teach you?

I'll give classes. And I'll get local experts to teach trade seminars. People will find new hobbies, things to do on cold winter nights that will bring them extra money. Maybe we'll have a lecture on birth control so women won't have more babies than they can afford. We'll have some classes just for fun — landscaping

*your yard, or maybe a powder puff mechanics course for the
girls. Or one on problems of marriage and let men and women
express their views. We'll work together . . .*

*Jane Boey is laughing at me. A mean, ugly laugh. No, maybe
she is smiling faintly, but she doesn't move. Maybe she is smiling at something that happened earlier. The hawk that flew over
the valley. Maybe she remembered it.*
*What is a hawk, Jane Boey?*
*A hawk is a nasty bird that eats chickens.*

Matilda . . .
*You was mine, I'd wup you with a stick. I'd break me a switch
and sting them skinny little legs good. Then I say, Tildie, the
devil will have you for it. That child just sit there good as gold
and you wanting to take a stick to her. The only Fitzgerald with
the name and likely to stay that way, because I'm betting Miss
Evadell won't be having another. Girl don't keep a name for long
and that's the end of it. Frowning at me as much like that old
woman as ever a child was. What you got to frown about? Never
gon have to lift a finger to do for yourself. I ain't able to hep myself. That look didn't come out in your daddy. I look at that little
Jean and see that old woman's hateful look, scrunched up in
that little face. Do this, do that, Matilda, and me so tired, Lord.*
*Change is a-coming, but Tildie won't live to see it. That old
woman Fitzgerald think she gon live till the end of time and she
might do it to spite me. They had her dead twice before when she
decided agin it. Move over and let the younguns in. Tildie'll
move over when her time come, Lord. You just tell her when it's
her time to meet you up yonder.*
*Old woman mess in her britches and too proper to tell me,
then go and make a bigger mess trying to clean herself up. My
poor old mama so swole up in the joints she can hardly get
about, but she makes it to the commode, Mrs. Fitzgerald. What
your high society friends know about that? Tildie know. Tildie
know. Tildie know she don't love that little white girl one half as
much as that sorry dog using up half the heat come off that
stove . . .*

\*

Matilda's house . . .

*When I was little, I never saw the colored people in my town,
just Matilda and Juleous and Raymond and the maids. Except
on Sunday mornings when we drove towards town to church.
We passed the unpainted houses in rows behind the market.
Their dogs trotted in the streets, covered with soot from the rows
of chimneys. Matilda's sister burned herself throwing gasoline
on her fire in the winter I first went to kindergarten. I never
knew her. Her three children sat in Matilda's dressing room for
a week after she died, but Matilda wouldn't let them play with
me.*

*On Sunday mornings I saw the colored people pretend they
weren't poor. But only in summer. In winter their houses were
wet brown like a piece of wood floating in the ocean; the city sky
had no color. Their streets were as colorless as the pine-straw-
covered ground in the woods. I would have thought no one lived
there except for the smoke spiraling from the sides and roofs.
The market on the corner had its contents advertised on the
windows in white shoe polish, prices for meat and fish. I saw the
word "lard" beside a price and thought that was the word
Matilda whispered to herself. If they wanted to, the colored
people could talk so I didn't understand them.*

*When summer came, the shoe polish in the window told of
vegetables, green ones. Collards, turnip greens, and cabbage.
The door to the market would stand open yet it looked as dark
inside as a cave. With the names of green vegetables in shoe
polish came the smells that curled around the dirt streets, the
pots that were cooking for Sunday dinner. I remember my
grandfather's anger when Matilda, who was my grandmother's
main cook, cooked the green leaves in his kitchen. I had sat on
the sink and helped her wash the grit off the leaves. The stiff
leaves shrank up into a limp mass of green slime as they cooked,
letting the smell into Grandfather's house that I remembered
from driving down the streets in colored town. That was the only
time I ever heard him call Matilda a nigger.*

*I had learned about the green smell from inside the houses.
All the green smells in our neighborhood came from outside,
from cutting or watering the lawn, from the boxwoods, or when*

Raymond chopped back the grass that crept out onto the brick walk.

In summer the yards in colored town sprang up with calla lilies, leather-leaved and gaudy with sunflower heads between them, swelling and falling over to look at the ground. I was always surprised that the giant flowers could rise out of that hard beaten earth around the houses, swept and white earth, pounded hard by children running. I planted sunflower seeds that grew so stunted I believed they only grew right for colored people. Matilda said she just threw a handful of seeds out the door, but I didn't believe her. She thought the ivy in Grandfather's yard and on the house was "snaky." She liked a yard she could sweep.

In full summer the plastic came off the windows and hung like broken spider webs. Honeysuckle started to climb up the wood, clinging to splinters, peeking in and through cracks until it pressed inside those houses. I wanted to look in, slide through the crack on the vine. Matilda didn't want me inside where she had to live, but I went in once in the winter when she didn't want to leave me in the car in the cold. She was scared to leave the car running because it might be stolen.

Her house was as hot as the barns during the tobacco curing at the country place. All that heat came from one fat stove in the center of the house. An old woman sat closer to it than I could have stood. I thought she must be crazy but I saw an old dog as close as she was. When she opened the door and threw in a piece of wood, the heat blast hit my face. There were calendar pictures on the wall with dates on them long before I was born, but Matilda didn't take them down, because she liked the pictures, I guessed. Or maybe she put them up after people threw them away. There were dolls sitting around, those like you win at the fair, stamped out of plaster with their eyes and clothes painted on out of the lines. I thought of how the funny papers sometimes had the color put on out of the lines like that. I always tried very hard to stay in the lines in my coloring books. I tore the pages out if I slipped. I didn't like those dolls at all.

The furniture was covered with different pieces of cloth. I lifted one of the cloths while Matilda was in the back room and there was a hole underneath. The old woman clucked at me *when I did that. Matilda cleaned our furniture, but I figured she didn't learn how at home. When I went outside, I shivered until I got in the car because her hot house had made me wet all over.*

*The next Sunday, I saw Matilda on the steps of her Baptist church. I told my parents I saw her, but they didn't think I did. She had on an organdy dress, bright pink, that was starched and stood out away from her hips and she had on the hat I saw her take out of the bag and try on at Grandfather's. She tried it on with tissue paper on top of her head and I asked her why and she said it was to keep her hair grease off of it. The hat was like lace, only stiff, and it sat on her head like a cloud. She showed me the ear bobs she got to go with it and they were two tiny hats made of plastic lace that stuck against the side of her face like starfish. I put them on my ears but they pinched. They pinched her too, so she left them open on the table in her dressing room until Easter Sunday to ease up the springs on the clips. On Sunday morning Matilda looked like the others, Easter Sunday when they were all pastels with their bodies so black they were like flowers on a wet peach tree. That was the first time I thought of Matilda as another person from the cook whose clothes were so pressed and starched I could peel apart the folds in her skirt. I never saw her look happy at Grandfather Fitzgerald's like she did on the church steps that morning. Matilda would never answer my questions about her life and I started not liking her. It wasn't like she was telling me nothing; it was like she was lying to me. She slept in that house with that old woman, that dark, hot house she would never take me to again, and she went up the steps to the giant Baptist church and didn't take me with her.*

Evadell Fitzgerald . . .

*They had someone bring them up in a big fancy undertaker's car, so you know they were put up to it and didn't come up with the idea on their own. They've got their own churches and you know as good as you're sitting there, Emerson, they never would have even thought of it if someone didn't put the idea in their heads. Like a child up to meanness you know has been suggested to him. They're as clean as a Pine Hill maid on Monday morning, you can be sure of that. They told them to be clean because they had other things on their minds coming here than stirring up what people might say about that. They came here just because the law says they can and I hate that business worse than anybody, Emerson. You know it wouldn't have mattered if anybody was the better off for it, but not a person in the world is. I heard someone talking at the club about how history says that even getting out of being slaves didn't do anything but make things worse for them. It just seems to me that they were made by the Lord to have other people look after the important things for them. They don't know the first thing about money, and give them a car or a washing machine and it falls to pieces as soon as they touch it. They want all the things white people have without working for them and there is no way under the sun you can give people something and expect them to have respect for it . . .*

* * *

Our church was just up the street from Matilda's. My parents would drop me at Sunday school. After it was over, I would cross the street and spend the church hour reading comic books in the hotel. The hotel put up a sign that said, "This is not a library. Buy don't read," but I always planned to buy at least one comic, so the guy was nice to me. I would go in his restroom and stick it in the front of my underpants so I could get it home. That's how much my mother gave me for the collection, a dime, and the man there never charged me any tax. I just wanted to read them all to see which one I wanted. One Sunday — I was nine years old — something unusual happened.

That Sunday the shoeshine boys from the hotel kept hanging around the door. They stretched their necks, acting like they were trying to see the door to our church. Suddenly one of the shoeshine boys pointed and said, "Hey, man, there they go!"

Another of them got so excited he was jiving around and popping his rag. Through the crack in the shade on the front window I could see what he meant. Dressed in fluffy organdy dresses and big hats like Matilda's, they were going up the front steps of our church, three black women in their Easter outfits. I thought it was strange for black women to dress that way around white people. There was only one lady in our church who dressed like a colored person, Mrs. Heatherton, but she was crazy. She painted her lipstick off her mouth halfway up under her nose and she never got her eyebrows to match and one Sunday her earrings didn't match.

The shoeshine boys were all dancing now, like watching those three black women march up the steps was giving them their drumbeat. I bought a *Little Lulu* quickly and headed back across the street to the Sunday school room. The other kids were still on the stale graham crackers and canned orange juice so I was there early enough to march into the service. We didn't have to sit through the sermon because somebody always farted or started giving Indian burns, but they let the little kids go hear the singing in the first part. I hid my *Little Lulu* behind the crayon cabinet before we left to march in. I had to walk holding hands with this boy who was picking his nose with the other hand. As soon as the teacher quit watching, I threw his hand down and he started rooting in his nose with that one too. I felt like saying, "Use your handkerchief, dear" ; my mother must have taught me that in the crib. I changed my place in line until I was sure to get to sit on the end. I wanted to be able to look backwards around the edge to see where the colored women were sitting. They were in the back, all three of them, and I saw that one had her white patent leather pocketbook in her lap. She sat just like the maids who sat on the green benches in the garden. We used to play like we were falling down in the grass to see if we could see up their skirts where they had their legs apart. It was dark up there under their skirts, but I remember seeing that they rolled their stockings at the knee with garters. I knew white women usually put their garters above the knee unless they were real old and wore their skirts so long they figured you wouldn't notice. My grandmother wore hers below the knee, except on Sunday. Then she got so senile she didn't know or care anymore.

Later at Sunday dinner my mother was really upset. The only time we were all together was at the dinner table on Sunday and there was always so much fussing then that I learned to eat fast so I could be excused.

"What in the world is this coming-to-church business? If they ride the buses and need more places to sit down because there are more of them on the bus, I can see that, but what is this coming to church? They've got their own church and they were perfectly happy getting dressed up on Sunday morning and going to it until somebody put it in their heads to do differently. Sitting there in the back like they belong there and bringing those fans. Now isn't that niggerish? Sitting there swishing back and forth those fans they got at the funeral home when it isn't that hot in our church. It has central air conditioning, you know. I suppose it might be hot if you were fat as a hog. Just wait and see if they pick up a hymn book and start singing. We don't carry on with our singing like they do, and there is a time and place for every kind of behavior."

My father let her go on like a wind-up toy that would soon run down. It was hard to tell if he heard anything she said. Her father had been a get-rich-quicker, not old money like my father's family, and I often saw him wince at her mannerisms.

"Did you see Minnie Heatherton? She prissed right up to them after the sermon and welcomed them to the church, just like the old fool hadn't noticed they were black as tar, and invited them to join the church. I think they had better take away her right to do that and just go ahead and admit she is senile before she gets the church in more trouble than they know what to do with. A younger person ought to have that hostess job anyway. It gives the church a bad name.

"If I was the minister, I would just close up the book and say that there will be no service today, and I bet everybody in the sanctuary would be as proud as could be of him and not a soul would hold it against him. And then they could go home and be forced to tell people they didn't get to hear a sermon in a white people's church. But that is what they want, isn't it? They just want to stir things up and it is best not to let them know you even notice them. Just ignore them like they aren't even there."

My father finally spoke. "You're right, Eva. All you have to do is ignore them," he said. "They aren't going to keep that business up if no one pays any attention to them. They'll tire of it. The worst thing you can do is get upset and let it show. They've got it all planned. Don't you think they just happened to come to our church. I'm willing to bet they dropped niggers off at every church in town."

"Emerson, don't talk like that in front of the child."

I'll always remember that shoeshine boy saying, "Hey, man, there they go!" I think it was like a time bomb and they all knew when it was set to go off. My father knew more than my mother.

I don't know my father very well. I've spent almost no time with him, just vacations, and there was more to do then than be with him. When I think of him, I think of instructions. Even when he used to write a P.S. on my mother's letters to me, it would just be instructions on how to do something or how to drive somewhere. He is a living manual. He has never been affectionate. When I was younger, he liked to rub his rough beard against my face. That was his way of showing affection, my mother said. When I started getting pimples, it would hurt when he did it. I got pimples right before I got my first period. That was when I was eleven. I didn't know what it was. I was playing canasta with a friend of my mother's while we waited for her to come from the beauty shop. I thought she was a stupid lady because she moaned with pain when she rinsed her cocktail glass with scalding water. I told her to use cold water, I remember that. But I didn't know her well or trust her enough to tell her that I was bleeding to death, so I had to suffer until I was alone with my mother and her newly lacquered hair that made her look like a pumpkin on a stick. She swore she had already explained to me that it was going to happen. It wasn't like she had ten daughters and couldn't remember if she told all of them. I was it.

I couldn't believe I wouldn't be able to swim every day anymore and had to wear that dumb thing to hold the pads that was an old one of hers with bloodstains all over it before she went and bought me one. I figured she sent the maid to get it and I hadn't wanted her to know about it. Then I thought that when people would ask a girl's age and she would say eleven or twelve, they were thinking, "Aha! we know what's just happened to you." I didn't want to be a woman. I couldn't think of a single woman I liked or a single reason to want to be a woman. Until that very moment, even though I knew I was a girl, I had a secret belief that maybe I could grow up to be a man. I knew from that point on I couldn't change things; I hate things you are stuck with, like it or not. I read that movie stars had their noses changed. I thought maybe my mother had done that; that's why I had a big nose and she didn't.

I never knew parents much different from mine until I went to Holbrooke. The ones at boarding school were all like mine, but Holbrooke had variety. My roommate Clara's father mooned the people at the dinner table at the American Legion hut. Some woman told his wife that he had the prettiest little butt she had ever seen, skin smooth as a baby's. I told my father the story and he didn't think it was funny. Sometimes I think I never laugh either, that I'm as humorless as he is. I hear myself laugh at the movies, but if I were in an empty theater, I wouldn't laugh. I have no memory of what a laugh from my father sounds like.

My father is a perfect dresser. He has on his casual clothes and everything will be perfectly crisp. He can go out in the country to look at his cattle and he'll have to have creases in his blue jeans. The girls at school are always telling me what a handsome father I have and someone his age has to be really good-looking for a college girl even to notice. He looks a lot younger than he is. He would never think of starting out a day without a shower, not that he was ever dirty. I think that he wants to wash so often he'll never know what it is like to feel even slightly dirty. And stink. He doesn't want to know what it is like to stink, but everywhere he took me, some dog was rooting his daughter in the crotch. I don't know why dogs did that to me, because I almost always took a bath every other night. He's never made reference to my looks, but he must think about it. Why it happened since both of them are good-looking.

I did something bad to him once, but I didn't mean to. He was teaching me to drive. We had this straight-shift sports car and I was having some trouble letting the clutch out without it rolling backwards. And he was so goddamn impatient, yelled at me for everything I did. We were at this stoplight. He took me that way because he knew it was the worst hill in town. I was trying to make the light and he started yelling for me to slow down, so I missed it. Jesus, I hated to stop that car. Then I was sitting there waiting for it to change and he was bitching at me a mile a minute. Then this car pulls in behind, a real wise-ass driver who gets up close like he's going to eat my bumper off, so I figure I gotta let it off right or I'll smash the hell out of him. The whole time, my father was telling me about a million things and I was begging him to tell me one thing at a time and let me concentrate on it and he said you can't drive a car if you only have the mentality to think about one thing at a time. I thought of pulling up the brake and getting out and telling the guy back there he should back up and get the hell out of my way because I didn't know what the shit I was doing. He was one of those drivers that made his car look like a dog getting ready to fuck. I saw the light start to change on the other side, the yellow through the crack, and I really let it go. I had the engine revved up full blast when I popped the clutch and I didn't hit the guy behind me. I just went roaring off and smashed into three parked cars on the other side of the inter- section. I told that story a lot at school. I guess I should have been ashamed. I was at the time.

It was pretty expensive. And my father made me wait a year before he let me have a car of my own and sent me to driver's education, which I wanted to go to in the first place. But the thing that was bad about it was he got this little cut and he would moan and groan about it every morning when he was shaving (his bathroom was right under mine) and he would make my mother come in and shave around it for him so he wouldn't cut off the scab. I have to know now for the rest of my life, every time I look at him, that I made that mark on him and that it's permanent. It's causing physical pain to someone else that gets me. Like Raney Fletcher. I stuck him in the arm with a pencil in the second grade and he showed me at the ten- nis courts ten years later that the lead was still there.

I used to imagine my mother getting a phone call saying my

father had died on a business trip. Once it was a motel swimming pool, once a golf ball in the temple. I don't do that anymore.

* * *

Clara's father . . .

*Matilda dropped me off in front of the building where I took tap dancing. There was a note from my teacher; she was going to be twenty minutes late, so I played on the monkey bars in the public playground until I saw her go up the steps. I was ten years old.*

*I saw poor white children who smoked and cussed. I played by myself and they didn't bother me. I hung by my knees, so they did the same thing. There was a little boy who had a bed sheet tied over his head and to his arms. He was sobbing as he walked restlessly around the swings, unable to play because he kept tripping over the sheet. I asked one of the older girls why he wore the sheet. She said that when he wet his bed, his mother took the sheet off and made him wear it until suppertime. He couldn't have anything to drink until after supper, and then only one glassful. I looked at the little boy and his lips were parched and cracked. I wondered if he might die of thirst. When I saw the yellow stain was on the part across his forehead, I could smell the urine.*

*He ran from the playground and up the steps of his house; it had a window fixed with cardboard and the red bricks were covered with smoke from the factory. The older boys started chanting after him, "Ku Klux Klan, Ku Klux Klan." I went for three days before I asked my father what it meant because I thought it might be something I shouldn't say. I had asked him what "fuck" meant when I saw it written in the water fountain. When I said it, his eyes jumped like the glass eyes did on my teddy bear when I picked it up. He said he might move me to another school. When I said Ku Klux Klan, he looked it up in the encyclopedia and gave it to me to read, but nothing stuck in my mind until years later. That was when my roommate and best friend, Clara, took me to a Klan meeting during our second semester in college.*

Clara's father is a farmer but he also runs a service station and the family lives in an apartment above it. They live where people in Raleigh refer to as "down east," the flat, humid tobacco lands of eastern North Carolina. But Clara has money. Far more than my father sends me to spend.

I remember the weekend when her father came to get us. He was driving a late-model Chevrolet. It had no fancy gadgets inside and no decoration, but was very fast. He said little during the hundred-mile trip. I couldn't imagine my father not trying to make conversation. When we got to Smithfield on the outskirts of town we saw a large lighted billboard: "You are entering Klan Country. Support the Knights of the Ku Klux Klan. Fight Integration and Communism." The sign had a knight in a suit of armor mounted on a rearing horse. In his hand was a long stick.

Clara's father saw me looking at the sign. "Whatcha thinking?" he asked, his eyebrows raised.

I smiled and said, "Just wondering what the big stick was for."

"That's his nigger knocker," was the reply. Then he rustled with his hand down under the seat and pulled up a piece of garden hose. "This here's mine."

He handed it to me and it dropped heavy in my hand. I tipped it up and saw that it was filled with metal. "Lead," he said.

Clara's mother: A car drove into the station while I was being introduced, popping on the bottle caps in the drive. Mrs. Tippen reached in a drawer of the cash register and took out a key marked "Ladies." "Excuse me," she said to me as she went to the door to meet the women who climbed out of their Oldsmobile, "I have to keep it locked to keep the niggers out." The women moaned when they stepped out of their air-conditioned car. "It's real clean in the restroom, if you'd like to use it," she offered, handing the fat one in front the key. "I just scrubbed it and no one has used it since." The woman took the key without expression.

At dinner I watched Mrs. Tippen through the kitchen door, switching the silverware arrangement back and forth, looking at it and trying to decide which way was right. Then when we sat down to eat, she said, "I'm left-handed and I never can remember which side things go on." The way she served the table, moving behind everyone and not eating until we were finished, made her seem more like a maid than a mother.

The apartment: Expensive furniture but nothing matching; in the corner of the living room a huge color TV; the pictures on the walls — flowers and nineteenth century ladies in oval frames. But I hadn't really expected them to hang Clara's paintings. Clara's father had said her work was about what he expected he was spending all that money for: "looked like a monkey poured paint on a sheet of paper." I think parents don't know their children at all. If I had a child, I wonder if I would always be afraid of the unexpected he might do.

Only a few hours after we had arrived at the Tippen home in Branch, Clara and I headed out onto the highway in front of their service station, swinging around a large piece of farm equipment that hovered over the center line. I looked at the farmer on the tractor and wondered if he was going home to put his tractor up so he could attend the meeting. The air was heavy with insecticide — a fresh crop of mosquitoes was hatching in the swamps beside the road. After about a twenty-minute drive down a dirt road, we arrived at the site, a field with a circus tent set up in case of rain and in case it became necessary to make the gathering look like a real revival, Clara explained. I saw the cross, an awkward apparatus with two silver tanks at its base. Clara told me that they used the same gas they cured tobacco with to light up the cross. The burlap and gas-soaked crosses couldn't be used in the county without a fire permit.

We sat in the back. There were lights mainly around the speaker's stand, where a man was fumbling with a microphone. In the darkness in the back of the tent were several lightning bugs that drifted up and down in the stuffiness of the tent. Around the chairs were broken stalks of an old crop.

After about twenty minutes the speeches started. The first speaker was a gaunt woman, her hair pulled tight into a braided bun, her navy-blue dress shiny with recent iron marks. She had pinned on a small white hat as if she were in church. She started by reading a poem about white chastity, then told the story of a " . . . certain sorry local girl that I don't need mention no names who's taken up with a nigra man." The woman *started her speech in fairly general terms but soon ". . . and they live in a filthy stinking house with rats and roaches running on the porch, and in the food and beds, and there are two poor little white children she had before she took up with that nigra living right there in that filthy stinking mess with the nigra children he had by some nigger woman . . ." I noted that her "nigra" changed to "nigger" as she got more agitated, but she spoke it softly, almost as if she were whispering a curse word.*

*"Somebody ought to git over and do something about them little white children or there won't be nothing to do but hope God in his forgiveness will find a place for them in his heaven, because they can't help what is in store for them. And the house probably ain't got a divider or nothing with those little white children right there having to see their trash of a mama get in bed with that black thing . . ." The woman's voice began to quiver and her face burned red beneath the powder she had applied for the gathering. I wondered if she had embarrassed herself by telling the story she had told only to small groups before and only to women to an audience filled with men. She tried to speak some more but she had started to repeat herself and her audience was getting bored. A man tapped her on the shoulder in the middle of a sentence and she said thank you to the audience, folding up the papers she hadn't looked at. She walked down the steps with her chin high, her head shaking with a palsy her speech had generated.*

*The next man to speak was not from Branch, North Carolina. He had been imported to speak at this meeting and others around the country. He said he had been convicted of first degree murder by a jury in Alabama that had six blacks on it, but the judge had the good sense to let him off. He was devoting his life to traveling to tell his story. I supposed it was somewhat different from the story he used before the jury.*

*"And these smart-ass college students come in first," he related, "and got people all ruffled and stirred up and then they got out before we yanked a knot in their asses. But they left them niggers thinking they were hot shit on a stick. So one of them come out with this petition, see, that he said had three hundred nigger names asking for more money and I told him there wont*

*three hundred niggers in the whole state of Alabama could write their friggen name." The crowd began to cheer and laugh.*

*"... and there wont twenty-five worth what they were getting paid now, so to git his black ass in gear and git out of my office. So I got a bunch of fellows together, see, and we went out riding in this '49 Caddy convertible and we went over by the roadhouse where they hang out and drove up beside one of them all duded up for Sa'urdy night, pants hiked up, socks shining out the bottom, you know what I mean, you know how a nigger ass sticks up. He had this smart-ass hat tipped over on one side and he was strutting and jiving," the man began to swing his hips and roll his eyes for a few laughs, "so me and Jaroy, who was in the back seat on the shotgun side, both took a swing with a piece of our gardening equipment, you know, and I'm telling you, I knowed at the time we got him good, because my right arm was laid up till Wednesday . . ."*

*The meeting continued with a collection of tales of blacks and Yankees. There was a brief speech against Jews by a member of the American Nazi Party, who spoke with a German accent. He marched out of the tent when his speech was over and the audience heard his car start and leave. Soon the audience was getting restless, not so much from boredom as the need to move around and get rid of the energy that the speakers had generated. The outlet tonight was the usual. They broke up to go out and dance around the cross.*

*The music began, a scratchy rendition of "The Old Rugged Cross," over a loudspeaker. I had seen the woman handling the record player wipe the dust stirred up by the crowd off the record with the bottom of her skirt. She had on a cotton slip with eyelet holes in the lace and stockings that were gartered just above the knee, squeezing her flesh into blue veins. Children danced around inside the tent, already clad in their sheets, playing ghosts, jumping behind the chairs to spook each other. Just as I moved through the tent flap to go outside, I looked down into the face of a boy of about ten, his teeth rotted across the front as if they had been slashed with brown paint. He ran his hand across my shaved calf and made a noise, "woo," then darted outside.*

When we drove back to the Tippen gas station, all the lights were still on but a "Closed" sign was in the front window. Clara's mother met us at the door, her hands wound into her apron.

"Your father is still out. How long ago did that meeting break up?"

Clara looked at her watch. "Close to two hours. He's probably at Bailey's having a few beers and playing cards."

Suddenly the pickup of Mr. Tippen turned into the station.

"Oh, thank the Lord," Mrs. Tippen muttered and went to meet him.

He pushed her out of his way and went towards the door of the station. "Enjoy the meeting, smart-ass college student?" he said to Clara. I could smell the beer on his breath. I thought he seemed nervous. He stopped in the doorway. "Some nigger got his ass shot full of holes trying to break in Belks. The niggers around here been watching too much television."

"You mean like the riots?"

"I mean like the riots and they going to find out we treat their sweet asses different here. If they burn down their houses here, they can sleep out under a tree."

"Who shot him?" Clara asked.

"I didn't," he said flatly and went in the house.

Lanette Tippen . . .

Every one of them safe and asleep right here under my roof, but I won't sleep a wink all night. I know it. Now she'll go back to Raleigh and say she was really down east, those Tippens were the most down east she ever saw. Clara taking her to the Klan meeting like that's what we do down here for 'musement, and Harold coming home acting so smart about nigger killing. I've never been so ashamed. And all his ugly talk right in front of the girls. What got into him, I declare, I don't know about all this that's going on. There was a time not so long ago we didn't have to have a thing to do with them. Pump a tank of gas when they showed the money to me and sell a cold drink or a Popsicle, and old Uncle Hop, who set out front on the bench till he died and didn't bother nobody. I shooed off Hop's grandson and he stood there glaring at me like he wont moving, till I told him Mr. Tippen would see to him. They put ideas in their heads. I know it.

Harold betta watch out. They can do things to you for that. Goes to them meetings thinking they got the world by the tail, just talking big and puffing theirselves up like bantam roosters. The federal man is going to git them. He don't care who he gits. He don't have no friends and no kin here to answer to. He just picks up his paycheck. You pay him to catch a man and he puts a white man in the jailhouse quick as a nigger. He comes up and tells me how I'm going to run my own store till I just took the stools out in front of the counter. Now everybody got to suffer. I know people. People don't care anymore, long as they git their money.

She's got the money, I tell you the truth. I heard of her before Clara got put in the room with her at school, because of that building downtown her granddaddy built. He was something at the bank, and you can be sure it was big. I was folding up her things and I guess they're finer than Clara's, but these young girls all look the same to me. I had her money, I would buy the finest. No, I wouldn't. I'm just talking big myself. Harold Tippen taking every cent he can spare out of his pocket, sending it to Clara trying to make like we're well off. Going to spoil her even rottener than she is. Don't he know that girl seen enough money to know when she ain't looking at it? She could buy and sell Harold Tippen ten times over. I ain't ashamed. She can eat at my table just like anybody else. That's a lie, Lanette Tippen. I'm ashamed right down to things she probably don't even take notice of. I worked my fingers to the bone cleaning and polishing up this place spotless, and I bet she looked right over it. Both of them strow their things, just drop them where they took them off. I don't straighten my back up a time in that room, picking up after them. That room of theirs at school is the biggest mess I ever seen. Clara has been raised better than that. I don't know why I bother. I don't know. Why do I git up mornings, live one day to the next, all anybody cares about it, and that's the truth. She ate what I put in front of her. Liked my rhubarb cobbler, she said, but she's just acting like she's been taught. I got too much sugar in it to suit my tastes. But manners is better than none at all. Clara don't act like she's been taught any.

Come tomorrow when those two are gone back, I'm going in

*my sewing room and I'm great minded not to come out till I finish that new suit I been putting off out of the linen I've owned for six months. I'm doing something for me, and Harold Tippen and the rest of them can just go about their business. I don't give a hoot and a holler if he has to look in the icebox and warm over his own supper. 'Spects it on the plate in front of him every day of his life. Sheriff Staley come out here, I'll say I don't know nothing about nothing. He can just ask Harold or them other men. I just take care of my house. I got the pattern on that linen and I'm cutting into it right or wrong. I got to git over worrying and fretting. If I mess up, I'll just buy me a new piece. Ain't the end of the world. I got money of my own and if I cut it wrong, I'll just go down to Belks and buy me another piece just like it . . .*

I just fixed myself a dinner of peanut butter and crackers. I graduate this May and today was the first of my interviews for jobs next year. I want to be in the mountains where I like to hike, so I have applied at a public school, my old boarding school, and a new government project in the mountains called the Appalachian Corps. I am too tired from today's interview to get dressed up again and go to a restaurant, but I feel like writing in my notebook for a while. The weather has taken a turn and a cold front is coming in. Asheville is the coldest city in North Carolina, always ten degrees colder than anywhere else. It's a dreary place in winter; I remember that well from the years my parents sent me here to prep school. The city has always had an abnormal number of discount and used-clothing stores, and the streets where they are located are filled with gaunt mountain people with run-over shoes and rotten teeth.

I opened a hot Pepsi on the bathroom door and it spewed out and dripped from the plastic curtain over the bathtub. While I ate, I looked out the window through old curtains, worn out from many washings but starched to hold their shape. This boarding house is one of the old city mansions, decaying and still occupied by an old white woman. Her china cabinets contain the few unbroken pieces that remain of her family dishes. Her name is Mrs. Upshaw and she knew my Grandpa Fitzgerald.

It isn't dark outside yet. There is a black woman starting to pace up and down in the street. This same woman keeps passing my window, a middle-aged, heavyset woman with a purse in her hand. This is a side street, a cut-through that is used only by people who live here. The temperature is dropping fast, the sky turning the slate gray with pink at the bottom edges that means snow. I wait for the bird screams at the end of the day, the rush for cover and food before the snowfall, but it is the black woman who paces in the street and has started to talk that I hear. I can't understand what she is saying.

The black woman lives in the house next door where I watched a starling putting sticks under the gutter of the rotting structure this morning, the clumsy bird starting a nest before winter is half finished. The woman came out in a thin pink robe and swept the trash off the sidewalk in front of her house as if winter didn't touch her either. She took scraps of aluminum foil out of the pocket of her robe and wrapped them around the limbs of a little tree by the sidewalk. The tree has a crude fence around it made of coat hangers and old silverware. It appears to be a shrine.

"You can't draft my boy out of the world, I say." The woman's words are at last clear enough to understand. "I say that to the Lord above and Mr. Johnson, that you can't draft him out of the world." The black woman is starting to give a speech.

She steps aside to let a car pass on one side and then the other. I am not sure if she actually saw the cars directly or just felt their presence. She has on a white cap and a nice coat. Her shoes are leather and shiny; they match the large purse that she carries pressed up against her side. She stops to spit. I get close to the window and look to see if it was a long brown snuff thread, piling in a slippery puddle between the cars to be stepped in. It wasn't. Just hot spit that is smoking on the cold pavement.

"He's eighteen years old, my boy. Treat his mama like a dog. Now he's gone for good. Walk on her friggen children in the friggen street. That's right, Mr. Johnson." She is screaming now.

She looks up at my window, snapping her head suddenly as if she had seen something threatening. There is no light on in my room and the window might be too dirty for her to see me watching, but I pull my face further behind the curtain.

"Don't throw your rocks through my window. I paid my money. Don't come knocking on my door.

"Going up to New York. My husband going to be up there working for me. I worked for fifteen dollars a week, I'm telling you. You better git ready for us, white people. Don't you come to my door. Wash your shit off your white commode. Wash it off your own white ass. I ain't washing it for you, I'm telling you for the last time. I'm telling you."

Her voice is trailing and she has walked from the street now that the traffic is heavier. The neighborhood is coming home from work. "I had my first child thirty years ago," she says, standing on the curbing. "I'm forty-eight years old. You don't pay my mama and papa. They worked like dogs for a meal on the table. But you ain't going to do it again, no, sir. Mistreated. Tell them! Let them know!"

The woman's voice is moaning now, crying, like a little kitten being made to cry for its supper. She is acting scared. Her words are turning up something in her brain.

"I'm forty-nine years old." She has aged a year. "White folks have mistreated me every day of my life on this earth. They say to me, 'Elsie, you're a good worker.' Who's a friggen good worker? Huh? Huh? They crucified me with Christ. Wash their own shit out. Give me thirty days in jail. I sued for it. Somebody told a lie. Somebody's nasty lives here." She points at the house I am staying in.

Now the black woman is back out in the traffic. An old white man is walking by on the far side of the street, but she doesn't act as if she sees him. Two little black children start teasing her, running in and out like puppies looking for someone to play. She shoos them away with her purse and they laugh and run to hide between the parked cars.

"My husband don't ever ride me nowhere in his big car. Gone up to New York. I feed my children. He don't ever send me a check. I paid cash for my dress and coat. My money. My money in this dress and coat." She opens her coat to show her plaid housedress, then snaps it shut.

It is starting to get dark and the first flakes of snow are flipping in the wind with the gray city ashes. The woman is preaching now and quoting the Bible: "The Lord is my shepherd, I shall not want. He maketh me to lie down in green pastures . . ." There is a young woman, probably her daughter, on the porch.

*When the young woman reaches the sidewalk, the older woman stops preaching and walks to her side. They are talking, but I can't hear them. The older woman is still waving her hands and pointing at the houses on the street. But if I hadn't seen the performance, I would have thought there was nothing abnormal about her actions now.*

*Now it is night-black and the street lights are on; the two women have walked up the steps into the house. All the people in doorways and windows who were watching have gone back into their houses like the wooden dolls on a weathervane house when rain is coming.*

*This morning a cat was dead atop the snow, its long black body stretched out and its head up high and resting on the curbing. The trash man threw it up in the truck with one hand like a frozen log. I saw the woman back outside at her shrine. She wore the thin pink robe of the morning before, and the snow was over her bedroom slippers and still falling. She was scooping the snow from inside the fence around the little tree. The limbs had already been cleaned of snow and the foil sparkled in the morning light.*

\* \* \*

The morning of my second interview I dressed and went downstairs early. The woman who rented me the room had told me that for a dollar extra I could eat breakfast there. When I walked into the kitchen, the old woman was preparing breakfast.

"I thought you would come down and join us when you smelt the bacon frying," she said. I smiled at her and sat down on a kitchen stool. That friendly voice with the sneer at the end. Homey cheeriness. I didn't trust this old bitch. I figured she really meant to say, "I see you've decided you're not too good to eat breakfast with us."

"I apologize for the oratory you had to listen to last evening. They have put that crazy nigger up countless times, but she never stays up."

"Why do you think the woman is deranged?" I asked her.

"Oh, she's just a crazy nigger, honey. Haven't you ever seen a crazy nigger before? But I guess you haven't had to live and see this happen to your neighborhood like some of us have." She wiped her hands on her apron and went on. Maybe she sensed that I would ask another question if she didn't. "I heard that she lost one of her boys in Vietnam and he must have been one of her favorites. How can it matter so much when they don't know or care where half of them end up or came from, you know what I mean? She was just looking for something to rant and rave about. You know how nigras are. You don't know what goes on in that crazy head."

"Is that what the tree is decorated for? Maybe that's his grave in her mind."

The old woman put a plate in front of me, two eggs and country sausage with biscuits. "You're just as good at guessing as I am. Isn't that the foolishest mess you ever seen out there on the street, hanging trash on a tree? I'm ashamed for people I know to see it. You'd think it was going to bear the apples of the Lord the way she carries on about it. Well, now, there are finer things to talk about in the city of Asheville. What do you think of our town?"

I looked up from my plate and swallowed my food. The food was good and I was hungry.

"Very nice," I told her. "I went to Allenmont School here for three years. I have two more interviews today, then I'll see if they like me."

"Well, now, you do say. I'm sure they will. Your granddaddy won't be forgotten around here and they will be pleased as punch to have one of his grandchildren in their system. I taught in the public school system for forty years. Then they let the niggers in, and I'm too old for that, if you know what I mean. Your granddaddy, God rest his generous soul, would be a grieved man today if he could be alive to see how they've taken over Fitzgerald Park. I guess you know he gave it to the city out of the kindness of his heart. Now there're niggers just swarming all over the place until a white person doesn't feel safe to go take a walk over there anymore. I used to go feed the ducks. And come summer when the swimming pool opens, there's going to be more trouble than we know what to do with. Times have changed in this town. There was a time you walked out down the sidewalk feeling that there was no finer place on earth."

I asked her if she had known my grandfather well.

"As well as most people did, I suppose," she said and went on to tell me she had been hired by him one summer to tutor Mary, my father's sister, in mathematics. "I suppose you were a little girl then. I remember all the little grandchildren were cared for by that old colored mammy. What was her name?"

"Baa." I didn't remember the teacher being there with Mary Jane, but I remembered Baa. I'll never forget Baa, coming up the hill to our playground from the servants' quarters, grinding her hips around and puffing with each step. Her shoes rolled over and her ankles bent until her feet didn't look like feet at all, but like blocks she moved on, like the wheelless boxes I saw mules pulling to drag the tobacco out of the fields at the country place.

\* \* \*

Baa . . .

*Baa hurt my eyes, especially in the sunlight when her white clothes were so bright they could make me sneeze. Only her brown face and hands stuck out, ashy looking with a whiteness that made her look like she was dusted with flour, not like the chocolate Aunt Jemima that hung on the wall in the kitchen holding a note pad on her apron and the wooden mixing spoons in her hands. No one looked like Baa.*

*Baa was layers of white: apron, long dress, and big baggy bloomers that Matilda made for her for Christmas, the bloomers filled with pockets for her to carry things. Mainly for her money, which was knotted so many times in a handkerchief that most people got impatient and paid for what she wanted before she got all the knots undone. Which is exactly what she wanted. Somewhere inside her brown-pink lips was a wad of snuff that, coming up the hill, she would spit like bug juice.*

*Baa settled often on a stool in the kitchen and I would go in to hear her talk to Matilda or one of the housemaids while they ironed. Baa was only supposed to look after the grandchildren now that she had gotten so old. All the other children were in kindergarten except on weekends, so she didn't have much to do.*

She bragged so much that I was no trouble, I was afraid not to be good. Baa was so old she had already outlived five husbands and she said she was too old to find another one. She was a hundred years old, because she could remember that her mother was a slave.

"My mama belong to Mister Fitzgerald's great-grandfather back when he owned the land that hold half of what this town sits on. We would skin 'maters come off twenty-five acres of the finest land you ever seen, many as twenty-five tubsa boiling water with those juicy things bobbing in them. Make you smack your mouth. Had a sweetness you could eat out in the field. I kept them tubs filled for my mama and she would squirt the 'maters out of their skin and pass them to Maisie to core them. Folks' property ain't come to much." She would roll her bottom lip out when she frowned, then spit her snuff in a tin box she carried.

Baa always talked about how much more people used to have, as if the plenty of Grandfather Fitzgerald's land was as much her mother's as his. Grandfather Fitzgerald had five colored people other than Baa working for him, three women in the house, Raymond for the garden, and Juleous to drive his Cadillac and the station wagon with the wooden sides. My father had said that was a passing thing, those wood-sided cars, and that Grandfather was going to be sorry he let some salesman talk him into it.

My grandmother was always sick and then she outlived Grandfather. Hardly ever was she sitting in the car when Juleous came out of the driveway, and sometimes I saw her in the flower garden with her walker, moving so slowly I could barely tell she was moving. Grandfather had an elevator put in the house for her because she was afraid of the stairs. He had a place dug as big as a room under the ground and put furniture in it for her to go when there was a thunderstorm. I don't see her use the walker a lot anymore, but she still goes into her shelter. I went down in the shelter only once and it seemed to me more frightening there than outside.

I heard Baa say once that Grandfather seemed to like menfolks as good as womenfolks, whatever she meant by that.

One day when Baa was sitting with the grandchildren, I saw

*her get angry. My dog was with me and we were all running around and making a lot of noise. I was about nine then. My dog was playing with us too and he jumped up on me and started rubbing up and down on my leg, his front legs latched around my thigh. I said he was dancing with me, and Baa came running over as fast as I had ever seen her move and beat him down, saying something about his having his business out. I didn't like her hitting my dog, but Baa had a fierce sense of what was proper.*

\* \* \*

Three years ago my grandfather died. The day of his funeral I was walking by the road with my cousin, going to the store to buy our Uncle Trextal some Pall Malls. My cousin Charles hadn't wanted to go with me, but the family suggested that I not walk alone. The country high school used the road for their drag strip. The cars went by and sucked my clothes, pulling them away from my body and snapping them back at me. I had on a dark suit that I'd never worn before and never wore again. I didn't want to look at the cars. Sometimes I could hear a radio blast the fragment of a song and I would try to guess it to give my mind something to do. Sometimes a voice would say something to me, or to my cousin.

"Hey, man, she's good. I fucked her last weekend."

*"I can't git no satisfaction; I can't git no good reaction . . . when I'm riding in my car and a man comes on the radio . . ."*

When you got in a car you were the aggressor, I thought. The one out there on foot was the unprotected, the prey. They got in a car and it was like a cowboy shooting Indians from a horse. I didn't like walking beside that country road.

The ditch was filled with day lilies, washed into clumps, their orange flowers open like silent mouths crying from beside me, faces lined up to watch a parade. They reached up in rows, all the same size, height, and color, and their heads bobbed when the cars passed or when a breeze dashed down the ditch. When dusk came they would roll up and pinch their lips shut.

"Hey, baby, wanna fuck?" Another voice came from a car.

"No, but my cousin does, so send your mother over," I snapped. Charles didn't flinch. I was probably trying to shock him, now that I look back at it. I didn't want him to walk with me. He had zits all around his neck. He didn't have many on his face but I could tell he went real easy shaving around his neck, missing a lot of the whiskers. There was a dark-brown blood spot on his collar where he cut one of them some time ago, because his shirt had been washed since and the hot water set the spot in. He had his collar turned up. Not by accident. He meant to. My father would call him a skin. Maybe he would just as soon have me as a son like Charles.

The old man is gone now, and it is different. I had been used to his being there when I went to ride. I let him keep all my horse-show ribbons in the case at the farm because he liked to use them to tell stories about the horses he had owned. The week after his first stroke, I went out to see him. He had on a plaid shirt. I thought he looked strange, the veins showing in his neck and his Adam's apple bobbing like that of a rooster reaching up to crow. Then I realized it was just that he didn't have on a white shirt and tie and I had never seen his collar undone around his neck before. He seemed vulnerable, as if someone could grab his neck and choke him.

Baa is dead now too. Matilda works for my mother, but she is getting forgetful and crabby in her old age. My grandmother has kept the other maids and has hired a nurse to live in. Juleous works for someone else. I have seen him several times, driving a white Cadillac now. He tips his hat when he sees me. I hoped he would stop and talk someday, but he never has. When I made my debut and got back the photographs of my bow, I was surprised to see that Juleous was one of the black men dressed like coachmen who were holding the door that I walked through.

Maybe my grandmother misses her husband, though I have never heard her say so. She needs her servants more than she needed him. She has always acted like the only thing that mattered to her were her children anyway, that my father meant more than her husband. Maybe because they were part of her. I don't really know how mothers feel.

I had my Allenmont School interview my second day in Asheville. The school looked the same as it had when I was a boarder there. Yet except for the dean, all the administrators were new, which is probably why I got the interview. I ducked past the dean, but I think she had forgotten me anyway. This was the job my parents were hoping I would get, a teaching job at my old boarding school. My grandfather had given the school a lot of money. I had seen the job listed at the placement service at school and wrote without mentioning my grandfather. But the reply mentioned him and that they would be pleased to interview one of their "distinguished alumnae." Some distinction. They expelled me in the tenth grade for kicking my biology teacher in the shin when she was shocking a frog, and my father had to use his pull to get me back in. The teacher had removed the frog's brain and was giving it an electrical shock to prove it still had reflexes. The jumping legs would quiver and kick. But the bitch kept doing it, long after she had proven the point. I always have been fond of frogs.

That morning as I reached inside my VW for my window scraper, the snow dumped off the car into my boots. While I worked, the crazy black woman came back down the steps and began to sweep the wet ground around her shrine. I looked up at her, expecting her to scream, "Wash your own shit out!" but she said nothing.

"Looks like the snow is going to melt pretty quickly," I offered. She continued to sweep, intentionally turning her back to me. I walked to the back of my VW and knocked the snow off the grille over the engine and off the taillights. When I got in the car, the woman turned and looked at me dumbly, as if I had spoken to her in a foreign language. But it was more than a confused look; her face was twisted in anger. I started the engine and warmed it a moment while the woman went back up the steps and into her house. The mother of the children that I wanted to teach. There was more than snow in my boots to give me cold feet.

In mid-February I got a letter from my first roommate at Holbrooke College. I remembered her well, though she was there only one semester: Christina, born in a town in western North Carolina. After her marriage she moved back home to a mountain town near Rocky Gap, which is where I had applied for the job in the Appalachian Corps teaching project. Christina spent hours grooming herself, which was an odd habit on a girls' campus. At Holbrooke there was no reason even to comb your hair until the weekends, when the male schools and the Marines descended on the campus. On weekends I couldn't even recognize my friends. But Christina never let up. I learned to study every night to the sound of her hair dryer. She would pluck her eyebrows before she went to the library.

One of the black girls in our dorm liked to visit in our room. She was the first black my own age I had ever known. I watched her move in front of the dresser, making faces at herself in the mirror. Her name was Garnet Ruby Anderson. She said she was lucky her parents weren't Amos 'n Andy fans or she might have been called Sapphire. Her nose spread as if it were made of modeling clay and pressed into place. Her nostrils moved when she talked and seemed too large for the air she needed to live. Garnet loved to put on her bikini and go out to the sunbath court to get a few laughs. She would drop her straps and complain about the sun line. She had the same ash that Baa had on her skin. I remember once watching Garnet take Christina's hand lotion and expel a large white drop on her hand that she rubbed into the brown until it shone like wet mud and the ash vanished. I studied Christina to see if her face changed. I thought I saw her tiny nose twitch.

One of the other black girls was tall and honey colored, with carefully straightened hair in fat rolls of curls that framed her face. Her face was beautiful but sullen. She refused to be friendly and left every weekend for an all-black college until she transferred. I wondered aloud then about her beautiful skin, the shade of a dark tan. Christina had said when she worked one Christmas in a drugstore cosmetics department, they bought jars of whitening creams "to suck out their blackness, and tons of this greasy stuff to straighten their hair." I remember saying I didn't know why the girl wanted to look like white people when she obviously hated them. Christina looked at me in amazement.

But Garnet talked a lot and I was intrigued by her wide, flat mouth. I used to imagine her with a giant tube of lipstick, trying to paint over the area. Christina said Garnet looked like a monkey and I agreed; it seemed to me Garnet wanted to look like a monkey. She chattered constantly and, in fact, once did an imitation of an organ grinder's monkey, using a coffee cup and the lid off a bath powder box for a hat.

One afternoon when Garnet was doing the usual fingering of the articles on the dresser while she chatted with us, she began to put Christina's curlers in her hair. I watched her put her coarse black hair around the pink plastic, rolling it up and down and laughing at herself in the mirror. She dropped the curlers on the dresser and kept talking. When Garnet left Christina leapt from the bed, threw the curlers into the sink, and turned the water on full blast until the steam rose and fogged the mirror. Christina didn't wash and roll her hair that night. The next day I saw the pink curlers in the wastebasket as I had expected. Christina had bought a new package at the drugstore.

After one semester Christina grew more and more unhappy and homesick, so she decided to marry her high school boyfriend, who was attending the technical institute back home. During the three years after she left, I got two baby announcements. Then I got the letter this February saying they had separated because of another woman, that Christina had gotten suspicious and phoned to find he wasn't enrolled in the night school he said he was attending. Christina had lived a whole adult life and I was still the same age I'd always been.

In the same mail was a second letter:

Dear Miss Fitzgerald:

This letter is in reference to your application for a teaching position in the Public Schools of Asheville next fall. After going over your test results and interviews, our committee on recommendations for hiring reached the following conclusions.

The committee felt that you might be placed in the suburban schools and your name has been added to the waiting list. It was uniformly felt that your background would not prepare you to deal with the very difficult situation in the lower-income area here. You have never attended a public school. In addition, your grades in the social studies

and psychology are not outstanding. To support these feelings, our statisticians found your test results indicated
that you possessed prejudicial feelings towards the black
race to a degree too great to consider you for a position at
this time. These are difficult times and we must seek only
the most qualified personnel available.

We will inform you as soon as possible if a suburban
teaching position opens though we do not anticipate a res-
ignation at this time and suggest you make further appli-
cations elsewhere. Thank you for your interest in the
Asheville Public School System.

Sincerely yours,
Reginald H. Sullivan
Asst. Superintendent

I guessed I should have expected it, especially since Reginald
H. Sullivan asked me why none of the black Holbrooke
graduates applied to teach there and I told him they could
make twice as much in northern Virginia. He had decided I
was disadvantaged because I wasn't born disadvantaged. Mine
was a token interview. He had no intention of considering me if
a black wanted the job. He must have had his secretary write
that letter. His grammar wasn't that good.

At home for the weekend I watched a black man take a lawn
mower down out of the back of his pickup, an old and dirty
lawn mower covered with dead leaves and oil. Matilda said he
was a friend of hers and would do the lawns until Raymond was
back on his feet from the gout. Raymond had sent word he
didn't want anyone using his mower, which was padlocked in
the tool shed at the country place. The man's truck fender was
wired to the bed and started to vibrate when he removed the
mower. I had seen trucks like his leaning beside the road with
a flat tire, down on a knee with no spare, a muffler hanging out
on the pavement like an afterbirth. Sometimes they were like
dead dogs that belonged to nobody, so nobody buried them and
they got shoved off in the woods to rot.

Through the open door, I could see a burlap bag that was
covering the springs to keep them from sticking in him. While I
watched him struggle with the unruly machine, I thought of a

question that was on the prejudice test that I took when I applied at Asheville: Did I think there were obvious anatomical distinctions between the races? Clara's father told her the reason that blacks wore their pants so short was because their asses hiked them up, and they had to walk like they were shaking loose shit down their pants legs. Clara herself said it was because they liked to show off their red socks. That man was my father's height and weight, but if he had had on my father's clothes, they wouldn't have fit the same. I'd seen my outgrown clothes on the maids' children. I answered yes to the question.

I saw the black man in the yard move my lawn chair out of his way so he could mow. He'd torn holes in his clothes to cool him, and his arm stuck down where his sleeve used to be, his veins looking like mole tunnels in a flower bed. I watched him get hot and shiny as he mowed the grass. Then he stopped and started looking for something. The hose, for a drink. I thought maybe I should set out a glass of ice water, but he might see that I was here alone. Matilda was shopping. Then I saw that he wasn't alone. A little boy about six years old climbed out of the truck and walked towards him when he picked up the hose, and the man ordered him back in the truck. I made two iced Pepsis and took them out in paper cups. The little boy finally came on the sun porch and I drew him some animals to color with crayons. When his father called him to leave, he quit right in the middle of his horse picture and ran out the door to the truck. He never said a word, but he had sung a wordless song while he worked.

I knew I could no more communicate with that child's father than someone who spoke Russian. Neither could Mr. Sullivan, for that matter. I was less afraid of that man than I would be of a poor white man, but he would make me angrier than a white man if he said something smart to me. I was only less afraid of him because he was afraid of me. The test had a question about fear too. I should have lied.

*   *   *

*I have left school on a weekday before. After you get your senior jacket and fit your commencement robe, they'd be embarrassed not to let you graduate. I only have one exam left. Besides, I need* a change of scene. I want to sit on a verandah and listen to bees buzzing in wisteria and drink ice tea with mint leaves in it.

I was thinking of Matilda today, one summer when I rode with her in the back seat of Grandfather Fitzgerald's air-conditioned Cadillac to Florida. She never talked to me on drives; it was like the inside of the Cadillac was a church. All of our communication was through actions: a pat on the knee, pulling my hand down from playing with my hair, shaking her head. Charles and I counted on our trip to Nags Head once and found she made more gestures than she said words. Then suddenly, when we were going over the Savannah bridge, she looked out and said, "Whew, I glad I ain't living down in that hot hole, uh um." The hot hole was Savannah and fat Tildie was like a bird in the sky.

This morning when I loaded up my car, I didn't put much thought into what I was taking because I didn't know what I would need or where I was going. At first I never left school because I was afraid. Now I leave in order to be frightened; I like to frighten myself so I will want to go back to the secure place I started from.

Today going south everything around my car felt like movement, the water sloshing in the canals, the palmetto leaves clashing like knife blades, the trees, a noiseless breeze going through them — a movie without sound. But that was an illusion. I was the one who was moving, the wind hissing through the front of the door of my bug-spattered beetle. The car stirred the insects into a scream, until once I stopped at a roadside park in South Carolina, shut the engine to be sure it wasn't the car that was screaming. No, it was bugs, crying from every direction. I listened until my skin began to crawl with the yellow and green and occasional pokeberry purple juice on my windshield, my washer bottle empty and squeaking, mouselike. I looked through the ugly mass, wondering what would happen if night came and I was sealed over with them, unable to see out with the door glued shut.

The frequent thump of a June bug taking a bouncing ride hit at an emotion somewhere because I had always liked June bugs; Raymond, the gardener, would loop a string around their shells and make me a living model airplane. Today while I rested my

*hand on the open window, a yellow jacket caught between my
fingers and made me swerve to the shoulder. I remembered my
mother's father, who had leapt from a car on a mountain road to
escape a bumblebee. My mother said I was like him, impulsive,
always leaping first and then looking. My grandfather had
jumped from a T-Model, so he only suffered bruises and a
burned rearside. He used to slip down his pants an inch at the
waist to show me, pulling them back up again with an expression not unlike the man who arrives outside our dorm every
Thursday night and yanks his pants up and down for the girls
in the windows. A drive is like a dream, I decided; you can't
keep the subject from changing, or thoughts from repeating.
And you don't really reach any conclusions.*

* * *

There was a red flash on the dial. The idiot light. I fumbled
for the manual in the glove compartment, new and untouched,
looked in the index under "red light": *Decelerate speed and
bring the car to a workshop.* I turned off the motor quickly.
The bugs in the South Carolina swamp were as loud as my engine had been . . . *an indication of a loose or broken fan belt.*
Up ahead, behind the sign, "Stop fo' yo' coffee break," Aunt
Jemima holding a steaming cup, was a building. The car
ceased to crunch tar bubbles under the tires; I beat on the dash
but the car refused to roll the rest of the way to the building.
Something ran through the garbage in front of the building;
half of the neon light in the window buzzed. There was a rusty
gas pump.

I turned the steering wheel in the direction of the pump and
got out to push the car. The gnats stung my legs, heading for
the sweat in the pockets behind my knees. The sun went
through my hair and began to sting the part. I wondered if the
Florida tourists knew about that heat, the ones who never get
out of their air-conditioned cars except to go to the bathroom or
to eat and sleep in their air-conditioned Holiday Inns. I took a
deep breath; this place smelled like the water in a pot of dead
flowers.

I put my hands on the fender to push the car; hot, so I swung
my hip into it. The heat came through my dress. The car rocked

but stopped like it was nailed down. In gear. I took it out of gear and threw my hip at the fender again; it crept forward. Suddenly it began to roll so fast I almost fell. I saw the gas pump in its path. I ran and grabbed the door, sprawled across the seat and beat on the floor until I grabbed the brake. The car slid to a stop. I looked at the building again. Stinging on my leg was a fresh cut. There I was, soaked with sweat, a cut leg, and the place appeared to have been closed for ten years. I heard the same noises I heard by the highway and there was no one anywhere.

I heard a sound, an animal crying, like my dog when he wanted to get in out of the rain. I walked towards the noise, to a shack beside the station, which had had plastic over the windows before something had flown through and left it shredded. I looked inside.

"Hello?" No answer in the dark. The kind of feeling when I picked up the phone once and no one was speaking on the other end, just breathing. Something was breathing hard.

I spoke again and two large yellow eyes appeared in the dark, a growl, and I was running and yelling back to my car. I jumped in, rolled the windows up, and locked the doors on both sides. Then I was startled again, this time by a man who walked to the door of the station. He had appeared out of nowhere. I rolled down the window a crack to hear his voice.

"You want something?" He sounded mean, not like I was a customer, but like I was a trespasser.

I thought a minute, at first not remembering why I was there. "Yes, I think I have a broken fan belt."

"Ain't got one to fit it."

"Well, it might not be a broken fan belt. It might be something else. That's what the book said when the red light goes on . . ."

"Sounds like the generator to me."

"Maybe that's it."

"Ain't got no generator to fit it neither. I don't do no work on them things."

I thought the generator sounded bigger than the fan belt. I had belts in my suitcase that might get me to a town where there was a dealership. He didn't have on a belt himself; his pants were hooked over his hipbones. He stood looking at me, waiting for another mechanical suggestion so he could say he didn't have one. He wasn't old, about thirty, but his face and hands were sunburned like an old farmer's, as if he didn't spend most of his time in that dark station.

"It's one of them foreign automobiles."

I jumped when he spoke without being questioned. I wished I could say that he was wrong and that it was made in southern Georgia.

"Yes, it's German."

"I wouldn't have it."

"But it's a wonderful car. Very reliable."

How could I be sitting helpless in a South Carolina filling station and say something like that? But he didn't comment, just smiled, which was worse. Probably didn't know what reliable meant and thought I was showing off.

"Tractor trailer hit you, you'd be a greasy spot on his windshield."

"Isn't there anything you can do to fix it? Patch it up, anything?"

"Don't know what's wrong with it."

"But will you look at it?"

He walked to the front of the car, reaching under the bumper for the latch, when I got out and cried, "No, the engine's in the back." He shook his head as he turned the engine handle and picked up the lid, mumbling something about Germans and the war.

"Busted fan belt," he said and pulled out a handful of black string. "I wouldn't go nowhere in no foreign automobile without no fan belt. Now take in that station. I got belts for Fords and Chevies, Oldsmobiles . . ." He named everything Detroit had ever made except an Edsel. "Even got a couple for a Model A, if they ain't dry rotted. Strong enough to git you home, ifin you had a Model A. What's a girl doing riding around by herself without no fan belt from . . . North Carolina! You really off from home." He had looked at the license tag.

"Yes, Raleigh. My parents live in Raleigh. And I'm going to see them."

"You ain't even going the right direction. How'd you git

yourself in such a mess?" He shook his head. "You sure your daddy knows you coming?"

"No, he doesn't. I mean I'm not going straight home. Savannah. I'm going to Savannah first. And my father is the very one to fill my car with trouble lights and things to inflate tires and tear-gas guns and fire extinguishers . . ."

"Your daddy do that?"

I nodded.

"Well, he's a smart man." He pointed at the trunk, so I opened it for him. "Now you take this. I seen a automobile burn to the ground for want of one of these." He removed the fire extinguisher and undid the tool kit, lifting out a round black loop. "Here's what I was looking for. Your daddy's a smart man."

My father didn't do that. That had to have been in the car all along; the Germans did that. My father never put in anything I could use.

Something growled behind me and I jumped again and ran for the car, only to see that the mountain lion in the shack had turned into a giant dog, a female with a litter of pups tumbling along behind her as she walked up to the man.

"Easy, girl, she ain't going to hurt your pups. I put this here belt around her neck and twist it if she does."

The big dog walked over and pushed her head under his hand. "She's a beauty, ain't she?" Then he said, "Sit!" and the dog rocked back on her haunches and sat immobile even with her pups nestling around her. Her face looked miserable, like she was caught in a trap, but she wouldn't move until he snapped his fingers. Then she trotted back towards the shack, her puppies trying to catch up with her.

"Yeah, she don't talk back." He began to cackle as he started working on the car. "Best kind of woman there is. Yes, sir, the very best kind. Yeah," he went on, "good to see some gals got some spunk. I admire a gal strong enough to push a automobile clean up to the station. At first I was betting now she's as tall and scrawny as a weed and she ain't got enough meat on her to make it and she'll push on it with it stuck in gear till she's wore out. I was betting you'd bust out and cry, that's what I expect a gal to do, bust out and cry.

"See, this thing has to have its own tools. Germans can't

make something to fit your tools. They got to make them just a
hair off so they won't fit. I bet I got a hundred wrenches in there
and not one of them to fit that nut."

"Does the one in the set fit?"

"Yeah," he frowned, "I reckon it does."

He started to work under the lid again. "It fits but it won't fit
nothing else. Yeah, I expect a gal to bust out and cry, break one
of them little red fingernails pushing on a automobile and cry
her heart out. Woman come here once, you coming here made
me think of it. Can't say you bear no likeness, though. She had
the tiniest little hands. Them little nails looked like they'd
snap off if she moved too fast. Painted them up just as careful.

"She wont big as a minute. Wont like you, not a bit like you.
First off she didn't have no automobile, and if she had, that little bird of a thing couldn't have pushed it out of its tracks. She
was on foot, high-heeled shoes at that, and I seen her coming
up the road to the station. She was wobbling in the sand and I
seen her stop, pick up one foot then the other, and flick off them
red shoes, and I could as good have told her she was going to burn
her feet up on the pavement. She had this hairdo that was
leaning this way and that and come to find out most of it come
clean off. I was trying to reason what to do. I don't want no
trouble, you understand, and was fixing not to go out, but there
wont no way in this world I could stop her from coming to my
place, now was there? Naw, sir, not with her heading towards it
and not another house for ten miles."

He took his head from the engine compartment and bumped
it on the lid. "Shit!" He looked at me, twisting his mouth.

"Well, she started into telling me what happened to her and
you have never heard of anybody having such a terrible time.
Somebody had stole her automobile. You could tell it must
have been a nice one because she had on fancy clothes with
shiny things sewed acrosst her front." He made a dotted line
with his finger across his chest. "Then she started telling me
how she had give these girls a ride out of the kindness of her
heart because they got stranded in Florence by some men who
left them, and the next thing she knew, one of them girls took
out a knife and ordered her out of her own automobile and just
left her right in the middle of the swamp, where she could have

died or got snakebit for all they cared, kept talking about that, gitting snakebit, like there was going to be one hanging out of a tree with his mouth open soon as she got off the sidewalk. Well, I told her I'd take my jeep and go in and git a sheriff, but she wouldn't have it. Said she had let the license run out and she would be in a mess of trouble if they found out, and I thought wont that just like a woman to think a fine for letting a license go is worst than losing your whole automobile like that. But I let her come on inside out of the heat to see if her mind might start working better, but didn't git a bit of improvement. Well, after a while she lit into the kitchen and started fussing and banging pots around, yanking stuff out of the pantry, and come out with one of the finest dinners on the table you ever seen. Hot biscuits melt in your mouth. I wouldn't have thought she could take the lid off a can . . . Start the motor."

"Huh?"

"Git in and start the motor and see if this thing is going to work or just flap right back off. I wouldn't cut my grass with this puny little motor."

I got in and started the car, looking at the dash for the red light, but it didn't come on.

"Now don't that sound like it ought to be thrashing wheat?"

"I guess you fixed it. How much do I owe you?"

He went around to the front of the car and put the tools back, slamming the lid. "About a dollar labor, I reckon."

As I reached in my pocketbook for the dollar, he walked up beside my door and said, "You got to leave right away?"

I turned off the engine, a reflex, and as soon as the engine was silent, realized my mistake.

"What you got to rush for? Come on inside and I'll fix you a Co'Cola with ice."

With ice. I got out and followed him in, feeling not unlike the dog with the pups, her tongue hanging out of her mouth. But my teats weren't big enough to swing. I was surprised to find that he had a counter inside, like a small soda fountain, with four stools. I sat down while he went around to fix the drinks, and I looked over my shoulder at the door that was only a few feet away. The car was outside and would run if I needed to escape. A fly started buzzing around me, so I snatched at it like I used to do back home on the porch and, to my surprise, caught it. Then I said, "Your South Carolina flies are pretty slow. Now if that had been a North Carolina fly, he'd be sitting on the ceiling laughing at me."

While I was contemplating removing the fly's wings and watching him buzz around on the floor (my cousin Charles used to do this), it slipped through my fingers and flew up to the ceiling. I looked over at the man again and saw he was frowning.

"If you had to live in this heat that don't let up when the sun sets even, you'd be slow moving too, I grant you."

The man walked around and sat on the stool beside me. I waited for the rest of the stranded-woman story but instead he pointed to a postcard in the rack.

"Recognize that?"

"Looks like Spanish moss."

"That ain't just Spanish moss! That picture was taken right out there in front of the station. You can tell by the way the trees is setting. The station is right here," and he pointed to a spot in the air beside the card. "If they'd got that camera over half an inch we'd be right in it. Don't know how in the world they took it without me knowing. Guess if I'd taken the time to put a coat of paint on the station they might have put it in."

I looked at the rack and saw that except for a few assorted cards picturing black children on piles of cotton, and one with a cotton boll in a plastic bag, one night shot of Savannah, and an assortment of cartoon cards — "You have to do what?" husband says to wife in rowboat — that all of the cards were just alike: a picture of trees draped in Spanish moss.

I looked at him then and confirmed what I'd thought earlier. He wasn't too ugly. If I had seen him in a western movie and he had been a lonely cowboy, I might have been in love for a couple of days; but somehow sitting beside him here didn't have the same effect. At first I don't think I was bothered by his stupidity, not even by his dirty fingernails and shirt and the fact that in tighter quarters he smelled like a dirty sock. There was something nice about a man that would have to go to a lot of trouble to be with a woman, even touch her. As my roommate Clara would say, you know he's either going to leave you alone or try to rape you, no sneaky stuff.

But he was pitiful. So strong and tough and here he was, an absolute sitting duck for any female who happened to come along. If I could have taken a picture of him with his dark skin and yellow hair and blue eyes with crinkles around them, a color picture that was slightly blurred, I could have had Clara and the rest oohing and ahing over him, telling me how lucky I was to break a fan belt. Then I laughed at myself for thinking that, thinking every male that happened to come into my life was a potential catch, the instinctive glance at the left hand for the band of gold. This is the Nevada Kid, Mom. He rescued me from the swamp.

"You better watch yourself down there in Savannah. Don't know as you should go there by yourself."

I jumped when he spoke because it had taken so long.

"Oh, well, I'm not going out after dark." Then I realized how stupid that sounded.

"Then why you going?"

I stammered around, searching for another scenic attraction of Savannah, when he said, "Well, that ain't none of my business." I appreciated him more then than when he got my car started.

"But you watch yourself now. Not that you'll get took for being a bad woman. You ain't got that filled-out look yet. But that was what happened to her."

"To her?"

"To the woman with the red shoes I been telling you about."

I was sure he looked down at my shoes then, size eight and a half: big feet equal fidelity, dainty feet equal wild woman of the streets. My grandfather said they turned off too much of my legs in feet.

"Oh, don't worry. I won't pick up any hitchhikers."

"That ain't what I meant. She got herself took a lot worse than losing a car. That was just the beginning of her troubles. Wont long after that when I seen her over in Savannah in one of them cafes, not one of them nice ones that'll set you back a pretty penny, but one of them sorry ones that a woman who's got any opinion of herself won't set a foot in to git a hamburger. Idn't it something, as big a place as that and I find her right off? But I never told you how she left here."

I shook my head and waited. I was starting to want to know the rest of the red-shoe story.

"Well, she got up so quiet the next morning I didn't even wake up and she slipped out of here and left me a note: 'Forgive me for taking the money from out of your pants,' she says in this note. 'I would never have wanted to take money from you sinc't you showed me more kindness than I've ever knowed, but I got to be gitting back.' More kindness than she'd ever knowed. She didn't know no kindness, I can tell you that. She didn't put down no name and to this day, I don't know her name except if maybe it's really the one off the picture out front of the place where she works — Lily. Sounds like a made-up name to me. But what I was telling you, that rather than go and admit she forgot to git a new license and git her automobile found for her, I figure she went out and got her one of them truck drivers to take her into this town and got her a job in a place like that."

I was beginning to feel uneasy. I decided I didn't want to hear the rest of the story. I wanted to get out of there. Just five miles down the road was all my car had to take me, five miles and he would never even know I had existed. I was wrong about stupidity not bothering me. There was something about absolute and complete stupidity that was starting to frighten me. I wanted to scream at him to stop, not destroy himself in front of me. He had proven he knew more about cars than I did and I wished he had stopped at that.

"And she won't talk to me. I come up and she won't even let on that she knows me, and sure as I'm setting here, she does know me. She knows me real good."

He sat back; I thought he was falling, but there was a stool behind him I didn't know was there. He tapped the ice back and forth in his cup and it made noises like snow slush disappearing back into water.

"Are you thinking she took me for a ride?"

"I don't know what I'm thinking," I said quickly and that was true.

"There are people that would do that," he said, almost a question. "Take your car and things."

"Yes, there are," I said. He was starting not to look convinced himself when I added, "There are people who will tell you a big story trying to make you think they are different from what they are, too."

"Yeah, yeah, you're right about that. You mean like women. I know you're right about that. It just seemed the right reason, you know, for her to be out walking all dressed like that. She looked right fancy dressed, if you was to see her out here. But I'm not to be a judge of how she'd look down there in Savannah. They say you could come from out here dressed in a millionaire's suit and one of them city people would look how your hair was cut and know right off, you know what I mean? That's what I heard people say who know."

I nodded.

"I wouldn't know. You could fool me, living out here. I mean you probably go to college somewhere and your daddy buys you what you want. You don't look like no mature woman though you're probably old enough to be. And your daddy don't let you git too fancy. I can tell that by the car. He bought you a sorry car so you won't act biggety."

The man crunched a piece of ice. "I won't go back many more times, don't know that I'll ever go again, to tell you the truth. It's a good hour-and-a-half drive from here." He was silent, reaching into the cup for the ice, the water beading on the grease on his hands. "Didn't think that before. I mighta just said it before I thought. Didn't think that before you said what you did."

"What?"

"About people telling stories. Don't know why I was thinking a pretty girl wouldn't tell me a story as big as the next person. She was probably real good at telling stories. Tells them to every fool she meets. More fools than you can count on both your hands." His eyes brightened as he said, "So many fools she don't remember all of them. Just them little faces on the bills. Them are the kinds of faces she remembers."

I laughed. I couldn't help it, but he did too and my feet hit the floor to walk just like the last note of a song had been played. As I walked to the door, the dog moved out again, still giving me chills on the backs of my legs. An oily blue pickup pulled up at the pump.

"More fools than you could shake a stick at," he mumbled.

It was getting dark out, red between the trees. I didn't look at him until I heard the car engine start. Then I saw him beside the man in the pickup, who pumped his own gas, lifting his hand about waist high to wave. I waved as I drove out into the empty road, no one coming from either direction. I wanted to start down the road fast, but my little car struggled through the gears as always. I wanted to cut his voice off, not listen to him anymore.

I began to tremble a little as my wet clothes touched me, but it was still hot. Blacks walked by the side of the road, frightening me when I moved past a child on a wobbling bike, dark clothes, not there until I was on him and past him.

I started to look in the next town for a place marked "Guests." A motel would not do; I wanted to be where an old lady would watch the late show and where I could hear men and women singing to each other in a twenty-year-old musical, all coming from the front room, where the old lady would sit until it was time to turn out the light on her vacancy sign. I found it, a place where no one else would stop, where I would be with the old lady, or maybe the old lady and her husband. When I checked in, I heard her talk to someone, who grumbled a reply from in front of the TV.

*   *   *

The woman with the red shoes . . .

*I stayed in a motel once in Savannah, sitting all night in a chair. I only got up once from the chair and went to the window to see if it was raining. I wanted to get away from the bed and the room but was afraid to move. It was not a fantasy that I had watched from my motel window in Savannah, my time there before, a woman walking by in the morning, tucking in her blouse. She was carrying her red shoes, walking in stocking feet on the sidewalk, with the thermometer billboard over her head already reading eighty-five degrees at dawn. I had seen a woman in red shoes, had laughed out loud when I saw her before I knew the story, or rather the story that might have been her story. Then I trembled, afraid the boy might wake up and speak, and I couldn't blot him from my mind, the boy asleep who was so angry with me, who hated me, he said, lying there cold and* stonelike, turning frozen to me when I chickened out. He and I weren't like Red Shoes and the Service Station Man. He didn't know me real good. But I hated him for really believing I wanted to go through with it in the first place.

No, I can't blame him, not anymore. That's not much reason to hate, though it seemed to be at the time. I can't keep blaming him for my guilt and embarrassment. The experience I had with the boy, that by definition was no experience at all, was a year in becoming real. Now it takes on another layer and becomes a memory. It seems to no longer frighten or perplex me. I feel nothing about him. There was a time when I imagined ways that he could be killed and take what we knew away in his dead brain. Then I could forget my embarrassment.

I liked that man in the gas station; but I'm glad he's not here. I wish he could have seen that woman taking off her shoes and tiptoeing down the pavement for everyone to see her through the crack in the shade in Savannah. I laughed at her, and she would have laughed at me. The service station man would have sat beside me and watched her, saying, "Damn, would you look at that. There's some people who would tell you a story, ain't there." And I would agree and feel completely safe.

But when I was in Savannah with the boy, I went in the bathroom and wrote on the back of the paper bathmat. The next morning what I'd written didn't make any sense, so I used the mat to step out on after my shower. I took it with me, the ink running like a bruise on the white paper. It is still there in my box of notes and I thought several times I might take it out and read it. But I only think that when I'm not near the box. When I'm near the box, I write more to put in. Maybe I already am what I am now and can't change it or figure out why by going backwards.

\* \* \*

# Part II

I DOZED WHEN the plane finally leveled out after leaving Kennedy. My father gave me a summer trip to Europe for my graduation present and for once let me make my own plans. That was why I flew Icelandic instead of taking a tour. It was a small and noisy airplane. That was what cheap meant. When you live rich, you are cushioned from noise and you have somewhere to put your legs if they happen to be overly long. The plane's engine may have been made by Rolls-Royce, but it made my VW sound like a Cadillac. See, hadn't even started my Europe trip and already I was the ugly, affluent American. I needed to watch myself there.

A stewardess said something about red wine or pineapple juice when I was half asleep, and I said no, only to realize just a few minutes later that I had refused a hot meal. I tried to sleep again so all the clicking silverware wouldn't make me hungry and awoke hours later to a stewardess asking did I want an apple for breakfast. Survival of the fittest.

Columbus was right. The world felt round when you climbed up and around it like an inchworm on a beachball. The clouds were such a dirty brown color that at first I thought they were land, miles of unlived-on, unused land with no life, green slime cut with dry rivers. On the way to Iceland, the airplane moaned like a rusty cable car, never reaching any summit or relief. When I first realized we were getting closer to the mainland, I saw the water below take on a shallow color. Soon there were bits of land, real land this time, scattered in the blue. Then Iceland. The main isle was stained around the edges by farms, with a few fragments broken off, gathering fishing boats like ants around a bread crumb. When the mainland appeared, it was patterned and divided with water in pools flashing back at the sunrise. Only a few minutes before, I had felt as if we could have been orbiting the moon.

After we landed and I went through customs, I boarded a bus to the hotel at Reykjavik. Another bus went past and I realized we were on the wrong side of the road. Out the bus window there was nothing. Miles of nothing. My perspective left almost immediately and it was hard to define the surrounding landscape as anything but nothing.

\* \* \*

*First item in a new journal. Iceland is their something; my nothing. Maybe because there are no trees. I would not require road markers and billboards, but it seems that I notice immediately that trees are missing.*

*No one I know for ten weeks. I can't wait. I must not be like my old roommate Clara at all.*

*In Iceland there is only an occasional tiny blue flower squeezed out between the rocks. Someone has taken a giant paintbrush and made the country brick red, covering everything. I read that people don't live long here, that even though they get used to the place year after year, they die sooner than they would somewhere else. They live double day now, double night in the winter. Last night I shut my window and pinned the shade to shut out the noise and light as men worked building streets while I slept.*

*It is cold here. I left summer back home. The children swim in warm-water pools while I shiver, wrapped in my coat. Their swimming holes steam like hot pots on the stove. Their limbs are white as the bean plants I raised in the dark in Biology lab. I have no contact here, no connection. I am watching life go on, but I see so little of it because I don't understand why. I saw men with wood and hammers in a riverbed today but I didn't know what they were building and couldn't ask them.*

*When I hiked in the country, the ground bubbled at my feet, fat yellow bubbles that rose and swelled like yellow half-balls, glazed and sleepy-looking like old eyes. Then they popped and* smelled of sulfur. My ankles were swollen from sitting so long on the airplane and I walked with care through the bubbles, fearing the ground might explode and scald me, a geyser minefield. The bubbles started to pop faster, then spurted like a broken vein, spewing hot yellow through the air that the wind twisted and threw at me, hot drops on my face. This is the landscape of hell.

But there is something very nice about the bubbling ground. It makes you look down and watch where your feet go and not take it for granted under there or it will burn you. Pay attention to where you are, it is saying.

A storm of orange sand whipped across the lava where I walked, the lava that splashed and froze as it fell before I arrived, like a movie cut off, struck silent as it spread all the living things under with its red earth icing. There was a break in the earth, half a mountain to one side, half to the other. I yelled and heard my echo, a language strange to the rocks. I walked into the crack and I shivered to think how little it might take to upset this earth again. There were craters on the earth moon, bright aqua-blue water at the bottom, with a color that would be untrue on the artist's palette, a color you would never think to use in a nature painting except for a small flower, for a speck not a pool. There were red and green lichens, three feet deep, pubic hair sprouting in giant crotches, primitive life come to grow on top of the lava. The ground shakes, almost every day it trembles enough to be an earthquake, and one day an island rose up from the sea. I can see it off the coast, but they say it may fall back again, so no one has plans to live on it.

The food is cooked in sheep blood to warm you, but I am not warm. Even when I roll in the white feather-bed cover and see the light of day come through my window at night, I am not warm, because I can hear the wind blasting the building I sleep in and the crunch of the glacier that I saw move when I stood still in the wind. The wind would blow me away here. It is that strong, strong enough to turn my body over and roll it if I lost balance as it blew.

The people won't speak to me. Maybe that is why I am so cold. Only the guide, and I paid her to speak. She was fond of telling *of the chopping blocks where churchmen and Danes lost their heads.*

*The rooftops are red and yellow and green. They glow day and night because the sun is always there. The lichens are red and green. The sheep are white and black. The wild flowers on the lava are bright blue, almost purple. There are no trees to hold to in the wind. I stand as close to the geysers as I can because I am cold and want to warm my hands and feet. I want to see a rainbow in the yellow bubble. I know what I am doing. I know what I always do when I get cold. I think in colors. It is hard to think about myself, to worry about sorting my problems out here, because there is so much else to see. Maybe I won't have to.*

*At supper in Luxembourg I looked for a long time at the bowl of water with a peach and a pear floating in it. Finally at another table I saw the people fish out the fruit with a large spoon. They meant for me to wash the fruit, that's all. So simple and I didn't understand. I shouldn't have been walking alone last night. I hope this doesn't mean I'll be afraid to go out at night at all. I didn't think about it being foolish, even after a child ran out of an alley and pulled my hair, didn't think until then that I was totally unprotected and had no one to run to. I had to run from a drunk. I ran further than I needed to, into a crowded open-air restaurant where I sat down and ate ice cream I didn't want. He was too drunk to catch me, but he did grab my arm and I knew he was strong.*

*On the train to Germany today I saw a yellow field, some kind of ripe grain, and over it flew black birds. For a long time I just looked, feeling something familiar and trying to recognize it. Then I thought of it. It was van Gogh's last painting, the birds over the field, his vision of his death. What was in van Gogh's head at that time, his insanity, could go into my head seeing those black birds in the blue sky over the yellow field with paths that went nowhere. It is vain and stupid of me to think I could have seen it if he hadn't told me it was there.*

*World War II was only in words for me, not pictures. I watched me appear after the war when I listened to the tic-tic of my father's movie projector. I saw the date 1949. He edited his home movies so carefully I felt as if I were watching myself in a newsreel. There were others in the movies, but I must admit that I mostly watched me, in wonder that there was a time in my life that I do not remember and that I do not see from the inside out. I bent around a railing over a creek in the park, my underpants showing, next to coal-black bell-bottom trousers, polished black shoes, and a face that looked from under a white sailor cap, so young I wonder if he did not have thoughts of the two-year-old flirting with him as more than a two-year-old. Did he wonder what I would grow in to and how old he would be when I was ready? Probably not. But I was pretty cute in those movies.*

*West Berlin is a giant electricity bill, the main-street shops cluttered with colored lights that are never turned off. But enough is still there to tell me of the war before my time: the brittle spire of a church, its rose window a gouged-out eye, staring half blind and half alive like a cripple in the midst of healthy children. Inside that church the battered mosaics are seamed back together; shrapnel holes in the walls are filled with cobwebs.*

*When I first saw the wall, it seemed unimpressive, like an ordinary prison wall. But then I saw the people and something was immediately clear: why should they be prisoners when they have committed no crime? On the other side of the wall, I walked through a burned-down city before I came to the fresh concrete of East Berlin. I went to a museum where the Indians and Negroes were recorded as mistreated and Harry Truman as waiting to see who would win before deciding which side to take. And the market fell to show what happens to capitalists. There is a giant photo of a Wall Streeter jumping from a window. The proud part of the museum is the German worker, industry. The word "imperialist" is everywhere. There seems to be nothing in their history but war. A sign outside says the museum was restored after the Anglo-American bombing, no mention that Russia was one of the Allies.*

*I looked for a long time at a thing in a glass case, an insignificant-looking thing, leatherlike, tanned, a crude shade for a lamp, I thought. My mind leveled and stretched and the German words on the card made my head hurt. I heard someone* come up behind me, an old woman. All of the guards were old women who walked heavy on flat feet; she rocked the uneven floors and made the thing in the case vibrate. The thing. I saw her face and wondered did she think I might steal it when even the market on the east side had much more to attract me than what was inside the glass. At once my body shuddered with the sight of her face, saying more than all the letters put together in a way I could not read, and I screamed like a child.

I think I screamed, but there was no noise in the halls. I fooled myself. There was no scream, just the shudder of my body as she stood beside me and the tears burned my eyes like acid. I didn't understand. I didn't know the person in the leather lampshade in front of me, a man or a woman. Polish, I think she muttered that. Or that the shrunken head in the case was a Pole. She pointed the head out to me and pictures of medical experiments being done on children. Forty-eight years ago, she told me, she had had a baby. They took it from her arms. She told me the years with her hands, then she cupped her arms and hummed to her baby and she moaned when suddenly the imaginary child was gone. I understood her. I told her I understood and I would carry what I understood back outside the wall if that was what she wanted me to do. I didn't know why she told me, I told her. She didn't understand me, but I don't think it mattered. It just seemed so important to her that I know what she was saying that she did it again and again. She was called away by one of the other guards. When I left I waved to her. She nodded, but in a very businesslike way.

I left and went to the Greek museum. I wanted to see some art. I didn't know I was going to a history museum when I went to the other one. I was overpowered by the Greek museum, columns, statues, whole temples. What is it doing here? Why don't the Greeks have their history in their own country? There was an old woman there too, a visitor, tiny with bright blue eyes. Her feet wouldn't touch the floor when she rested on a bench in the museum. She smiled and seemed to be enjoying things very much and I smiled back at her. Something about her looked a bit insane.

In the daylight I watched soldiers in funny hats like the one my cousin Charles played in as a little boy. It was no joke to try to make them laugh like at the changing of the guards in England. When I went to the Tower of London with my parents, I tried for a long time to make one of them smile. I tried until I got mad and my father laughed at me. Here, if you don't know it is O.K., you don't do it. The soldiers walk in the new East Berlin city without girls. There is an occasional church left standing, but they appear dingy from disuse, not war. The soldiers looked at my short skirt with eyes like adolescent boys'. They look the same way at a Mustang in the square. They disapprove, even the young. I wonder if they are jealous of people who have Mustangs. Maybe I'm imagining things, just like them, seeing what I want to see. It was easier to think about the war when my mind was outside beside the sailor over the creek. I wish I had watched him more closely. When I go home, I'll watch those movies again. I remember other things from the projector, relatives I don't know, a line-up of cousins, and the ones who died in the war are pointed out, the one who never had to leave Cherry Point, the one who can't sleep with his wife because he hurts her during his bad dreams.

Young couples do not seem to have children. Only one child swims, nude, in the fountain. A child would build a wall. I saw one pregnant girl and I wondered how it would feel to know you were going to have a baby but it was going to be born behind the wall. Is it as if it were never born? I wonder how she reads what is in her museum. I know how she reads it: "We have done no wrong. Life is one continuous war between the haves and the have-nots. Good people are have-nots. Good people will always be poor and have to struggle, but we are going to give you a country that loves poor, struggling people and you will never be hungry again. We already have the best factories in the world and your baby will be a good Communist."

Sometimes I am really simple-minded. I don't even know what a Communist is. I wonder how she would feel if the old woman in the museum told her about her baby. The crazy black mother in Asheville was forty-eight too, and her child died killing Communists.

\*

*I went to Dachau today. It is not the oven that seems horrible to me. Cremation seems dignified, not to want to clutter the earth with a plot of ground marked for people not to step on with a stone to remind them that you once lived. I think I would want to be cremated, for my corpse to vanish. Someone told me of a practice in Switzerland of burying people in a park with no markers and the decaying bodies fertilized the flowers.*

*I started to take a photo of the outside of Dachau, but I stopped after I looked through the camera and realized no one would be able to tell it from the army barracks at Fort Bragg. Outside, maybe, I see why it all happened with no one knowing. But for the statue, an abstract of people twisting in black iron sculpted long after the war, there is nothing significant about Dachau from the outside. The statue, thin, drawn bodies stretched across a square, is not really abstract at all. It seemed to move in the drizzling rain.*

*The pictures inside will stay wedged in my head for a long time, black-and-white photographs. An old woman stood close to the enlarged photos, tracing down the rows of faces with her finger. They showed a movie taken when the war was ended as they took the bodies away in wooden wagons, the men with gas masks on as they led the horses, the horses' nostrils open to the smell. People bring small children here and lead them through without speaking. One of the photos shows a mother walking with her three children to their death; she had dressed them warmly in coats and hats like it was any day and she wanted to protect them from the weather. Some of the murderers were women. I always thought a Nazi was a man, with a woman as a poor, dumb mistress like a gun moll.*

*My father says things about Jews just like he does blacks. It is always a nigger dog that wet his white side walls or a Jew cat that woke him fighting at night. He signed a petition to keep Jews from buying land in Windy Pines Resort because he said they would turn it into a little Miami.*

*After dark the night before last, I watched men in boats out on the lake in front of the hotel at Lake Como. They were using flashlights and gigging for fish. The air was gutted with bugs,* the flashlights drawing them to the water and bringing the fish to the top to strike. I heard the men arguing later when I was trying to sleep and could see a circle of bald heads under my window hovering over a card game. After I finally got to sleep, a storm came through, a violent thunderstorm that must have been a surprise even to the people who live there all the time because all of the furniture was blown from the porches. I watched one of the waiters trying to fix a ripped awning in the morning. When I woke up, I saw that my bed was filled with mashed bugs — probably the bugs that dropped on the water for the fish had come in the screenless window when the storm hit, and I mashed them when I tossed and turned trying to sleep while the storm crashed outside.

I needed to come here to Switzerland. Maybe I'm easily depressed, but after the concentration camp, I started combing every town I came to for war scars, wondering every time I saw a man with a missing limb, wondering why the trains had special seats for them. Sunday in Germany was good for my mind too, the rows of huge white bellies poked up at the sun beside the Rhine, the little children in the parks dressed all day in their Sunday clothes. Over here it's like a party on Sunday. Even eating an ice cream cone felt special. I haven't been by myself long enough to start feeling lonely, so it was pleasant to watch other people happy.

Last night they celebrated a holiday here in Bivio. They played the national anthem and sang and shot fireworks. Everywhere in the windows I saw round red lanterns with the white Swiss cross on them. On top of a mountain was a big bonfire. People ran down the streets from house to house, shooting fireworks and moving on to the next house to enjoy each person's fireworks one at a time. I walked along with them. I'm starting to feel as if I'm supposed to be here watching all of this, that I really have a purpose. Maybe writing all of this down gives me a sense of purpose.

Yesterday afternoon I went up on the mountainside behind my pension. There were ox-eye daisies everywhere, yellow and white just like on my grandfather's farm and in Colorado, everywhere in the world you can find them I bet. The flower colors seemed to change with altitude; the forms were the same but at each level a new color appeared, all blue, all pink, all orange. There is great beauty up close in the little things, and the mountains in the distance are almost more than I can comprehend. I have trouble describing things I really like. I walked through a field of mown hay, strong smelling and soft, and I sank in it like quicksand, almost to the point of panic.

I kept hearing bells, single bells like wind chimes. Then I looked up when I heard them come closer and behind me was a brown cow with horns, and around its neck was a bell. Each cow had a bell of its own. That was a good feeling, that each one was important enough to be given its own bell so it could be found if it were lost. When they walked they made a beautiful music.

I ate my lunch that the hotel packed for me, sitting by the trail. While I was there, several old people walked by. One old lady looked at me and said, "You know not to put that trash on the ground, don't you?" That kind of stung, but it didn't ruin my day because nothing could. I did start to think about the people here, their isolation policy and neutrality, their protection gained by being passive. I could make these observations to my father, tell him about the museum in East Berlin or Dachau, and he would raise an eyebrow, look bored and unshocked, and I'd feel like an idiot. I would be telling him the marvel of something he already knew. Maybe that's why I like to write here, because there is no one to call me stupid.

I am going to stay put for a few days and do some hiking and cruise the lakes. I'm not sleeping well and that's unusual for me. Usually I can sleep standing up. I need to unwind. I wake up at night and wonder where the bathroom is.

Yesterday I talked to an American boy on the train, who said he was going to take a scenic trip through the Bavarian Alps today. We were riding through farm country with big houses where the farm animals lived on the bottom floor under the people. Men were putting down new rails, six of them swinging a log against the iron. The American boy made fun of a girl who got on and rode for a short distance with a big cardboard suitcase tied shut with rope. She was a farm girl, her hands large and chapped from hard work. She wore thin nylons that wrinkled on her unshaven legs, the kind of nylons that I didn't think they made anymore. She had a friendly smile and turned her head away shyly because one of her eyes was damaged. I wondered if she ever looked at the light blue broken eye with her good eye. She wore no wedding ring; the eye probably turned away her suitors. Maybe her father damaged her by accident with a pitchfork or a fence wire. Like a man in our neighborhood who was tossing his daughter a ball and she looked up as it went through their picture window. He spent a fortune and couldn't fix her eye back right.

Today on the TV news I saw a train stacked like scrap metal as I walked through the hotel lobby, a wreck in Bavaria. The American boy was probably on that train and the big farm girl was already at her destination, maybe praying with relatives because she hadn't waited until today to ride to see them. The Germans in the hotel were standing in front of the TV and moaning as the scenes flashed, each one worse than the last, of cars broken and twisted. On the window of one I saw the sign for smoking and the sticker that means no cigars. Someone didn't die because he smoked cigars and another died because he didn't smoke. A lot died, because they were cutting them out of the metal and carrying away stretchers. The TV cameras over here don't censor death. They photograph everything at the death scene. And I watched, waiting to see if I saw the American boy, but I didn't. Everyone was watching, so I didn't feel guilty. I know I wasn't watching because I cared about his life.

If you were the engineer in the nose and looked down the track, how long would it be before you knew something was wrong and pulled on the brakes? If you were the one at fault, would you have time to think it was you who didn't wait in the last station long enough? You were going to kill a lot of people and didn't want to. You were like a drunk driving into a crowd and couldn't stop yourself, but you didn't mean to be a killer. Or would you have time to hate the other engineer for making the error because you knew you were going to be dead in seconds?

I had been telling myself my alarm was false when I trembled as the other trains passed, rattling our windows, that my fright *was my ignorance. This is the way it is. You travel roads that people died on today and will die on tomorrow. You fly in airplanes and read that others crashed at an airport you used. I don't think about it unless I make myself. I look at those broken train cars in wonder and think that I looked in the windows of those compartments for an empty seat and now they are turned over at strange angles. I wonder if the seat I used was a survivor's seat. That is all the unknown. That is not the way that I fear death.*

*I walked by the tracks today and saw a sign that had a lightning bolt. "Danger of Death." Electric trains. All as out of your hands as the airplane the moment it moves from the gate and becomes managed by a complex network that can, but rarely does, fail. Some people are blind with fear that it will fail when they are inside. My father is. No smugness there. After every business trip he is smashed when my mother picks him up at the airport, and he isn't an alcoholic.*

*I don't know why I thought I could just go out and walk down the tracks around the lake. I only did that one other time in my life, on old-fashioned American tracks in the mountains.*

*There was a trestle. The trestle was of the Clinchfield Railroad, high over the Nolichucky River near the North Carolina–Tennessee border. The river was running high and muddy for that time of the year, an unusually warm and rainy February day that was melting the winter snow. In the sandbars were Clorox bottles and plastic milk jugs, trapped in the snags by the hundreds, white plastic bubbles like eggs tossed up from the water. I had my lunch in my knapsack.*

*When I asked about the trestle to Lost Cove, an old man told me, "There's a man in there with a thirty-thirty who shoots anybody who goes in. You don't want to mess with no man like that. He wouldn't think much of some young girl come walking in there. Soon shoot you as look at you."*

*I laughed at the man, half believing him.*

*"I'm not telling you a tale," he insisted. "You don't know nothing about people like him."*

*"Do you think I believe that some old bearded codger's in there sitting on the porch with a gun across his lap?" I asked.*

*"Naw." He laughed too. I watched the tall gray-haired man in corduroy pants, his gas station and grocery store behind him, Poplar, North Carolina. His face softened quickly, none of the surliness in his manner that was found among the flatland farmers where Clara lived. He wanted to keep me out, but I felt his concern for my safety was real. A kitten came from under a bench, a clean white kitten running across clean, white swept concrete. "Naw. Real reason is I don't want you on the trestle. I'd worry till I seen you back out.*

*"Girl died on there. Train run her down before she knew what hit her. I seen what it did to her, us counting pieces till we figured we had enough to make a whole girl. Worst thing I ever seen, and I was in the war. Ain't been long. And she won't be the last." He looked up at me while lighting his pipe and puffing steadily. "You got good sense. You can see as good as you're standing there, where you going to git off when the train is coming? Not a thing she could have done with all the good sense in the world once she got out there and that train come bearing down on her. It's near 'bout a quarter-mile acrosst that thing." He had worked up his emotions while he talked, thinking about the girl again, and his voice had started to tremble. When he stopped talking, his lips continued to move.*

*I looked at the trestle; the concrete sides curved and had no footholds; it was built skimpy, only enough material in it to hold the train. The river was fast and rocky below, moving with such speed I looked away and felt dizzy.*

*If I had to, I thought, I could lie flat between the rails. No, not with all those things that hang under a train reaching for my back. Holding until a hundred cars passed, the train shaking the trestle, the river rushing below, who has the mind or strength for that? He was right; there was nowhere to go in that quarter-mile, should I get caught. But I had come a long way and I had told everybody I was going to make the trip.*

*I left him, passed the gauging station, and started the walk across the trestle. A dog followed me down the tracks, but it stopped dead still, whimpering when the river was under the crossties instead of earth. I started to call it but had second thoughts about taking someone's dog across the trestle. The animal waited a moment, then turned and ran back towards the* station. I was sure the old man was thinking I didn't have a dog's sense as I picked my way on the crossties. Four miles down the track was my destination, Lost Cove, North Carolina, a deserted village. It was said that when the passenger trains were cut off from the cove, the village died, its houses still furnished, its orchards, gardens, all left behind for the animals. Then the freight train was cut back on, roaring by the little village without slowing, making it harder to go in than when there was no train. A wall of mountains, the Bald and Unaka Mountains, that quarter-mile of trestle, and an irregular train schedule separated the town from the rest of the world. Lost Cove could be seen from Flattop Mountain, the one-room schoolhouse, the church, the cluster of houses, like a miniature town in an electric-train set, even a chicken running somewhere, or maybe it was a deer. I had viewed it from there early that morning and it was hard to judge the size or condition of anything. From the top of the mountain it was a perfect village, protected — or trapped — by the river and mountains.

On the trestle walking was hard. The rail was narrow and hard to move fast on; the crossties were too regular, spaced too close for my step. The top of my body with its backpack got ahead of my step. I wobbled when the wind swept against me, feeling light, as if I could be swept over the side. The river underneath was deafening, brown-red with eroded topsoil, moving between the cracks at my feet and pulling my balance from under me when I gazed downward. I looked forward and backward over my shoulder for the train that might come before I reached the other side. There was a dead fox, his body dried and wrapped around the wood ties like a tacked-up skin, the scent almost gone. My feet kept moving, leaving the fox behind.

Halfway across, there was a sound. I was sure I heard it, a whistle. I ran, the ties falling under my feet, my pack beating my back. When I reached the other side, I jumped to the ground beside the rails, running away from the two metal runners. My side ached and my pack had made sore spots on my shoulders. I felt like a child who had jumped into bed and slid under the covers to escape an imaginary monster, safe for a moment, but the monster was still there if I were to look out at it. I turned and stared at the trestle; it stood between me and the outside like a thread.

The man at the gas station must have thought I was a child, or that I had the mind of one. I could no longer see his station or him. I knew that sometime that day I had to face the reality of recrossing the trestle when the hike was done, because I was not equipped for overnight. But for then, I was over.

As I walked down the tracks, the side too narrow to keep a footing, I looked back for the train, nervous until I could see a large section of track and knew I would have enough warning. Soon there was a rumble, a sound like large rocks rolling somewhere, a huge machine coming down the river. A train, the whistle in the distance had been real. Its direction was impossible to judge; the river spread and lapped noisily at the rock cliffs below, the track was cut into the rock with little more edge to stand on than the trestle. I tried to guess the width of a boxcar, how close against the rock I would have to press to let it pass. The rumble got louder until it was above and separate from the sound of the river. The train appeared, large, black, and strange to someone who had seen a thousand trains, larger than life when there was so little ground to stand on. I got off the track far too soon, because the train moved very slowly, struggling, teasing. In the shade beside me, icicles popped away from the cliffs, melting and wetting my sleeve as I pressed against the rocks. Finally the train passed me; I abandoned the car count at seventy-five because there were so many more than a hundred cars, carrying pipe, steel, new cars. A man in the caboose waved as I stepped back on the rails, knowing it was safe for a while. But the trains were irregular; they followed each other, faced each other, and only the man on the switch somewhere knew where and when they would appear next. The rumbles kept coming, giving me chills each time I sensed a roar above the sound of the river.

I moved on, seeing the scattered bolts and pieces of iron between the ties, broken couplings, rusty. A huge nut and bolt lay beside the rail; trains were giants. And they kept coming, one after the other.

After four miles of track, I reached Cane Bottom; my map showed the next bend would hold the village. It would be up from the tracks and the water, in the cover where it became lost when the passenger service was cut off. Seedlings and sage formed a scab over the clearing below the houses. I left the rails and soon passed a fallen house, another one, large angles of the roof broken and collapsed. Then I saw a whole house, a row of houses, a bare and twisted apple tree. For a moment they seemed as strong as houses in a lived-in village, houses with wells and privies, paths from one to the other. There was a chicken; several of them scratching under a house and ignoring me. Chickens with no one to protect them; it didn't seem real. I remembered the man with the gun. I stood still; animal sounds rustled and whistled from the woods. He wasn't there; no one was there.

I saw the school, a rotten bell tower over the one-room schoolhouse, the Mountainview School. There was a graveyard; the stones of children were numerous during the years that smallpox killed the Indians. The last stones were dated in the thirties. On the door of a house was a sign that seemed fresher than the brown house it hung on, "Jesus Saves." The houses were furnished, beds with tall ticking mattresses, lumpy and, since the inhabitants left, slept in by the sweat- and blood-stained bodies of hunters. All the heavy things were still there, wardrobes, chests, beds, but the lamps and pictures and scatter rugs were gone; clean squares were spaced on the walls where pictures used to be. Anything that could be carried was gone. The walls were papered with newspaper to seal out the cold, papers now riddled by silverfish, dated also in the thirties. The cabinets still stood, with fresh coffee cans left by hunters, the doors ajar.

What do you look for when there are no people? I imagined the people, but if they had been there I couldn't have roamed freely in and out of houses, rooms, without asking anyone. It was a strange feeling, and at each new doorway I hesitated. Usually a rat or bird rustled out when I first appeared. Inside a kitchen, an oilcloth curtain sucked through a window; outside the room a dark trap, the mountains, an unbroken wall as far as I could see. Still, it must have been hard to leave behind what was yours, and the window was built facing the mountain wall *in the first place. A woman had worked there, washing and cutting fruit in a white enamel pan, looking at the mountains, listening to the hollow sound of sliced apples against the pan, the knife moving towards her and pressing against her thumb, using a knife in a way that gave her husband chill bumps.*

*Leaving the village, I felt movement all around. Between the trees light caught on the brown of deer, springing along beside me, watching me but not running away. The string of animals seemed endless, does and fawns speckled like the filtered daylight, more than twenty of them. I stopped, they stopped; I moved and they moved. I sat down by a creek to eat my lunch and saw them watching me from behind every bush. I don't think I would have seen them had I not known they were there, not when they were still. One came closer and I got up to go meet it, a dried apricot in my hand. It matched my step, one back for each step I took forward, the perfect form, round eyes and nostrils, tiny legs, an idealized form. I put the apricots on a rock, and when I went back to the clearing, the deer moved cautiously in for the food. They ate daintily, one apricot at a time, but they pushed each other away with force.*

*I slid my pack back on; I knew that the light had grown weaker, because soon I could no longer see the deer among the trees. The trees were thick, the creek clear; Lost Cove was built in a beautiful valley, more beautiful than many living towns, I was sure. It was like so many villages that I had seen in the mountains; a house tucked away in a cove, put into the side of a mountain, some hundreds of years old. I believed the reason for the site had to be romantic, a home built by a man who loved the view of the hills, fog covered and green, changing with every season, not by a man who looked first for a place to farm. East or west of those mountains he would have gone for that; if he had looked for a farm, he would have looked for level ground, deep topsoil, and a long summer. The land was rocky; it ran from black loam to clay, its water as unsettled underneath as the layers of earth that shifted to make the hills, its growing season short, its winters brutal. The soil was thin now, washing down just like the hills. Those mountains were as rugged as any to live in, but they were smooth and old, soft to the sight.*

*I followed the trail until it ran out, and like the village of Lost*

*Cove, it seemed the trail was never there. The deer sounds disappeared. I walked to the creek, moving down the rocky banks knowing it had to empty into the Nolichucky, taking me back to the tracks and the way out. Even with the creek there was a directionless feeling, surrounded by trees with no light patches to be seen; that was how a lost child must feel, a tunnel of trees with no end; my own noises as my feet came down on twigs were magnified. Soon I heard the big river again and saw the tracks as the creek dropped faster down the cliffs, the rails black in the fading light. The way out now was down the manmade path of the rails. The mountains shielded the sunlight rapidly, the well-worn rails no longer shiny. I was running out of time. Going back, while I was thinking about the trestle and hoping to get there before complete darkness, I was forced to leave the tracks to let two more trains pass. In a pocket beside the rock wall was a dead doe.*

*I must have walked by her before when the light was strong; she wasn't newly dead, her eye already pecked away and maggots encircling her spine, her brown coat dulled by rain and snow. The train caught her with nowhere to run. She must have tried to scramble up the walls and fell onto the rails; the rocks may have been slick with ice, or maybe she couldn't stand to wait through the terrible sound and vibration of the train. Like the girl on the trestle, I knew how the deer must have felt; it didn't seem shameful to have panicked.*

*The small trains that started to appear moved faster than the early trains, sneaking up where the turns were tight. At dusk there were no animal sounds, just the river and the breaking and crashing of icicles. There was a feeling that the world was dying around me, or maybe a feeling of being the only creature left alive. The houses in Lost Cove, intact after the people were gone, dead shells; I was looking forward to seeing a light in a window. And the infrequent inhabitants, the man with the thirty-thirty, hunters for deer that moved beside me instead of hiding from me. They violated the village. But so did I. Just curiosity, nosiness. All of that to see a giant mistake and misfortune. And knowing none of the victims.*

*I moved out over the trestle without hesitation. The water was dark but still moving quickly. I went as fast as I could, my pack lighter but my ankles not as strong as at the start. No way to predict the train, its direction, its size, its frequency, its speed. I walked numb; the air was getting colder as the sun disappeared. One foot in front of the other, as fast as I could go. It was like time had stopped and I was on a treadmill. Over halfway across. Crazy, crazy, crazy, I whispered aloud as I moved my feet. That was a kind of suicide. My mother said I was reckless, liked to tease danger. Not then. I only liked to before I got in it. Then I was committed. Counting — one, two, three, four — each number brought me closer to the other side. I started to run. My legs hurt and I had to be careful, but I knew I had less time than I did when I started. I couldn't let myself fall. My pack banged against me. The end. There was earth beside the rails.*

*When I jumped off at the end of the trestle, a door slammed shut behind me. It was all over. Just for a short moment I stood to recover. I couldn't stand long or my tired legs would cramp. It was over too fast for panic to go from my legs to my brain, too fast for a feeling of relief to give me a second wind. It was strangely light on the outside, the sky pink still, everything clearly defined where the mountains rolled and let the light through. The dog met me and trotted beside me. I patted him this time and he left his smell on my hand. I saw farmhouses at the base of the low hills, windows orange with shades; I heard buckets rattling, hungry animal sounds as the farmers fed up.*

*I gathered an armful of dried milkweed pods and cane; the man at the gas station was watching me, standing under a light bulb. He waved. I got in my VW and headed down the dirt road towards the highway, the backs of my calves aching as I pressed the pedals.*

*I had seen a dead village. What made me work so hard to see a dead village? As I turned onto the highway, I thought of something funny. When I was a little girl, I planned to give all my aunts hand-embroidered towels for Christmas. I sewed and sewed and when only a week was left admitted defeat and bought them all bottles of cheap perfume. My father saw my unfinished work and teased me, so I worked all summer in every spare moment until I finished every one and gave them towels the next Christmas. He forgot he had made fun, in fact he probably thought I bought them with my allowance. I never had the courage to ask him if he remembered I failed the first time. But it made me mad when he said, "Bit off more than you can chew," and happy when he called me "bullheaded." If I started something, even if it was wrong, I'd finish it. I almost split myself open when I was twelve, diving off the high dive at the club pool. I didn't know how far it was to the water until I got up there, but I had to go off because everyone was watching. It seemed a fate worse than death to have to climb back down that high-dive ladder.*

*But this was different. This was like when fat Uncle Trextal used to pick me up and toss me in the air until I was so hysterical I got choked. I would never go back across that trestle. Any trestle. Unless I meant to die and the train was coming. Like a woman I read about in England who stood with her back to the engine, holding her baby, and let the train run them over. Maybe in the long run the experience of the village was worth it, like a trip to fantasyland that I won't be given again. Maybe a village just like it is tucked away in these Alps. Now, in remembering, the impression of the village is stronger than my memory of the fear. I know I've been frightened before and I'll be frightened again. I'm glad I did it.*

* * *

Dear Clara,

Today I saw them like nowhere else I have been. Dissertation on the American tourist: "Don't photograph that one, Agnes. It says here that it's a copy. It's so small, Agnes, didn't you think from the picture that it would be larger?" she says, looking under the male statue's fig leaf. Would you believe a middle-aged American man had a gondolier sing "Volare" to his wife while he filmed it with a sound camera? And the Great American Tourist definitely brings out the worst in the populace. Everywhere someone is trying to sell you junk. I took the free boat over today to see the glassmakers and I have never seen such a collection of gaudy junk in my life. I don't even want to believe that there are people who buy that junk, American people. I have seen kewpie dolls that you won at the state fair when the man couldn't guess your weight that had more class. Gift ideas for wedding presents for people you hate.

On the way over I saw a floating cement mixer. That made my day. I thought that was so neat. One guy had chickens on his boat and grass in tin cans. You might be wondering how they bury Venetians. Well, I'll tell you anyway. They have a floating graveyard. Also, another truism bit the dust. Remember how we used to say the blacks were all good runners and had a natural sense of rhythm, then we met Garnet Anderson? Be it recorded here that all Italians are not dark and handsome with beautiful tenor voices. A gondola went under my window this evening, and the oarsman was singing, all dolled up with a hat with streamers, and even his mother would have dumped garbage on him.

You'd really hate the Venetian women, Clara. They come out at dusk pushing these huge baby carriages with lace all over them — baby, the carriage, everything is lacy but the wheels — and they are so fucking beautiful you'd want to push them off in the canal, baby and all. They don't even sweat in the heat. They're even more feminine than Carolina coeds. They don't perspire, and furthermore they don't even glow.

This place is falling apart really. I don't see how it can last long. In some of the buildings water is already going under the door into the first floor. Pollution has eaten the faces off the statues. The floor is so buckled in St. Mark's it's like walking in a fun house instead of a famous cathedral. Under the weight of the columns it's two feet lower. The big tower in the square has already fallen at least once. As I look out my window I can assure you that if it falls in the next ten minutes, it will claim ten percent of the American Jewish population, four hundred ninety-two pigeons being stalked by three hundred cats, and two hundred Italian beggars afflicted with miscellaneous maladies. I saw one today selling these little dogs that squeak. Made me think of the story my grandfather told me, one of those things that got his goat about sixty years ago and he spewed over it to his grave. Bad to hold a grudge when dollars and cents were involved. He bought this little dog that could talk, laugh, cuss, sing, you name it, from this guy at a carnival, and when he got it home, it was silent. Seems the man was a ventriloquist and long gone the next day. Only difference is here the tourists are the ones who are gone the next day. This year yo-yos that glow in the dark are in. I can see them all over the square now that it's dark. Don't worry. I bought you one.

About out of space, but I've got to tell you this one. I passed this old man today, really a neat-looking old guy with a beard and a guitar and about the bluest eyes you've ever seen. He gave me a big, toothless Italian grin that said at ninety he'd still pinch your ass. Then about two hours later I passed him again, only this time he was sitting on the bridge playing his guitar and he had this leather bag hooked to the handle for money. And he had on a pair of dark glasses. Do you believe it? Crusty old son of a bitch, more power to him. So anyway, thought I'd pass the technique on to you in case things get a little rough in the Village next year. A blind painter ought to really get sympathy.

More later,
Jean

\*   \*   \*

*The water laps against the wall under my window when the gondolas go past; there are muffled voices, a few tenors singing. Mosquitoes are humming around my head and hang on the wall, basking in the light from my lamp. When I wrote Clara tonight, I saw two me's: the one that had been writing in my journal and the one who wrote Clara. Even though she is my best friend, the voice here in my journal isn't for her. I'll write a few words about my real day before going to sleep.*

*I saw a woman today, a girl actually, about fourteen, holding a baby. She lay against the wall like a rag doll. The baby was* covered with sores, and flies clung to the crust on its eyelids. It was wrapped in a dirty rag; its belly rose like a small melon and its limbs were dark. I stopped and looked at the child, and the girl knew that was her chance. Her palm went up and she made whimpering sounds like a little animal. I put money in her hand and it shut tight, pinching my fingers with a strength I didn't think she could have. I wanted to keep looking, but I didn't want to hurt her and I was afraid she would notice my stare. When she put the money inside her dress, the baby shifted. I think back on it now and I'm sure of it. The way the baby moved when she dropped the money into the front of her dress. The smell that came up from her was not just dirt and urine. The baby was dead.

I held something dead not so long ago. Not much different in size from that baby. I held it while its life slid out slowly. A dead thing is warm and loose for a long time. Then the stiffness comes slowly. It was the weekend I took the ferry across the sound towards Okracoke Island. The ferry's World War II submarine engine struggled with weight and age, but I felt no rush. I had three more days at the shore before I left for New York to take off for Europe.

The desolation of the Outer Banks isn't for everyone, the strange colorless beach with miles of sea grasses and pilings in a hopeless battle with an ocean that is eating it away like a starving dog snapping at a carcass. I had known about the shipwrecks along the coast of the Outer Banks for years, every North Carolinian did, the bits and pieces scattered and half buried in the bleached sand. This was the Graveyard of the Atlantic. A map I saw once in National Geographic showed ship noses pointing upwards, a solid string of sinking ships the full length of the North Carolina coast. Sometimes in the bits of wood from boats there would be a carved piece, trimming, or ship furniture that was dashed to bits on the sandbars.

That day I looked at the ocean water differently. I was scared of the water off the Outer Banks. The day before I had gone in to swim as always, just as I had done years before with my parents, diving out beyond the breakers so I could float along up and over each wave until I drifted in, dumped into the breakers again. The undertow would carry me down the beach and I would have to walk back, looking for the cottage I used as a marker or my mother's red beach umbrella. I never had any fears about swimming alone.

That day I thought the water seemed unusually sandy, gutted with uprooted grasses and broken shells. I thought there must have been a storm at sea or a whirlpool or earthquake down under. My feet were placed flatly on the underwater sand. Then I felt the sand suck out and the ground go unlevel under me. At first it seemed a novelty, but I began to lose my balance in the holes that were ripped beneath my feet. For a while I went with it, not fighting. Also I seemed to be pretty far out for the water to be so shallow, but I figured the tide must be coming in. Soon I started to tire of the water, of struggling just to enjoy the wetness of it. I started to sense that it was stronger than me. I was falling and getting nowhere. I looked at the beach that had seemed close, but I couldn't get closer to it. I was beginning to swallow water on my falls because I wasn't on my feet long enough to get air. My eyes were stinging from the salt and it had gone in my nose and made the top of my throat raw. I don't remember how long this went on; at first it was frustrating. Gradually it became serious. There was no one on the beach to call to, and I would not have wanted anyone to come to me any more than I would have called someone to join me in a pit of snakes.

It still seems basically absurd, why I couldn't just stand up and walk in. Momentarily I believed that I was close to drowning, but my mind couldn't handle the fact that it might happen in water only a few feet deep. A few feet deep but thousands of feet sideways as I went down again and again, like a giant had put chains on my ankles and was amusing himself by yanking on them. Finally I reached water shallow enough to crawl in and keep my head above the surface, coughing until my sides hurt and moving like a baby to the dry sand. Crying like a baby too, as I dug my hands in the wet sand, clawing and inching forward. When I was safe on the dry beach, I stretched out on my stomach and lay there for a long time before I could walk. My knees were bloody from broken shells. And I ached all over.

The next day the water looked the same. I looked at it down through the surface to the sand and saw the flower face of a sand dollar. But I would never think I was seeing through that sur-

*face again to what was really there. The ferry I was on that day kept moving over dangerously shallow water. I told myself that the man with the beard and the Irish brogue up there must know what he is doing. Then he jammed the boat aground and had to grind the engines for thirty minutes, with the automobiles on board bumping each other. I wondered if he had studied pictures of the typical old salt in a make-up book.*

*The gulls dove in while we were stranded, easily taking bread from my fingertips. I felt that had they been larger they would have been plucking people from the boat in their hungriness. I looked at the perfect white gull bottoms as they hovered over me, suspended. I got dreamy feeding them, the motor groaning and filling the air with more burned fuel than the wind could carry away, my eyes fixed on the floating birds. Their air was stable, the water underneath me rocked. There was a moment when time had stopped and the hands of the clock were spinning in place like a merry-go-round. But I felt relaxed, not afraid. The crisis was someone else's problem. I had a secret satisfaction that someone else was struggling with the ocean, not me. His misfortune and the jokes of the people on board pleased me at first. Somehow it felt evil and good to see someone else make a mistake, a public mistake. But soon I was back to normal because I felt sorry for him when the other ferryboat passed going to the mainland and everyone laughed. I figured the passengers' laughter didn't matter that much to him but the other skipper's did.*

*I leaned back on the railing and focused my mind on the variety of white gulls. There were three or four different kinds. They flew differently. Some of them were more aggressive, some made sounds. My mind had exhausted itself with my body the day before. It didn't seem to want to do much.*

*We unloaded at Okracoke and I started the drive down to the main part of the island. People were rushing away and passing my VW as it whined through the gears because they wanted to be the first to bargain for the limited number of rooms on the island. Ours was the last boat that evening. I pulled off to let them pass and to look at the ponies out in the brush. Soon I had to get back in the car because my legs darkened with mosquitoes starving for a thin-skinned human. The rough ponies, their thick coats matted with sea water and burrs, hadn't looked up when I walked towards them. There was little left now of the former herd, only a few lumpy-headed mongrels. I remembered the book I had read in the seventh grade, the horse club days when I believed in Spanish ships and Arabian horses swimming bravely to the North Carolina shore after a shipwreck. I could feel a real kinship with the little ugly ponies if I thought about it long enough. One of them was beating the ground with his foot, digging a hole. He dropped his head in the hole. Something I had read was true. They did dig holes to drink.*

*I put my tent up near the water, as close to the surf as was safe. I wanted all the wind I could get to blow away the mosquitoes and sand fleas. The mosquitoes weren't in abundance on the ocean side, only where the sound slid in and stopped in pools between the marsh grass. When I finished my supper and took a walk down the beach, I noticed the sun set strangely for the East Coast. It seemed to be setting in the south. I could see the lighthouse from Cape Hatteras and watch the strange currents, the zigzagging whitecaps. People on the boat had talked of the rip tide yesterday, the four drownings down the beach. I was glad that was history before I knew it.*

*As I turned the bend, I saw a dead bird covered with dry sand from the wind, not the water. It was a strange bird, a duck of some sort. I did not see why it had died and when I touched it a chill ran through my body. It was very warm, from within, not just from sun heat on its feathers. I looked up and down the beach. I saw more lumps. In the distance a boy and girl bent over one of the lumps and touched it as I had done. The ducks were everywhere, dead. I hurried to catch up with the couple. They met my distressed glance.*

*"Pollution," the boy said. "I bet that's what killed them."*

*I asked him why only one kind of bird was stricken by it.*

*"They were migrating. Over two hundred migrating birds stop here. They must have all stopped to eat in a poisoned field or in a poisoned stream. Some insecticide could have done it."*

*"This type of duck would never have been here, near people," the girl said. "It's a shy bird that always lands in the marshes. I know because last season we walked five miles through the swamp to see it."*

*I noticed they were burying the birds, scraping sand over them with the wood on the beach. I walked in the other direction and covered two bird bodies myself. Buzzards and crows were already coming. The ducks must have been dying all day. A black form walked on the beach ahead of me, spearing the sand with its claws. I wondered if poisoned meat would kill a buzzard.*

*Back at my tent before I got ready to get in my sleeping bag, I saw another of the ducks. It was still alive. It was sick, staggering towards me, a strange whistling sound coming from it. Its webbed feet bent under because it could not lift them high enough to step. The bird fell on its chest, got up again, an armless struggle as if its wings were welded to its body. It seemed determined to make it to me. Each time the duck's legs bent and buckled, it pulled to its feet again. I ran to meet it — an old friend come to me — and lifted it onto my lap. I sat in the sand and held it in my arms; it trembled a little, not fighting my grip around its body. It relaxed and lowered its weight off its legs as I talked to it. The bird was warm enough to make my arms wet its feathers with sweat. A hot liquid spewed from its mouth and dried stiffly on my arm. Soon the whistling stopped.*

*I looked at its feathers shining in the moonlight, the color patterns and texture so intricate, each feather folded into place. It seemed an object that had taken a long time to be made, from a liquid egg to a down-covered duckling, growing, learning to fly. Maybe it had been a parent, maybe several times, maybe this year was going to be the first time. I didn't know if it was male or female. It seemed more complex than if I had just seen it flying. I couldn't tell if it had ever felt happy, if ever in that last minute it had felt comforted. The wind died down and I sat with the mosquitoes biting me until I was sure it was breathing no more. It stayed warm for a long time after it was dead, long after its neck was limp, its head to one side.*

*I have never had to hurt for someone I loved who died before his time. I wonder if I would hurt worse for a strange human's baby who crawled into my arms to die than I would for my own. I think grief for my own would be less honest because I would be crying for part of me. Would it seem not as bad as seeing an arm or a leg being cut away, because you could grow another baby?*

*Maybe I don't give mothers credit for recognizing the separate life of their child. That girl today in Venice never really had a separate life from her child, though it was outside her and had breathed on its own. Her poverty kept it part of her. She killed that baby because she was too poor to have it. Jane Boey killed herself instead. I think I feel closer to Jane.*

It reminded me of a cave, damp and musty smelling inside as if it had a leaky roof and was rotting, as if there should be spiders and slimy creatures curling up in the dark corners. It was in strange contrast to the gaiety of the Via Veneto. Inside were the friars, as dingy as their home, padding about in dirty wine-colored robes with hoods. On the wall a sign read: "The crosses which mark at several places the interment of the few that are buried and the remains of some, which are preserved as mummies, lying or erect, with their sepulchral decay, speak eloquently to the visitors about the drama of a life which is passing."

There were plots of earth inside the building, dirt brought there from the Holy Land. Each monk who dies is buried in this dirt, rots, and is dug up. Faced with the unpleasant task of re-burying what has now amounted to four thousand people — monks and villagers who donated their bodies — an inspired eighteenth century friar started a design with the remains. Heart shapes, arches, a clock with leg bones for hands and Roman numerals made from short straight arm bones. Leg bones are stacked into an arch for a mummified friar who still seems to be dried flesh hanging inside his robe, maybe because someone died too soon and needed his dirt, his arms cut off for the coat of arms. On one wall are flower designs, white bones like a giant lace doily. I don't really know how to react to this.

On the way out, I heard two Americans talking and instinctively turned towards their voices. They were priests. I walked over and asked what it all meant. The priests smiled and one explained that the enclosed cemetery was a major source of income for the Capuchin monks. It had been closed by Pope John but was now reopened. The priest said he once knew of a member of this Franciscan order who kept a skull on his desk.

He said, "I saw it there and was affected by the strangeness of it. But the belief is simple. If we surround ourselves with reminders of death, we live better."

*   *   *

Dear Clara,

Cute postcard, huh? At the entrance to this place is a snaggle-toothed friar who kept pinching me on various parts of my anatomy after I asked him where several of the bones were located. I figured you wouldn't believe me if I told you, so I bought one of his cards. I was filled with regrets today that I didn't go grave robbing for my senior art project. I can hear Mr. Pollard now, "Miss Fitzgerald, I find this subject matter exceedingly trivial."

Your pal,
Jean

*   *   *

I will always laugh about the disregard for the human shape that goes into a black bikini; a three-hundred-pound mama swollen with thirty-five years of pasta and baby dropping stretches the elastic over her rolling skin just like the blooming eighteen-year-old. And she doesn't notice that anything seems strange. Maybe that is good. Something in my culture keeps me from seeing it as good, but she has fun in the gentle sun, tossing rocks in the water, so what does it matter?

*   *   *

Dear Clara,

What looks like a giant white beach ball with two black stripes?

Answer: An Italian mama in a black bikini.

Your friend,
Jean

*   *   *

I wound back through the little town on the hillside, Sarre, going back to the hotel for the night before the darkness caught me. A little cat went by me, and part of her pink insides hung

*out under her tail. Fires blazed brightly on the sea below, I think
for shell fishing. I wondered why there were no people in the hill
houses. There were people smells up there, cooking and urine,
and some noises, but I couldn't tell from which house. There
were people below by the highway at the hotel.*

*My eye caught a figure. A small, bent woman in black whose
face was turned downward. I smiled instinctively. I meant her
no harm and thought I might be walking through her yard.
Probably the last thing she would expect to be confronted with
was an American walking through her yard. Why would an
American come here? She walked in my direction, not looking at
me. Her face turned up for an instant; I caught the grimace, and
it went back down again, saliva on her chin, saliva on the sleeve
of my shirt and shining on the back of my hand. I wiped my
hand against my side, still walking, and I heard her utter a
curse behind me about an Americano. She was gone around the
corner of the house as I went quickly back to my hotel.*

*I did not meet any of the eyes in the lobby as I went to my
room, locked my door. But no one there knew she had done that.
I would tell Clara about the woman, but I know I would just
make a joke out of it. I didn't feel like laughing. I went to the
sink and washed my hand. Why did she do that?*

*Last night my stomach tore apart. I stumbled to the public
toilet again and again, my head swelling with the effort of remembering the right room. Each time I would touch something
of mine when I returned, my shoe, feeling for the knot in the broken lace. I took paregoric and slept finally. In a dream I picked
up the little cat I saw last night. I stuffed her pink insides back
into her with my thumb. When I placed her gently on the stones,
she looked at me and spat on my hand.*

\* \* \*

Dear Clara,

Picture this. The end-all case of the green-apple-quick-
steps and I'm sharing the bathroom with fifteen people,
and some old bird is in there about ten minutes trying to
grind one out. Could have had something to do with the

dead dog floating in the local water supply. I took this paregoric stuff and tripped out. Opium derivative. So now two days later I'm solid concrete inside and need a dose of Drano. I hope your postman is enjoying this bowel dissertation. I wrote it especially for him. I have decided to bask on the Riviera for a week to recuperate.

Take care,
Jean

\* \* \*

*Even though the Spaniards go out every weekend to watch the bullfights, just as regularly as stock-car races and baseball games back home, the set for the bullring seemed impermanent. It seemed just that, a set. There was a dinginess about the personnel; the parade was like a circus, costumes that had been worn threadbare and gone too long without washing, weeks of sweat dulling the colors. The horses looked tired, draped with the heavy padding that we're supposed to think is there to protect them from the horns. Hemingway says it is there so we won't see the animal's guts hanging out, that the horse gets hurt just as badly through the padding and the pads are holding the guts in place that were gored out at the last event. They did look like half-dead creatures. I thought of the little horse who was beaten to death in the dream in* Crime and Punishment, *having to pull too great a load. They live like a bad dream that won't end until one morning they don't wake up.*

*The first sight of the matadors was almost comic. They looked like spindle-legged little boys. And so cocky. I don't think in all my life I have seen human beings as cocky as the three matadors. When they left the ring, there was a clean moment when the sky was very blue and the colors of the crowd on the other side were crystal. The crowd seemed new and fresh, the performers worn. The sand glared like a desert; in the center of the arena was a man in a dirty clown outfit cleaning up after one of the battered horses. Then they do feed them, maybe with the hopes that they will live another day. Painted on the sand were two large blood-colored rings.*

*There was a nice jingling sound over the noise of the crowd. It* was from the bells on the harness of a team of mules, healthy-looking mules. I found out later they were for dragging away the carcass of the bull.

I thought I was ready. I thought that I had my mind cleared, my tenderheartedness was not to come out. I was viewing a national sport that was none of my business, that would go on whether I objected or not. That morning I saw pictures of bull heads in the market downtown and saw that they were selling the meat of the bulls who died in the ring. I thought that it must be tough meat, but I also thought how good that it was not wasted. We never see our cows except when we play cow poker on the way to the beach and they are grazing peacefully in the fields. Then they are bound in Styrofoam and cellophane in the supermarket; nothing that happens in between meets our eyes to remind us that this is a murdered animal. The in-between here was the death in the ring. I don't know why exactly, but I felt better when I saw the meat for sale.

My feelings surprised me when the first bull ran into the arena. He ran to the center of the ring and heard the people cheering. He looked up at them and wondered who they were and what they were doing there. He turned around in circles, churning the smooth sand into a dust cloud with his hooves, his instincts telling him to be afraid of noises. But soon he knew he was surrounded. His motions sped up and his skin began to twitch. He was an animal, a living animal moving in ways special to him, his eyes rolling, his skin flicking away flies, his tail slapping his haunches, slime coming from his mouth as if he had been given a drink before the fight. A living, moving animal given a drink. For a moment I thought that I had never seen anything killed before. Maybe a squirrel that my father hit with the car, but never had I seen something so big and bursting with life and known that even if I ran and hid my head, nothing would stop him from being killed.

Then the men on horses came out and I felt an ache that stayed with me the rest of the day. They tried to get the bull to make passes, but the bull wasn't interested. He was still looking at the crowd, tossing his head and drooling every time a sharp voice was directed at him. The picadors rode by and pierced his shoulders. Each heavy spear stuck in, its weight flopped down-

*ward and around, eating into his shoulders. He started to panic. Why are they hurting me? They kept hurting him. Soon he was mad and bleeding. Then the matador appeared.*

*Even though his blood ran red down his shoulders, almost black against his black fur, he didn't want to charge. They couldn't make the bull hate enough to make the matador look good. The crowd disapproved. I heard a man say he was a bad bull, not bred wicked enough. It seemed to take forever, the slaughter. That was all it was when the poor bull finally dropped from the sword. A slaughter. When the mules came and pulled him away and his huge body swept a path in the sand, I felt relieved and I put on my sunglasses and cried. Finally the poor soul could rest.*

*The sun moved from overhead and the shadows grew sharp in the sand. The last bull was brought out to fight, the red circles broken now from the dragged bodies and horses' hooves. This bull was huge, a giant. I wanted him to live just to watch his muscles move as he pounded around the arena. I wondered if a bull could leap into the stands. If any could, it would be this one. He was beautiful, and the crowd thought so too, cheering with approval. The matador appeared and looked like a small bird flitting in the sand. I felt my first sympathy for the man. But I was thinking, don't die, pretty bull.*

*Much of what happened next is still not clear. Two passes went smoothly, one of the horns almost catching the matador as the bull passed, rumbling by like a freight train. But the third pass stopped. The bull planted his forelegs and the man was tossed up, a piece of cloth on a windy clothesline. For a moment I thought the bull had pierced only the cape. Then I saw the tiny legs kicking. Before he came unhooked from the horn, he looked like a child having a tantrum. The clowns were fast, instantly luring the bull's attention away from the man on the ground. When I looked back to the spot where he fell, the man was gone. There was a patch of human blood near the old bull blood. This bull left proudly and rapidly after the brown cows sent to lure him out, his balls swinging under his tail. I wondered who would be brave enough to remove the spears from his shoulders. The crowd screamed as he left. I felt confused. It was as if the tiny man had never been there at all.*

*Today I looked in the newspaper. The pictures of the goring distorted time. It had happened too fast to be seen in such detail. I couldn't read the Spanish. I wanted to know if that magnificent animal was declared the victor or did they run him out and slaughter him like the lame bull, maybe with a shot in the head while he mounted a brown cow. Or maybe he would be the father of more bulls that would win.*

*I am on the train from Madrid, wedged in the sleeper with my purse pressed against the back of my berth. It is strange to be sleeping with three people I don't know. To my side is a fat Frenchman, already asleep and snoring. For a moment I imagine what it would be like to be married to a bulk who snores and farts in his sleep, to stare at the ceiling and wonder if you can face another day. Beneath me are two boys, Americans and probably college boys, one of whom talks loudly. The other mumbles his replies. Maybe they have been traveling together long enough to be tired of each other.*

*"You know when they make those movies," the loud one just said, "the gangster ones, and they kill so many people the movie is called violent? People have holes made in them, neat little round red holes that aren't even big enough to mess up the costume. That is so damn phony. A patrolman was shot trying to stop a bank robber near my house. My dad said he was a rookie and thought he was going to be a big hero. I rode there on my bike when I was in high school, after I heard all the sirens, and there was blood as far as ten feet. The movies make you think there is no blood in a person. They don't let you see how much comes dumping out when you don't plug up the hole."*

*"How much is there?" a weak voice asked.*

*"Ten pints, five quarts, six quarts. I don't know. Guess it depends on how big you are, but a lot. I heard about this guy who was traveling over here and ran out of money. He heard you could give blood and get money. He was in Morocco, Tangier. That's one of those places where they run people down in the streets and don't stop for them any more than if they were dogs. If you hit somebody in the lower class, you just keep on going. It's worse to stop and let the peasants tear you apart, and the*

*police don't care if you report it or not; they figure one less peasant, one less problem. Anyway, they strapped this guy down who was giving the blood, he was English, I think. His traveling partner never saw him again. His family tried to find out what happened to him and they found his passport on the black market."*

*"What did happen to him?"*

*"His blood. They took all of it. Ten pints, five quarts, whatever it is. They took it all."*

*"Jesus!"*

*The boys are silent. He can't top that story, and it is sufficient to take care of my and the other boy's dreams for the night. The Frenchman snores on, his tone changing and getting louder as he turns his mouth towards the space between us. In the thin light I can see shiny saliva spattering out on his pillow. Wonder if he would be drained dry in the night? How much water is in a person? I now know how much blood. Wonder what it would be like to travel with someone and be tired of them and tired of telling your own stories. Always having to ask, have I told you this before? What point was there to it anyway, wanting to tell people stories? To control what they think of you. To tell them who you are the way you want them to know it.*

*Who am I? Well, I am Jean. I don't need the last name. Already I say where I come from as soon as I open my mouth. But here they don't think I'm southern unless they are American. In some places they think I might be English, not American. I wouldn't know if a Spaniard came from Puerto Rico, Mexico, or Spain. Or Spanish Harlem for that matter. I don't want to tell anyone about me. Unless I tell them a lie. I do enjoy telling lies, the way I used to flying home from prep school. I think I learned that from* The Catcher in the Rye. *I like to talk to my notebook. I have a feeling I'm going to meet those boys whether I want to or not.*

*I wonder what I'm missing that's going by in the dark outside now. Spain was pretty, what I saw of it, green and plentiful looking, and it seemed strange for it to be poor. The government, the religion, the heat, I'm too dumb to know why. I'm too lazy to go read and find out. I did expect a red desert. I think that so much of what I see is wasted on me. It all started when my smallpox shot didn't take. No one to tell stories to, so I make jokes with myself. I'm rocking to sleep. In the treetops, clickedy-clack, clickedy-clack. The boy below is finally going to shut up.*

When I woke up this morning, the boys had already gotten up and left the compartment. The Frenchman still slept, the pillow by his face soggy, his lips dry and cracked from the night's snoring. I hadn't heard him all night, not after I concentrated on the sounds of the train. When I walked in the snack bar, the boys were already there, Pepsis and potato chips for breakfast.

"Hey, there's the girl you slept with last night, Juke," one said, and I recognized him as the big mouth.

"No, she's the one you slept with." The other boy sounded shy. They laughed in a friendly way, so I smiled and sat down on the stool next to them. Since people never go the same way, I knew I didn't have to worry about seeing them again.

"You're both wrong. I slept with a sexy Frenchman," I said.

The boys had just come from the bullfights in Barcelona. They had been there when a matador died, they said. The bull had hooked him through and carried him around on its horn.

"He lifted this guy up like he was a doll, and his horn was right through his gut. The guy acted like he was alive for a while. He wiggled like a grasshopper I pinned down in Biology. Only his juice was red, not green."

Lovely breakfast conversation, I told him. The sort of thing my father used to make me leave the table for. Then big mouth said, "You must have a real class father. Mine never made me leave unless I turned over my milk and it got on him, or if I farted, out loud only. You could pin the strong, silent types on the baby or the dog." I wondered if anyone around us understood English. I hoped not. I don't feel like an ugly American when I'm alone, only around other Americans.

The boys were soon talking about Amsterdam. I asked them if they had been to the van Gogh museum, if that was where the black birds over the wheat field was kept. They hadn't and looked at me oddly, so I asked them to tell me about Canal Street, what it looked like.

The boy with the acne spoke up quickly, eager to change the

subject. *"You really ought to see it. I mean, girls go down there. It's not like skid row or anything. You see a lot of tourists sitting in the sidewalk cafes just watching the show. They stand all along the street, the whores, I mean, dressed in hot pants and high boots, and they are really good-looking. Young too, like some of them are teen-agers. Only thing wrong with their looks is their bellies stick out."*

*"That's because they're pregnant,"* big mouth interrupted, *"and are earning money for an abortion."* I decided I didn't like him.

*"No, it's not. It's muscle. I read that, that a whore gets really big muscles in her stomach."* The shy boy was asserting himself. *"Anyway, I sat there and watched them reject these guys who were kind of crummy-looking."*

*"Worse than Juke, even,"* big mouth stuck in.

*"They almost always turn down the Orientals who have to go off the main street and down the back street where the uglies are,"* Juke continued, *ignoring the other boy's comments. "The uglies are about sixty years old and have bruises all over them. Black women are back there too, and Orientals. I mean, you could start thinking all whores were beautiful blondes and redheads if you saw just the front row."*

*"They decorate their rooms,"* the other boy interrupted again, *"with colored lights, or they have this phony leopard skin in there, and some guy stands there looking through the window getting up a head of steam, knowing that all he has to do is put down the bucks and he can fuck that pretty little thing, right there on top of the leopard skin. They're just like the side shows at the circus. From the outside you think you're going to get the works and then you get inside and she wants more money, or she won't take her clothes off and you just get a hand job."*

They got quiet then. I figured Juke was embarrassed again because his neck reddened. He must have gotten a hand job. I ordered a doughnut and offered that I read most of the whores were divorced and had children and they worked for a few months out of the year to support their families.

*"Where did you read that?"* big mouth asked.

"National Geographic," I replied. Both boys were silent then. I probably took the edge off their adventure. I could have said

Family Weekly. *When the train stopped in Belgium, I said goodbye and got off. I would never see them again.*

*On the giant boat crossing the English Channel, everyone was served the same food at long wooden tables: greasy French fries and a large fish with a lidless eye that looked up at me. I tore at the hard bread that was put in the center of the table and watched those around me before I cut into my fish, hoping they would reveal which part of the fish was meant to be eaten. There was a small boy at my table. His face was shiny and chapped from rough wind, from an outdoor life before we left the shore. He ate a little of his fish and potatoes and then he was scolded by his fat mother. Soon I saw that he was going to be forced to eat it all, a mound of food that would probably fill five stomachs his size, but it was going to be stuffed into him as if he had reserve drawers, where he could hold it until tomorrow when he would need food again and it might not be in front of him. His eyes began to bulge, but still the mother crammed the food in his mouth. He ran from the table once and she waddled after him, seating him again and starting the stuffing once more.*

*Then it finally happened. With a great triumphant burst and gag, it spewed out of him onto the table, first the half chewed, then the half digested, and his little body crumpled to the floor with his back shaking in sobs, as he held his stomach that probably still had more than it needed to last his day. The mother scraped up the vomit in a pile and covered it over with her napkin. She rolled the uneaten fish and potatoes into his napkin and put the bundle in her purse. She was not ashamed of that or of her child's agony.*

*The boat moved into the gray water, the final train to the docks having dumped its contents of blocky people, who had shuffled on board; buttons that stated "Poland Express" were on their clothes. They were not jovial, and I wondered if England knew they were coming. There were few seats on the boat because the large behinds took up more than their share on the benches. I saw a space and took it. It was too large for me but there was room for a child to sit beside me, should one need to. I started to fall asleep.*

*Soon I heard a woman, her harsh voice fussing at me but in a language I did not know. It was obvious that she was mad, but I didn't know what I had done. The other Poles were also angry at me, one shaking a finger. It seemed to be more a dream than real. Another woman, I think an Englishwoman, frowned at the Pole and said: "There are no reserved seats in second class. First come, first served. You left your seat and she has just as much right to it as you do . . ." I heard the Englishwoman talking until all sound became muffled. In my lap and in my face was a fish-, sweat-, and urine-smelling bulk, soft in my face at first like a pillow, then smothering. My legs were pressed into the hard wood of the seat and the circulation began to stop. The woman had sat on me.*

*Soon I was pounding like a small child on the bulk, pinching skin between my fingers. She seemed to have no feeling no matter how deep my nails dug. She was hurting me, crushing my legs, cutting my breath short. I squirmed out; I think I was helped out by the nicely dressed Englishwoman, who was very angry at the Pole and swearing. I thanked her and went to the railing and looked out into the dark water, my legs slowly coming back to life, and stayed there breathing the fresh air until the gray morning came and I saw the ferryboat pilings waiting on the English shore. The woman never left the space again, and every time I looked, she was glaring at me. I slept all day today. I know the meaning of that old phrase, I feel as if I've been run over by a truck. I think I came very close to doing what the little boy did, spewing out my fish and potatoes along with the rest of my insides — like a cockroach under a shoe.*

*I saw an Indian woman on the boat. She was beautiful and her little boy was beautiful. She was wrapped in silks and her hair was in a long black braid, the same as all Indian women. She must not be poor because she would be in India, not here. She seemed to have no traumas, no choices, nothing to do but bask in the beauty of herself and of motherhood. Then a strange thing happened. A drunken Englishman was entertaining a little blond girl. Scores of people were enjoying the show as he rolled and bounced her in a stroller. The little Indian boy was watching with unchildlike restraint. The drunken Englishman made several gestures for the little boy to join them. The boy* made a few hesitant steps forward. Then I noticed the mother, the agony in her face. Her son waited for her command as if her word to go forward would release hundreds of years of prejudice. The Englishman insisted, she gave the word, and the two children, the dark and the light, giggled together in the stroller. But I watched the woman, staring like a mother cat when one of her litter is being handled by a human. The agony, partly hidden under a thin smile, did not leave her face until her boy was back at her side and the Englishman and blond child were gone in the crowd. I wonder if she hoped her child would forget how much he enjoyed that.

The preacher at Hyde Park Corner was a middle-aged woman, fifty perhaps. Her face was very pale, even her hair appeared to have been powdered. Her clothes were black except for a white lace collar that reached up around her throat like tiny fingers trying to strangle her. She held up a Bible as she spoke, its tight, worn black binding looking very much like her.

She clamped her mouth shut suddenly, a fearful look spreading across her face. I thought she had spotted the devil himself in our presence, but it was only that another box had been put up near her. The crowd began to cheer as a short, stocky woman climbed onto the box, her hands on her hips. She was dressed like a maid and looked as if she hadn't changed since her last scrubbing job. She grinned widely at the men gathered around her, exposing her two stray teeth. Although the other woman began to preach again, she was obviously shaken.

"And the Lord has said, 'Come to me as . . .' "

"Aye, and what does she know about coming." It was the woman on the other box speaking in a heavy Cockney accent. "I can bet ye she ne'er come in 'er life, eh lads?" The men began to laugh. "A bit o' verse for ye, lads, and it ain't to be found in the Good Book:

"There was a young lady of Kew,
Who said, as the curate withdrew:
  'I prefer the dear vicar;
  He's longer and thicker;
Besides, he comes quicker than you.' "

*The preacher woman continued in a louder voice. "The Lord has said, 'Come into My flock . . .'"*

*"Into 'er frock, lads! She wants ye to come into 'er frock. Aye, lads, she's tight as a jug. Pinch it off ye, ye don't mind 'er lads." The old woman made a scissors motion with her stubby fingers in front of her crotch.*

*The evangelist clasped her Bible to her chest. "There are those among us who can only think of sex and filthy . . ."*

*"Hear 'er out, all she does is think about it. I can tell ye folks that 'er poor old man broke it off trying to put it in 'er, she clamped him out so tight."*

*The crowd was beginning to get rowdy and the boxes started to rock. The bobbies who had been standing in the background walked up and asked the women to move along, that their time was up for the day. The evangelist was gone in an instant, but the Cockney lady stood her ground with one finger raised. "Ah, lad, ye 'andsome bugger. I'll be on me way with one last bit o' verse for the folks:*

> *"There was an old girl of Silesia,*
> *Who said: 'As my cunt doesn't please yer,*
> *You might as well come*
> *Up my slimy old bum,*
> *So Jimmy the tapeworm don't sieze yer.'"*

*After that one the crowd dispersed. I wrote the limericks down in my notebook while an Indian gave an agitated speech in broken English.*

*On the train I ate a scone. I remember them from English novels. They sounded so exotic when I read of them. (They taste like Matilda's biscuits with currants added.) Like all those blustery moors and heaths covered with heather, the haunted castles. When I asked a man today if out the window was a field of heather, he told me it was cabbage gone to seed. Everywhere a mist hangs in the air and collects in people's lashes and brows like clear jewels. Today on the coast I saw ponies caught where the tide came in and left them galloping on bright green domes threaded with streams of sea water. The waves smacked the* banks of the green domes, panicking the ponies and filling the air with spray. The fences of stone were toppled in places, their tops set with spiked rocks that were intended to make them unclimbable before time broke them through.

Today walking in the rain to the YWCA, down the streets of Edinburgh, I saw the old city high on a hill to my left and to my right a new shopping street. I fed some scrap bread to a pure white pigeon, and while I watched it eat, I saw what looked like bodies covered with canvas. An old lady walked up and read my thoughts, as the Scots are able to do, and told me the bodies were from the monument of Sir Walter Scott overhead, that a gale had blown up and toppled off a number of them, so they were all removed for renovation, the black statues of Scotland's heroes.

I went to the zoo and was the only person there besides the keepers. The animals were lonely; even the cats stopped their pacing and came to the bars to meow. It seemed so useless for them to be caged just for me to see. I talked to all of them because they seemed to like it. A chimp tried to make me feel sorry for it by pointing at a hurt place on its arm. I acted sorry and talked to it because I could tell by its expressions and nods that my sympathy made it feel better. I watched the penguins for a long time. I wondered if they looked at me and envied my long legs and knew that if they were better equipped they wouldn't be in that pen. But animals don't reason. The cats hate, I think. The penguins didn't seem to care.

When I left, all the animals made lonely sounds in the distance, crying up the hillside for some attention. I felt bad about leaving each cage by itself as I went by, even the hyenas that are hard to love. I felt like the only person left on earth.

It was a day for animals. On the way to the Y, I spotted a cat approaching a fish in a shop window while the proprietress had her back turned. I tapped on the glass and gave the cat away just before it slid the fillet in its mouth. The woman leapt like a comic-book character, shooing it away. I didn't feel bad for the cat because it has a better chance of living there if it doesn't do wrong.

*

On the train across Scotland I started to watch the people as much as the scenery. The woman across from me put her suitcase in the window seat so no one could sit there. There was the odor of alcohol and she did look like the typical drunken landlady. She frequently took her bottle out of her purse, poured a little into a plastic cup, and sipped away at it. She ate her lunch and threw the paper wrappings out the window of the train.

"You ought to hem up your britches, you know?"

I said, "I beg your pardon." She caught me off guard.

"Those britches. You're putting your heel right on the hem of them when you're stepping."

She reached down and lifted up my foot into her lap. "See what a mess you've made of 'em, picking up all the filth off the sidewalk." The woman held my foot firmly while she reached into the big net bag beside her on the seat. She took out a needle and thread. "Now you hold it right there," she said to the foot in her lap while she threaded her needle, as if the foot would run away as soon as she released it. The woman began to turn up the hem in my pants. "You need to take little teeny, tiny tucks, you see, as you go. What makes the youngsters wear these foolish bell bottoms? Like the American sailors during the war. I thought they looked a bit silly myself." I shifted so the woman could do the other leg. I thought I heard the people in the seat on the other side giggling as the woman struggled to stitch with her trembling hands.

"Are you a schoolgirl?" she asked.

"Yes, ma'am. I mean I was until this June when I graduated," I answered.

"Ah, and I bet you're to be a schoolteacher or a governess."

"A teacher, sort of. I have a job when I get back to the States, working with the poor people in the Appalachian mountains."

"People ought to carry their own weight. I don't like that business of people not working. They ought to put some control on immigration, don't you think?" She bent over towards me, whispering the "don't you think?" very loudly. There was a handsome Indian in the next seat. I just nodded slightly, but the woman was determined, winking at me and nodding towards the Indian man. The man had been frowning the whole trip, I had noticed.

"I don't know much about it," I said weakly.

"Now do we ever go to their countries and put ourselves on them?"

"I'd like to go to Japan," I said quickly. "And I'm over here putting myself on the English."

"To Japan! How can you go to Japan after the atrocities those people committed during the war! I can't pass one on the street without wanting to knock him over in the drain. Slant-eyed devils."

She finished her hemming and pushed my foot off in the floor, dusting off her lap with exaggerated gestures, as if I had put the foot there against her will. "Thank you very much for fixing my pants," I said.

"Don't mention it. You're not a married lass, are you?"

"No, ma'am."

"Well, it's a good thing and don't you ever let anyone tell you differently. Far too many of these young marriages, to my mind. People are having too many children, you know what I mean? I never married and I'm glad of it."

The woman stood up and started to rub her body all over. She was very strangely built. She rubbed her body a long time until people were looking at her. "Hard to get your blood going again when you've been sitting for so long. Traveling will ruin you."

She bought a Pepsi from the boy walking through the aisle and poured half out for me in a cup. "You've got a lot of class about you, lass. Don't you go and get married to the first buck who comes along asking. You can see your raising."

The woman reached into the bag again and took out a wet cloth, washing her face and neck. She took a brush and flattened her frizzly red hair and then stuffed it under a green beret. Then she took out a mirror and put on bright red lipstick. Soon all her things were gathered up and the train jarred to a stop. "You mind what I told you, lass."

"Yes, ma'am. Have a good day," I said.

The woman grunted and banged her way into the aisle ahead of everyone. I saw her again when the train was pulling out, her arms full of bags, her coat long, barely showing her spindle-legs. After all her sewing, the hem was hanging out of her own coat on one side. I caught her glance and waved from her window seat. The green beret and smiling red lipstick looked more like a retired schoolteacher than a drunken old landlady.

After we left the woman in the station, I noticed that outside the train window people were beginning to bundle from the cold. The water falling down the hillsides looked cold, and the meadows filled with mountain flowers. The population began to thin as we traveled north. There was only an occasional reminder of the bombing, a hollowed-out factory that was never rebuilt. It seemed that this was not a small country, not crowded, as the miles of green pastures went by. Coming into a town, I saw a cage of parakeets on a porch, swinging back and forth in the cold wind. An old woman struggled to put a flapping sheet on a line. She was yelling at someone. I saw the someone, a child, an idiot child with the puffed face and drooping mouth of a mongoloid, stumbling with arms outstretched towards the train. The child ran into the fence around its yard and crumpled to the ground. I caught one last glimpse as the train left the woman and child behind. The woman did not leave the clothesline, and soon a white ball of a face appeared at the fence top as the idiot child stood back up, its features blurred in the distance, around a corner, and it was gone.

I don't know what to make of the people here on the coast at Largs. I went out this afternoon to get the feel of the place. All the people look very much alike, very fair skinned, many red-headed, all with chapped faces, even little babies bundled in blankets with faces so chapped their cheeks are peeling away. They are fat people, healthy looking, and you would think cheery, but that's not true at all. On the pier I was looking at the crab nets; one had a dead gull woven in it, and a man was trying to take it out. A child with red paint on her hands was screaming. I thought at first she had hurt herself, but no one seemed to be upset in that way, especially not her mother, who was scolding the man who struggled with the net. "You ought to mark it, you know. You can't just go around painting where you please. Somebody could ruin a fine thing on it." The man kept *working, weaving out the bones of the gull while the woman chattered away.*

*I went to a recreation center and there it was finally evident that the Scots didn't know how to enjoy themselves. I wanted to laugh. Everywhere they were playing machines, loud, ringing machines which erupted with all sorts of responses while the Scots fed in their money, pokerfaced.*

*The square is filled with old people sitting on every wet green bench on newspaper and holding newspapers over their heads. The women wear net scarves around their thin gray hair. All about them on the ground are shopping bags. They are singing or trying to sing. None of them can remember enough of the words to get through a whole song. Their tired legs stick out everywhere, old men's white veinless legs above their sock tops, old women's legs with rolled stockings and veins broken from the weight that has piled up over them. Here they are now, count heads, twenty-seven. Next year there will be twenty-four, twenty-two, on down until the square is empty and the green benches glow in the drizzle.*

*A cat just walked through the crack in the door to my room. She acts as if she stays here often, jumping up into a chair that has a cavern that fits her body. When I call her she jumps in my lap without hesitation, purring as soon as I stroke her. Her loose hairs float in the air.*

\* \* \*

Dear Clara,

In Fitzy's *Guide to Europe* there is a new entry. NEVER order food that you can't identify by name. Picture this. Holiday weekend. Scores of glum Scots with their general pissed-off-at-the-world look on their faces. The waitress was so bitchy I just pointed at the first item on the menu. The food comes, and there I am, so G.D. hysterical I can't control myself. On my plate is this giant tongue, garnished with tomatoes and onions, like somebody had cooked my grandmother's hot-water bottle. My mother's douche bag? I guess you'd hafta been there.

Out of room,
Jean

*   *   *

When I write Clara, my mind seems to snap back to the reality of home, to familiar things. Yet when I go out walking, I search for and relish the unfamiliar. I went to the Dublin market today. The competition was fierce, old women hollering, one bobby, two bobbies, calling each other names between the bargaining. They were holding up chickens, freshly plucked, with their heads and feet still on them, covered with flies. I saw a barrel of snails. They kept crawling over the top, and an old woman would scoop them up and sling them back in before they got away. There were stacks of fish with no ice under them. The smell was overpowering. The old women who scream at each other seem to have young eyes, as if their bodies weathered around them like unpainted houses. They have tied their legs up with rags, their hands are burnt red from scalding and plucking chickens. They bring their produce to market in battered baby carriages. I watched them hack up stingrays, pushing away the slime to find the line the knife would follow. I thought of my Irish grandmother, who never chopped up anything more menacing than a radish. These women would never shut themselves away with a walker and a Bible. They'll be hacking those stingrays and plucking chickens until the day they die. Their Bibles probably have greasy pages.

I saw Dylan Thomas' grave today in Wales in a graveyard stacked into a strange hillside. The stones were all aged and proper, carefully crafted by a stonemason, all but the grave of Thomas. On his grave was a cross made of lumber painted white, "R. I. P Dylan Thomas." Someone forgot the period after the P. I wanted to carve it in with my pocketknife but didn't. He slept in the Mermaid Inn. "We will show you to his room and you can stay there," they told me when I came here. I think more likely he slept downstairs on the floor of the Mermaid Tavern, face up under a table, smiling when a barmaid spread a tablecloth over him.

Today when I walked from a castle, black birds wound out and over my head, rooks. The fields were green and unreal, as if they were lighted from underneath. The cows were dark. All the *colors were cold. The birds made a strange sound as they soared over my head, the sound a dying man must think he hears when the buzzards circle. Yet a buzzard is silent. I would die silent here, chattering in front of my grate. I can write now, but I think I am too cold to talk aloud if there were anyone to talk to. No one would hear or know where I was until the maid came in the morning to clean the room.*

*I roll into the feather comforter, and soon my body throws its heat back at itself, the feathers like a giant sea gull I've crawled under. My writing hand is getting tired; my elbow is under the cover. I can't think when I'm cold. It would kill me here. I love the sharp scent of the air, the raw ocean wind, the evergreen smell; but soon it overcomes me and I shake all the way to the center. But I have found a white mother hen to sleep under. I am glad this is the end of my trip and not the beginning.*

\*     \*     \*

# Part III

I TOOK MISS TRIXIE out at Grandfather Fitzgerald's place one day in late August not long before leaving for Rocky Gap and my job with the Appalachian Corps. I don't think anyone had ridden her since Charles left in July. The grooms said they exercised the horses, but I think they only did that when my father came out to check on his cattle. And they never had to worry about him changing his schedule and catching them, not Mr. Clockwork. Trixie had always been my favorite because she learned her gaits following her mother through the pasture. They seemed completely unmanmade, though I suppose a horse wasn't the first to come up with more than a walk, trot, and canter.

It was strange that I no longer cared about form and appearance; I just liked to be outdoors riding. I can remember it wasn't so long ago that I was after perfection. I had gone over to the riding club a couple of days before to watch the dressage competition and I couldn't remember ever having been so bored; I was critical for a little while, trying to do my own judging to see how the riders compared, but pretty soon I couldn't even arouse myself to be critical. I did think I was better than anyone I saw, but it would take more than that to spark my interest again. I think it happened one day my junior year at the school competition; it all seemed so pointless. Even after the riding master said I was the best at Holbrooke, it seemed only a hair more significant than holding the record for flagpole sitting.

While I was working Trixie in the ring before we started out, she threw her head and got me in the face, not square on the nose or she would have bloodied it, but enough to hurt and make me go put a martingale on her. She had never done anything like that before or I wouldn't have been careless with her. Then as I was taking her down to the trail, she sidestepped and took down the mailbox on the caretaker's house. I would never hear the last of that.

It was a good day though. The leaves were starting to scud across the trail, and she felt good and wanted to go all the time. I could feel the silk of the spider webs as we went through the woods. No one else had passed through there that day, at least not anyone high enough to be on horseback. I brought her home covered with suds, but it was her doing and Sam knew that. He knew I wouldn't run her too hard. I helped him wipe her down. We knew she would roll if we let her in the corral but Sam and I agreed it made her happy, so we let her do it. She puffed at the ground predictably, picking her spot. Her legs, looking like little more than hair-covered bone, buckled like a horse shot in a cowboy movie. Sam remarked that she was one of the few who rolled all the way over, that most of them went down on one side at a time. We each took a side and brushed the dirt off her before we blanketed her in the stall.

I have a funny feeling about horses. I've been around them all my life, all kinds. Grandfather liked Tennessee walkers at one time, then hunters and five-gaiters. I have a real fondness for Miss Trixie. I talk to her when we're on the trail and when I'm grooming her. She snorts and nickers softly at my voice. But I know damn good and well she knew better than to slam me in the face. She knows I wouldn't hurt her like that. Maybe that's her way of telling me that she hates me for having control of her. Then again, I don't think horses are that bright. They're supposed to come out tenth on the intelligence scale, way below cats, dogs, and pigs. Maybe even chickens. It's hard to believe something that big and beautiful is that dumb.

Sam wanted to know if Trixie was going with me to Rocky Gap and if he should start planning on loading her up. I asked him why he thought I would be taking my horse, and he said I always did before when I went off to school. I told him I had graduated, and he said my mother told him I was going to do some more studying, maybe be a veterinarian. I had told my mother once, when I was about twelve, that I might be a vet. So I figured she was ashamed to say what I was really going to do. I confronted her that night, and she said she told him that because she knew I would tire of my job quickly and probably go back to school. Sam would be proud of me, she said, if he thought I might be a vet. She patted my arm and said what harm could there be in making Sam feel good, that he liked me best of all the grandchildren. I told her that was like having a favorite weasel.

The next morning all of her charge cards were on my dresser. She had done that every fall as far back as I could remember and again in the spring. It was her little signal for me to go buy a whole new wardrobe. There were a few times when I enjoyed that, I admit, felt a certain thrill when I saw those cards to do with as I pleased. But the last few times I'd felt nothing. I took them and put them in her room. I wouldn't be making a lot of money, but it would be mine and that was what I'd spend.

Maybe I was going to find it harder than I thought. I'll admit, too, that I never thought how much it cost to do something once I decided to do it. Like that wilderness training school. I thought I would be able to get someone at school to go along with me when I read about it in a brochure, but they all looked at the price and said it was too much. I never bought a sports car or thought much about clothes, yet I couldn't remember anything that I couldn't have either, at least not because it cost too much. I had money left over after my Europe trip because my father gave me enough to go first class. I made myself go get measured for a custom-made leather outfit in Spain just to make my mother happy. Maybe I could want those things if they were harder to get.

Clara's money seemed to have no strings attached. I get things in the mail that I have to sign and have notarized, stocks and trusts and junk that my father sends me that I have no idea about. I follow his instructions like a blind person. And it isn't because I'm not interested. I asked him if he'd like to explain it all to me and he said no, just let him handle things and when he was gone the lawyers would take care of it. Maybe he didn't want me to know that I was just something he used like a tax deduction. That must be why he puts that stuff in my name and gets me to sign those tax returns every year. When I told him about my job, he acted like my salary was just one more complication and told me not to sign or fill out anything without contacting him first. One night I said to him, "Show me a rich man who enjoys his money," and he replied, "Yes, and I'll show you a man who won't be rich long."

I liked having my horse with me and I knew my father would pay the stable rent if I asked him, but that would make me still feel attached. After returning my mother's cards, I applied for new ones in my name. The application forms asked for my salary, which is so low they probably won't even give me cards. And I'd told my mother I was not taking anything with me that wouldn't fit in my VW except for some books I was shipping to myself. I thought she would be happier when the embarrassment wouldn't be around to show herself. She started crying after she found the charge cards I returned to her room and said that the last decent thing I did for her was make my debut.

I told her I didn't see anything decent about my debut. I told her that in the dress she picked out for me I looked like a female impersonator, or worse yet it looked like the dress was still on the hanger. She has these pictures of my bow all over the library. My collarbone sticks out so far over that low neckline it looks like my chest was dirty. I never minded seeing myself in my horse-show pictures at Grandfather Fitzgerald's. In fact I was proud of them, but my mother wasn't interested; she is terrified of horses. Maybe I don't mind those pictures because you don't have to be pretty to look good on a horse. It's possible that Lady Godiva could look a lot worse than I do on a horse. That's not true. I guess it depends on who's looking and what they're looking for.

My mother made me have my hair done for the debut and I came out looking like those dummies in the early-American clothes at the Smithsonian, which I guess was what she was after. On the way over to the ballroom, I pulled the whole works down and put the rubber band off the evening newspaper around it. If I'd had scissors I would have cut it off before we got there and left it like a mat on the floor of the car. I suppose I wouldn't have ended up looking like such a fool if I had taken any interest in the whole business before it happened. So I ended up being my mother's creation. Perfume on a goat. One Sunday I looked through my father's *New York Times* trying to find a picture of an uglier debutante than I was. Actually I found a couple. Even with the best touched-up pictures that money could buy. My mother planned that bow for ten years. She signed me up for ballroom dancing school. I went to one lesson. I was standing beside this blimp — we were the only girls who didn't have partners — when a boy came up and said to me, "I'd rather dance with a skinny one than a fat one. Come on." I walked out and spent the time for the next nine lessons looking in windows downtown and reading movie magazines in the drugstore.

I remember back then my hair kept getting knotted up when I was riding. When my mother sent me into town to get it trimmed for my four hundredth permanent, I had it all cut off. She was horrified and said I looked like a boy. Later a man walked up to me in the yard and said, "Son, is your father at home?" I let it grow back out. After I had given up wanting to be a boy, I didn't want to be mistaken for one.

On the way to my training session for the Appalachian Corps, I stopped for the night in Mrs. Upshaw's house in Asheville. She acted as if she wasn't too eager to rent me the room for only one night, probably because the law said she had to wash the sheets even if they were only slept on once. I walked down the sidewalk, thinking that the neighborhood was decaying at an almost visible rate. The house that the crazy black woman lived in looked the same, but the yard was draped with narrow white paper. At closer glance I discovered she had made a fence of adding-machine tape. Her shrine was still there, but it had changed. The fence around it had grown, new bent forks and knives had been pressed into the soil. A sheet of transparent plastic was draped around the little tree like a tiny tent, stretched over the top of the fence and secured with rubber bands. Something had been growing under the canopy. When I stood close, I could see the unpicked paperlike blooms of jonquils that had grown from their bulbs and died under the plastic trap. Then at the end of summer the foliage was starting to rot. The whole structure gave off an unpleasant stench.

At first I didn't see her sitting on the porch because her pink robe of last winter had been replaced by the plaid housedress she wore when she gave her speech on the streets of Asheville. Since then her dress had faded, and she did look as if she came from that street, a beaten old woman with rolled-over stockings and splitting shoes. She looked like a woman in a trance until she sat up suddenly in her chair and pointed her finger at me. "God will get you!" she shrieked, but she didn't tell me why. Maybe Matilda was right when she heard I applied to teach in a black school: "What got into Miss Jean, wanting to do sech a thing."

After three days of lectures for the Appalachian Corps trainees in Bristol, Tennessee, I knew little more than what form to fill out and how many copies to make. I didn't have much in common with the other trainees. Most of them had sociology backgrounds and were political activists. I guess I expected them all to be recent graduates, but most of them weren't. They all had had experience with other projects. I hoped my grandfather wasn't the reason I was hired.

There was a seminar on model mountain villages, describing the ideal community as one that made use of the natural abilities of the people. In other words, the government didn't have to send many welfare checks. It was their premise that all villages in the mountains were alike in resources, give or take a few minerals or timber, so what separates prosperity from poverty had to be attitude. I was assigned to spend three days observing the model village of Coppertown near the North Carolina–Tennessee border, where the townspeople had a profitable wood-carving industry.

The road into the valley was narrow and empty of traffic. I met no cars leaving, passed no one coming in. On the way into town, I heard an interview show on the radio, asking local inhabitants about the moon walk. "Now you don't expect me to believe that. They did that out in Hollywood," one old lady said. The announcer was hanging up the phone, but all the listeners could hear her raving that he must have thought she didn't have the sense she was born with to believe in the likes of Buster Crabbe. How come she went out every night when they were supposed to be up there and couldn't see them?

At first sight, the folk school was a well-kept, prosperous farm that could be the home of a wealthy gentleman farmer. I went into the main building that housed the carvers' workroom. I found a glass case containing a wooden fawn with a speckled back in a sun-flecked clearing. An old man came up behind me and said, "Don't she look real as life? Don't know as how I could shoot one." His fingers that rested on the side of the case were scarred by his jackknife.

I heard the booming voice of a woman carver who turned out to be Gay MacKensie, long famous for her owls, frogs, and deer. She was broad shouldered, with arms as muscular as a man's. It seemed more likely that she would be swinging an ax at the sawmill than doing the delicate carvings.

In contrast to Gay, I then met a soft-looking lady in a pink dress. "Come in and join us," she said shyly. "My name is Sadie Jennings. I do piggies." She took cherry carvings from her basket and set them on the table, rooting, snorting, squealing piggies.

"You know," the old man said, "I heard one on Gay, how she tied her poor old hen up on the porch post so she could git a better look at her. What you gonna do you start carving bears, Gay? I can see you trying to tie up a bear on the front steps."

"That's a striped-looking piece of wood, Chuck. You out to do a zebra?" she retorted.

"Naw, a litter of baby skunks," he laughed as he rolled the wood in his hand. They talked of the smells outside, how when they were small and got out in the morning, they could smell people frying meat, just sniff, and know what so-and-so was having for breakfast. "Where did it all get to?" they wondered aloud.

"The meat just ain't got the flavor anymore. I can tell you that much. People got too lazy to do it right," Chuck said.

One carver had been down to the state university to see his

son graduate as a highway patrolman, but his interest had been distracted by the squirrels, his animal specialty, that lived in abundance on the campus quad. They weren't so plentiful up here in the cold hills and they wouldn't come up close like the spoiled and petted campus creatures. He learned a lot about squirrels that trip, just sitting out there under the trees watching them. "That's what they learned me down at the university," he chuckled, holding up a bushy-tailed squirrel.

Another man, who spoke in short sentences with a grin on his face as if he were always kidding, told me he started his carving in 1936 with a goose. Now he did horses, thin-legged perfect little horses. When he brought out his week's work, I noticed the response was different, the admiration evident. He was the master; the horse with its tiny legs would foil most carvers. You wonder how many times one miscut and the leg snapped away, the horse ruined.

"I'll tell you about carving them little rascals. Now a three-legged horse'll set anywhere. A four-legger will start rocking and set unlevel to spite you," he told me. When asked by one of the women carvers how he was able to get so much done in a week, he grinned and said, "Wife does all the work. She does the sanding. I'd sand it out of shape. She does all the work and I take the credit for it. Sanded every lick of that horse. I just whittle and rasp them. She can set in a certain place. I jump around." The women shook their heads and he added, "I tell the truth whether it's so or not."

Gay MacKensie's grandson pranced around the room, smiling at everyone. "That boy'll make a politician or a preacher." He added, "Can't tell which. Wait and see if he likes chicken."

They continued to talk sadly of the carvers who had died. I was sure that no one at the table was under forty. Finally I got the nerve to ask about their children. "The young ones won't seem to git going," one man said flatly.

Last night before I started to drive into the downtown section to my motel, I decided to stop and fill up with gas so I could get an early start for Rocky Gap the next day. I noticed a bench outside the service station that had knife marks on it.

"Did the carvers work here?" I asked the man who put the

gas in my tank. He was fairly old. He asked me to repeat what I had said, then he frowned and cleared his throat.

"Carvers, humph! Bums. I painted that bench three times till I swore it wont no use. Only carvers I know are over at the school place."

I was surprised that his station was so close to the school, yet he considered himself in a place apart from it.

"Do you know anything about the school?" I asked.

"Communists."

I was caught by surprise.

"Communists," he repeated firmly. "Bunch of foreign Communists come in during the war and holed up there and packed up bullets to shoot at us, right here in the good old U. S. of A."

I walked inside behind the old man to pay my bill. A forest ranger in uniform stood there. "Telling her 'bout the Communists over at the school. During the war, remember how they acted like it was agin their teaching to fight, and they made like they was boxing ammunition for our side. I seen it at the depot marked for Russia." He nodded at the ranger. "Let Jess here tell you. He knows more than me about the foolishness up there, all that community farming. That's Communists, ain't it, Jess?"

I asked the ranger what he knew about the community farming while I waited for my change.

"There is no way they can justify plowing up one square inch of land in these hills. Every clod they turn over ends up in Hiawassee, Georgia, or halfway down the Mississippi on the way to the ocean before they know what hit them," he said.

The old man interrupted, "Many the time I seen a boy bust up the land set on planting, then he seen something better and upped and left 'fore he got seed one in the ground."

I asked the ranger if he thought they should plant trees and he nodded.

"They ought to thank the Lord they still got their own land," the old man added. "Them people up in West Virginny ain't got a square foot 'cause of Rockefeller and the coal."

The ranger spoke up again, "And you see what happened to them when they sold off their timber. Poorest people in the

124

whole country living in what could have been the timberland of America. Places up there where half a mountain fell on the town. They cut the trees and let them do strip mining on top of everything else. They didn't have the sense like folks around here not to sell off their wood."

"Money burnt a hole in their pockets," the old man added.

I got back in my VW to drive into town. I saw the ranger and the old man through the window still talking, the old man slamming his fist on the counter. I easily read the word on his lips — Communists.

Communists. They saw the folk school as communistic. My mind was too tired to piece it all together and to wonder if they were just crackpots. But they were two different people who felt the same way. I lay in bed that night, watching the neon light from outside flicker on the ceiling until it was turned off at midnight. I had just been going along with it all, loving the people I met, the carvers, Gay MacKensie. I didn't have any reason to believe there was anything that I wasn't seeing. I was trying not to be naive, to be realistic and critical of my own plans for Rocky Gap. Before I went to sleep, I had an uneasiness, almost a guilt. If they hadn't mentioned Communism, I would never have thought of it. Then I became scared of my own stupidity.

*   *   *

Gay MacKensie . . .

*You think you like hit here? Don't git fooled 'cause hit's pretty to look at. I seen the summer a-coming and I said hello, goodbye, for all the long it last. Come winter, you git holed up in here, like hit or not. Nothing bigger'n two feet in a pair of waders going through that mud. I got shet up and started out whittling to give the little ones a trifle to play with. Hain't had a hand fit to look at on a woman sinc't. In my 'magination, I seen old Gay MacKensie a-standing at the Pearly Gates, shaking hands with St. Peter. Then come up the preacher to shake hands with the Saint. St. Peter says, "Come right on in, Gay. And Preacher, what you been doing all your life?"*

*When I started out whittling, I was hard put to figure hit was* *worth a dime. But as old Poley Derryberry used to say, "Hit's worth right smart to have something to do." A rich lady come here wanting one of Poley's chairs and was taken aback at the $2.50 price tag, when Poley had spent better'n a day on hit. Old Poley says, "Now I wouldn't want to charge nobody more'n I was willing to pay."*

*Hit's hard to git the wood. Got bastard pine to carve to your heart's content, but hit's not good for much. Hit'll pop out on the rug if you throw it on the fiar, and just soon drop a limb on your head as look at you. But the knots make hit good for turtles.*

*I do me some teaching. But folks lose interest in things like the school. They stay home a couple of times on the cold nights, watch TV, git attached to some special program, and the first thing you know, they git outa the habit of going. You got to watch students; they'll make a neck on an animal ever' time. Now I don't want to be doing what hain't lifelike. Animals hain't got no neck. Got to take a good look at things. Can't fail if you never try. I knowed how when I started. Didn't have no teacher standing over me telling me what to do. I like drawing my own patterns. You work with the group and they don't want me to do nothing but the same thing, over and over, and if hit looks the least little bit different, they don't want no part of hit. I don't know what's the matter with folks doing the buying. They say I want a frog just like the one I seen at Mrs. So-and-So's, and 'spect you to turn up one you can't tell apart. Even the Lord don't make two frogs alike.*

*We have a hard time gitting wood, though, on our own. You could kiln-dry hit in three weeks if you had the oven, but we got to wait three years for hit to air-dry to keep from checking. They git you stuck up at that school. I think they make you carve too slick myself. But you got bills to pay, hit's best to do what they say . . .*

Christina . . .

*He came back for three days. Three days and I have to take a carburetor off the breakfast table before I can set it. Greasy mess on my hands. I made fingerprints on the eggshells when I took them out of the carton. If I put my butcher knife through him,* they'd find my fingerprints in the trash bag and send me to prison. His back feels like iron. My knife would bend on it, and he would grab me and throw me across the room. I cracked the first egg on the edge of the pan. The pan wobbled on the burner, my thumb stuck through the shell and the yolk oozed oval shaped in the pan. Two tries. I take the worse-looking one for me. If I was fixing for me alone, I'd just scramble it right quick and forget I had any intentions of making fried eggs. But that's how he has to have them. The second one came out smooth, a quick crack on the edge of the stove, sliding into the pan and whitening around the yellow. I watched the clear bubbles swell in the white while he walked across the kitchen to his chair. Scraped the floor and made a streak on the linoleum pulling it out.

I saw something. In the center of the yolk was a heart, a tiny heart with veins thinner than hair that ran from the red spot. I wondered if the three days he had been home had put a tiny heart in me. I bent over it to see if it would beat for a second before the heat killed it. It only moved from the hot grease. I hovered over it so he wouldn't see, as if he would look at me any more than if the kitchen had been empty. Maybe he would have if I was covered with goose bumps in those baby doll pajamas he liked me to wear when we first got married, freezing my behind off in the cold kitchen. I turned it over, over medium, and he would never know he got it. I couldn't eat that one, knowing what I know. It would make me upchuck just thinking about it. But he'll never know. I couldn't help but stare when he ate, trying to guess which bite he ate the little heart, wondering if he might suddenly flip it over and see it and slap me across the face before I could run . . .

\* \* \*

I had been shocked when I first saw Christina. Actually she looked exactly the same as she did our freshman year, the same careful eye make-up, teased black hair, painted nails, the little frown between her perfectly plucked brows. The shock was that while her face looked the same, her clothes had changed. She was wearing woman clothes, the kind of silky blouse buttoned down the back that my mother might wear, plain black slacks, and sling shoes. I thought if you bought a blouse that buttoned down the back you were either showing off that you had a man to button it for you or you were double-jointed. Her voice sounded a little different when I called to see if she was home, more mature, but maybe that happened to everyone's voice, even mine. The only physical change appeared to be in the width of her hips, which had never been any too narrow, and a small roll around the middle.

If Christina was shocked to see me, she didn't show any emotion. She let me in, fixed a cup of coffee and offered me some. Neither of us had drunk it our freshman year; I still didn't. She told me I was still skinny as a rail.

The baby gurgled in the back room while we talked, but Christina didn't offer to show it to me, which I appreciated. It seemed more honest somehow not to pretend that either of us was really interested. Her little girl played in a pen in the corner. I felt strange around children sounds and the smell of urine and sour milk. I was surprised that Christina talked the way she did in front of the little girl. I didn't know how much awareness a child that young had of its parents' language. The child did seem more unaware of our presence than a pet might have.

Christina had had few friends in her short time in college and had always talked to me in a way which made us seem closer than we were. That manner had not changed. I could picture Christina telling her deepest personal problems to someone who happened to sit beside her on a bus.

It wasn't long before she was talking about her ex-husband. "He said we'd take a trip to Florida someday to ride the glass-bottom boats at Silver Springs and show me off in my bikini. That trip, that's just like wishing for a million dollars, even if we had had the money. Besides, he wouldn't have taken me anywhere if he'd been rich as Rockefeller. I always fixed up so he'd be proud of me. I had lots of other boyfriends who were proud of the way I looked. I told him I should never have married him, no more respect than he had for me.

"When we were going together, he used to make a fool of

himself over me. He put his arms around me in public, teasing me in front of my parents until I got embarrassed and said something to him about it. He would want to be with me every minute as soon as school was out, every weekend. You know how he was when we were in school. I never got a weekend to myself."

I remembered. I remembered how Christina paced the floor for the mail and her daily letter, and her anger when he said one weekend he might not have enough money to come up. She called him and he borrowed the money to come. Christina read those letters with a bored look, sometimes letting them get three days deep before she opened them. It didn't matter what he said; he just owed her that bit of himself every day. I always wondered what you could find to write about every day. "I got up this morning. I took a pee. I brushed my teeth. Then I thought about how much I loved you in that beautiful pink sweater." But he did appear to love her then.

He was a basketball player. One night when Christina and I had gone to a game, the chain had broken on her high school ring that had been thumping against his sweaty chest as he ran down the court. He stopped playing and crawled around on the floor until he found it, the referees and players staring in amazement. Then he brought it to the sidelines and gave it to Christina to hold. The crowd went wild, the boys making fun. But the girls were jealous because it was so romantic; Christina acted embarrassed, but she loved it.

"When I was in high school, I was planning to get married to this other guy when we graduated." Christina told me this today as if I'd never heard it before. "Then I met Travis, who was at Fort Bragg. I probably never would have gone to Holbrooke if I hadn't met Travis. I had had sex drilled in my head at church since I was a little girl and I always said to myself that I would never get messed up, that I might not be the most beautiful woman in the world, but when I found the man I wanted I would be sure." Then I saw the new Christina. "What a joke," she said bitterly. "How do you know he's the one? — that's the catcher. I thought three guys in high school were the one before I got engaged to Travis. But I'm not saying I loved sex. I didn't. It felt great until we went all the way and then that was nothing. For me it was nothing but a mess, having to go home with stains on your clothes and wash them out before your mother saw them. Then you worried to death about being pregnant. I remember one night I thought Roger's rubber had broken, and he threw it out the window and wouldn't go check and told me if I wanted to know to go look myself. But he was nervous, I could tell that. I told him I wasn't going to go tromping around in the ditch looking for it and scratch my legs up. But I never got pregnant until Travis. You didn't know that was why I left school? I thought for sure you would have guessed."

I didn't know. It had never entered my mind. Christina was so religious, I figured they just necked. I thought she got married because she was insecure and hated school. She had never told me about the sex before. It was hard to imagine that a girl like Christina could have kept that inside her, unless she hadn't admitted to herself it was happening.

"I bet you didn't know that two of my ushers at my wedding had gone all the way with me too?" Christina was laughing. I laughed too, but I was uneasy. This was a cynical Christina I hadn't known.

"But I'm telling you sex was nothing. For them, they were like a dog with a juicy bone. I'd be ashamed for someone to see me that way, panting and sweating like an animal. I was ashamed until Travis, but he changed me. For a while I thought we were really onto something. Then he got tired of going to the trouble for me; slam, bam, and maybe a thank you, ma'am, if I was lucky and he was feeling generous. There were a few months there I just couldn't wait until night to go to bed. We'd count the times we did it. We did things I would have thought I'd of gone to hell for in high school. I was a different person then. Now I'm back to thinking I'll go to hell for them. Or maybe I'm already there." Christina laughed again.

"So what does it all come to? I gave up my youth to him. Where can I go with two kids? Who wants to date a girl who's got to find a babysitter? People around here used to say that I looked like Maureen O'Hara; that was when I had red hair. You didn't know me then. Bet you didn't know that was me in that picture." She pointed at a photo over the couch; her hair was tinted an auburn color. I stared at the picture while she talked and imagined her painting her black hair red with a large brush. "I was homecoming queen in high school. I did just one little streak right through the middle at first with peroxide and I thought it looked cheap, so I did the whole thing. Even Elizabeth Taylor has a weight problem. She is very short like me, and when they told her she was the most beautiful woman in the world, she said she was too short of arm." I remembered that quote. Christina had read it to me from a movie magazine our freshman year. She read every one of them on the stands and talked constantly about movie stars as if they were good friends. It got embarrassing when other people were around, and we all made fun of Christina after she dropped out of school.

"But I know she doesn't have a problem as big as mine. My hips have been too big since I was twelve years old. People are never satisfied, are they? I would be if I looked like her. The doctor said it was inherited and I'd probably never be narrow even if I starved myself, but it would mean I could have kids easily. He was wrong there. I almost died with Michele. My husband, ex-husband, that is, said it was because I sat on my ass all the time, but he would never do anything with me. Everything he bought was for him alone. And he will say to this day, 'What about the boat you kept asking for?' He bought it last Christmas and said it was for me. I rode in it twice. Both times he just went out and started fishing with me sitting there and not a damn thing to do. You know how I hate the sun. I almost burned up, and all he did was say, 'Why don't you fish or shut up, one? So wear a hat next time.' Sweet guy, huh? I tell you, they change when you marry them. I gave the best years of my life to him, and then someone comes along who is just out for a good time and out to see if she can take him away from me and he is just like a fool. They repossessed his goddamn boat. I showed them where the key was that he chained it to the garage with."

That was the first time she had mentioned the other woman since the letter she wrote to me. "He can't see that she doesn't want him," she went on. "It was just a challenge to her to get him. I know her. She looks kind of like you, real tall and thin and more athletic looking than feminine. She just signed up for classes at that college to get a man. She's a secretary but she calls herself an office manager, you know, like a maid who calls herself a housekeeper. She was like that in high school, went to all sorts of extremes when the best thing she could have done was spend her time doing something about her personal appearance. She even tried to get on the track team just to be around men. She was that boy crazy. And they wouldn't look at her until she started putting out. He would get mad at me when I tried to talk to him about things and then she came along and he acted like he was meeting a long-lost friend. He couldn't help but talk about her. He even started making fun of her being so flat chested and skinny. Don't let anyone ever tell you they don't talk about the person they're messing around with."

Christina looked directly in the mirror across the room. She had been looking in it for a long time watching herself get mad, but she didn't know I knew it. I had noticed that habit at school, how she found her reflection in everything — spoons, windows, rearview mirrors — and studied it. I used to find my reflection on the bathtub faucet and make faces in the distorted image and be glad I didn't look that bad. Christina always kept a mirror in her pocketbook that could be located and plucked out in seconds. She knew every pore in her face. She plucked her brows knowing every hair and where it would spring back and how soon. I used to wonder if Travis would feel differently about her if he saw her putting on the make-up instead of always seeing the finished product. I had watched her at school work for an hour, then take the make-up off and start over, reading magazine articles on the art of eye shadow and how to make it appear you have high cheekbones. She was pretty, almost perfect looking if somehow unreal. When I arrived there was a small red splotch on her cheek. She was generally so perfect that you would notice a blotch. She never had problems with her complexion in school. There were always tufts of Kleenex on the dresser, stained blue, pink, and black, the colors she applied to that perfect face. Nerves were ruining her health, she said, mentioning the red spot, which made me wonder if I had been staring.

Once at school she had been half asleep and dreamed she was in the bathroom, and she wet the bed. She swore me to secrecy over and over again. She was a shaky person. I think maybe all the labor over her looks must have been lack of confidence. She had a terrible fear of criticism. There was a lot about her that could be criticized, but she set her own standards and achieved her self-conceived idea of excellence. Appearance was king. She failed only if she broke her own rules. Maybe we're all like that.

She pointed to the child in the playpen. "No matter what you want to do, that little thing is always there and you have to put her first." The child looked up and laughed. Christina made a face at her and she laughed again. "But we didn't intend to have this last one. I got off the pills for a while because they made me gain weight, and the old way didn't work anymore. With all my worrying, it did perfectly well in high school, but I might be more fertile now. And he never realized he was a father except when he was complaining or yelling at the children. And I think of how he sneaked. Of how I trusted him out at night, and he sneaked with her and made a fool of me in front of this whole town. I hope she cheats on him. She will. She's done it before. I could tell him a few things about her.

"I can hear the two of them now, making fun of me. He was the one who wasn't enough; he wasn't man enough for me. He never once made me feel secure and protected like I had a man around the house I could count on for anything before dark. I will not get a job. It is his responsibility to take care of his wife and children and he is going to have to do it. I just bet he wishes I would get a job; that would make it a lot easier for them to play around. Let him know that he is a man with responsibility. I'm not clerking in the five-and-ten. He's going to keep me up if I have to send him to jail."

Christina got up to fix some more coffee, again offering some to me. She lit a cigarette and looked out the window while the water was heating. There were three full garbage bags by the back door. The door was blocked by them; it might have been days since Christina had been outside.

I told her about my trip and about some of the people she knew from school. Christina hadn't heard of the dead woman that I found near there or she would have mentioned it. I didn't. It seemed right then that it would probably upset her more. Christina kept changing the subject back to the other woman, getting more and more agitated until I felt that any response would bring her to tears, even to quietly agree with her would trigger an outburst. I wondered how long it had been since she had had anyone to talk to or anyone to listen to her.

I spent the night at Christina's and I had a dream that stayed with me a few minutes after I awoke. I had driven to Bryson City in the dream. I drove to the house of Jane Boey's sister, Alice Faye. When I got there I saw that the yard was full of children. There was a woman on the sidewalk, so I asked her which ones were Mrs. Boey's children. I remembered only two. The woman threw her head back and laughed hysterically. Soon she regained her composure enough to speak.

"All of them. Every goddamn one of them. Three of them are by one of the ushers at her wedding. That one is by the forest ranger who found her."

The woman went on, designating which children belonged to which man. "She comes back every now and again to take care of them. A mother has responsibility."

I was shocked that the woman didn't know of the death. "But she died last winter, up on Le Conte," I told her.

The woman began to laugh hysterically again. "Then why is she setting on the porch yonder? They let her unthaw so they could stretch her out flat in her casket and she got up and walked away."

I looked at the porch and there was the long black hair hanging over the back of a rocking chair. The chair faced the wall. The girl with the blue hand was rocking and alive. Her hands were still a pale blue. Soon I was standing at the base of the porch, talking casually with her. I wanted to talk to her awhile before I asked why she had pulled such a trick. All of the work to sort the dead girl out in my mind was meaningless because she wasn't really dead. The girl in the chair swung around quickly. She had the same laugh as the woman on the sidewalk. But not the same face. I looked at the face a long time until I was sure. The face was Christina, with her hair long and black. I woke up then. I heard Christina talking to someone. As soon as I was awake, I knew Jane Boey was still dead.

I got up and went to the bathroom. I heard Christina's voice from the other room, but she wasn't laughing like in the dream. She was on the telephone. I saw the back of her teased black hair, inky black like unbuffed shoe polish. She didn't look at all like Jane Boey.

"That's right, two hundred dollars, and I need it by noon today," she was saying. "You know I can throw the book at you. You've abandoned us as far as the law is concerned."

Christina was quiet. Then she said, "You're goddamn right I'm threatening you. You come back and promise to me that you'll never see her again and we can take it from there. If not, you can just start paying off. Who do you think you are?"

Christina's parakeet started to flap around in its cage, kicking out seed hulls and feathers and turds. I thought it might have been agitated by the loud talking, but as I passed I saw it pecking its image in the mirror.

*   *   *

*This morning I drove over the narrow bridge into Rocky Gap. On both sides of the structure were holes like rotten-toothed mouths, where cars before me had driven against the barrier. If a truck had been coming from the other direction, I felt I could be shoved into one of the holes like putty. The water that I had seen on the roadside cliffs coming in, running down rocks that were cut by highway machines and dynamite, staining them black and feeding the rock plants, turned to yellow in Rocky Gap. The yellow isn't that of the topsoil that runs off the ridge farms; it matches the dark yellow of the late summer flowers that are stiffened already by the cold nights. It is dye yellow. Yellow that comes washing down out of nature is dull and aged-looking like old piano keys. This was bubbling from a pipe somewhere at a mill, too potent to be dispersed by the rush of water over rocks. Tomorrow the river may be red or blue, with bubbles that swell and crack in side pools like blisters. The yellow river cuts Rocky Gap in half, and only one bridge crosses it.*

*Somewhere cloth soaks in the colored water until it is tinted; a child wades in the river and stains its ankles and feet while its mother dips her hands in the factory pot. It may be a premature observation, but after the bright green of Coppertown, Rocky Gap looks feverish and unhealthy, born sickly.*

*Summer did not repaint Rocky Gap. At home in Raleigh, summer is when the streets are relined, the pock-marked pavement smoothed over, the curbing repainted. Rocky Gap has been worn down for many winters, its private and public enterprises. No one ever gave a thought to scaling the brick wall of the Dixie Hotel and redoing its letters. It wouldn't take a bomb to level Rocky Gap so an architect could start over in a vacant space; all it would take would be a few hard shoves on the major buildings to send it down like a house of cards. In the front window of the Dixie Hotel Cafe, dead flies are stacked with their feet pointing upward, looking like black tacks. In the front sign, once neon that no longer burns, starlings have stacked nest in unruly nest until there is a teetering haystack of bent sticks and straw. If winter doesn't knock down the bird tenement house, maybe the female will fall over with it in the spring and break her eggs. I think that a starling would probably flap down and suck up the egg goo, wondering why she never did it before.*

\*   \*   \*

When I stopped in the gas station at the end of Main Street, I noticed that the modernizing of Gulf Oil Corporation had not reached Rocky Gap. Standing iced with bird shit was the flat pumpkin sign that had been hauled away from all the city and interstate stations and replaced with the fat orange pie off the sixties' drawing board. I bought a blackberry pie out of his case that I figured must have been delivered when the sign was put up. My father would never have stopped there. He would have said, "Old stations that don't get their tanks filled regularly have condensed water in their gas." Something he read in *Popular Mechanics*. My mother would have turned up her nose at that pie if she hadn't eaten in a week, wrapping it in a Kleenex and depositing it in the trash. Actually it was pretty good.

My Rocky Gap journal might become public property. We were instructed to keep our impressions, dating our progress, for our final reports. I couldn't imagine they would want to go inside the heads of Gay and Christina, yet as soon as I saw them I wanted their voices in my journal. I was to be paid four hundred dollars a month and given a cottage to live in that was formerly occupied by a forest ranger. If the area school for adults became a reality, then I would be given quarters on the campus, probably a house trailer, and raised to another pay level. But that was a long way into the future. First I had to find a site and determine if there was any potential for a school in this area. Rocky Gap was chosen because of the large number of unemployed people who seemed to possess no usable skills. Some were feldspar and mica miners, many were disabled coal miners from further north, but the area had been mined out years ago and the former miners who still possessed any semblance of health worked in either the cloth or the paper mill. Some were farmers, but the growing season was extremely short and they produced little that brought income from outside the area. Almost all of their groceries were trucked in over narrow roads. One winter during a serious snowstorm, the government had to airdrop food. As far as Washington was concerned, the area received a continual stream of checks: John L. Lewis checks, Social Security, Workmen's Compensation, Black Lung checks, and it appeared that there was little to no information being fed out of the area. There were so few people that the congressional candidate came through once, gave a speech from a truck in the square, had dinner at the BPOE, and left.

When I stopped by the post office to rent a box, I noticed the floor was littered with envelopes from government checks. The windows were unwashed, and overrun cardboard boxes were used for trash baskets. My office was to be in this building as soon as the estate of the lawyer who occupied it before was cleared up. Until then I was to operate out of the cottage I located after a two-hour search through back roads of Olley County. No one, it appeared, even knew there had been a forest ranger living there. That might have been a bad sign; maybe no one would know there was a teaching consultant either.

*   *   *

*Tonight I want to attend a local revival. When I was looking for my house, I saw a sign: "Jesus Church — Revival tonite — 7:00 — All invited," and a large circus tent. The tent was in the center of a field on the main highway. If I can find my way back out again, that should give me a chance to see the population of Rocky Gap. Then I will have people other than myself talking in my journal again. I will know them sooner than the people from my past if I see what is here through their eyes.*

*Not much to say about my house. It smells musty like the old playhouse with the leaky roof that belonged to my father's sister. No one had come up to air it for me, but I guess no one should have. In the bedroom the mattress reeks of damp nights, even after I covered it with two mattress pads and my clean sheets. I have started to make a list, spray air fresheners, moth balls. The white feather-like insects drifted off a rag in the floor of the wardrobe. I plugged in the refrigerator and listened to the motor whir on. They had turned on my electricity. My father suggested that I write and send a deposit, and he was right again. I don't have the stomach to open the icebox door and smell the old rubber and pasty enamel. Or maybe there's even something spoiled in there.*

*Outside, the trees smell fresh and the wet ground smells clean; it is as if the grove of trees I am in doesn't like my little house and is going to rot it away like the leaves at the tree bases. When I walked back to the house steps from the woods, I heard nuts cracking under my shoes. Something made me shiver, maybe the wetness. I wore a sweater until I got too hot.*

*There was a dream house that I had once. I had it when I was very young, because I was always going to live in it with the boyfriend of the moment, a companion who changed frequently. The longest one to live in it with me was the boy who used to bring me presents when I was ten. Brian. He brought me a china doll with a handmade dress, then a bottle of perfume that my mother said was expensive. When he brought me a stamp collection already mounted on the pages, all stamps of flowers and butterflies from foreign countries, my mother got suspicious. She called his mother and found out that he had been stealing something every day from his sister. They had been blaming it on the maid. I met him every day at the end of my neighbor's driveway for my present. I guess I had to give them all back. I don't remember, but I know that soon he was not living in my house with me and I was living there alone.*

*The house was not much larger than the one I have now, but this one would never do because it has places that are rotten and stains that can't be fixed. My house was covered with ivy and had a thatched roof that goats ate on, but all the wood trim around the windows and fireplace was new and painted with shiny red paint. The yard was in tiers, and on each one I planted different-colored flowers so that when you stood at the bottom and squinted the colors would merge like a rainbow. Inside the house, fishbowls were placed so light shone through them. One tall, thin bowl was used for a wall. My dog lived there with me. When he lived there I never thought that he would ever be dead. Maybe that's when I stopped thinking of things to put in my house, when he got run over the second and last time. It was impossible for me to imagine being as old as I am now, to know that even without a violent death my dog could not still be alive.*

*I put boxwood bushes around the house because I liked the smell. They never had the brown-yellow dead spots on them where dogs had peed like the ones at my real house. There was a special square of boxwoods that I used as a graveyard for the fish. That seems strange to me now because I would have thought nothing ever died in my dream house. But I remember having funerals, making caskets out of jewelry boxes for my goldfish and guppies, making a headstone and putting flowers in pots out of my doll house. I guess I had a graveyard because I enjoyed the ritual of fish funerals.*

*Everything was in perfect order inside. Each item had a special cabinet and shelf. There were flower and mushroom decals on all the doors and labels to locate things. Maybe that is where the dream house has merged with my real house. I come into my real house now and I am like an old maid. I organize and stack and label everything. I even make note cards so I will be able to find my books without looking through the boxes. I'm not as bad as I was in college. I can remember when I wouldn't go to sleep if a door to a closet or bath wasn't shut all the way. And my shoes had to be placed beside each other perfectly parallel, left-right, left-right. I think we talked about that in the psychology class. It was supposed to mean something, but it must not have seemed to matter, because I don't remember it.*

*Since I got back from my trip to Europe, I have dreamed every night that I am still traveling. When I was at my parents' house for a few days, I dreamed I was sleeping on the train and had slept through my stop. I had to pee bad and was lying in bed thinking I couldn't go to the toilet because the aisles of the train were blocked by people sleeping on the floor, the way they had been one night when a strike caused the train to be overloaded. Then I woke up and saw my bathroom at home only a few feet away. The family cat watched me pee. I never felt rested after those nights at home and the nights since in motels and at Christina's. I wake up slightly and squint, trying to remember where I am from the patterns of light through the windows. There is no light pattern here until after four. It is starting to form now. The trees are thick and old. I'm as hidden as a mouse in a hole. I haven't slept a night here, but it seems I've been here a long time.*

\*   \*   \*

Only one day in Rocky Gap and my "sleepy little town" changed complexion. There was a big difference between seeing the buildings and seeing the people for the first time. They must have all been there, all the voters and churchgoers, and children and millworkers on a cool September night. I felt as if I had returned from a carnival. But the act was real.

I dressed carefully for the revival, putting on hose and a small hat I brought. I figured there was no need offending the local people on the first night. I drove down the bumpy dirt road from my house and back to the highway. I stopped a moment at the highway, memorizing the area so I wouldn't miss my turn coming back. There was a Clabber Girl Baking Powder sign directly across from my turnoff. I was proud of myself for remembering to do that.

I found the tent with no difficulty. All of the cars and pickup trucks in Olley County were going in one direction, stuffed with people. When I parked, I noticed I had the only foreign car in the parking area. As I walked into the revival tent, I had the strange sensation of having been there before. I slid into one of the folding chairs near the back and looked around me. The tent had started to fill, and unlike the usual church, the front seats were filling first. I caught my foot under one of the cornstalks beneath the chairs. The Klan tent down east near Clara's house — that was why the scene was familiar.

This gathering appeared to have attracted more women than men, their hair wound into fuzzy braided buns or tied back with rubber bands. There were only half a dozen or so with lacquered beauty shop hairdos. Up front, wooden speaker stands were temporarily constructed for the entertainers who would perform for their weather-beaten audience. There was a religious cloth of some kind, soiled and spread like a tablecloth over a large wooden box at the front of the tent. Hanging on the front of the structure was a stained-glass window replica made of construction paper. I guessed that must be the pulpit. At first impression these people seemed poorer than those down east and in the bigger mountain towns like Asheville, less jovial in their responses when they nodded at their acquaintances, sterner and more old-fashioned. I looked around as much as I could without appearing to be staring. My guess was that Rocky Gap was not a very happy place to be.

Soon the preacher came in and called the congregation to order, asking them to all rise and turn to the song on page forty-three. They fumbled under the folding chairs for the hymn books, and as the pages rustled, the pianist started to play. The piano was out of tune and the woman in front of the keyboard made three loud mistakes in the introduction. On the third one she shook her head. She seemed ashamed she hadn't practiced more; maybe she didn't know which ones he was going to pick. Many of the people gave up looking for the page number and held the book by their sides. The singing was shrill and tuneless. It was so unpleasant to listen to I sang loud enough to hear my own voice come back to me. The old woman beside me moved her lips and made no noise.

The service went like all services, slow, boring, the same Biblical quotes. It was like those dull Sundays when I was a teen-ager and let my imagination drift as I went through the motions. Yet most of the people listened intently, their necks bent and their heads tossed back like birds trying to let water run down their throats. Probably they couldn't read, so this was their chance to find out what was in the Bible and remember what little of it they could. I was getting restless, but those around me didn't seem to be. They had little for amusement and this man with the slightly northern accent had them under a spell.

Soon he started in on serpents. There was a snake in the garden. From the beginning the Lord put snakes in the world. Christ's disciples took up serpents. How many of you here have handled a snake? The woman beside me began to whisper, "Git the power. Git the power from the Lord." Then I realized why the people had sat closer to the front. They wanted to be up close to get a good look at the snakes. He didn't need to give an interesting sermon.

A couple of hands went up in response to his query. Then when he said, "Now I mean a poisonous snake," his head cocked and his voice pealed out like a first grade schoolteacher asking her brood if they remembered to wash their fingers after using the restroom. The hands floated back down; the little children had prematurely told the teacher they knew the right answer and were ashamed. Those two old farmers in front of me had probably thrown garter snakes out of their corn rows or lifted a black snake out of a hen nest on a hoe handle and watched it sliver like a noodle on a fork. I rode past a sleeping black snake on a rock once with Miss Trixie snorting and tossing her head, and I saw Sam carry a wiggling one out of the horse barn on a pitchfork. He said he didn't kill it because it ate mice, that there were good snakes and bad snakes. The preacher continued to talk while we all framed the snakes of our lives in our minds. It was obvious he was referring to the bad snakes.

"I have taken up enough serpents in my day to fill a bathtub ten times over." They were silent. He had better think of a better container than that. Most of these people had never filled a bathtub with water much less knew how many serpents it would take. If he had said five bushels, they would feel their skin crawl and check under their blanket before they slid in bed at night.

"Enough snakes to stack your corn crib to the ceiling. Hundreds of snakes. Every kind of snake the Lord sent to this earth. Rattlesnakes, copperheads, cottonmouth moccasins. Once I had a friend send me the deadly viper and I handled it too. The Lord anointed me and gave me victory over the serpent."

"Some friend to send you a viper," the boy behind me said. The girl with him started to giggle.

The audience was beginning to rustle with anticipation. The snake man was here in Rocky Gap. He was telling them about victory, about how he had been bitten five times and the Lord had told him it wasn't time for his death to come. There was death in the box in front of him. But if his death ever came from the snake, the Lord had willed it and he would be proud to go meet the Lord.

The boy behind me whispered, "If I stick my head in the stove and it burns off, the Lord willed me to die." The girl giggled again but the people around them told them to get quiet. They wanted to hear this man out. He had a courage beyond their comprehension. Finally the moment they had waited for arrived. He opened the box. It was a wooden crate that had held chewing tobacco before it housed the snake. When the lid was laid aside, the congregation became so silent that I could hear a thump inside the box. When I heard that thump, I started believing what was going to happen. I thought more than one snake must be in there and they were squirming and hitting the sides of the box. A shiver ran through my body. I felt the hand of the old woman next to me rubbing the skin on my arm, her calluses raking me like a currycomb. I smiled at her when she patted me on the hand and left her fingers touching me. She needed a friend because she was afraid to be alone. I saw her pale old eyes dancing around, the rest of her face stone still.

"If you have no fear, the Lord will let you hold the serpent in your hands." The preacher pointed at the people and they began to clap and moan in rhythm. The piano player started to hit chords. Soon they had a steady rhythm going. It made me want to move my body like a hula dancer. If I were the snake, I would have risen from the box like a cobra from a snake charmer's basket.

Suddenly he reached into the box and lifted it up, golden and brown and licking around his arm. I was amazed, stunned by the reality of the snake. Its body was thick as a child's arm. The flat head moved over the preacher's hand and pointed towards the congregation, its tongue zipping in and out, testing the air and the surroundings with its pronged tongue, a new place, new faces, but maybe after a hundred performances they all start to look the same to the snake. Yet the snake didn't look like anything these people had ever seen, except maybe in a nightmare of hell, when they woke up screaming and pounding on their mates. The people leaned backwards in their seats, moving as far away as they could get from the deadly snake but continuing to chant and clap, softer now as if not to awaken the evil in the snake. For what seemed an eternity the man let the snake move around his hand and arm while he talked of victory. If the Lord had anointed you, you too could handle a snake. The old woman next to me gripped my arm with both hands. I stroked her hand; she hummed to herself as if in a trance. The people began to jabber, jumping from their seats and talking in an unknown tongue. I got chills on my arms as the congregation around me broke away, entering another realm and leaving me alone. Soon the old woman pulled her hand away and pounded her palms together.

For the first time I noticed the group behind the preacher. They must have been his family. Yes, the two boys had the same face, except the fear their father didn't have was etched in their young skin. They seemed older than the man with the snake, as if they knew from experience not to touch a snake. The woman with them held her feelings tight, a neat woman dressed much nicer than the local women. When the serpent was lowered back into the box and the white hand of the preacher lifted out and replaced the lid, the congregation began to move again, free from the clutches of the serpent, but with its twisting body in their memories. The preacher had his victory over the snake and over these people. They felt the power. The singing started, the preaching got louder, and I saw the people work themselves up to a high pitch, sweating in the cool night. The preacher started to pound on the snake box in rhythm. Soon feet were stamping, strange voices in a steady beat. The old woman beside me had started to clap loudly and beat her lap. The noise became dizzying in its regularity. I watched the faces in my row. Their tongues were zipping in and out, and saliva hung and drooled from the corners of their cracked mouths. White diseased old tongues unlike the young pink tongue of the serpent. The collection plate was passed, hardly noticed by those who put their money in except for the boy behind me who said, "Pay the clown for his performance," but he spoke quieter now. I was sure no one else heard him and he didn't sound so convinced that this man was a clown.

Soon the preacher lifted the snake box over his head and the crowd grew quieter. Was he going to do it again? Yes, he was. What strange ego had driven him to do it again? They were with him; he didn't need to risk it. He put the box down and the people tried to be quieter. No, he didn't want that. He pointed his magic finger at them and made them jabber again. I saw two women batting their tongues against each other, the saliva hanging off their chins from their strange kiss. It was harder now to reach the rhythm. Their emotions were ragged. They were tired. The lid came off. Out came the snake. It was lifted, up high and wriggling, until a short scream broke the silence. I saw the man's face change. Was it the scream? Did it scare him, give him that fear he said he didn't have? Or did it frighten the poor, dumb snake, who was snatched from the box for an encore, crammed into the hot box with people screaming around him, and then yanked out again?

The snake struck quickly, a simple act that took no training. It hit its target without practice. The snake was dropped to the floor and I saw the blood ooze from the man's wound. But there was no stampede to clear the tent. Only one old man who smelled of alcohol and urine stumbled down my row towards the exit. The old woman beside me shoved him past, muttering, "Git out from in front of me, Leon." When Leon was gone, our eyes searched the stage for the snake. One of the sons grabbed the box and turned it over, holding his foot atop it as if the snake trapped inside could lift it up. There had been only one snake after all, and the boys then did what not a man there could do. While the box was held on its side, one boy took a chair leg and bumped the snake in and the other slid on the lid. The snake was captured.

The preacher, who had continued to talk of victory while the snake was boxed, finally collapsed beside the pulpit. The boys and the hard-faced woman went to their knees, lifted and carried him from the tent, smoothly, as if this were part of an act they had performed before. But they were playing roles in a real tragedy. That was real blood that I had seen coming from the two holes that let the venom inside him, real blood popping up on the man's hand in a circle no bigger than a quarter.

* * *

Leon . . .

*Cornstalk caught in my shoe sole I pull it out but can't git over swimmy I fall on my head they throw me out of here. Say Leon's drunk sorry Leon not worth a tinkle damn but I ain't had nothing today 'cause I got no money. My head is aching and swimmy that singing is hurting me I don't go to no church and have to listen to that and I didn't come here tonight to be at no church. Git on with it I say preacher man. You acting like a preacher but you better bring out that snake soon or Leon be long gone 'fore you say Jack Rob'son. Sleeping in Sweet Peach in that Sweet Peach box.*

*. . . I been off to sleep a bit I declare 'cause things is changed thinking of that old snake all curled up and snoozing. People's leaning different and starting to rustle he said I bet it is time for the snake in the garden got to tell you about the Bible but that ain't why Leon come here. Have I handled? Handled a dead snake preacher man after my hoe come down square. Head here rest there slick and cold and dead. Is that live snake hot like a chicken on the chop block pick him up burn you like a sausage frying? Naw sir. Not with no head still on him barehanded I never handle bathtub full like a bucket of worms bathtub out in*

*Saul's field got water in it for the cows in the bottom could be maybe one old snake snake full. Who fill it up you preacher man? Talk big. I seen one in the crib onc't et mice whole but didn't have no pisen five times. Bit five times. You lie. Man don't git bit but onc't. Man the devil let a snake bite him. Snakebite on my snake hee hee. Death in the box. Sweet Peach. I heared it bump. I heared it bump and off the lid oh he is out oh Lordy look at him come out of hand around arm yellow and hot he is hot and alive like he gotta arm with no bone three arm man oh no that's a snake. That's a real big snake. O Lord it's real and alive and it looks at me looks around. I run. Cornstalk under the chair don't you push me back down sonavabitch tongue coming after me tongue reach so long it git me oh my God. Yeah Lord Lord yeah Lord yeah Lord my God. He put it up. He put it up. I have wet my pants and it goes down around the seat of my chair inside my sock smell it hot didn't come through in front good cold spot goose bumps like a skinny snake go down my leg hot.*

*oh my God oh my God*

*Don't beat on it don't make it mad throw off that top and come out don't make it mad please sweet Jesus he has it up again my throat is powder yell I couldn't yell if my life depended but I did I bit him where'd he go on the floor hungry after me. Out. The chair is over bang chain on my foot stop shoving me and I run and run and run and fall. I'm dead. Pull out the cornstalk bit him bit him bit me.*

\* \* \*

The morning after the revival I went into the local store to stock up my refrigerator. I walked over to the bins where the vegetables were stored; battered, unwrapped, and handled by all the hands that came in. I guessed if you arrived more than a few hours after the delivery by the county farmers, you bought what had been in every crusted hand in the town and tossed back into the rack. The cornhusks were peeled open and the yellow grains bore the scars of fingernails that had pierced the grains and spattered out the juice. The bins were stained with vegetable and fruit juice that was years old.

I passed the revival tent on my way into town, the center post already gone, the men working to roll up the lopsided canvas. I thought I might stop and ask them about the preacher, but that might have been a mistake. The word could get around that I thought the preacher was like everyone else and could die from the snakebite like any mortal. I should be careful of what I asked, since people were likely to be suspicious of me. The snake faith was infallible; if you didn't get bitten, God was with you — if you did, God willed it. If you survived the bite, God said it wasn't your time; if you died, God was ready for you in heaven.

A middle-aged man stood behind the counter, corn weevils fluttering around his head and drilling into the Indian corn that was tied in bundles of three for the tourists who never got there. Bunches of yellow and red bittersweet had shattered on the floor and only the stems were still inside their wrappings. A middle-aged woman stood at the counter in front of him while he counted her purchases and stuffed them into her shopping bag. I had a moment of panic that I was going to offend him because I didn't bring my own bag until I saw the stack of paper bags on the shelf behind him.

"Leon, git out of here. You smell like a skunk!" the storekeeper yelled suddenly. "You want a bottle of wine, git the money from Dwayne."

I saw the bent man who had run out of the revival, his ears red and twisted, shuffling out of the store. The storekeeper shook his head and said to the woman in front of him, "How he thinks he's going to steal a bottle of wine from me. All you have to do is sniff the air and you know Leon is in here someplace." The woman didn't look at the drunk as he went out, holding her head stiff, as if she would sin if she looked over her shoulder at him. I recognized her as the piano player from the revival.

She said, "Did you see him last night, knocking down half the row trying to git out of the tent like he was the only person in Rocky Gap worth saving. But Mollie Burcham is our shame. We won't hear the last of that crazy old fool. She seen that snake once, and when she seen it again there was no call for her hollering out like she didn't have good sense."

"I know what you mean, Mildred. Just what you mean," the man replied. She was looking at the prices on her goods carefully, and I thought it was a strange contrast, the casual talk and the intense watching of the register to see if she was being cheated. The storekeeper knew how carefully she was watching, but he continued to chat. "Dr. Thomas says he figures the Reverend will come or go 'fore evening. The Doc made him comfortable as he would allow, but his faith is so strong he won't even swallow a pill to ease the pain. The Reverend admits he don't want to leave his sons and his wife, but God may have decided it is time for him to die. He's already talking about seeing Jesus come to walk beside him to heaven. Doc was in here this morning . . ."

"Mollie Burcham would turn up a copperhead in the woodpile and just as matter o' fact chop his head off with her gardening hoe. Then she gits where there's somebody to take notice of her foolishness and she lets out a whoop loud enough to raise the dead." Mildred was obviously not interested in the preacher's condition.

"It raised the living, I'm telling you," the storekeeper exclaimed. "It raised the living in that snake. There's them who say them preacher fellows don't carry about none what still got their pisen sack. I remember when Miss Effie Gilliam come 'fore sech was even talked of and I seen her handle a half-dozen snakes big as her arm right on that very spot where they set up the Reverend Willis' tent yesterdy evening."

"I declare, Mr. Bigham, I would have died of the fright, that slimy cold snake got his teeth in my skin. Mollie Burcham is going to have to answer in hell for her whooping. You'd think she be feeling some shame, and I already seen her this morning out chopping through her sweet potatoes again and I walked by her and didn't git so much as a how-de-do. The Bible says you ain't got good sense, you can't go to heaven."

After Mildred left, I introduced myself to the storekeeper. He seemed friendly enough. He had a daughter about my age, he said, eighteen, that was married and had two children. I told him that I was a schoolteacher in a new government school for adults, which I wasn't exactly, but that would suffice for now.

"Did I overhear that the woman who screamed last night is called Mollie Burcham?"

"That's her. She lives in a shack up by the mill. You should try giving her some learning," he said with a laugh. "Learn her to keep her mouth shut. We'll git blamed for that preacher gitting bit, you wait and see. Every state 'round'll say it happened in Rocky Gap, North Carolina, where people ain't got no more sense than to think they're in a side show. I'll say it made me wish I'd set back two or three rows, though, when that snake popped him."

"I know what you mean. I was in the back and glad of it."

The storekeeper began to laugh in a friendly way as if he were enjoying my company. "What you think of the crazy people 'round here? Snakes and hollering."

"I think I'm going to like it here. The people have been very friendly."

He was a bit taken aback. Maybe I had been excessive. Actually he was the first person I'd talked to. "Just don't go gitting friendly with the wrong kinds. There's some sorry ones come down from West Virginny and Kentuck when the mines give out. We'd just as soon they go somewhere else, but the word is the cities won't have 'em no more. You watch out for them kind. They live on gov'ment checks and wouldn't lift a finger to scratch their heads. They won't take for teaching and learning or whatever it is you're planning to do."

"I'll be careful," I said. He sounded like the mountain version of my father. Maybe the storekeeper needed to do that because his little girl was already in the hands of another man and didn't need him to care for her anymore. He got shortchanged on the number of years that she stayed his little girl.

I left the store and drove back to my cottage. On the way I looked for Mollie Burcham's house. I noticed a small unpainted shack beside the mill. Behind the house ran the yellow river. In the back yard was an old woman in skirts to her ankles with her hair tied back with a rag. She stood up to tuck her hair under the edges of the cloth, scratching her behind with the other hand and watching my car pass. Three big dogs started barking and jumping at a chicken-wire fence as they sighted my car. As soon as I had unpacked my purchases in the refrigerator, I decided I would drive back to talk to Mollie Burcham.

150

\*　\*　\*

Mollie Burcham . . .

*When the warm days finally come, I'd wake up mornings a-thinking maybe it wont to be too bad. We didn't have money no more and had sold off all our readymade clothes and curtains and rugs for the nearest nothing to git a bite to eat. The sun was a-shining, and I could hear the chickens and bugs in my back yard and people wont a-living right up on your doorstep like they was in town and I'd tell myself today is gonna be the day to change Mollie Petry's life to good.*

*But I'd git out in the field and I'd see me there wont a whole man to be found nowheres. Nothing but a bunch of broke-up cripples or they wouldn't be out there in that hollow, all of them a-waiting to tell you ever chance they git how it come upon them and how ifin they had knowed what they knowed today, it wouldn't a been. Then off they go a-hopping on a cork stick of a leg or they pull off their shirt to show you where their arm come off and the sink hole it put in their side.*

*And I was always one to look right at it. I was the only one of my sisters could do that. When a man come in doctoring or a-selling something, I would marvel to look at a whole man who had all his members that were rightly attached. Soon as the whole men 'round me got to working age, they was off to town to the mines and like as not to stay on the Sa'urdy nights and Sunday a-drinking up what they earnt. I had me a baby by one of them whole men, Sarah Mae, who died of fever 'fore she was outa the crib. Like to have kilt me, li'l Sarah Mae dying, not big as a minute, but I was just a child myself. Found her dead and swole up one morning like a dead kitty 'fore I ever had it clear in my head she was to be a person.*

*I declare I believe what drawed me to him was to tech on a man what was all there and not have some old bastard a-telling me to come up and thump on his leg hard as I could, then cackle his fool head off when I sprung back with my fingernail a-aching from the hard wood. Man made me poke my finger down in the hole where onc't upon a time he had an eye like the rest of us and askt me what it felt like to me. I told him it was like poking in the inside of a eggshell, round and sticky, and it made my finger smell bad, and he used to call out ever time he seen me past to come dab my finger in his eggshell. My brothers and sisters like to have laughed their britches off at me about that. None of them was likely to let somebody a-made them do that. But I was always the one to jump off in the water first . . .*

When Mollie Burcham was only five years old, she said, her hair grew like cotton wisps on her head like an old whore woman, or the aged woman she is now. She grinned and asked me if she looked like a witch, and I saw her two green-yellow teeth and couldn't answer. She chuckled at my silence, taking the rag off her hair and shaking her head. She had let me in her house to visit without question, like a lonely grandparent. When I looked at her, I thought her hair looked as if it could break loose and blow in the wind like thistle seeds, leaving the slick center knob bare. Mollie told me she tied her hair in a rag to hold it to her head. She could pin it in curls until the pins would rust her scalp, and it would never take curl. Her face glowed pink in the sun, so she wrapped her arms and wore a bonnet when she had to do the picking. I watched her pull up the stretched sleeve of her sweater, brushing her arm to show me how her skin flaked away like ashes. There was almost no pigment left except in tan ovals on her wrists.

She talked about her life without being questioned. Once her brother took her down by the pond and piled her head high with mud, to make her beautiful, he said. She sat with her body drawn tight and her eyes closed, seeing visions of the beauty she would have, while he gathered black-eyed Susans and stuck them about on her head. But she couldn't resist looking, and when she did see her reflection in the water, her mud head snapped forward. The mud head fell in the pond yanking at the cotton wisps until she let out a yap like a kicked dog and dissolved her visions into brown water.

I liked Mollie from the first time I visited her. I think I may have liked her partly because I didn't like Mildred, the lady in the grocery store who had it out for Mollie for screaming at the revival. I had to think of my own Grandmother Fitzgerald too, *carefully closed off from what she saw as the hard things of life, like cooking her own meals and starching her dresser cover. Mollie spent the same days tied up with rags tromping through a field, her feet rotting in the dew. Both of them must have figured that was the way life was supposed to be. Mollie has this funny little bright-eyed look that makes me want to watch her expressions, as if she's right on the verge of saying something she would call sassy. She said she has always been ugly as a wart toad. I know you have to be young to think age can have any beauty. The only thing I don't like to look at is her skin in the joints because it seems it will be a short time before the skin breaks and the bones will poke through. She's still tall, even though old age has taken a lot of her height. Maybe that's why we got 'long right away. We both knew that tall in a woman equals ugly.*

*She told me when she was courting, her mama would come onto the porch in her bare feet to embarrass her, parading back and forth across in front of her young man with her dress tucked in her crack to make sure he would know they were country. Her mama would lift her skirt and spread her feet in the field, urinating in the dry soil, wiping herself with her skirt. Once while a young man was visiting Mollie on the porch, she told her sister to go into the house and get a snapshot off her chest of drawers, that she wanted to show him how many cousins she had in the war. Her sister laughed and said, "We ain't got no chest of drawers. You know we ain't got no chest of drawers." Her family was determined not to let her "git above her raising."*

*I see Mollie at the point she is now, seventy years of life. Then I think of the mountain woman on Le Conte, Jane Boey, who has been out of my mind for a while and who was frozen young forever, her hair still thick, her skin smooth. Something made Mollie different, made her not give up. She has been a woman for seventy years and she is a survivor. If she dies in her sleep tonight, she still survived. If I tossed a hot coal at her, she would throw her old hands over her eyes because she is still watching everything happen. An old man would cover his withered genitals even after his penis was good for nothing but urinating. I think Mollie would want to see what was around her if it were only the rotting walls of her house and the snow piling up on the road and the path to her privy. I think she is the history of these hills if she will keep talking to me.*

\* \* \*

Two of the local women's club leaders stopped by to welcome me. They were bored and boring. They gave me a bank calendar, a Gideon Bible, and a free set at the local beauty parlor. On the way home I stopped off to see Mollie. We had a good laugh over which one of us should use the beauty parlor coupon, since we both have our thin frizzy hair in braids.

\* \* \*

*Today Mollie talked more of her mountain girlhood. She asked me if I was tired of listening to an old woman, that she would know she had run me off when I didn't stop by again. Mollie said she grew up scared of her daddy. She remembered him to-day, back when she lived in Kentucky, which was really her home, Hazard, Kentucky. There folks didn't think they were too good for her like the ones in Rocky Gap. The residents of that dismal Cumberland town knew they were in Little Hell and the poverty they were born with had sent them there.*

*Her daddy plowed around the graveyard on the farm they set-tled for as many years as they thought people in the community would remember there was a family buried up there. Then came the spring of 1900 and he broke the graveyard land. Time for a new generation, he said, at the turn of the century, so he planted it in corn. If their bones were close to the top, they would be like powder, he figured. There was bone meal in fertilizer and it ought to be good for his crop, he told her with a laugh. If they hadn't been lazy and had planted their kin deep, he'd never reach them with his plow. The Lord would make him pay, Mollie's mother said, and his corn would grow dark green from their bones to spite him and have kernels on their ears as hard as a dead man's teeth. Mollie said her mama had strong feelings about laying aside room for the dead. But the corn didn't grow* greener; the corn was the same as in the other fields. All that there was to spite her daddy was his little girl, Mollie, digging around his stalks with a spade. He snatched her up by the back of her dress and it made a tear, out loud, at one of the rotten arm seams. In her mind an animal had grabbed her, and she could never think of her daddy without being afraid to turn her back on him.

"You going to leave the roots bare to the sun." He scolded her and shook her until the spade fell from her hand.

"No, Papa," she said clearly, hiding her fear of him. "I'm going to dig out the grave of the little girl. She was near my age, they say, when she died of the pox and they buried her with a china doll. A real china doll with white slick legs and arms. Her dress might be all gone now in the dirt and even the blue eyes and red lips a-painted on might be wasted, but I figure that china lasts longer than bones."

"I wanted that china doll bad," Mollie told me seriously, and every spring at land-breaking time she walked the furrows looking for it. She had found it a thousand times in her dreams and it was beautiful. She ran for every white root and cutworm that turned up with the plow, thinking it was an arm or leg of her china doll. She was shamed for telling her daddy. He laughed loudly at her and teased her until he broke her doll dream to pieces in her head and she never had it again.

I looked at Mollie's hands, wondering how she could ever have wanted a china doll or even felt its slickness, how she was once a soft child. The sides of her fingers are crusted from whittling in the winter, making toothpicks and sewing quilts without a thimble, or from pulling husks off corn. She is always doing something with her hands when we talk. Her skin looks like an old piece of wood that the water has run over for years; the hard flesh is left in ridges and the soft has worn away. It appears she could be snapped apart like the sticks she uses to kindle her fire.

The women here are so different from those southern ladies that wear gloves for everything they do, church, washing dishes, gardening, as if their hands must never come in contact with anything coarser than they are. Gay MacKensie's hands were scarred and callused from her jackknife. I watch Mollie use her hands as tools. I've seen my mother buy tools for what Mollie does with her hands. Grandfather Fitzgerald's maids had far more money than Mollie. We used to give them lotions and perfumes for presents. The maids always had extra time to sit around and rest their bodies. I don't think Mollie has ever stopped being busy, even now when there's only her left.

"Women here don't want what they never had because they don't know what they should be wanting," Mollie said. It didn't offend her to talk about being poor. "I'm speaking of the hard-up ones. Some of them in town never wanted a day in their lives." She went on to talk about how radio and television were presenting to people wants and dissatisfactions they never had before. To know that everyone wasn't poor was a bad thing; it didn't give you ambition, just bitterness. All boys wanted now was a fast automobile, and the girls wanted to marry the one with the fastest automobile whether he had a "lick o' sense or a dime in his pocket. They start a-thinking they ought to have what ever'-body else has." I listened for the edge in her voice, wondering if that comment was meant for me because I came from outside.

I finally asked her about outsiders coming in, why there was such a resentment towards people from other places, was it because they came in fancy cars wearing nice clothes and built expensive houses? Mollie changed when I questioned her directly instead of letting her ramble. She tightened up her lip and told me what a fool I was. That it wasn't what the outsiders brought in; it was what they took away. She said the fruit was stripped from the plant and not even a seed was left. Their hills had been plucked clean by outsiders with no respect for who was there first. I felt the fool she called me.

I'm attached to these hills in a different way from hiking. I think the mountain people have to go nowhere else to know that what they have is prettier or just as pretty as anywhere in the world. The Appalachians are special mountains, worn down and covered with vegetation. Often the houses are impractically located — the view from the porch not sacrificed to shorten the walk to the fields. That must be unusual for poor people, to consider the beauty of the surroundings before they consider water, land, wood, and whatever they need to survive. I don't think their placement of their cabins could be by accident, not from *what I saw from the house windows in Lost Cove. I said that to Mollie and she just grunted and said, "They wont still there, now was they?" I better keep my idealistic dissertations to myself for a while.*

*Mollie told me there were seashells printed in the rocks on the plateau, that she wasn't "pulling my leg." This was all once an ocean, and when the ocean went away, it left the coal. Her daddy told her that. He never saw the real ocean and neither had she. But he hadn't told her that when they had taken all the coal away, they would leave the people buried under mud from the strip mine slides. He didn't live to see that. He thought the coal would never run out. Mollie gestured at the coal scuttle beside her fireplace as if the contents were so foul she didn't want it near her, instead of something to bring warmth from the cold. The slag, the mud slides, men coughing till they died, arms and legs gone from the explosions. There is no love from the mountain people for the black mineral.*

*She told me one horror story after another. I had set her mind off churning up the bad memories she had buried. The men in Kentucky went down in the mines and worked in hell every day of their lives, hating what was bringing them what little they made, hating the coal and hating the owners. The owners took the coal away, and with it went a chunk of the life of the people for good. And in return they got barely enough money to stay alive and keep digging. Every railroad car that went out left the people and the land more wasted. It was hard for her to tell if it was worse after the coal was gone. She had left Kentucky and didn't want to see it again to find out.*

*As I was leaving, she asked if I'd heard about the Reverend who was snake-bit. I had. He had died because he refused medical treatment. Mollie sat back in her chair at the news and hissed through her teeth without emotion. "The fool. He knowed a snake could kill you."*

*"Seven years. Look at where it goes and it ain't so much. But ifin a man come and took it and said you owed it to him, it ain't the same as spending it yourself. Take it at twelve and you a grown-up 'fore you through."*

*Mollie mumbles sometimes. She talks as if there is no one*

*there trying to understand her and her words mean no more
than a song. Maybe that's the way she is when I'm not there and
she has trouble adjusting to company. She's been alone a lot.
Today when she was trying to say something about seven years,
I thought at first that she must have meant the part of the Bible
about leaving the earth bare every seven years, but that wasn't it.
She was talking about England. I wouldn't have believed she
knew England existed. Her mind is like a history book with the
wind blowing over the pages. You never know where she is in
time, how long her words are on one subject or when she is going
to flip back and repeat the same page.*

"Little chillen runnin ever' which way in England, running
in the alleyways, under the bridges, picking pockets and stealing as fast as birds gitting crumbs. No cutting up, running to
their alley to see what they had made off with and figuring how
many pennies it might bring. Naw, sir. They knowed they was
as good as hanged. They seen it. Seen their little playmates
swinging on a rope. I was told some tales. I git too big for my
britches, my great-grandpa tell me a tale make me see Mollie
Petry on a rope swinging in the wind till it made me hurt to
swallow just thinking on it."

Mollie said folks got misled by a country that punishes the little ones with a spanking or a switching, instead of snapping
their necks at the end of a rope. England hanged them with no
mamas and papas there to grieve for them, her great-grandpa
said. Every year their mamas would pump out a bloody shiny
baby, until one year there was too much blood and all the other
little ones were left alone, leaning like a thin picket fence watching the midwife cover their mama's face.

"Like stairsteps, each one seen the one the step afore him 'fore
he was old enough to know what made him. Their papas was off
to the wars or to the mines, dying for somebody else or locked in
the debtors' prison. Then bad men come for the chillen, herding
them in ships like no more'n sheep, numbering them and selling
them. I bet folks down east led you to believe it was just niggers
that their kin brung over to do the picking. But it wont. Where
they think we come from? Ain't no fine cotton plantations and
fancy dresses behind the likes of Mollie Burcham."

*Seven years. That was the promise they gave her great-*

*grandfather. At twelve he was told he could put in seven years of his life to pay off his ticket to America and stay out of English prison. Indentured servants. That must have been in the pages I skipped in American history, or the pages that weren't there. Could this be why people hid themselves off in these hills, why I was told not to accidentally hike into certain unfriendly areas? They wanted to be away from neighbors. Even if they could suck the blood of those who had more, they would rather be left alone, free of those who think they own them. There was a time when mountain land was free for the taking. If you were strong enough to make it here, it was yours. But the government owns them now. All those checks at the post office buy them. And the coal-mine and sawmill operators have gotten all the land that is worth anything. They may have been strong people, but they're the losers.*

*I had asked Mollie before why there were families she told me not to go around. The storekeeper had hinted there were certain ones to stay away from. But he might have meant to stay away from Mollie. Mollie doesn't tell me anything direct, which seems to be the standard manner of people here. They tell you things in such a way that if they tell you something they shouldn't have, they can disclaim it. I guess the reason she was telling me about the ancestors of the people here — the orphans and criminals of England — was to explain why, hundreds of years later, they are so mean. It's their excuse. Or if all the people who collect those government checks emigrated again, this time from the Cumberland Plateau, they were in conflict with those who were here first.*

*I think what she was saying to me is that the easterners came over thinking like landowners, while her people never thought of themselves as anything but runaway serfs and street urchins. They aren't the easterners' kin; they are stray dogs. The feudal system was here, too, under another name, but after the Civil War there were laws to protect poor people from its enforcement. Then the mine owners came in and the poor people were called miners, not serfs, and the blacks in the east were tenants and sharecroppers, not slaves. The only difference is now the owners don't care whether their workers stay alive or not because they aren't owned property and there are plenty to take their places. When they are old and sick and crippled, no one wants them since there is no affection.*

*Grandfather Fitzgerald wouldn't have left Baa with nothing — or any of the servants who were with him for years. They had earned a security by the time they were old and useless. Maybe there is little difference between the poor whites here and the blacks in the east. Maybe there is little difference between being poor anywhere. No one feels any affection or gratitude towards them, so all they have left is a government making unemotional gestures to keep them alive until they die of natural causes. And they sent me here to change things. I think I see why the government stays in trouble. I also think I should keep journals like my father keeps his business records, one for them and one for me.*

*"Pshaw," Mollie grunted. "Gov'ment give me half of what got took, I be a rich woman. All gon be square up yonder. It's written in the book. The Lord ain't a dealer in coal. He don't have to buy and sell no land to heat up His hell. Seven years ain't a day to eternity."*

\* \* \*

When I saw Christina in the supermarket, I waited a moment before speaking because I couldn't be sure it was her. We were in the only shopping center in the area. A scarf over her hair spread over giant rollers, making her head seem to totter back and forth like a water head. I walked around to look at her face, half expecting a drooping mouth and retarded stare, only to see the familiar plucked brows, her hair yanked up and her forehead puckering from the tension of the rollers. She smiled broadly when she saw me, overly expressive for Christina, and my first thought was that she might be terribly lonely, that she would pounce on me and try to resume a friendship that never really was. But it was the same with Christina. She slapped down the reaching hands of the baby who rode in the small container of the market basket.

"Would you please quit pulling at me? Jean. You certainly don't wear out your welcome, do you? How long has it been, a month? Never thought I'd run into you here. Figured a free woman like you would eat every meal out. Oh, I see. TV dinners. Next best thing, huh? I'd eat them myself, to tell you the truth, if I didn't have the brats to feed."

We talked for a while, the other shoppers pushing into us as if we were stalled cars on the highway. Christina was fingering a bottle of blue liquid. She told me it was expensive but it said on TV that you could hang it in the back of the toilet and never have to put your hands in it to wash it. I could visualize Christina washing the toilet with a brush on a ten-foot stick. Then she spoke in a whisper, looking around to see if the other shoppers might overhear.

"You know what I hated as much as anything about him? He couldn't hit the commode to save his life. His precious thing that he thought he could just shake and watch the females of the world drop their pants in unison. He couldn't have hit the bathtub, much less the commode. Down on my hands and knees, scrubbing the floor with the stench about to make me upchuck, the honeymoon is over, as they say. I never have been able to get on my knees in front of the commode without thinking I'm supposed to be vomiting in it, and by the time you get down that close, the smell would do it to you whether you had to or not. Every week now I'm cleaning up the bathroom and it's like I'm just putting a shine on things, no more kinky hairs on everything and his dirty razor and the towels just piled up wet to turn to mildew. He even turned the toilet paper over to roll the wrong way, irritated me to death. But you wouldn't know about that, Jean," she said bitterly, but not without a hint of gladness. I think Christina was in her own way glad that she knew someone female, her age, who hadn't suffered bent over a toilet dirtied by a man. It was almost as if she saw me as a victory for our sex.

\* \* \*

*I had a funny thought tonight about Christina, a memory that I probably suppressed because I thought it was one of those things you aren't supposed to notice. I remember how even though she did her hair and face with incredible precision, that Christina would sometimes wear the same underpants for days. When we got our week's laundry, often she would have only two pairs. She hated the steamy bathroom because it made her hair frizz. She would carry her towel and soap down and come back in minutes, deciding against a bath because of the steam.*

*I thought of someone else tonight too: the black woman in Asheville. Wash your own shit off your commode, white people. Elsie's not going to do it anymore. Christina's not going to do it anymore. I wondered if there was the man who had ever washed a commode.*

\* \* \*

I occupied an office in the Rocky Gap Post Office that also housed the courthouse, the jail, and its one cell. The cell always contained the same man: Leon, the town drunk, who was left in there with his door open most of the time. He was allowed to hang a calendar with a fully clothed pinup and keep a radio, which he played loudly when the socket at the end of his long tape-patched extension cord wasn't needed in the post office.

Once he was playing a church service loudly, and when I walked by the end of the hallway to his cell, I could see him standing on a wooden box with an electrical cord in his hand. As the music ended and the preacher began to speak, Leon wrapped the cable around his arm, clasping it as if he had a snake by the throat. Leon was imitating the snake-handling preacher. Suddenly he fell over and crashed to the floor, yanking the plug out and silencing the preacher in mid-sentence. I started to go help him up, but I saw him crawl onto his bunk. His imaginary snake and his drunkenness had bitten him at once.

I heard the man who ran the Rocky Gap Cafe say that they were thinking of finding a room for Leon at the Dixie Hotel just in case they ever needed the cell for a real criminal. Leon looked out and smiled at me every day when I arrived. He was hard to look directly at because his face was as red and raw as internal organs.

I ate at the cafe every day, the same thing — an untoasted egg salad sandwich and a Coke, with the pie of the day for dessert. People in the town treated me friendly enough, it seemed, although most of their comments indicated that they just thought of me as passing through. Maybe that was the way I thought of myself. I was surprised to find that the courthouse cleaning woman was the revival piano player, Mildred. In a town as small as Rocky Gap, the same paths crossed often.

Since my house was so small, a narrow, three-room cottage with out-of-date furniture and kitchen appliances and no shelves, I filled my office with my books from school. I thought of hanging several of Clara's paintings but decided to wait and see how her wild, splashing primary colors might affect the local visitors. I had plenty of bookshelves for my books in what had been a lawyer's office before he died. Even when I visited my grandparents as a child, I carried a few of my books so I wouldn't feel alone. Some of the paperbacks from my courses were falling apart from use; my philosophy books were untouched and stiff as boxes.

The first three weeks of my job were spent reading the real-estate listings and looking for a suitable and cheap piece of property to locate the school on. The rough plan was to bring in a portable trailer-type school for the trial period to see if the local population was going to respond favorably to the idea. I was to look for property that would require little tree cutting, in case the whole project had to be abandoned. Until I located my land and got the trailer, I would use the grade school art room if I could collect an interested group of children on weekends. Actually the reason I wrote little for my Washington notebook was there was little to report. I soon found that in the overtimbered area a clear stretch of land was not a rarity. Rare, on the other hand, was the thick forest land I had seen near Coppertown. In Rocky Gap the fields stretched like rolling deserts, often rutted from the heavy rains with foaming puddles at the bottom of every ravine. I wrote up seven possible locations. All I could do was wait for them to act, though it had been two months since I got there.

I also reported for the Washington notebook that my other instructions were ludicrous and basically useless. *Get to know the local population and their educational desires. Try to give them an awareness of the skills needed for today's world. Do not use technical language when interviewing and if possible keep the interviews informal. Mountain people have traditionally been known to be suspicious of strangers* . . . Carefully canned instructions from Washington. Who writes those things? Suspicious of strangers. They've also been known to tack government-worker hides on their smokehouse walls.

In mid-October, seven weeks after I arrived, my supervisor was scheduled to visit, but I got a mimeographed note with my name filled in and a date; her arrival was delayed for six more weeks. I suppose that would have pleased your average government employee. I was able to put off writing up my first report. I had stacks of penciled notes and comments from people, mostly material from Mollie that I would probably never show them, but still very little idea of what to try to set up in the way of beginning classes. I had hoped to use local people for teachers, but those with skills, such as electricians and carpenters, didn't need the extra income from a teaching job and didn't want to train any future competition. Both of those reasons were so logical I didn't know why I hadn't thought of them myself. One woman mentioned cooking classes, but another snapped when I repeated the suggestion: "What does any grown woman need to learn how to cook for? She knows how. And they teach the teen-agers that over in the public school home-ec classes." They have no time for weaving or vegetable dyeing. I met not one person with the sensitivity of the Coppertown woodcarvers. Crafts were only worthwhile if they had to be done. If people could afford to buy their synthetic cloth in the piece-goods store downtown, there was no need for doing it themselves. In fact the women saw no beauty in the bulky hand-knits and subtle colors that drifted out of the hills into university homes in the east. I asked about using local wool, and a woman frowned and said, "You won't catch me wearing that scratchy ugly stuff. I like double-knit polyester."

Several women in the garden club wrote me notes on paper decorated with rose photographs like those in garden catalogues. They expressed an interest in flower arranging and the growing of potted plants. I forced out a semi-interested reply since it was the only positive suggestion I had received. Night classes did not appeal, they said, because they wanted to be home with their families and watch television, especially then in the fall when it was getting cold and the new shows were starting. Day classes were possible, but only for the idle women in the garden club, the wives of the few professionals who had all attended college anyway and considered me a wet-behind-the-ears child. Besides, they weren't the ones getting the government checks; they were the middle class. The only one of the poor that I got to talk to me was Mollie, and at her age she deserved to be cared for. In Rocky Gap you either worked in the mills or ran the mills along with the few people who operated the stores that took the mill people's money.

I searched through all my texts and read all the data on the subject of course offerings, but I was starting to feel panicky. I wondered if my four years of college put me any closer to the answer that I couldn't find. I couldn't believe that the lady who started the folk school at Coppertown had faced this. I remembered what one of the carvers said: "We knew how to carve before she came." Maybe the people in Rocky Gap knew they didn't want to know how to do anything before I came. I hated to admit it but all I found was the same "bad" you found down east, and none of the mountain "good" had been preserved. Woodcarving was inherited.

When I applied for the job, Clara had made me think of something — that we had never bothered to question our image of the mountaineer. The man square-danced and played a fiddle, the woman made quilts and preserves. The black sheep made moonshine. They had self-respect. They were proud and self-reliant. Public relations bullshit. I saw Leon from my office window, behind the Ridge Bar draining all the discarded beer and liquor bottles into one, until he had a few inches of brown liquid in a Mason jar. He drank it all in one swallow and stumbled back into his cell. I thought of visiting Clara one weekend to see the mountain people who made the crafts. To see them make anything but a trash pile and babies.

*I think Keats said it: "I wrote my name in water" — or maybe it
was carved on his tombstone — "Here lies one whose name was
writ in water." A week ago the garden club asked me to judge
their art contest because they needed an unbiased judge. This
morning the weekly newspaper came out with a photo of the
winner with her painting. The painting was not the one I had
put the blue ribbon on. I went by the paint store where the paintings were displayed, finding second and third not my choices
either. When the storekeeper commended me on my judging, I
told him I thought it was pretty good too, but next time I'd buy
some of his epoxy to attach the ribbons. He didn't get my little
joke.*

*I got a letter today from my cousin Charles, who is in law
school at Carolina. He said that a friend told him there had
never been a sheriff's election in Olley County where one of the
candidates didn't get shot. It's hard to believe that about this
quiet little place. Bloody Olley. The county was caught for
ballot-box stuffing in the last election. Although it might appear
that there is only a cabin on every other hill, according to the
record books in the courthouse Olley County has the population
density of Harlem. Every man, woman, child, and maybe even
dog that has ever been born, lived, or died in Olley is still a registered voter. I'm sure Charles sent that information to my father
and they both had a big laugh. I bet they're making bets as to
how long I'll last at this job. I cut my hair because it is too hard
to wash long hair here and sent it to my mother in a braid. She
phoned, and you would have thought I had mailed her my arm.*

*I took a walk this afternoon down one of the roads that the
Forest Service cut for fire vehicles. I felt like getting away from
what I've been talking about for a while. I hear myself talking in
front of those groups. They act like they understand and care,
but the group today was smaller than it was at first. They send
their friends with excuses for them. I can't remember which ones
of them have left but there are more empty seats. I probably have
left in attendance only the most idle and bored women in Olley
County. But I'm not supposed to let that worry me. If I can relate*

to the ones who are there. The fact that there is a spark of interest of any kind in this area is supposed to be a wonder, and worth my four hundred dollars a month. I have a nightmare of finishing one of my talks and noticing that Clara was on the back row the whole time.

In the dark woods that I walked into on a path, the leaves were deep green and wet. The last fall flowers were pale and stunted and hung onto their plants like dirty paper. Clara would have been terrified there, but I have always felt comfortable in the woods, to look in every direction and see nothing made by a person. At the wilderness school we had to spend three days out with nothing, no tools, no food, no sleeping gear. But that didn't make me fear the woods; it taught me what I needed and what I didn't need. A sixteen-foot house trailer and a TV I don't need, but a sleeping bag and boots are nice to have. I feel safer in the woods than on a city street. I feel alone in the good sense, really totally alone with no one there for me to be frightened of.

The naming of things is special here, it seems, the names of mountains and rivers. Old this, little that, Big Stone, Flattop, or Iron Mountains. Then there's Ripshin and Skint Knee and Broken Back Knobs. Those are mountains that conquered someone's body. I suppose a person could spend a lifetime just studying the naming of things. Walking today was a relaxing feeling, to feel I was seeing something on my own in the area that wasn't negative.

Then the whole good feeling vanished with a strange sight. I came to a clearing where a road had been started. I walked down as far as it went and it became obvious that it had been abandoned. There were deep furrows where the soil had eroded after the land was cleared. It appeared to have been left open to the weather through all the summer rains. Then, near the end of the bulldozed section, I noticed the side area had been burned, the grass and trees. When I got to where the road stopped, there were three large earth-moving machines charred like dead black dinosaurs, their giant rubber tires burned down to a frayed metal cord. They leaned on their weak sides. Like a fire bomb had hit.

I noticed that one had escaped the fire, its sides still bright yellow. When I walked closer I saw that its rubber tires were flat because holes had been ripped in them. They looked like bullet holes. And there were bullet holes in the cabs. Crazy. Somebody went wild and killed a bunch of highway machines. If killing them was what they had in mind, then that's what they accomplished because the road stopped. On the other side of the battlefield was nothing but woods, untouched woods.

I went to see Mollie Burcham again today. She never seems to tire of talking to me and I always like to listen. I wanted to ask her about the road machinery but I didn't ask directly. She loves to talk but resents being questioned. Mollie talked about what it was like when she was a little girl in Kentucky, before REA came through, she said.

I think Mollie rarely leaves her house. She talks a lot about her family, her grandchildren in Kentucky, but I get the impression they don't come to see her very often. Like a Coppertown woman told me, her world is as big as the chicken lot and the hogpen. When I mentioned the rough roads in the hills, Mollie said now we think of cars getting stuck on the muddy and snowy roads through the hills. She remembers when the roads were so bad you couldn't walk places, couldn't even pick a path around the mire. I didn't have the nerve to ask her who stopped the road machinery. I'll ask one of the men in town. I guess I fear that thin thread between us might snap when she is reminded I'm an outsider. Roads from outside. Roads to see each other. Somebody decided to stop them.

Leon . . .

I yell whoopee! whoopee! when it went up. That's what they told me to do holler up a storm Leon like a bunch of wild Indians. If they was there make 'em think half the woods' coming down on them. I did. They was gone like skeered rabbits no sign of them. When I jumped pretty soon it quit rubbing hard up front and come squirting and some went tickling clean down inside my knee made my pants stick and let go when I ran. Wanted to tell Dwayne see I wont too old but he might git mad. He didn't see. He didn't take no notice of it if he did. Dwayne blowed a hole in the water truck so big it looked like it was shooting up water outa hose and it come down siss when the fire started into going. I don't know for sure what Dwayne meant to do 'bout that fire 'cause I think he was just intending to start up one and he got two of them going and one of them come at his pickup not more'n fifty feet away 'fore he took notice pay attention to me next time and decided we better take out stinking black diesel smoke.

I 'member a good fire best next to this one Dwayne told on me sure as you're standing 'cause Pa thought he done it was me and they put me up at training school for three months but that wont bad 'cause they had a pool table. Dwayne was so sorry when I told him that he wished he'd gone 'cause Pa give him both our work to do ha serve him right. Birds come squawking out of it and some things running by rabbit bump into my leg and fall down sprawling and take out again and one thing big enough to be a deer. Didn't git a good look and didn't have no gun noway. But that was the yellow field that went up woosh and snapping like firecrackers and hardly a acre of little trees never amount to nothing. Nobody come near till I was done and squirted it outside with the skin so hot it burnt inside my pants when I put it back only this time I was skeered to git it out and made a wet spot I seen for a while that got dried stiff it got so hot 'fore we was back to the blacktop.

Here down in the dark where they come out to sun on rocks I seen them and heared them singing like they penning you up in a circle throwing their voices and I walked up on one just as peaceful and walked backwards hurting between my legs I got so skeered but when the fire come they all come running out like a dumped-over can of worms and one the biggest I ever seen I can tell you come sliding head-on into Dwayne's back tire and it made it so mad it stuck it and got its teeth hung up and the air come out and blowed that snake out like a string. I yelled Dwayne come quick Dwayne we in trouble now without the pickup and he come and looked and I thought he was mad enough to snatch that old snake out and pop his head off with his bare hands but he got in the truck acting like he was going to leave me but I hopped on the back quick as a wick and he drove out with the tire flat and I smelt the rubber burn as it come apart but it wont the fire like I was skeered it was at first but just that

*tire no air in it and when we pull up side of the road off the
highway and took down the spare I said Dwayne would you look
at that you tore his body clean off big fat snake and nothing left
but his stupid old head with his teeth still stuck in that rubber
acting like he was still alive just biting away and no sign of a
body to go on that head. I was skeered that head could still bite I
wouldn't tech it.*

*We got them dozers though didn't we Dwayne do you reckon
the fire will keep burning and he said no it would stop at the
crick if it got that far they'd be in a surprise come Monday and
they come in with their lunch boxes thinking to spend a day cutting that road up where the best timber in Olley County was
standing. I said I skeered them off but Dwayne claimed they was
gone already. No it won't burn up. Dwayne was gitting tired of
me worrying 'bout the fire I could tell and Dwayne was right it
didn't burn nowhere but I went back and seen them. Black as tar
and yellow paint come off like peeling skin and the seat on the
big one was burnt up so bad they better be mighty glad there
wont no ass setting in it when we got through with them mighty
damn glad I told Dwayne and he said right Leon we showed
them sonsabitches . . .*

\* \* \*

I drove down some of the farm roads in Olley County one day
in late October, the ones that weren't on the state map, following the numbers of the mailboxes on the stands at the edge of
the main road. Many of the boxes weren't lettered with a name,
but serviced, I guessed, by a mailman who knew one old beat-
up box from another when he delivered the biweekly government check. It had been dangerously dry for some time and the
dust spiraled behind my car. The leaves had all turned and
most had fallen, but the winter rains hadn't started yet and we
hadn't had a hard freeze. When I heard the rocks cracking together under my wheels, I wondered if they might set off a
spark. Maybe it came from Smokey Bear commercials, but
since I was a child I've had a horror of starting a fire and not
knowing it. I had a dream once of reading in the paper about a
forest fire in a woods where I had camped the day before.

There were dozens of cars junked back there on the side

roads, some of them in models I didn't remember. I saw a man beating at a copperhead with a hoe, the snake flipping its thick body, its movements gaining momentum as it died. Through the open door the junked car seat wiggled like a bucket of worms and made chill bumps on my arms though I had the heater running. I noticed that almost every house had the privy built too close to the well, some of them actually built above the well, so the ground water from the outhouse must have flowed right into their drinking water. They weren't immune either or toughened by it. These people had diseases that were a thing of the past outside the hills. As I drove through, the people stared at me blankly from their porches. Almost no one was doing anything but sitting, even the children. I couldn't make myself stop and talk to them. I didn't know how I would explain who I was. I felt overcome by the hopelessness of it all. If I went back, they might ask me why I came through once before and just stared at them.

I drove past rows of wooden shacks covered with sheets of tar paper with printed bricks. I wondered if the inhabitants thought the paper looked like bricks or if maybe their eyesight or their taste was so bad they believed it could pass for bricks. Or maybe the tar paper just kept out the cold, and some Madison Avenue type who wouldn't cover his doghouse with it figured it would sell better if it looked like bricks. There was no doubt that the brick house was the status symbol in the hills. A brick house meant that you had erected something to inhabit that was strong enough to take the daily beating of the mountain weather. And that you expected your house to last as long as you did.

When I was looking for my way back to the main road, I saw what appeared to be a body in the ditch. I stopped without thinking. It could have been somebody setting a trap for me, but I'll always be the kind to fall for that. Since there was no traffic, a criminal could have waited all day for a victim. When I was about five feet from him, I could smell the odor of his unwashed body, a living body, not a corpse. I could see his sides going in and out and I knew he was alive, even though he was face down in the light soil collected in the ditch. I stooped and put my hand on his shoulder, and when I did, I saw an empty mayonnaise jar under his chest and could smell the alcohol. I said, "Are you drunk?" and Leon rolled his head around at me with an energy I didn't know he possessed and said, "Does a cat haffa ass?"

\*　　\*　　\*

Soco . . .

*"My pappy stole him an Indian woman. It was told that the white women here in the hills was so ugly and so few that a man had no choice when the sap begun to rise. He seen her walking with two braves. He never knowed whether they were her husband and brother or two brothers or what not, out collecting herbs for medicine, and he shot one then the other and took her screaming home with him. Kept her three years 'fore she run off, three children, my two brothers, who worked in the mines till they died, born together. They would come looking for her from time to time, the savages, and he would turn loose his dogs on them."*

*Today I went to see Soco. I was told that she had known F. Scott Fitzgerald when he was here for treatment of alcoholism and when Zelda was in the institution in the mountains where she burned to death. Soco had also talked often to Thomas Wolfe, they said. Soco is very dark and withered up, a human prune. She made me wonder if Wolfe and Fitzgerald would look like that now if they had lived. Almost better that they got to die while their images were handsome. When I asked about them, she said disappointingly little. Fitzgerald was a showoff; she saw him hurt himself on a diving board for a young girl who had just won a beauty contest. When he loved himself, he loved Zelda; when he hated himself, he hated Zelda. They were as alike as twins, but only one, the boychild, was the favored one in talents. Soco didn't put much store in beauty anymore. When she was young, she did, because when she was young, she had never seen beauty crumble with age. When she was young, she believed that old had always been old. There was a picture on a shelf of a young Soco who never had any beauty to crumble, standing beside a giant man. The man, she told me, was Thomas Wolfe.*

*Soco is a fortuneteller. She has a sign in front of her house*

172

with a large hand painted on it and the word "Palmist." I have
seen this sign all my life beside the road to Florida. I thought
she might be a Gypsy, but after I saw her up close and saw the
bones in her face, I knew that she was more native than the Eng-
lishmen who emigrated here. I asked her about her Indian blood.
Choctaw.

* * *

The fortuneteller, Soco, looked at my hand. When she got
close I smelled the odor of her body, the decaying odor that
came from everything in the room. Then she displayed the look
of surprise that I expected from an actress like Soco. She had
decided not to favor me. She shook her head and made clucking
sounds as she traced my life line to a stop. Then she leaned
back in her chair and packed the side of her mouth with snuff
from a box with colored-glass jewels and a small white bone.
She sat a moment and lit a pipe on top of the snuff. Her teeth
and hands were stained mustard yellow, but white teeth would
have been too shocking against the rest of her coloring. She
started to mumble, her sentences not coherent enough to piece
together, making me wonder if she were an actress after all or
just senile. Owls and spiders.

Over the door to Soco's palm-reading room were nailed rem-
nants of the men in her life. There was one photo of a pilot next
to a World War I airplane, with a cocky smile unlike the inno-
cent soldier faces I saw in the oval grave frames in Italy. There
was a collection of shirt tails, cut from the men each time they
shot at a deer and missed, with a penciled description of the
deer and how close the hunter was. There were several
homemade guns, dusty and probably unserviceable. I felt that
Soco didn't need to protect herself with guns, that she could lift
that stained hand and strike me dead. Yet maybe a strong
hand could split her greasy skull with an ax, like Dostoevski's
pawnbroker. I asked about a hairy collection nailed along the
side of the window, wondering when I asked if I should have. I
shouldn't have. Scalps. Five generations of scalps.

They weren't all Indian, but it was sure the ones with deep
inky-black tufts of coarse hair were. Soco told me the more mel-
low colors, one of them a dirty blond, came from King's

Mountain the day the mountain men slaughtered the king's army. Because the mountain men were too crude to know how to fight fair and because they wanted to further curse the defeated British, they scalped the fallen redcoats. Soco was amused by the notion of proper conduct during a fight. Soco showed me on a shelf a red jacket that would have been in a museum but for the huge bullet hole she ran her yellow fingers over. There was loose hair scattered on the unswept floor, straight, curled, light, dark hair from an army of scalps. I laughed at the thought of our Smithsonian Institution with its carefully labeled collection; at Soco's house was history that could put even the East Berlin museum to shame, the hair and flesh of a war, not polished armor and guns. And it would rot into the ground with Soco because that is not the way we preserve our history.

\* \* \*

*After I left Soco's house, the foul-smelling room of memories of death, with her assurances that my death was going to be untimely and violent, I went for a walk in the woods. I was quick to notice the fresh outside air that was beginning to grow chilly in the late afternoon. There are fewer forests here than on the other side of the mountains where I used to hike, the big trees gone to be timbers in the mines or sold to the furniture factories in the east. I am no longer able to turn inside my mind to get away from these people, the people that get away from me with such ease. The woods are like the poem, dark and deep. There is always a water sound, water coming from the ground, from banks, off the trees, chilling my body with the sun-shielded wetness. There is a pleasant decay here, natural and never human. Where the people have been, the woods come back very slowly, but they'll make it. I saw trees today, higher than the chimney of a fallen cabin, growing where a family once sat in front of the fire.*

*In the deep woods where the sawmills haven't been, the trees live for three hundred years, only an occasional one fallen from a natural disaster, lightning which struck the protruding top and burned the core of a single tree down to the trunk. Inside the trunk is a dark house with colored mushrooms on the walls, where animals can live. An owl looked at me today with a very superior expression and no fear. He sat in a dead tree as still as one of Gay MacKensie's carvings. A few of the trees have fallen from disease; in the high altitudes the balsam fir is covered with a soft green growth spun by insects, which would be beautiful were it not so deadly. But mostly, the deeper you walk, the trees stand tall, blocking the sunlight from the woods floor, the giant poplars, beeches, and nut trees, and flowers grew underneath in summer that can only live here in the cool, damp dark of the woods. The trees have weathered and aged with dignity; they even die with dignity and power.*

*The flowers are gone now, but for a few dead ragged blooms on the full-leafed plants. The berry trees are heavy with fruit, so winter will be hard, Mollie says. I guess I go to the woods because I know that the effect will always be good; that there is enough there to distract me from thinking on what I am doing wrong on the outside. I don't go there to think about things that are troubling me; my mind is cleared. All of the hills would be like the woods if the coal hadn't been underneath for men to destroy the trees and themselves getting to it. I'm starting to believe that natural beauty, supposedly the most free thing in the world, is only for the affluent to enjoy. I haven't seen a single poor family preserving anything that was already there. They strip clean a spot for their house and their garbage and they sit there until they die and pass the spot on to their children. Maybe I'm starting to hate civilization.*

*The women I meet try to fill me with fears. Like the women who told me of bugger bears when I was a little girl, the maids at my grandfather's who were trying to make me play in the yard and stay away from the woods. I was to be scared of this and that, they told me, just to keep me from wanting to leave their sight. There was a bugger bear of some description in every forbidden place and I can remember feeling his presence when I did what they told me not to. I'd say, "Hi, monster. I came here anyway. Hope you don't mind." The monsters were always male, never witchlike like Mollie and Soco. Why are they trying to make an adult so scared of things? Is it because they are? Soco sees my life line snapping very soon. Mollie picks at me constantly about living alone up in the woods. When I mentioned that she lived alone too, she said no one was interested in mess-*

ing with a poor old woman as they would be a rich young girl. She came to my house and looked at the things I had sitting around, junk lamps I got out of my parents' attic, and said I must be "well off."

She looked in my bedroom and asked me if I could see the mirror from my bed. The looking glass, she calls it. I told her the reason it was there on the mantel was I only had one clock. I could see the clock face in the living room from the bed and know if it was time to get up. So Mollie says I have condemned myself with that mirror by seeing the reflection of my head on the pillow, until the first snow covers these hills. I may be lucky and the snowfall will be early, or I may live in peril through the Indian summer.

Mollie's daddy quit farming to become a miner. Her mama's first husband had been a miner, and until he died she had money to spend. Her mama had urged him to leave the farm because she had been in the commissary store in town and seen people with cash money. When they farmed, if they couldn't make it or grow it, they couldn't have it.

But while Mollie's daddy was still a young man he got ruined by the blackdamp, methane gas that seeped into the mine where he was working. Some of the men died from it, but Mollie said it didn't do him the mercy of killing him; it just ruined him. He would go into twitches the rest of his life, sometimes having spasms so bad that her mama would pull a heavy chair on top of him to keep him from breaking up the house or falling off the front porch. They lived in the row houses then, built for the coal people. Some of the mining-town houses were built of unpainted wood, but the row she lived in was the colors of the rainbow.

"When I first caught sight of them," Mollie told me, "I declared there was nothing prettier under the sun than them little houses a-painted the colors of kept flowers in a garden, not them damp rotten-wood colors and water-beat siding I seen all my life. They had a wood floor built in them you could walk barefoot on in the winter. Me and my mama and sisters would take Pa's money from the mine afore he got laid up and buy curtains and rugs and what not from the commissary till we had the place fixed up the prettiest you ever seen. Ain't got a rotten scrap to show for it now 'cept for a few snatches in my bed quilt.

"My mama used to cry ever' time there was a thunder and lightning storm because her first husband was blowed up in the mine. He had been good to her and give her money 'out the asking. She used to think that lightning flashing behind the mountains looked like the day she was on the porch and seen this big tongue come out of the mine like the devil spitting fire. It got set off by a spark in the coal dust and blowed up twenty or more men, and the ones it didn't blow to kingdom come got crushed underneath the carts and fell on by mules in there to do the pulling. She was always partial to her first husband, she confessed at me, even 'fore Pa got ruint. She got religion after he passed, she told us.

"Then after Pa got hurt, they tolerated him a bit longer, but he was worth next to nothing. He'd start out in the morning as good as the man besides him, wont two hours and he'd be down and shaking and crying to go out in the daylight and they'd holler for Mama to come git him. I seen her lead him acrosst from the mine many a day, him limp as a sack of feed. They give us ten days to git outa the house so they could set up a new family. Mama waled him with the broom and hollered at him to stop that twitching or she was gonna kill him. I think she was a-hoping somebody else see fit to kill him or he'd take sick and die on his own accord. She was wanting to marry up with a man could work and we wouldn't have to move out of that house. Ours was blue, as blue as a robin's egg."

I've gotten Mollie to leave her house more often. I take her into town with me because she likes to go in the stores and "feel of things." It must make her remember being a little girl with money to spend in the commissary. She reaches into the freezer and handles all the packages of salami and bologna and clucks with amazement at what people pay for "sech a little bit of meat." I thought about buying her some, but I don't know how she'd feel about my spending money on her. Also it might give her a bad impression of me if she thinks I spend good money on trinkets. But she grew up spending every penny they had. She said her community never had a bank and you better spend your money fast on something too big or gone too soon for stealing. She said the bank in Rocky Gap was for rich people only, which shows how little Mollie knows about banks. But I think it's too late to try to explain that. The government sends me here to change things and I don't even want to change Mollie where she's wrong. She appears to have adjusted to life a lot better than I have.

After her father was injured, I think Mollie's life went bad on her for good. She talks very little of being a happy child. She started developing a hate for men then because it was a man who caused them to leave their blue house and go back to the hollow. She told me that living in the hollow again wasn't like before; the hollow was filled with the crippled rejects from the mines. Being forced to go back to the hollow was like a prison sentence, like being told you were crippled too and not fit for the life outside where people could hope for a good life. Mollie was a woman in good health, but unless she became attached to a healthy man, she had to live in the hollow.

When I stopped today, Mollie was in a fret, mumbling to herself while she peeled potatoes. She took the peelings and put them in a jar of water, to keep them soft, she said, just in case her check didn't come and she had to eat them. She will never get very far from what happened to her in Kentucky. She doesn't really believe in the government that sends her the check twice a month. She thinks it will die or go lame and crazy like everything else around her. I thought today of my father. He doesn't believe Mollie should get those checks. He will never see this old woman alone in her mountain shack and he doesn't think she should be kept alive. She'll never see him and she doesn't trust him. She's a wise old woman to be uncertain about the arrival of that check.

Today she was talking about Joanne, how worried she was about Joanne since the doctor had gotten her so upset after her examination. I tried to figure out which of the women in town it might be. It wasn't one of her granddaughters, but nothing she told me about Joanne was familiar. After about thirty minutes of listening to Mollie, I realized the mysterious Joanne was in the soap opera Search for Tomorrow. Mollie thinks that her TV set is like a window and that she is allowed to be a peeping Tom between commercials. She has never questioned that they might not be real. I asked Mollie what she used to do before she had

*TV. It is on when I get there; she turns down the sound while she talks to me, but she keeps watching it, and I hear it blast out before I get off her porch when I leave.*

*"When we first got radio, morning till night I kept it tuned listening to the stories. I loved those stories. Took my mind off'n my own story, if you want to know the truth — my husband up there in the mine, me figuring out where we was going to git money for food. And that radio was where I first tuned into the preaching. There was one for the niggers that I listened to a time or two just for 'musement sake, of all the hollering and carrying on, like listening in on a birthing. There was this other man, a white man who didn't take hardly a breath and could put words to you faster than you could git holt of them. Sometimes he'd make me drop what I was doing so I could put my mind on it and catch half of what he was saying. I kept telling myself I was going to quit listening one day. He made me feel so bad about things, for the life of me I couldn't do no better. But when he started in to talking about heaven and I would forgit all that damnation he was preaching and start planning on gitting me a place there. He could make pictures of the Good Place come in my head, with golden streets and angels playing on harps and floating around not feeling no pain. He wont for doing the dancing, business of the devil. He was told that God didn't approve and I hear they was hardly gitting enough together to make a round onc't his show come on."*

Mollie came to Rocky Gap in the fifties. So far as I can tell, she was one of the last to give up in the hollow. After the men were replaced by machines and her younger brother got out of prison and left to go to Detroit, she never saw him again or heard whether he lived or died. Her last summer in Kentucky she planted a garden in the thin soil.

*"I scratched me up a little garden. Dirt was deep enough to plunk a seed in 'fore you hit the yaller, but I scraped out the chicken-house turds and spread enough guano to burn your nose out. I had me some plants started to bust ground after a rain or two. But that rain I was a-hoping for was the end of me. The mining company was long gone, six months gone 'fore we knowed what hit us. I didn't have no husband living, so I wont*

*keeping up on what the mines were up to. My three boys left me
for the city, but I wont for a-blaming them. Man couldn't feed a
family. Come to find out it had froze up in the winter, the sides of
the mountain that they left loose. So come the thaw, dirt and
rocks and ever'thing a body could see was gonna come barreling
down, hell bent with the rains. Had us a good rain. My bean
plants were speckled with dirt and I went out and throwed me a
little rotenone on them to keep down the beetles and went to bed
like a baby, saying Mollie Burcham do all right for herself, not
suspecting a thing in this world come dark and the rain hitting
the roof just as peaceful. Then there come this big rumbling and
the whole mountain fell down upon us. My porch, that were five
feet in the air, I walked out level with the ground. By morning I
wouldn't have swore to you where I had planted my garden to
save my life. Whole trees, roots and all, rolling down on that
town. Knocked down my chicken house and drownt three of my
hens 'fore they could git out of the water that got damned up by
them tree trunks. I couldn't have told you it was coming. When
the last company left, all I could see was they took a sight more
trees off'n one spot 'cause you could see daylight acrosst the top
of the mountain. Took the sun a mite longer to set. They let
something git into the water that only stinked a little, but it
turned up the frogs like the palm of your hand. But it wont my
land to talk about when it was up on the hill. That was their
land. Somebody else was fool enough to sell it to them. Not me.
Didn't have none worth selling, to their minds. But then their
land ended up atop my land and they was long gone. That ain't
treating folks right but git mad as a hornet and not have a body
left to take it out on. I knowed what the preacher man would
have said ifin I could have asked him. The Lord works in
strange ways. The Lord was telling Mollie Burcham that was
her last summer in Kentucky."*

\* \* \*

Every time I went by Leon's cell, he called my name and
wanted to talk. I made the mistake of talking to him once and
he became a pest, especially when he was so drunk he ran his
thoughts together and I couldn't understand him. One day in

early November I didn't answer him because I had some work I wanted to get done in my office. I ignored him when I passed, though he was shaking his unlocked door. About five minutes later I heard a tap on the glass window of my door. I turned to see a mass of flesh, hair, and fabric pressed against the glass, like meat wrapped in cellophane at the supermarket and as red as Leon's face that grinned at the top of the window. Leon had dragged up a box and exposed himself. No sooner than I turned and saw him, he lost his balance and fell off the box. I heard him scramble to his feet and shuffle back to his cell, leaving a greasy spot on the glass. He clanged his own door shut.

I had to ask Mildred Persons, the cleaning lady, to remove the greasy spot: "What makes people put their filthy hands on the glass," she complained, "instead of turning the knob like they're supposed to."

I told Sheriff Whitcomb about Leon, but told him I didn't want to press any charges, I just thought he should know in case it happened in the future with a stranger. The sheriff dropped his face in his hands and sighed, "Wish he'd pick a stranger now and then. It ain't the first. It ain't the last."

I found that Leon did it on the glass at Ruby's Beauty Parlor a week before while the mayor's wife was getting her hair fixed. The sheriff thanked me for telling him. Leon was going from public nuisance to public menace. Now, he said, he had to figure out if he was dangerous and where to send him.

I stopped by to see Christina and got the shock of my life when I knocked on the door. There he was, the guy she dated in college; her husband, Travis, had come back. He asked me in, then turned and walked away. She was the same as before, constantly yelling at the children, complaining about the cost of things, complaining about everything this time but her husband. He moved about the room as if none of us were there, going to the table and resuming work on what appeared to be a car part. He had newspapers on the table, but I saw him slide a stack of greasy pieces onto the uncovered part. That little frown appeared between Christina's eyes when the metal tinkled on the Formica top, but she said nothing. When I used

Christina's bathroom, I saw his razor in a puddle of foam and black hair stubs on the side of the sink. I lowered the toilet seat thinking that he was the last one to use it. There was a ring in the tub and dirty suds around the drain hole; in the bottom on the white enamel were three black hairs coiled into circles.

Travis and I had as little to say to each other as we had had when Christina and I were in college. I couldn't even talk to him about problems with my car since he dismissed them because it was foreign made. She asked me to stay for dinner, but I declined, saying I had a lot of paperwork to do. As I walked out the door, Christina smiled and said, "Enjoy your TV dinner." When she said that, I could smell her chicken baking.

\* \* \*

*I thought of someone tonight who hasn't been on my mind for a long time. J. T. Boey. Because of Travis, with his slicked-back hair with grooves from a wet comb, a stiff piece broken loose and sticking up like Dagwood in the comics. Travis wore short-top boots and his ankles were thin, sticking out under the pants legs that sprawled under the table.*

*I guess he is good-looking, a kind of reckless good looks that you know he will use, that will make him even more cocky. I've always been afraid of men with looks like Travis', but Christina seems to have no fear of that, her feminine frailty up against that, between the sheets now that she has let him back in the house. Christina's fear is of the mental abuse, of knowing that he doesn't prize her looks like he did and that her looks aren't the prize they once were.*

*I wonder if J. T. Boey ever went back to Bryson City, if Alice Faye Hutchins got to say, "You don't believe me, you walk out to the graveyard and see what's written on the stone you didn't pay a cent for."*

Christina . . .
*He lies asleep on the sofa and I watch him, wondering if he'll feel my stare through his eyelids and his eyes will flick open and catch me. I'll look back at my magazine. On his arm is the watch that had the broken band. I bought a new one and took off the*

182

*rubber band that was holding it and fixed it. He never mentioned it, just buckled it on the same as before. He wears the clothes that I washed, the shirt I ironed a wrinkle in the pocket of and tried to get out, but I see the wrinkle, with his cigarettes showing through the cloth. He shaved with the razor I bought, and the shave cream. I bought the shampoo and set it on the tub. But all with his money. Maybe that's why he says nothing.*

*He lies there sleeping like a baby. I maybe could kill him if he didn't feel my motion in the air; there's only about five steps from me to him. What could I kill him with, not that gun he tried to teach me to shoot that made my hand black and blue. He loves me in his way, I know it, or he wouldn't think to come back to me. Take away all that I bought or touched and he lies there naked as a newborn, sleeping with his mouth open.*

*I have touched the naked too. And gone without it touching me, or with him touching when my mind was as far away as I could put it, hoping I wouldn't make an irritated noise and make him mad as he does it with me but without me. When you are very young, you don't have to be afraid to live without that . . .*

*I am now the proud owner of a hundred-and-eighty-dollar hound dog. A man at the vet's told me he'd make a good "bar" dog. His name is Sam. He looks a lot like old Sam, the groom at my grandfather's, the same pushed-in face. He is black and white, and I found him up on the scenic route after he'd been hit by a car. Had to be a tourist who ran him down because no one else is up there. Guess they hit him and either figured or hoped he was dead. So with three broken ribs, a broken leg that had to have a pin put in it, and various bruises and cuts that already had maggots by the time I found him, Sam is mine.*

*He's real friendly now. I took an awful chance, now that I look back on it, picking him up and carrying him to the car. But he didn't bite me; he was too miserable to move and had decided to die there. I almost didn't look at him because I thought he was dead. But when I backed up and checked, he was panting. At first he was scared to death of me, I guess because he figured everybody and everything was out to hurt him.*

*He went in Leon's cell today and acted friendlier than he has* with me, but I think it is because he thought he'd found another animal. He rooted all over him, going after the worst-smelling places until finally he started to howl like he had something treed. I had to go in the cell and pull him out. He still ducks when I go to pet him, but he's got that tail going. I like having him around. I can talk to him without feeling like an idiot talking to myself. He's already sharing his fleas with me. And he hears things coming up the drive long before I even know they're there. He's a little slow getting up on that bad leg, but he's improving fast. He's got his foot caught under his flea collar. Old Sam ain't taking too good to civilizing. Wait till he jumps on my mother's white couch and licks her in the face. I'll be real disappointed in him if he doesn't.

\* \* \*

One night when I went to the Laundromat, I took a walk, looking in the windows in Rocky Gap while my clothes went through the wash cycle. It was a strange night, too late for Indian summer but far too warm for November. There was a restlessness in the air and I could hear an uneasy rumble in the distance. I kept my eyes on the front door of the Laundromat to see if anyone went in where the four washers and two dryers were, because the week before Clara had written me from Hedgerow Craft Colony that all her wash had been taken while she went for a beer in the local tavern. She said she was loving it at Hedgerow, though, the hardest work she'd ever done. She liked the school so much last summer that she never even went to the Village, and took a part-time job at Hedgerow as a switchboard operator. Hard to believe that before I got back from Europe she had changed the plans she had for four years. She said all the hair was burned off her arms from learning to blow glass. There wasn't a bad teacher anywhere; just people who loved their work. Clara was learning to do things that had form: pottery, glass, and jewelry. She was getting excited about materials. I'll admit I felt envy when I read her letter. When she said materials, she meant silver and porcelain, not the construction paper and Elmer's glue I used in my art education courses at Holbrooke.

When I walked off Main Street, the street turned to dirt. The store windows were never changed to new displays. They sat like an attic or an old room that no one cleaned up with any intention of attracting attention to what was inside. Soon the rain began to swish through the dust and sing on the pavement as I walked back on Main Street. It thundered loudly, and the space between the flashes and the noise shortened as the storm moved closer. When I stepped under the eaves of a building to get out of the rain, I heard music, like church music. I walked down a short alley and saw a lighted room. At one end was a giant Budweiser clock like the kind you see in old bars. A man was singing into a hand microphone, and on the front row was a woman, her hair braided into a tight little bun. A fat woman with tangled hair was banging chords on a piano. I recognized her and the music; it was Mildred Persons, the lady who cleaned the courthouse offices. The three were singing loudly with whining voices.

In a moment the singing stopped and the man shut the mike off. He was looking at the giant clock and counting on his fingers. A sign on the door said: "This is a church. Behave properly." While I was trying to decide if I was behaving properly, the man saw me and said, "Would you like to join our worship service." He did not say it friendly, as if he were really inviting me. He said it like "I see you sneaking over there and you had better come in and sit down so I can watch you better or git the hell out of Dodge." Mildred didn't indicate that she recognized me. I sat down and listened to him start to preach; he was shaking the mike and watching that clock. I saw from the clock that I had ten more minutes on my wash cycle.

The two women would chant and scream occasionally. He talked like an auctioneer, breathless and constant. "I hear you Lord, I'm asking you, glory be, and I said, praise the Lord, listen to me, I beg you, I'm a-telling you . . ." Every time there was a pause, one of the phrases slid into the silence, usually "Praise God, praise the Lord!" He was running a race with time that he would lose if he left silent spaces between his words. He was saying that the Lord had "touched down," citing the different items in the county struck by lightning.

I slipped out soon and went back to the Laundromat, where

my clothes had already twisted to a stop around the center knob. As soon as I got them in the dryers, the power went off and all of the machines stopped. I sat in the darkness for what seemed like an eternity. The lightning would flash and I would see the white forms of the machines and see that no one had moved close to me in the dark. When the power came back on and the dryers began flapping the clothes around again, I got impatient and took them out before they were done. They would get wet on the way to the car anyway.

I believe the reason I left was I got scared. I was thinking of that big clock and the service being over and wondering if the Lord had touched down and stopped the clock. I was thinking of that man and the two women coming out into the empty streets of Rocky Gap. I was thinking of being alone and wanting to be home in the safety of my house with Sam. I wondered if Christina felt safer with Travis home. The year before, I didn't have Sam or the house and I wasn't afraid. But I wasn't alone either.

The next morning I went to see Mollie, Sunday morning and she had her radio on. It was still raining, but the lightning and thunder had stopped. On the radio I heard the same voice I heard the night before. I listened in amazement as Mollie rocked and moved her lips while the man preached, repeating all the sites I heard him mention where the Lord had touched down. Two old women. That was his entire congregation and he said this was the morning worship from the Faith Tabernacle. I listened to the singing, the same singing I heard the night before from one man and two women, and it was supposed to be a whole church. He could have fooled me.

In the background on the radio the night's storm rumbled, but Mollie's house stayed dark. The service had been one of the main things I was going to talk to Mollie about. But when she cut the radio off at the end of the service, I didn't mention it. She went to the door and looked out at the rain that splattered on her unpainted steps.

"Why you reckon we got thunder without lightning?" Before I could explain, she said, "The Lord ain't got time for Olley County."

*

Every day going home I passed by that string of signs, reading them until I got to the end, then trying to fill in what must have been on the missing sign. The last sign in the sentence and the Burma Shave were gone, knocked over by a plow probably, maybe years ago. I don't even know if they make Burma Shave anymore, but I could remember reading the signs on the way to Florida. *At intersections/Look each way/A harp sounds nice/But it's/Hard to play. Twinkle, twinkle/One-eyed car/We all wonder/Where/You are.*

One afternoon in late fall I parked my car and walked down the stubble between *When you drive/If caution ceases/You are apt/To rest* ... I crawled around in the dead grass like an idiot, looking for sign number five, until finally I found the end of a stick. I tugged on it, pulling it out from under the ground, and broke off a hell of a splinter in my hand. I rubbed the dirt off the rotten wood, looked at it for it must have been thirty seconds before it made any sense. I would have scored minus ten on an IQ test that day.

*... in pieces.*

I didn't look for the one that said Burma Shave. Another of life's little mysteries was solved. I was wrong. I thought it would say *in Hades.* It was a bit more graphic than I figured.

# Part IV

*I* DREAMED *I was drawing on a blackboard with colored chalk. A beautiful Technicolor dream with chalk that would respond to my every wish; it moved like water and lights and knew no bounds. I started my drawing in an empty room long before art class was to start, but soon people began coming, people of all ages, and they sat behind me like a jury. Their presence killed my water and light colors because I couldn't work with people around me. From that point on I never saw my drawing again. Soon I was aware that I was copying the whole thing from a newspaper. The pages kept rattling and the sections came apart. I had even fooled myself into believing it was original. The drawing had been more elaborate than a cartoon. I was frustrated at the difficulty of hiding the newspaper as more people came in. I knew they knew I had copied. I took a rag and washed it all away. It was gone and I agonized that there wasn't enough time before class would start to do one on paper. Why had I used the blackboard? What had been so much fun at first suddenly seemed stupid. A blackboard isn't permanent and the result can't belong to you.*

*We drew on the blackboard in grammar school, but those drawings were smeared and worn out before the janitor got around to washing them off. I learned to draw by copying the funnies. All my women had figures like Daisy Mae and Moonbeam McSwine. Maybe I dreamed the dream because I used to draw the funnies.*

*Although the adults have shown little interest in classes, I have enough children signed up to try a weekly session in art. I remember very little about my own early art classes. I don't think teachers had any effect on me back then. They gave me things to do and I did them. I carved a self-portrait in a linoleum block, a face with pigtails; I remember the face in the linoleum better than my own. I stuck the tool all the way through my hand. After that the teacher made the whole class go back to paints on an easel; the paint was watery and ran downhill and messed up everything I tried to do. I told myself if I became a teacher, I'd never make little kids paint on an easel with runny paint.*

\*     \*     \*

The second Saturday in November, I had my first art class with the little children of Rocky Gap in my newly arrived trailer. I knew why they were in my class; their mothers didn't want to give them the money to go to the movies and wanted them out of the house to be somebody else's problem for two hours. The longest two hours of my life. First off, I had spent a lot of time the week before collecting materials in the community. Since I'd had no response from Washington on my request for money for supplies, I made an attempt to show them that art could be accomplished with found objects. I had planned to save the huge cardboard boxes I got at the furniture store to use the following week, painting them and making houses. By the time I got to my classroom trailer, the children who were dropped off an hour before class was to start had already discovered my boxes. My future houses looked like Hiroshima after the bomb. I had expected them to be shy and standoffish like their parents. The box destroyers were breathless, and the late arrivals were jealous because they had missed the fun.

I soon found that you never give children any material to play with that will not wash out with water, my second mistake. I rolled out colored ink for them on sheets of glass and told them we were going to make prints from found objects. I remembered that from one of those education classes I had at college. I sliced potatoes and apples for them to press in the ink for their first prints. They watched me demonstrate on a easel for a few minutes. Then, before I gave the signal, the mass printmaking started. There must have been three hundred prints made in those two hours and less than twenty-five were on the paper I gave them. Three of them are on the seat of my slacks.

When the time was drawing to a close — I was counting the last minutes — I looked at the back of the class at a little boy whose eyes were crossed. I was thinking they should have been repaired by a doctor and wondering if the one eye looking forward saw me watching. He had on corduroy pants that must have been handed down to him by an older brother because his belt was used to fold them to take up the slack. The reason I noticed the pants was because he had the fly down and had his pale little carrot in his hand. He smiled up at me like he was about to pull the trigger on his gun, and I instinctively moved out of the way. He didn't put it away, and I didn't ask him to.

For my final reward I was shown a woodcarving one kid's father made. Somehow I don't think the same marketing devices will do that work for the Coppertown carvers. It was of a man in a barrel, a clever combination of wood and rubber bands. When the barrel was lifted, up sprang an oversized penis decorated with red fingernail polish.

I sat and stared at my wrecked classroom for an hour after the last child left, unable to move. I had often wondered how Matilda felt when she looked at the dinner table after the guests were through. All the care, the polished silver, the china, became chaos, lipstick on a linen napkin, seeds, bones, food on the tablecloth around the plates. How did she muster up the strength to prepare it all again the same way?

Finally just after Thanksgiving I got enough people together for an adult class in art appreciation. I ordered free color slides from the National Gallery and used the ones I took in Europe. They seemed to be interested, but I couldn't be sure. I decided to wait and see how many of the twelve who were there came back the next week. I was able to use some of the material I learned at Holbrooke, but I felt uneasy up there because I kept thinking if I knew it, maybe the people out in front of me knew it. I wondered if they were thinking, That fool, she acts like she's bringing us words from the mount, and we knew everything she said before she said it. Maybe they knew a lot of it was misinformation and I didn't. I tried to read their faces while I was talking. The only time I felt secure was when I read the script from the National Gallery slides, because I knew those were not my words.

In early December word came from Washington that one of the Appalachian Corps volunteers in West Virginia had been arrested for drug possession. The local people had alleged that he was a Communist and went to his house for a search which netted them union literature, some Marx and Lenin books, and a Che Guevara poster, all of which was reported in a local news article. They also found two ounces of marijuana, which was the legal end of the volunteer. "Further incidents of this type could terminate the funding of the program in its trial stages," the report stated. I knew the organizers were worried or they would have hushed it. Probably felt their Washington jobs threatened if the troops out in the bush got out of hand. It was suggested that we use our Christmas vacation to reorder our lives and re-evaluate our purposes. Maybe the Washington office would send us a mimeographed list of New Year's resolutions.

Clara stopped in Raleigh on her way home for Christmas. With her was a girlfriend named Scott, whom she brought from Hedgerow. We were drinking beer in one of the bars near the State College campus, which was almost empty except for some foreign students.

"And now we have another study in loss of innocence, a familiar subject of the college girl that manifests itself at all girls' schools." Clara, who majored in painting, was getting drunk and had started to mock Pollard, one of the art teachers at Holbrooke. Against my better judgment she had talked me into venturing out of the teacher prep program to take one of his painting courses.

"Take note of the forlorn look in those once-innocent but now-knowing eyes. A rented room at the beach with plastic curtains and gritty sheets, a roach from under the bed scurries across the floor when the lights go out." She raked her finger-nails across the table top, imitating the way Pollard's roach fingers had scurried across my painting. Clara remembered the scene better than I did. "Fumbling with a sweaty adolescent while a car crunches by outside, a siren screams in the dis-tance. 'Is this where I'll lose it,' she asks herself, 'after guard-ing it and saving it all these years?'"

"That asshole," I said. "He tells us to do a self-portrait and he sees what he wants to see in it. I bet he had that speech pre-pared before I even did my painting. I saw one of his paintings in the traveling state show. It looked like he had framed the paper towel he used to clean his razor."

Clara was laughing loudly. She was getting pretty drunk. "Remember what I told you, Fitzgerald. Them that can, do. Them that can't, teach a twelve-hour week in a southern girls' school."

"Yeah, or they teach the social rejects of Rocky Gap."

I could see Pollard in my mind, hating him. His goddamn sport coat hiking up in the back as he folded his arms in front of my painting. "Half-baked, Miss Fitzgerald. I wonder if there is anything I can do to make you develop." His arm patches were sewn on with red thread and he had this scrap of bloody paper towel sticking on his face where he had cut himself shaving. When his coat fell open, his body odor would float over you. We always figured if he ever took off all his clothes, the smell would drive us out of the room.

"Fitzgerald used to crack me up, I mean it," Clara blubbered. "She did one of those 'Draw Me' things out of a magazine. This man came and told her she had great talent, pointing it out to her in a drawing someone else did. Fitzgerald entered every damn contest . . ."

"I won one. I won the Bugs Bunny Easter Coloring Contest when I was twelve years old."

"She has a picture from the newspaper of this guy in a bunny suit handing her the check, and he has his arm all the way around, trying to feel her tits. And Bugs Bunny said, 'I wonder if there is anything I can do to make you develop.' "

Clara's friend Scott wasn't very interested in our art background, that was easy to tell. I wondered why Clara liked her. Scott had been living in the Village and painting. She dropped out of college and came to the craft school where Clara was for a change of scene. She thought of herself as an artist. Maybe she was the first real artist Clara had ever known.

"Why did you go to Holbrooke College if you had any real intention of being an artist? Why would this Pollard be any good if he came to Holbrooke? All the Holbrooke Colleges of the world do is train you to be a society matron with a hobby to keep you from drinking."

I felt insulted even though I figured she was right. We could say those things, but when someone else did, it made us angry. Clara was too drunk and in too good a mood to be insulted, but she quit laughing for a while.

We walked red-eyed from the bar, Clara and Scott both bumping into me and getting us tickled. We were higher than we thought and laughing at everything and nothing. We walked down a rain-shiny street, trying to remember where we had parked my car. There had been no windows in the bar, and the noise of the band had kept the rain from sounding on the roof. It had been dry a long time and the rain smell was strong. I could see it falling in the neon light and landing in a row of cans filled with bottles and boxes, but the smell wasn't from the cans. I said something about the smell. Scott said she had no sense of smell.

I stopped walking. "Ever?" I asked. "Or just because you are drunk?" I was drunk and I could smell. I shouldn't have kept asking; I knew better, but couldn't stop myself. She shouldn't have mentioned it if she didn't expect me to ask.

"The doctors don't know why it is gone," she answered.

Clara laughed and retorted, "Sure they don't, Scott. They don't because they don't know about the cocaine."

Scott said she knew a boy in New York who had the bones eaten away in his nose and it fell in from cocaine. We laughed. A rotten nose collapsing on his face. A flat face. Why was that funny? I asked if food had any taste without smell but didn't get an answer. They were talking about something else. Someone at the craft school who couldn't weave without grass. I started sniffing like crazy, my key case, the steering wheel of my car, the wet fur on the collar of my sheepskin coat. I could smell them all.

We went to another bar that had a fireplace. I couldn't help myself. I asked if she could smell it.

She looked hard at me and said, "I know what it smells like because I can see what is burning. It's gum. We used to buy the same kind of wood for our fireplace at home when I was a kid."

With my bleary mind I tried to remember what a gum tree looked like. I thought of three-sided nuts, one side the squirrels left on the trail. My memory wasn't working. A gum wasn't a nut tree. Gums had pronged balls that jammed in Raymond's mower, but I still couldn't see the tree. I could smell trees alive thinking about them. I sat quiet for a long time with the fire smell, thinking if she couldn't remember, she had nothing but cigarette smoke burning her eyes.

Finally I saw a gum-tree leaf, five-pointed and sweet to smell when I rolled it into a ball. I sniffed the imaginary gum leaf in my hand. I didn't want to give up any of my senses; I wanted to go home. I'd be glad when that girl was gone. I wanted to ask if her sense of smell was gone for good, but something kept my mouth shut. I knew that it was, and that I didn't care.

Leon was down on his knees on the sidewalk across the street. He had been well supplied with liquor for over a week from the New Year's party garbage cans. The restroom down the hall smelled of Leon, even if he remembered to lift the toilet seat. Mildred cleaned it twice a week, but over the ammonia smell was the odor of an alcoholic's urine.

At first when I saw him crawling, I thought he was just drunk, but then I noticed what he was doing. He was trying to lure a cat to him with a plastic container that he shoved along in front of him on the sidewalk. I tried to go back to my work, but I was getting uneasy and kept looking up at him, wondering if he was going to hurt the cat when he got it to come close. Why would Leon care about feeding a cat?

The cat rubbed up against the front of the hardware store, the resistance breaking down in its undernourished body. It was black and white with the white dulled by the town dirt, its legs and tail seeming unusually long because of its thin body. I just knew Leon was going to hurt that cat so there was no use trying to go back to work. The cat came closer, sniffing the container and backing away. Leon resisted grabbing for it. The cat came up again, its sides sucking in and out as it dipped rapidly for what was in the container, choking it down in an uncatlike way. It was hungry.

Leon watched it eat for a moment, then suddenly scooped the animal up in his arms. Instantly the cat went crazy, scratching him until he released it. The animal vanished around the building. Leon sat there a moment, looking at his empty arms. I wondered then if Leon had just wanted to hold it. Soon he leaned back against the building and went to sleep in the sun. Neither the cat nor I knew what Leon really had on his mind, but I think the cat made the right decision.

That night when I left, I saw the cat under the bushes in front of the post office, eating a motley pigeon that was either slowed or stopped by the cold. I hurried to my car to get out of the winter wind that whipped up the back of my coat. Black ice was on the pavement; the mountains were in a hard freeze. It had been a year to the day since I found the frozen mountain woman, Jane Boey.

In mid-February I was confronted in my office by the courthouse cleaning lady, Mildred Persons. Since she dusted my books and put them back in the wrong place, I always knew when Mildred had cleaned because I had to reorganize my shelves. I did notice they were replaced right side up, so I figured Mildred could probably read. I had asked her to bring her children to my Saturday art class, but she had never shown any interest. She was a grouchy person, complaining to herself while she worked, her shapeless fat body moving in quick jerks.

"Good morning, Miss Fitzgerald," she said that morning.

"Good morning, Mildred," I replied. I'm always uneasy when someone older than me calls me Miss Fitzgerald. I noticed the question that was in Mildred's voice. She continued to stand there after greeting me instead of beginning her work.

She turned to my bookshelf and put her finger on a purple box. In it was the white Bible my mother's mother gave me. I never took it out or opened it, leaving it in the box to keep it clean.

"I see you have a copy of the Good Book."

"Yes, that was a gift from my grandmother. She's dead now."

"I see. I see. And do they still study the Good Book in school?"

She caught me off guard. Religious questions always made me edgy. Christina used to make me feel guilty when I displayed my ignorance of the Bible. Since the tent meeting I hadn't attended church. I slept late on Sunday mornings, which was probably bad public relations. Also Mildred had never mentioned seeing me at the Faith Tabernacle, where she played the piano. "In Sunday school," I answered, "not in the public school."

Mildred continued to stand there. She was getting at something and I began to grow nervous. I wondered if it was the prayer in the schools problem. Maybe Mildred thought the federal government had sent one of their heathens to Rocky Gap. Maybe she thought there was something sacrilegious about my accidental appearance in her church. When I turned back to my desk, she made it known that she didn't intend for our conversation to end there.

"I was wondering if you would tell me about some of them other books."

"Which other books, Mildred? There are all sorts of books there. You are welcome to borrow any of them." I was getting impatient but she stood her ground.

"I was noticing that a lot of them have foreign names, funny-sounding names, like that Russian who come over here, you know?"

"Khrushchev?"

"Him."

"No, I don't have any of his books. There is one about him

that tells of his life. There are a number of Russian novels there, if you are interested. You might enjoy them. The characters in them are mostly farmers and . . . they have interesting lives." The end of my sentence came off flat. I caught myself before I said ". . . are all poor." I didn't know why Mildred was bothering me so. I told her again to help herself to my books any time, and turned back to my work. I heard her voice whining to herself as she started cleaning.

That afternoon when I got ready to leave for home, I noticed a space in the shelf. Mildred had come back during my lunch hour and taken all of my Russian novels. The books that I had bought for my philosophy course were also gone and there were several gaps I couldn't identify. I laughed at the thought of Mildred with the philosophy course books, how I had faked my way through that course by memorizing the lectures and how impossible the translated German had been to read. I was curious to see how she reacted.

Three days later a copy of a letter was on my desk. It listed the books that Mildred had taken. It had been sent to the county judge from the city magistrates and the school board. It alleged that Miss Jean Fitzgerald, a federal employee, was using tax money to spread Communism in the Olley County community. I was, the magistrates concluded, in all likelihood a member of the Communist party, and the above-listed literature was being held as evidence. I checked the last names of my accusers. None of their children were in my class.

\*   \*   \*

*I have just read the letter again. I have to admit it to myself; it's real. Of all the stupid things. I am getting the pain in my groin I always feel when I'm afraid. I can't laugh it off. What have I gotten myself into? Did it happen because I was trying to impress these country people with my bookshelf? What a ridiculous thing to have to explain. What does Mildred Persons see through her simple mind? Does she go out of her cabin one morning to dump out slops for her hogs and see the black metal shape of a Russian submarine rising out of the French Broad River? Mildred Persons, standing frozen there as the death machine surfaces and moves to the shore below her cabin. An army rushes out, armed with bayonets and hand grenades, coming full speed up the banks after her, tearing her limb from limb and throwing her to her own hogs. Or maybe the sky fills with black metal birds, and she hides in the woods, watching them blow apart her cabin, blast her '50 Ford, kill her best hen. There is no one to look after Mildred Persons, no army, no one in Washington, no one who knows any better than she does what evil lurks outside her mountains, evil that is going to come to Rocky Gap and get her like the boogyman.*

*Is that the way the Communist evil comes to Mildred Persons, or does it slip in slowly, carefully disguised as someone come to help, a young girl, somewhat awkward, unsure, with a basket of wares that she doesn't charge for? No matter, no need to pay. That's what Red Riding Hood said to Mildred. Send your children over. The government paid me to come here, so my goodies are free. And Red Riding Hood creeps in and like a worm drills to the heart of all the young children, eating it away, then the brain, until Red Riding Hood has control. Then the Russians don't have to send all those black iron things in the water and the sky. No need to waste them if Red Riding Hood can destroy without them. She learned how with those evil books. She never opened the Good Book in that purple box. That is the only book Mildred needs to get through life.*

*Mildred is no Chickie Little, not gone to say the sky is falling and having everyone laugh. She ran in with her stack of evil books and they listened — the banker, the grocer, their wives. Listened to the cleaning lady who plays the piano for the Faith Tabernacle. If there is a new and strange bug in your garden, kill it. Better safe than sorry. Especially if it is easy to kill. They turned against me fast. I didn't know they disliked me. I thought I was just someone to be ignored. I hope she comes back to my office. I hope she has the nerve to walk through my door.*

Mildred Persons . . .

*Walking 'round like a spook, like a old scarecrow wearing men's britches. She betta watch out, she never gon git a man, let herself git some age on her. What a man want with that, they'll say. She ain't gon have no choices, I can tell you that. What a woman want to live by herself out in the woods for? It ain't right, I tell you. And she never onc't come out on Sunday morning to give the Lord His day, up there in the woods sleeping and drinking on the Lord's day. She's a bookworm, that's what she is, and all she's studying is the filthiest books she can lay her hands on.*

*Mr. Walton on the board he say to me, "Mildred, you just find out about the habits of that one for me. See if she's got a Good Book. Take a check on her things when you're cleaning. I don't mean go snooping so she'll take notice or nothing, but just take a long look out the corner of your eye. Find out what you think's going on in her head and there'll be an extra ten spot in your pay this week." Well, he was good on his word. He didn't know I was smart enough to git him the evidence right there in my own two hands. All that stuff she reads on how to overthrow the government. My Otis says she's just the kind them Communists just love to git their claws in 'cause she ain't got no better sense than to be one.*

*We got to keep them out, Mr. Walton says, or we end up just like them people overseas during the war. Everything we worked our fingers to the bone for git took away from us without a thank you and give back out to them too sorry to work. Mr. Walton says they'll come up to me, say Mildred, give me a hen 'cause you got two more than that nigger Jones down the road and the government says you got to all have the same. Take my hens like taking my money, like taking right out of my pocket. Stealing from me and giving it to a nigger. I fightcha for that. I kill her she try to steal from me. I never took nothing out of that office that didn't belong to me, though she left pens laying around and even money in the drawer one time that I put back when I got to worrying 'fore she got back, though she got so much she probably wouldn't have noticed. She said I could help myself to them books. Wont like stealing.*

*The Lord says man and woman should be married in His sight and raise children, and woman is keeper of the hearth, and I wouldn't be cleaning all them things belong to other people, stay home and be cleaning my own if Otis wont laid off 'bout half the time. I can't hardly stand to look at her, them*

*skinny legs and arms. The Lord ain't letting her body fill out till
He sees her mind is set on being a woman and serving Him . . .*

*Last night I had a strange dream. I shot at a dove and it flew
away. But it spattered the green grass with red drops. I have
never shot at anything before. Yet in the dream I didn't seem to
have feelings about it. I followed the wounded bird, listening for
its rustling, trying to hear its cry, but it appeared to be gone. I
was looking at the gray side of a barn when suddenly I saw my
gray dove against it, fluttering up in front of the door with red
drops of blood falling to the ground like raindrops. They made a
noise like water on a tin roof. I raised my gun to shoot it again
and as I did, someone opened the door and it was too late to tell
my finger on the trigger stop. I never saw the person I killed.*

\* \* \*

I couldn't believe it had happened, that it was all real. I sat
there in that room at the head of a table and it was just like the
time I was going to be sent home from prep school. Or maybe I
wanted to think it was like that so I wouldn't be scared. All
those faces. People who were out to get me. Two of the women
from the garden club; I remembered them from the art contest.
One was the woman whose picture I saw in the paper, whose
painting I didn't choose mysteriously switched to first place.
Even the postmaster, who had always been friendly, was there.
There was no one on my side or even anyone who understood my
side. I'll admit I was uneasy before the hearing, but I thought it
would be a simple matter when they recognized their mistake.
But no one admitted to a mistake. I almost laughed when I imagined seeing Dr. Anderson sitting there, pounding on the
books that I read for his Russian literature course, saying to
me, "Miss Fitzgerald, can you explain why you have a collection of Communist literature in public view in your office? We
have all had experiences with Communists before, Miss
Fitzgerald. They came here trying to organize the mill workers, but they weren't like you. You are sneakier than they
were."

I sat there as they read quotes from the books, about the

state, about the capitalists, about Stalin. They read mostly the
quotes I had underlined when I was studying for exams. I
thought about an incident years ago when the religiously
fanatical mother and father of a boy I was dating made me sit
one evening and listen to them read a series of quotes from the
Bible. Those Biblical passages were all about sex and sin, but I
felt the same way, as if I would burst if I had to sit through
another second of it.

I was trying to organize the poor to rise up against Them, the
Rocky Gap property owners. Their federal taxes were paying
my salary. Their children weren't good enough for my classes. I
had to go outside of town to find the riffraff, whose minds I
could manipulate. What good were art classes for people who
were always going to work in the mill. Those people were being
paid more than they were worth already. If you gave them decent things, they wouldn't take care of them. I heard a series of
stories about how they clogged drains with garbage when you
gave them running water, how giant roaches ran through their
houses. This was their case against me.

They were obviously confused by my job with the government and the fact that the postmaster could verify I had gotten
checks from the government. Was the government infiltrated
with Communists again and did they know what the person
they had sent out was up to? Why hadn't someone older come to
check on me? They had their own schools paid for by their
taxes; what did they need outside help for? One of the ladies was
particularly offended by my use of the term "poor area."

"It may not be Raleigh, North Carolina, but we like it," she
snapped.

One man wanted to know who put me up to it, if I was the
front person for a group of union people that were to come in
soon. He told me about a union man who had come a year ago.

"He came with his family and set up housekeeping like he
belonged here. Thinking he was going to get a union going and
collect a bunch of dues from a bunch of stupid people. They
killed him less than two months after he got here. The very
people he thought he could get on his side killed him."

I asked him who "they" were and he grunted me no answer.
He was one of the higher-ups at the mill. No one who was there

to quiz me was lower than the upper middle class of Olley County.

I phoned Washington after the hearing was over. The only indication I had had that they knew I was still in Rocky Gap was the arrival of my trailer and my monthly check. I guessed only the computer knew about the check. I should have called them before, but I thought all I had to do was tell the board about the origin of the books. I also left word with Dr. Anderson's wife for him to send a course syllabus and a letter of explanation for the books. I was hoping she'd laugh about it and make me feel better, but she was completely businesslike. I found out that the board only heard what they wanted to hear and their minds had been made up before they saw me. I also wrote a letter to the main office in Washington so they could see in writing up there the absurd thing that had happened to me. The secretary said someone would phone me. But I knew it would be weeks before I heard from them. The incident would be twenty memos deep before they'd tell me what to do. I wished I could laugh. I wanted to say, "You stupid ignorant farmers, you haven't got the sense of a cow." What had I heard Clara say once, "Ten more points of intelligence and you might be declared a tree." I wrote to Clara. I needed to hear her say, "Now what is going on? I hope you told the mayor himself he was full of shit as a Christmas turkey."

Dear Clara:

You aren't going to believe this. You remember that course I damn near flunked under Dr. Anderson, Russian Lit from Pushkin to Social Realism? And Eighteenth Century Philosophy? They have come back to haunt me. A seedy old cleaning lady found the books on my bookshelf and I had to appear today to explain my obvious affiliation with the Communist party. And all I was trying to do was put out enough books to impress them with my learning. The cleaning lady was not impressed by my Bible with the uncut pages. She has a vision of hundreds of little slant-eyed yellow people with big boots, black hats, and sickles swimming over and hacking her to pieces. I'm their leader, Clara.

This letter has been sitting here a while, thus the bend in the center of the page from my typewriter. Actually Mildred, the cleaning lady, was just the one they used to set me up. It was the higher-ups I had to answer to. The ones who could destroy any chance of my starting a school here. I was just about to write you and tell you I was finally enjoying my work, especially the kids on Saturday. I think I don't know the real reason they want to get rid of me. Maybe my presence is an insult. They are not impoverished and are perfectly capable of ignoring the ones who are. I was going to try to be funny about it and write you and feel better but it sure as hell didn't work. What am I supposed to do now, Clara?

\*   \*   \*

*I took the letter out of the typewriter. I don't know what else to say. I find it hard to talk seriously with Clara. Tomorrow I will have to go back to work. I am not working for the local people. I am working for the federal government. They probably have no legal right in this town to interrogate me as they did today. My father would hit his legal ceiling if he knew about it, but I won't call him unless I get desperate. They can't take my job from me; the federal government is the only one that can fire me. I bet my father pays more taxes in a month than I earn in a year. I'm not wasting their money. They could refuse to cooperate, though, and destroy the whole idea of the school. I won't use my office until all of this is settled. I will just go in to collect my mail and check the city switchboard for calls. That is, if they will tell me I get calls or put up my mail anymore. I put my unfinished letter to Clara in an envelope. I'll mail it like it is.*

\*   \*   \*

It happened when I left the post office after mailing my letter to Clara the last Friday in February. I had gotten a letter from her, but it was just a typical newsy letter because she didn't know about anything that had happened. I walked over to my VW and opened the right door to let Sam in. A man with his back to me was standing beside the driver's door as I walked around. The parking lot was deserted.

"Excuse me, I need to get in my car," I said.

"You do, do you?" I recognized him when he turned. He was Dwayne, Leon's brother who often brought him liquor.

"Yes, I do if you don't mind." I didn't move any closer to my door and the man gave no indication of leaving. He was dressed in worn work clothes but not farmer clothes, mill-worker clothes. A chaw of tobacco gaped open one side of his mouth and rested against his yellow teeth.

"You the one who lives up off Ellis Creek Road, ain't you, Commie?"

I didn't answer. I didn't know what to say. He repeated the question, emphasizing the name of my road.

"It's none of your damn business where I live, and if you don't get out of my way, I'll go ask the sheriff to make you leave." My voice shook. I didn't want him to know I was afraid. I was glad Sam was with me. I hoped he loved me enough to protect me. My dog that I had as a child bit my father once when he was just playing with me.

"Shit," the man went on. "What you think Sheriff Whitcomb thinks about you, Commie? He's a good friend of mine. Known him all my life. You ever live in one of them communes?"

"What the hell are you talking about?" I said. My toughness was sounding less credible.

"I mean, you ever live in one of them places where all them stinking Commies smoke dope and fuck anything that happens to be in their bed? Or their spot on the filthy floor. You ever fuck that dog, Commie?"

"May I ask who the hell you think you are to start talking to me like that." When I tried to cuss to sound tough, I sounded just the opposite. I have never heard anyone talk like he was for real. When kids at school did it, it was very different.

"I work over to the mill. I seen this car over where that crazy old bitch Burcham lives many a time. What you and that old biddy got cooking up? You seen what we did with that union man who come in before? Tied him up like a pig and fed his nuts to the hogs."

I stared at him a moment because I couldn't think of a retort. He seemed to be getting a little uneasy, but his mind was in a frenzy.

"I'm getting a little bored hearing the different ways you people took care of that union man," I said finally. "Why don't you get together and agree on your lies? I heard it wasn't even the Rocky Gap mill, the last time I was told that story." I relaxed a little, enough to feel like I could move my body again, because he went on the defensive. I glanced around, but there was still no one else in sight.

"You think you're pretty smart stuff, don't you? You thought you could just . . ."

I couldn't stand it anymore. I pushed the man back and pulled open my door, jumped in, and locked it. I reached around Sam and pressed the lock button on the other side. Sam started to bark and growl like I'd never heard him. While I started the engine, the man pounded on the windshield of my car. I had to get it going quick before the shaking took over my body and I ceased to function. I had never seen a person so violent. And over what? I felt the car rock under his force as he began to push on the side. With his middle finger he made obscene gestures, driving it through a loop made with his thumb and index finger.

When I drove away, something clanged against the back of my car. Probably his foot, the bastard. Sam crawled over in the back seat and barked for miles. I checked my mirror. He didn't follow. My body was shaking so hard by then I could hardly move the gear shift. Sam didn't take him lightly either. What if he had a weapon? How hard would it be for him to find out where I live? He already knew what road. I needed the gun in my dream.

\* \* \*

*I feel as if I've been buried under an avalanche. Like when I was a little girl and had a recurring nightmare of mountains falling on me. I've been out looking for two hours and I can't find Sam. It must be the pessimist in me to go and look on the highway first to see if he'd been run over. I hope he would be too smart to let that happen again. Unless he was running a rabbit and wasn't paying attention. But he wasn't there. I have called him until I'm hoarse. I can't believe he'd leave me just like that. Especially after the way he acted when Dwayne threatened me. He really liked it here. Maybe a female dog in heat somewhere near. I'd forgive him for that if I could just hear his toenails clicking across the porch.*

\*    \*    \*

My father had a habit of cutting up the newspaper, pinning articles he wanted me to read on my bedspread or my bathroom curtains, articles about teen-age drug problems, girls being hurt on horses, the dangers of hiking alone. Anything he saw that registered in his mind as something that might make me unhappy because it cast fear on my way of life. In late February, a week after my incident with Dwayne, he located a news article. Since I wasn't in Raleigh, he decided to call me in my office. My mother was on the extension.

"Jean, you sit back and make yourself comfortable. You're going to listen to this." I was immediately offended by his manner. I hadn't felt his control over me lately and didn't even like being told to sit back, much less listen.

"Emerson, can't you just tell her about it? And then we can visit on the phone. I don't think you serve any purpose by reading all that gruesome . . ."

"You don't think, Eva. That's your problem. Here's the story, Jean. Charles found it in the archives. He did some research for me after he told me about the election irregularities in that area. There also appears to be an abnormal tolerance for violent crimes. They're very short on convictions up there.

"Olley County dateline, last February: 'Harold Atkinson, 42, was found dead late Friday night on the porch of his house that was destroyed by fire, the dwelling located west off Estes Road about two miles from US 23. Atkinson, a union organizer for the Unified Textile Workers, was pronounced dead upon arrival at Olley County Hospital primarily due to burns over fifty percent of his body and smoke inhalation. Atkinson's wife and three children, who escaped the blaze with minor burns, recalled an explosion of unknown origin before the structure was engulfed in flames. Mrs. Atkinson reported the blaze after a three-mile trip on foot to the closest dwelling, but rescuers were unable to revive the badly injured Atkinson. Investigation of possible arson is incomplete at this time.'"

"Do you recognize his name, Jean?" my mother interjected. "Emerson, I'm getting chills all over. Jean doesn't even have anyone there to go to for help. I wish you hadn't insisted on reading it aloud."

"If you're cold, go put on a sweater. I want Jean to hear this."

"Don't be so insensitive. You know why I don't like it. I worry myself sick over her. I never wanted her to go to that place out in the middle of nowhere —"

"Which is all the more reason to keep her informed on exactly . . ."

I felt as if I were listening on a party line. "Mother, I don't have anything to do with unions."

"It goes on," my father said, drowning my mother out, "giving some background on the fellow: 'a graduate of the University of North Carolina and former Peace Corps worker in Africa.' He made it through all those jungle bunnies, then came home and got killed."

"That isn't funny, Emerson."

"I wasn't intending to be funny. He was a man with some education and certainly some knowledge of the dangers of his work. He had been residing in the mountain area only a few months. Are you still there, Jean?"

"Yes, Daddy."

"I thought we'd been cut off, you got so quiet."

"I'm listening to you, Daddy."

"Well, pay attention. This next article is not a straight news story. It's by a reporter doing a study on the suppression of unions in the South. Seems he went to the area about six months after the incident and got a complete run-around. Found that the local authorities never investigated the fire, the fellow's family was long gone, and the whole thing got hushed into oblivion. What do you think about that?"

"I didn't know anything about it. It sounds pretty horrible."

"Pretty horrible, huh? Is that all you can say? Don't you get a newspaper? This came out in September of this year. You were there in September. Other people read newspapers. Ideas get in people's heads and crimes are duplicated. They found out that's the way to get rid of someone who decides to interfere in their way of doing things. They take the law into their own hands without any fear of punishment. I've seen it before. Where there's a pronounced lack of evidence and no cooperation by local authorities, you're dealing with widespread political corruption. How can you expect to do political work and not even read a paper?"

"I read the *Rocky Gap Weekly*."

"That's not reading a paper. Don't get smart. This was in the *New York Times*. They found a lot of notebooks and diaries in his house. The reporter went through them, I presume, until they were taken away by the FBI for evidence. It was months after the crime before anyone bothered to even search the remains of the house. Have you been careful of what you're writing down? Don't put down a word you don't expect the world to read on the front page."

If they read mine, they would read about Dwayne threatening me. They'd read about Leon and Christina and Matilda and Alice Faye.

"Emerson, Jean isn't dead. And she isn't going to be. Nothing is going to happen to our Jean. Jean, honey, if you never do another thing for me, would you please leave that awful place?"

"I'm not organizing a union, Mother. I'm a teacher."

"Those mountain people aren't like us. They don't appreciate you and your good background. You don't know how they get things twisted in their simple minds."

"I'm sending you this whole story," my father interrupted. "It's about three columns for you to study. For your information, that program you're in is going to be under investigation shortly anyway. That hasn't been in the papers yet, but you can believe it will be a splash when it hits. I was in Washington Friday and there's already talk about it being a mistake. There've been some drug arrests. I was suspicious as soon as I heard the names of the irresponsible bunch heading it up. You know as well as I do, they didn't give you a once-over. How about supervision? Did your superior ever arrive?"

"No."

"Now you see what I'm talking about. You're bound to get a bunch of misfits and subversives involved in these programs. It's the ideal setup for subversives because they can deal with the ignorant segment of the populace, almost totally devoid of supervision. Those projects never pan out. The news media get people all worked up with pictures of malnourished mountaineers, and the government creates another worthless agency."

"So what are you telling me this for?"

"There's more to it than meets the eye, I can tell you that. If you want my legal advice, I'd get out before the investigation gets started. Being associated with a program under investigation will make it hard to get another job."

"You don't have to work for a while, Jean. She doesn't have to jump into another job right away, Emerson. She can come home or take another trip. Go to the Caribbean and get out of those cold mountains."

"I bought you a little handgun, Jean, that you can pick up when you're home. Can't chance sending it through the mail. We'll go out to the country place and I'll show you how to handle it. Now, I don't want you to register it, and you can carry it in your glove compartment."

"Emerson, I don't think a gun is the answer. Girls shouldn't have guns. You never know when somebody is going to take it and use it on you. I'm ashamed of you, a man with your professional training telling his own daughter to break the law."

"Will you shut up."

They argued over the gun for about five minutes, until my mother said they could finish talking about it later, that they had called to visit with me. She asked if I had made any new friends my own age. I told her I saw Christina in the grocery store and went by to see her. She asked about the dog I mentioned in my letter.

"I think maybe he's run away. Or been stolen."

"Who in the world would steal a worthless mutt? Didn't you have him on a chain, honestly, Jean. You can't just pick up a stray and expect him to stay around like a good dog. Why don't you get a nice pet, so you won't get your heart broken by another stray? Mary Frances' Pekingese just had a litter of the cutest puppies."

Then they argued about dogs, my father wanting me to get a trained guard dog if I got anything.

I finally got them off the phone and for a moment felt relief from the noise of their voices. Then I remembered that I hadn't mentioned to them about the Communist inquiry. As far as Rocky Gap was concerned, my father's daughter was a subversive. I wondered if that might have been a big mistake, not to tell him. If I had mentioned it, I would have had to leave immediately as far as my parents were concerned. But not to mention it. I didn't know. The phone rang again while I was thinking.

It was one of the board members. They had received the letter from my professor explaining the books. The case was postponed. I asked why it wasn't closed, and the person said I would have to ask the board. I said I thought he was the board. The whole board, he said, not just one member. Before he hung up, he asked me if I was "kin to Fitzgerald Park in Asheville." I said yes and he made some comment about what a fine man my grandfather was. I didn't respond. He said goodbye and I just hung up. I had an empty nervous feeling.

\* \* \*

*I had to bundle tight to walk today, long johns, two scarves, and my hands weren't warm even in gloves until I had walked for a long time. March is still winter in the mountains. I did see a robin, but it seemed strangely out of place. Later I saw a whole row of robins, spaced apart, taking fast little steps, listening for worms in the still frozen ground. They didn't look up or fly away when I walked past. In one of the barren fields there were hundreds of blackbirds, pecking rapidly and moving like a wave of tar over the broken stalks. I watched as the black patch moved, almost oozing, the rear birds often leaping to the front to be the first to peck in the dead grass ahead. I wondered why a single bird wouldn't have the sense to go off by itself instead of fighting the others for food. There are hundreds of dead fields. And thousands of stupid blackbirds.*

*At the edge of the woods was a half-gone tree, a willow tree with a gaping mouth and long straight hair hanging down in back, a cartoon tree. I walked by and thought the mouth might say, "Hello, Jean. Surprised to see you are still here. Heh, heh, heh." Or maybe it was just yawning. Ice still hung in the creek* water, batting in pools as the muddy water moved past, and the dead grass was combed in the direction of the rush of the snow thaw. There was trash caught high in the tree crooks from the floods and snagged in the honeysuckle, tangled in the waxlike leaves that held on the vines through the winter.

I walked into the woods, stepping up high on the grass knots to keep my boots dry. The thorns and dead brush grabbed at my legs. It was like playing with a kitten with gloves on; they dug their claws in, but I was stronger. They couldn't hold me so they planted their seeds in the cloth of my jeans. I felt bad when I picked those seeds off, as if they were saying to me, "Take me with you." Maybe they had gone far enough, farther than they could have gone on their own. I am the crazy old woman of the woods. I talk to trees and to seeds. Worse yet, they talk back to me.

There was a family graveyard, set off by a fence. The people in this area were so poor it is a wonder that they had a fence to keep their dead in or the living out. They don't even have fences fit for their stock. Outside the fence, like skeletons thrown from the boneyard, were white pokeberry stalks, starting to sprout new green shoots like grass thriving on the hoof of a dead animal. I saw a baby grave and a mother grave. They died together the same day, April 12, 1892. Maybe death was taken more easily then because it was expected. Even though the baby killed her, the father felt strong enough to have someone make the baby a tombstone shaped like a cradle. The cradle sides went all the way around the grave, telling you how tiny its contents were. I guess what amazed me was that he went to so much trouble when the child was a girl.

Soon I knew I was near the people's house. I saw a car, its windows gone, laced like a giant honeysuckle planter. This is where they lived, Mollie told me, the union man and his family. She knew he died in the fire. His wife said there were at least three men, Mollie told me. All of those mutilation stories were bragging, she said; they firebombed him in his sleep. I asked her who did it. She said the men at the mill got put up to it, she heard, for an extra Christmas bonus. It must have been Dwayne. I believe he could do something horrible like this.

I felt rusted tin cans shatter under my feet, crunching like roaches. *Instead of thinning as the house drew nearer, the roof of which I could see, the piles of garbage got deeper and higher, newer. I soon saw the thrown-out household things, white enamel pans that had sprung leaks around blackened cracks, a thunder jug like the one Mollie keeps under her bed, half of a toy wagon, the front wheels and shank. Soon I started sneaking, walking slower and looking hard to see if it was lived in now. There was no path so I should have known that it was empty, but I felt fear start to come just the same. The porch roof was collapsed and the windows were open without cardboard blocking the cold air. No one had been there this winter.*

*The fire had started in several places from the firebombs. I looked to see if I could tell by the huge gaping hole if the fire had landed on the outside and burned inward, or did it blaze up from the inside and burn out the roof. No matter. The contents of the house were spilled everywhere. Mollie was right that they must have been sleeping because the mattresses seemed to be thrown first, landing near the house. The other things were further out, the chairs and kitchen things as if they had been pulled out and looked at by someone to decide if they were worth taking away.*

*When I stood there with all the furniture outside around me, I could feel the violence of it. The union man had come here with his family with plans to organize the workers for better pay. I wasn't just looking at things and forming impressions and pictures in my mind. This is where they lived for a few months. The house was a simple farmhouse, not like the houses on the ridge that belong to the owners of the mills and downtown stores. It was an old house lived in by families before them who had no wealth. Though the house was caved in in the middle, I tried to edge close enough, see if anything was still inside. No one was sleeping in the bed that I could see shoved against the wall. It had a handmade quilt rotting in the rain on the mattress. Worse than shooting someone in the back, killing them while they sleep. I still can't comprehend Dwayne, a person who would do that to another human being and be proud of it. I wonder if Leon was there.*

*I moved around, looking in each window, but there was silence. Windseed and cocklebur had snapped in the torn screens.*

No one was there. I didn't expect an old house to be so silent, no creaks in the wind or animals running inside. I started to be afraid the house would suddenly collapse on me, so I backed away.

The weather had stripped down all the insides that were in the yard. I stared at a chair because I could see that a chair was really only straw, wood, rusting nails and springs, lying swollen under a cloth covering. In all the clutter and ruin much was worth saving, picking out, if someone would come here, plates and bowls, a coffee strainer, an unbroken mirror, a bucket that sat still holding water. But no one had come to go through the material things that were left, only the reporter who beat me there and got the journals. He wasn't afraid to walk inside that house.

My sleeve brushed a broken plank reaching out from the house, and the sound of the nylon of my ski coat whistled like a call through the woods. That was when I really got nervous. I scraped my arm over the board again, just to be sure that it was me who made that crying sound. I thought of the trip in, how I walked over the honeysuckle net that made a bridge from garbage pile to broken bed springs. I had stepped carefully coming in, ducking under things, pulling limbs out of my way. I guess I got uneasy when I knew that to get away from the house I couldn't run a beeline as hard as my legs would go. I would have to pick carefully each step. What would someone think if they saw me there? That I was in cahoots with the dead man? I shouldn't stir the people up again; they seem to have forgotten the book incident that I can never forget. Would they do that to me? They have no affection for me either.

I saw the water pump and wondered about the well. I remember at Grandfather Fitzgerald's, the wood cover that was over the old well. Baa said if I slipped in or fell through the cover, I would go in the dark hole to China and there would be things living in the bottom that would eat me when I landed. If I had fallen in the well today, I would be there now and forever. That is part of the danger of being alone. There is no one to know you have gone somewhere and no one to know when you should return. It would be only accidental and too late that *someone would discover I hadn't returned. I tried to put my mind to the ways I would be missed. Maybe my box would fill with unclaimed mail, the milkman would wonder why I let the milk spoil on the porch, my phone bill at the office would be overdue, and the power man who comes to the house once a month would see no power had been used. That was not consoling, because I would be long dead.*

*I thought of Sam. If he was still with me, he would be running through that house sniffing things out with a reckless abandon that would send chills up my spine and fill me with envy for the freedom of a dog. I went away from the house slowly. I had no choice. Then I saw something very pretty that held my mind while I picked my way through the debris. Coming up through the garbage were jonquils and another bulb flower that I did not recognize. The jonquils were strong stemmed and bunched with fat yellow buds. Some of them were surrounded with snow patches like lace doilies. The few warm days last week must have gotten them started prematurely. They came back every year, pushing through the human junk around this house and they would keep coming back. They would keep coming back until the house and all its human possessions were ground into the dirt by winters. The spot that held the house would be slick and flat but for a few stones that had been brought from the woods for it to rest on. The lone chimney would topple and the red brick clay would crumble. The giant oaks overhead that had shaded the house would shade an open spot. The jonquils and the white bell flowers with the thin leaves would grow and thrive with iron in the soil. Honeysuckle would cover all the plastic that would not rot. Then it would be only a hole in the trees where a house had been.*

*I thought of digging the jonquils and bringing them to my cottage, away from that horror of a house. I thought of the patience of a plant. It would grow and its bulbs divide and it would thrive where it is. Jonquils are put near a house to make people happy, not to make the jonquils happy. I might not stay here long enough to see them come up next spring. I think I did all of that thinking about the flowers because I was afraid to think of what had happened to the people who were in that* house. *Rocky Gap did silence the road machines and the union man, two things that came to change Rocky Gap. I left that house believing the stories that I had thought were just boasts.*

*Why did I have to dream of that house? I hadn't dreamed of a house since my dream house with the rainbow tiers of flowers. It was on my mind when I fell asleep. In the dream I walked around it, the house looking as much like the cottage I live in as the burned-out house I visited yesterday. Suddenly my body began to drop, falling straight down very fast. I was falling in the well that Baa warned me about. It had to be. I hit the bottom, but I wasn't in water. I stood on something. It was a girl, hog-tied. A man died in that house, not a girl. I stood on her a moment, balancing like on a log. If I fell off, I believed I would drown. It didn't make me fall asleep, falling in the well. I fell awake for the rest of the night. And it had happened early and fast, a high-speed nightmare, because it took a long time for morning to come.*

*How could the air hold up something dead? It barely moved, dizzy and blind. A dead thing would fall faster than my eyes could follow. It would hit before I could think and it would disintegrate, blood, metal, whatever was inside, would spray and the sky would be blank. But in those seconds after I saw it over the dark buildings and before I knew what it was, the kite was something dead in the sky.*

\* \* \*

Four days after my parents called, I got a letter from Clara. It had a Special Delivery stamp on it, but was put in my box like regular mail.

Dear Jean,

I've been trying to call you, but there's no answer at your office and the operator says you can't have a house phone because there're no lines out there. Aren't you terrified without a phone? I can't tell you how much your letter upset me. You didn't even sign the damn thing. I tried to borrow a car, but Scott's bus wouldn't start. I told several people around here what happened and they said that you were in real trouble. Those people up there are dangerous. Those are mountain natives who told me that. Don't stay out there by yourself. In fact, why don't you come down here for a few days? There's plenty of room, and since Washington hasn't bothered to tell you what to do about the trouble you got in, they'll never know you're gone. I think of something my old man used to always say. Don't argue with a fool. You're not dealing with normal minds, Jean. Anybody who wouldn't know the difference between a bunch of books for a college course and Communist propaganda is dangerously stupid. You can't second-guess people like that. You don't know what is in their heads. They were looking for a way to get rid of you. What do they do next, since the book deal didn't run you out? If you think I'm trying to scare you into getting out of there, you're right. I hope it scares the shit out of you. The director here at the school said every union organizer that has ever gone into Olley County has been shot or burned out. And there has never been a trial. He said you could come over here for as long as you like if you wanted to get away because two of the students couldn't take the pressure and dropped out. I have to tell you this — your mother called me yesterday, completely hysterical, and told me about some guy who got murdered up there. I thought she was upset about the Communist thing, but she never mentioned it. Didn't you tell them about it? You couldn't have. She would have been up there dragging you out. Now I feel guilty for not telling her. Your parents are about to go crazy with worry. So get your ass out of there, Fitzgerald, until this gets smoothed over at least.

> Take care,
> Clara

* * *

*I've been nervous these last few nights, I don't mind admitting it, but it appears now that Dwayne's threatening me was an isolated incident. I can't believe they still think I'm a Communist, but I couldn't believe it in the first place. I'm so tired of everyone telling me what to do, Clara and my parents included. But where's Sam? Why doesn't he come back? I've been to the pound three times. They've promised if he shows up, they'll call me. I'm afraid to trust anyone anymore. I was so scared they would put him to sleep if he'd lost his collar. The dog catcher said he was probably in someone's hunting pack, that I shouldn't have tried to make a pet out of a hunting dog. I heard a car turn in my road last night. There were fresh beer cans this morning, so it was probably just a teen-ager parking. I wouldn't have even given it a thought if Sam were here.*

*I've started back to work, looking deeper in the rural areas for people for the school. I've talked to a lot of families now, the very poor ones, and they were more afraid of me than I was of them. But they don't want anything I offer because it isn't material. When I go into these hollows, through the vine-twisted trees and the creek beds stacked with uprooted trees from the slides, I start to feel that no one has been there before. Then I see the tracks of a pickup truck, and at the end of the winding road will be a house or two. A few feet off the road will be a trash pile, with the white enamel of a used-up appliance and a No Dumping sign. Sometimes I count the mailboxes at the end of the road to see if I can figure how many houses will be back there. The first and only house I went to today had seven old cars in the yard and only one that had been running. If the grass is pressed down behind the car, you can guess it has been out recently. The table was set for dinner, with hubcaps for plates. Out behind the house were piled all the tin cans and bottles the family had emptied the last forty years, just far enough to keep the rats and the smell from the house. The privy had so many flies it sounded like a buzz saw as the sun warmed the March day into the fifties and hatched the first spring maggots.*

*These people find the money for guns, though. I see them coming out of the woods holding brown and black guns, or riding with them in a rack in their pickup back window. Although I know they're just hunting, it still gives me a chill when I see the guns. The father takes the son out and his big moment is to kill something, then he's one of them. He can smoke with them and take a swig from a liquor bottle. They slap him on the back so he knows killing is good. There are none of those romantic boys up here who feel disgust and nausea when they see their first dead,*

*like a boy I dated in college who kept talking about hitting a
squirrel he was sure he would miss. The boys here would sling it
over with the gun barrel to see how solid the hit was, then kick it
back with no respect for something that used to live. And they
imitate the gestures, their voices cracking into manhood, of
fathers and uncles whose lives can only be a model to a son who
can't see beyond the door of his shanty.*

*The family today didn't mention my Communist troubles.
They're so far out from town they may never know. Or care. I
remember I wrote here earlier that the inhabitants must have
thought the place was beautiful or they wouldn't have put up
with the hardships here and would have moved on, west of the
mountains or into the long growing season of the east. Now I
don't think that was it at all. Now I think they just wanted to get
away from people and each other and never gave a thought to
where they'd put their house. I was wrong to even believe people
have to think about something like that.*

*I can't look at hills anymore as a backdrop in the distance, the
land of thin air, morning fog, and black-green trees. Now I
think they are a wall. They keep the outsiders out and they keep
the insiders in. They are between me and the outside too. And I
think they make a prison instead of a fortress, with people inside
who would cut each other's throats about as fast as the guards
and the visitors. I thought because the hills were my idea of
beauty that they were everybody's. I thought Jane Boey wanted
to see beauty before she died, and she may have thought she had
walked as close to hell as her living legs would carry her.*

\* \* \*

In late March I met a young lawyer at the lunch counter, in
to serve his time as prosecutor in Olley County. I liked him right
away; he was pleasantly homely and seemed uncomfortable in
a tie. When I was sitting beside him at the counter, I felt secure
and protected. That was when I faced for the first time that my
normal state of mind had been insecure. I knew I had been
afraid, but I thought I only felt it at night in my cottage, not
when I was downtown.

The lawyer said every male juror in the courtroom for his
last case was carrying a gun. They made sure he noticed the

bulges or saw the handles when their coats fell open. He had asked for the conviction of a murderer in a two man–one woman triangle, but to his surprise the jury let the murderer off. The jury knew the man did it, that wasn't it. They just thought the victim had deserved to die; the fact that he died of murder, with twenty knife holes in him and three bullets in the head, was not relevant.

When the lawyer was in Rocky Gap last year, there was a white man accused of raping an Indian girl. There were three witnesses to the rape who testified it was forceable, so it appeared to him an open and shut case. He was sure to get a conviction. Then three Indians came in as voluntary witnesses and said they had had the girl themselves, that she was easy and went around asking for it. The man was let off. One of the Indians who testified for the white man was the girl's brother. A week after the rapist was released, parts of his body were found in seven places in the county. They didn't want prison to get him; they wanted him for themselves. Civilized justice doesn't satisfy these people. I told him about Dwayne and he said he would have packed his bags. The lawyer left for the county seat at Haywood. Only Leon was in the Rocky Gap jail. No one was arrested for the death of the union man. I knew the lawyer would never want to come here unless he had to. I hardly knew him but I knew I'd miss him.

*   *   *

*I could get bitter fast here with nothing to give me perspective but the woods and flowers. I hiked often to get away from school and it always felt good to be cut off, but I'm not sure I'm honest in liking that feeling anymore. When I hiked, I cut myself off by choice. I remember something my grandmother used to say: a person was a dyed-in-the-wool liar or a dyed-in-the-wool thief. I know what she meant now, how what is in people goes deeper than their bones, not a stain, but a dye that penetrates to the core. I feel my life change so fast I am surprised to see how little time has passed between incidents. But women in these hills are like the ones before them and the ones before that. Only maybe for each generation things get more hopeless and a little worse.*

*Mollie told me that she always felt unprotected out in the*

*fields, that somebody could be sneaking around in the woods
and pick you off with a gun. It's been a hundred years since soldiers were in the woods picking off farmers with guns, but
Mollie's mother and her mother's mother made sure that she
didn't grow to be an old woman without that fear in her system,
whether she needed it or not. And she keeps that pen of awful
dogs that I have see her throw the raw carcasses of chickens and
hogs to. They rip into them with blood staining the dirt around
them, going at each other's throats for a bit of meat. She wants
them to love raw meat, living meat if need be. Where I come
from, if a dog eats raw meat and chicken bones, it's because they
accidentally got in a trash can, and their owners stay awake
nights for fear a splinter might snag the dog's precious intes-
tines. That is such a dumb thing to think. I just like to repeat
how irrelevant my life is. I think I'm learning what's really
wrong with these people.*

*It's hate, that's what it is. It takes the light out of a person's
eyes, that cold blank stare of hate. They get hungry, they hate.
They get cold or they get cheated, they hate.. They see people in
commercials on television telling them to buy what they can't af-
fort, they hate. It's the only response they have left when something makes their bad condition worse. What I used to feel
moved by, a sensitive picture, all those photos of faces in
Dachau, are here and real. In these yards, running around on
scaly bent legs, their feet black from dew sores and twisted from
misfitting shoes, is the next generation that will hate too. Their
eyes start life bright and their skin is still shiny and fair as a
bean sprout, but their first teeth rot in their heads, the baby teeth
just sore brown snags and their heads crawling with lice. Soon
the corners of their mouths and eyes start to droop and turn inside out with malnutrition.*

*The government sends me here to nurse the community back
to health and I watch it eat itself like a cancer. I'm not equipped
to fix it. I want to tell the young ones to leave, to run away from
their families, to get out of here before that school with the leak-
ing roof and splitting wall puts them too far back to catch up. Or
before they have put a baby in the pretty little snaggle-toothed
thing down the road and made their secondhand plans to raise
a family. I met a woman here who is a grandmother at twenty-*

*nine. But the smart ones do get out. I'm seeing what's left.*

*What did life give Mollie? Children she never sees. Dead in the war or gone to town to the factories, drunks. Fifteen years ago she had to pull her husband out of his bed and down the front steps, already cold and stiff, then work for three days to get a hole wide and deep enough to put him in, hoping the sun wouldn't come through the trees and make him start to rot.*

*"Before I put him under," she told me, "I pulled up that hand that had teched on me living and teched them ugly brown warts that growed on my hands and could near 'bout feel them starting to going away. Arm was stiff as a tree limb. I didn't know I'd be a-using my own dead husband's hand to rid my warts, but it was as good a hand as any, I reckon. I checked into his pockets one last time 'fore I throwed the dirt over him and come up with fuzz and a broke toothpick, which was as much as I 'spected. Took me three days to dig that hole, and with fifteen or more years gone, I would look at it and think it was burned in the ground by the devil hisself. Some days I swear I don't recollect spading."*

*But Mollie keeps trying. She had to bury her own husband in Kentucky and was still strong enough to get her things together and come to a new place to live. She has a fierce drive to stay alive and after all that she has suffered, she will probably die of old age one night in her sleep. I guess I don't know why she keeps trying. I'm not sure anymore if I would. Maybe her generation kept trying, but the new one, Jane Boey's, quit. Yet Jane was only one person, one strange person, who took an out never condoned, not even here. I don't know how I feel about Jane's way out now. Or Christina's way back in, her need to keep her life churned up and negative. There must be victims who want to be victims, who would have it no other way.*

*Last night I went to bed with the sound of nuts hitting my roof. They hit the tin top and banged down the pitch like running feet, and I sat up in bed, wide-eyed in the darkness. I knew there were nuts broken loose by the cold March wind, but my mind made me think they were being thrown at me, someone trying to lure me to open my door so they could shoot me. I am starting to be afraid more often and for less reason. I have started to be aware that I am alone day and night. I hear those*

*things in the night and know what they are. I beg my mind to rest
and say to me that they aren't human sounds.*

*I dreamed I found Sam's collar on my car antenna and
wouldn't believe it wasn't true until I got up and looked in the
morning.*

*I wondered from the first if Mollie knew anything about the
business with the Communist literature and the hearing. When
I asked her, she told me she knew, that Mildred Persons had
come by to tell her. When I asked if that changed her feelings
about me, she said she knew Mildred Persons didn't have good
sense, that she wouldn't know a Communist if he crawled in bed
with her. I said neither would I, and Mollie chuckled and got
that sassy look in her old eyes.*

*Mollie said she didn't know about Communists, but she re-
membered foreigners, the ones who came to work in the mines,
most of whom left and went further north when they started
shutting down. They kept to themselves, she said. They were
hard to talk to, but they were good workers. She knew about
union organizers too, but Mollie said she grew up suspecting
and disliking everybody, the people who were different from
her more than those who were like her, although there probably
wasn't a whit of difference between them. I asked her why she
was my friend. She told me I was good company for a talkative
old woman, which is the only remark that made me feel good in
quite a while.*

*I guess I really didn't want to talk about my problem with
Mollie, at least not my problem with the hearing on the books.
Our relationship seems to be above all that. Mollie's mind isn't
on anything I would say anyhow. She met me at the car, she was
so eager to get me to read her a letter from one of her boys. From
what little of it I could make out, he is sending one of his little
girls to live with Mollie. She didn't flinch when I told her that
her son's wife had died, but her face lit up when I told her she
would have a child to live with her. She asked me to read the
letter a dozen times. A little girl named Ola Mae. Maybe they
could switch names so the child wouldn't have to live her life
with an old woman's name. Mollie put twenty dollars her son
had sent in my hand and closed it, asking me to find a bed and*

*buy it for her. When I left I had a funny feeling, possessiveness, jealousy. I didn't want to share Mollie.*

*The long-awaited child is here. All of the city sophistication she had over Mollie in my mind vanished when I saw her get off the bus, bowlegged, with fuzzy blond hair. I saw her on Mollie's porch when I passed today and thought she looked like an old brown photo of the woman who lived in that house, another Mollie. I hope she wasn't a disappointment. An old woman like that doesn't allow her hopes up often. When I stopped off to see her, I noticed Mollie had made a hasty quilt for the bed I bought for her. I also bought a little unpainted chest of drawers that was still unpainted. When the child spoke to me I could see her teeth, already brown and rotten. She was old enough, about ten, for them to be permanent teeth. The hem was out of her dress on one side and her hair was matted as an unkempt animal's. She probably hadn't been cared for since her mother died.*

*When Mollie left the house to use her privy, Ola Mae began to speak at a rapid rate, catching me off balance because until that moment, except for a few grunts and yeses and noes, she had been silent. She had a mixture of a big-city accent and the mountain speech of her father. "I seen her git outa bed last night and hike up her petticoat and squat over this pot she pulled out from under her bed and I heard the dodo and peepee hitting in it and saw her whole behind . . ." The child continued to describe the act until Mollie returned, then went silent again as the old woman came through the door. It was as if the child had never spoken and was still the shy waif I had first met. Mollie talked as always, not including the child in her conversation, but smiling at her frequently, glancing in her direction each time the child moved. She was obviously delighted by her presence.*

\*  \*  \*

In early April Mollie waved me down as I passed her house. She had never done that before, so I pulled in though I knew I would be late for class. I thought the child might be sick, but it was worse. The child had run away. When Mollie woke up, she was gone. Mollie told me that she had been "stole," but I told her I didn't think that was it. When I said "run away," Mollie's face fell, not in disbelief, but with grief. The poor old woman had never even considered she had nothing to keep the child there. I told her I would find her. A little kid couldn't have gotten far, and I hoped people would have the good sense not to give her a ride. I drove around the area but didn't sight her, so I went into work and told the sheriff what had happened. He led me to another room, and there was Ola Mae, asleep on a bench. One of his men had picked her up on the highway less than a mile from Mollie's house.

The sheriff didn't know that Mollie had the child. He would contact the welfare agency in Asheville to find out why she was with a senile old woman. I told him why, and he looked at me as if I had committed a crime, telling me that I should have reported such a case. I told him it never entered my mind to interfere with the business of families. She was, after all, the child's grandmother. He thought a moment about that and nodded his head. I think he didn't want to bother with the child. I asked him what he was going to do and he said, "Take her back, I reckon. Guess Mollie Burcham has as much claim on her as anybody." By evening Mollie and the child were sitting on the porch, and they both smiled and waved as I passed.

I had promised to drive Mollie and Ola Mae down for a weekend at the Atlantic Ocean. The weather was still much too cool to enjoy the ocean, but Mollie was eager to please the child and wanted to go. Ola Mae ran out when I was halfway up the walk. When I first saw her face as she moved through the door, it was sullen, but it instantly spread into laughter. She ran to meet me with a friendliness that seemed strange, unearned. I had had almost no contact with the child but for her two visits to my art class, where she barely touched any of the materials. I thought after she stepped off the school bus, her days must be grim; the bus dropped only one child by that section of the highway.

I talked to the child until Mollie appeared. She shook her head when I asked her about new friends at school. Ola Mae looked clean now and almost neat, though I knew there was no bathtub or running water in the house. Mollie told me that she herself never bathed all over, and I know she never washed her hair.

Mollie's hair looked different today, waved slightly, and when she got closer, I could see reddish brown streaks through the white. Rust, I figured later; Mollie had tried to roll her hair into pin curls with bobby pins that rusted her white hair while she slept through the damp night. She had on her long-underwear top, and the sleeves were several inches longer than the sleeves of her dress. Her stockings, thick and patched, wound around her legs like loose skin. On her feet were the bedroom shoes her son had sent for Christmas. I don't think Mollie knew that the felt shoes were meant to be bedroom shoes. She handed me a paper sack to put in the trunk, their belongings for overnight.

"No need to carry our own water?" she asked seriously.

"No need," I replied.

I buckled Mollie in with her seat belt but she struggled until we were about ten miles outside of Rocky Gap, finally getting the latch undone. Then she sat stiffly, her feet flat and apart on the floorboard, not moving any more than if she had the belt on. The child was obviously excited, riding standing up in the back and leaning between the seats to babble to us about everything we passed. Up close I saw that the hand that kept grabbing my arm to show me things was as rusty as the streaks in Mollie's hair. If Ola Mae had had her way, we would have stopped ten times before we got to the interstate. I did stop once for her to see the statues at a roadside stand and the Mexican pots. When Mollie and I were looking at a plaster Negro boy hitching post, the child climbed into a giant pot. I felt a moment of panic as I eased her out, trying to hold down her enthusiasm so she wouldn't break the brittle pottery that would double in price at the first crack. Mollie popped her lightly on the behind as we got back into the car.

When we were on the move again, Mollie said suddenly, grinning at me: "One a-coming, one a-going, one a-shitting, one a-shoveling."

I asked her what that was and she said it was the slogan for the men on the WPA who built the roads into the mountain hollows. She had seen WPA on a sign as we passed the entrance to the parkway. Mollie had never indicated that she could recognize letters. The WPA had cut the Blue Ridge Parkway as one of the make-work programs for the starving mountaineers during the Depression. For years the road was an ugly open wound from almost any mountain top, but now was a scab around the hills, crawling with tourists who came to see the foggy mountains, hoping the fog wasn't so thick they could only see a foot in front of them. I remembered coming up as a child with my parents and my cousin. My father complained every inch of the way, wondering when the winding road was going to end and he could get off, and condemning Roosevelt for being a socialist and selling out to the Japanese.

A white cloud had enclosed our car, and my father pulled into an overlook, where I lost my lunch because of the curves. I remembered the tinkle of glass from the headlight as he smashed our car on a litter barrel. When I scrambled out into the bushes to throw up, my mother started screaming for me to come back before I was through. We watched a tangle of baby rattlesnakes over the rock wall at the edge, only a few feet from the overlook, woven together like living threads in a net. An old lady from England came up behind us, the kind with the argyle socks and baggy khaki pants, trying to pretend she was having a marvelous time out in nature, and said, "Oh look, the rattlesnakes are reticulating."

My cousin Charles turned to me and said, "Yeah, and copperheads copulate, but black snakes just screw." Daddy made us get back in the car. We never saw the mountains, but just before we got back to the place where the road started down, there was a huge buck deer in front of us, his mass of antlers lifted on his head like a dead tree, standing in the road more an apparition than real, flexing his muscles and disappearing as my father swerved the car, long after the deer had taken care of his own safety.

I offered to backtrack for Mollie and Ola Mae and take the longer parkway route when she told me she had never been up there. Mollie said that the parkway was just for the tourists who never came down to the gap unless they were lost or started the scenic route and got bored, thinking they were finding a way to get out.

I probably should have taken her up there without asking, because they would have enjoyed it. Sometimes Mollie just sounded bitter. I remembered some of the girls at school, how at twenty they were cynical and hard sounding if they had had trouble with a boyfriend or parents. Then I met Mollie. She had lived through events that were nothing more than answers on a history quiz to me, the world wars, the Depression. My parents had lived through them too, maybe with a slight discomfort, but Mollie felt the agony every hour of the day. My parents moved from upper- to middle-class comfort; Mollie moved from being poor to being a stray dog. Every time I talked of my life with the slightest edge of complaining in my voice, she got this knowing look on her face and I prepared to hear her one-up me. Almost any comment that contrasted our lives would set her off, even when I didn't realize the connection. That day I said, "Look how high the river is," as we crossed the bridge.

"You think it rains a lot. You think things git musty and wet 'round Rocky Gap," she retorted. Then she clucked and I got ready for her to make my attempt at conversation sound as empty as my mother's tragedies sound to me. The only real tragedy my mother ever suffered was falling into her sunken garbage can in the dark. My father's biggest was when he backed over my tricycle. For a few minutes of total panic while he pulled the mangled toy from under his car, he thought I had been pedaling along on it, but I was in my doll house. I guess my tragedy was when he beat the hell out of me for leaving my trike in the driveway.

"You think it rains a lot," Mollie went on. "I remember when the sky darkened with the dust outa the mines, a-hanging over where they loaded the coal and a-floating up like a black cloud that aimed to follow us ever'where we chose to go. Truth was, the real sky had darkened up too and we was unawares; couldn't catch sight of the real sky. I recollect that they had put the corn in the ground, it was the month of May, and when the thunder started a-rumbling, we thought the crops was 'bout to git a good start from the Lord. The rains would come from heaven and wash that black cloud outa the sky and take our misery away in the river. My mama crouched in the corner a-wailing about the thunder and lightning, and Pa was making a joke of her, saying 'Boo!' ever time it rumbled, making like he was what she was feared of. It was just nighttime when the rain started, and 'fore the sun come up the next morning, the sky had let go and washed half the men, women, children, chickens, and cows and houses in these hills to kingdom come. I seen whole houses floating in the river, with wild things and tame things a-holding onto the same roof for their dear lives. Water washed the corn field down to the bare bone and didn't leave 'nough fitting dirt to pot up a flower. Filled the mine over a man's head with foul-smelling water. I heared a man found a cow in his yard when the water went down that wont his'n and he looked close and seed it was the cow belong to his cousin seven miles up the river, washed clean down there. He walked her back, figuring he had some good news, and there wont a scrap of a house left. He found his cousin at the relief shelter in the commissary and give him his cow. But that cow never give another drop of milk. Washed her milk-giving powers clean outa her."

"What's a *c* with a line through it?" Ola Mae interrupted.

"Cents, that's the sign for cents," I answered. "Like a capital *S* with two lines is a dollar. See the dollar?" I pointed to a sign with cigarettes at $1.99 a carton. Ola Mae blew on the back window. I watched her in the rearview mirror making dollar and cents signs in the fog.

"There was grass wrapped 'round the treetops, ifin you're wondering how high it went," Mollie went on stubbornly, "and folks' belongings hung up in the tallest of them, and the skeeters like to have et us alive. My mama's icebox washed right off the back porch and we picked chickens for two days on end that was drownt in the yard and then watched them go bad on us 'fore we could git any ice, and we buried them like the sorriest trash 'cause Abie Whitcomb died, they reasoned, from hurt meat. There was folks worse off than us, folks burying more than chickens and folks who never found their kin. My pa found a nigger man drownt in our hog lot 'out a name or nothing on him, naked as a jaybird 'cept the collar of his shirt twisted 'round his neck. Buried him wondering if his kinfolks was still out looking for him like he was alive. He was a big nigger, I seen him, big as the ones who come to put down the railroads, and swole up even bigger. My pa got tired of digging 'cause there wont no ground to speak of left, so he took him and rolled him down in the honey hole. I heared him splash when he hit bottom. And it stunk so bad for weeks on end ever'where you went you would have tried to go without breathing ifin you could've.

"The higher-ups in the gov'ment started in a-trying to be helpful and brung in the most foolish things for folks to eat with them near to starving. Boxcar came in. We seen it from the hill and went running down to git our share, and my pa was guessing it was mushmelons and my mama said it was them big 'taters they growed in the flatlands, and we was a-watering at the mouth just thinking on the good things that train had brung us when we got down there and found it come up from Florida. It was filled with these hairy things, and ifin you could e'er git one bust open, it had a good drink of thin sweet milk inside, but the most tasteless white meat on its sides you ever seen. Looked like little nigger heads with eyes a-looking at you and was just as hard. We drove railroad spikes in the eyes to bust them and 'bout half of them was bone dry. And they give you the runs like you never seen the likes of. I was a-counting on some of them good oranges, so the next load up from Florida we figure we got some, but they had gone bad and was the sourest pale things you e'er seen, so bitter they'd pinch your mouth shet. But we'd of et any scrap we could git our hands on, we was so hungry thinking 'bout all them good roasting hens we fed to the worms. Pretty soon we didn't have our hopes up when the train come in."

"How come they got all them signs — peaches, tomatoes, 'lopes — and they closed up?" Ola Mae could read surprisingly well. Far better than the Rocky Gap children her age.

"Because they leave them up until summer. *Peaches* is spelled wrong."

"I know it," she said cockily.

"Them was hard times. We thought they was hard, that was '27, and then come worst times." Mollie wasn't going to stop. "Most all the mines shet down, and I only had one brother left a-drawing pay. We started into eating many a thing we'd of throwed out the year before. That was the year my brother got sent up to prison for two years. He went to the mines with his lunch pail and his thirty-eight beside his cornbread, and old man Burley talked ugly to him one time too many and he killed him dead. Said you ne'er seen sech a look of surprise when he took up that thirty-eight. There was others there who'd of done the same thing, but my brother took it upon hisself to be the one, and they didn't hep him a bit. They couldn't git down to the courthouse fast enough to tell on him and git him sent up. I ne'er forgived people up there for that. I knowed they wanted Burley dead theirselves."

Mollie glanced into the back seat, where Ola Mae was turned around, looking out the back window. "That was your great-uncle, youngun. Harley Blalock Petry. He's gone now. His heart quit him."

The child didn't respond to Mollie. "What's that one? The one with the lady in the apron? Some kind of girl."

"Clabber Girl Baking Powder."

"Clabber, clabber, clabber. What's a clabber?"

"Shut up!" Mollie snapped.

"Clabber, clabber, jabber, jabber," Ola Mae giggled and slid down in the seat as Mollie popped her weakly on the knee.

When we got to the interstate, Ola Mae had a brief moment of what I thought was amazement as she looked at the wide pavement, but then she sat back and started to pout. Mollie was still staring.

"What's the matter, Ola Mae?"

"Ain't no more signs to read."

"There are some signs; they're just further back from the road." I was starting to feel relaxed driving, although I would be uneasy the whole trip because of my unbuckled passengers. "Don't you like the smooth highway, though? Without all those bumps and curves?"

"I seen roads like this before. I been on them all the time back in Chicago." I realized that the lack of civilization was what intrigued Ola Mae, the country signs and pathlike roads. The city kid had spent her ten years sweeping past billboards of the same size down a slick stretch of straight asphalt. She recognized her old life. "I wist I was back in Chicago."

I glanced at Mollie but she didn't flinch. I think she was getting used to the little girl's dislike of her new home. As we left the tight trees and went into the clear light of the interstate, Mollie's old eyes looked older, tired. I asked her if she was enjoying the trip. "Much obliged, thank you," she said. Then I knew I was in trouble. Mollie was going to treat me like someone who was doing her a favor, her superior. Now she was going to ride quiet and, in her mind, nonoffensive. My attempts at conversation about the things outside started to fail. I tried to get her to talk about past things. No good. I was talking more than she was. Ola Mae had fallen asleep. It was going to be a long drive. When we passed Raleigh, I planned to tell them it was my hometown, but they were both asleep. I drove past pines planted in rows and people setting out tobacco seedlings. A pleasant blast of warm air came through the vent and I could smell cut grass and onions.

There wasn't a lot of daylight left by the time we got to the shore. I found a motel room on the ocean front while Mollie and Ola Mae sat in the car. Mollie acted as if she had on blinders when we came across the Intracoastal Waterway and into Atlantic Beach, as if her head wouldn't turn and catch sight of the whitecaps on the blue water between the buildings. Ola Mae's sight was caught by the scene closer at hand, the children crossing the street with their beach equipment: buckets, surfboards, and black wet suits for the cold water. She had seen the big water of the Great Lakes.

We drove down to the fishing pier and got out, Mollie as unresponsive while the ocean broke and soared around the pilings as she had been on the trip down. I remembered my first sight of the ocean and my fear that I would fall through the cracks in the pier that were ten times as narrow as my body. Ola Mae found some children to play with who were living in trailers and campers near the pier.

Mollie stopped suddenly, grasped the railing, and looked down the long pier. She moved along the railing and sat down on the end of a fishing bench. I walked around her and sat down next to an old woman who was watching the children on the beach. When the old lady smiled and spoke to us, her cheeks stretched solid like round balls. Her hands rested bent in her lap, as stiff as crab claws. One of the claws lifted to wave to a child, who said, "Look here, Grandma!" and held up something from the sea too small for any of us to recognize. I wondered what would take Mollie out of her reverie.

I asked the woman if the weather had been nice. She nodded yes, "A bit of a chill at night, but like summertime to home." I asked where home was, her accent familiar. Coppertown. She was the widow of Sam Q. Allbright, a gem cutter and wood-carver. When I told her of my visit to her town, she invited me back to stay at her house. We had only been talking five min-utes, and it was as if she felt a poor hostess and had to redeem herself.

Henrietta Allbright was her name. "I ought to of done a job of keeping up Sam Q.'s work. I declare I should have, but there are just so many little things, I'd be a-spending my life with a dust rag, and the little ones want to go off to the ocean ever chance they git. That there's my son-in-law's trailer and camper. Sleeps eight adult folks."

I had heard of Henrietta's husband, which pleased her. She said he had been well organized and had his collection in cases. Even installed a light in one that held glowing rocks. I asked her if she considered giving his collection to a museum. Hen-rietta wrinkled her nose. "They been after me for the longest sort of time. I know that museum fellow well. He's no paymas-ter. No kin in the world and just a-hoarding up all he gits his hands on. Just like to beat somebody out of something. Likes to think he can talk me out of Sam Q.'s stuff like I don't know what it's worth, talk me out of something then do me a good turn. I hear his niece's a trash mover. She'll spend it quick."

I watched Ola Mae, who was standing behind the other chil-dren, her fear of the moving surf evident, although her face was only a white circle from where we were. Soon she stooped and began patting the sand in an area near the other children, who were building a sand city. For a long time she patted violently and separate until one little girl handed her a shovel. Then she worked with the group, her white hair lifting like flower petals about to break away from the center. I should have thought to buy her a bucket and shovel.

Henrietta was still talking; Mollie was silent.

"Preacher's daughter moved from over to Asheville. She come up talking about how she was agin bobbed hair, and it wont no time till she done it. She said she wanted to be liked for herself, not her hair, and I remember reminding her the Bible says a woman's hair is her glory. She didn't like them short dresses, wore the cock-eyed things to her ankles. Mama cut your dress when you were in the mill sack. Me and her were in a wagon on the way to a club meeting not long after she come there, and I remember it just as good. She grew up fancy away from there, anybody could tell that. I was just an old country girl, and we might be rough, I told her, but we had plenty. She offered me a piece of cake in a slip of paper and I cussed her out good. Told her I had cake at home. She was throwing off on me, you see. She always did kinda shun me."

"I know what you mean; just what you mean," Mollie interrupted. Her voice sounded strangely eager. She was rocking back and forth on the bench as if it were a rocking chair. Something Henrietta had said had struck a memory. "Man try to give me a sweet onc't, a-wrapped in shiny paper. I wont a bit older than Ola Mae yonder, and my mama found the shiny paper in my dress pocket when she was washing and like to have beat the stuffings outa me. I told her I didn't buy it, but she wouldn't pay me no mind. I thought she was so peeved 'cause I was spending money on foolishness, you see, but she was agin being beholden."

Henrietta nodded. "I was just a strip of a girl, worked at ten cent an hour; eighty cent a day was good money. Picked berries at ten cent a gallon, hoed corn all day for twenty-five cent. But we paid our own way."

"I chopped many a day other than my pa's place for fifteen cent sunup to sunset." The two old voices droned back and forth, Henrietta's high and Mollie's raspy. They were forcing their speech louder because I sat between them and the waves thudded below us.

"I 'member them boys; they would pay five, ten, fifteen dollars for a box lunch for the right girl," Henrietta went on. "Didn't have none of that crepe paper to decorate with, but them girls dressed me up and the bidding started and they run the box up on him. I did all right for myself."

Mollie patted her hands in her lap. "My brother got whipped till he bled out his ear. He had the money from selling Mama's preserves, and it worked out of his pocket while he was plowing and he cut it under. Always believed them niggers picked it up. Grandpa couldn't talk, hardly make a grunt, and kept playing like he knowed where the money was at."

Henrietta took her turn. The two old ladies seemed to be enjoying swapping tales, although they listened more intently to their own rather than the other's, waiting impatiently for their turn to speak. "Grandma slept in her dress," Henrietta mused, "but Grandpa kept on his long handles. Had me a date all the way over to Knoxville and got stuck in the mud on the way home. Grandpa met us at the door, and the rear of his underwear bagged and it like to have broke us up, but them fancy city boys didn't crack a smile."

While Henrietta giggled, Mollie picked up the conversation. "They was some rough roads, mud up clean over your knees so you thought you was stuck up till summer dried it out. That snow would keep a-coming ever' time a spot of ground turned up. I 'member a bus wreck, only second time I been on anything wont a horse pulling, and it slid off in the ditch. I was in there with my brother, cutting up till my uncle come for us, and later we heared a nigger woman and her little boy were dead in the back the whole time. There was some hard times."

Henrietta nodded. "I 'member no 'lectricity, oil lamps with mantles, till REA come through. Fellow got drunk running the wires and sweated hisself to death. There was some hard times, but we made it through all right for ourselves. I got ten living children, five boy, five girl. Ever one of them turn out all right but Percy, and he be all right soon as he gits hisself straight."

Mollie was suddenly quiet when Henrietta jolted to a stop and turned to face her. "How many you got?" she asked. Then she was silent and appeared to wonder if she had asked the wrong question. "Three boys. That's my grandchild yonder." Henrietta looked at the single white-blond head that bobbed among her brood. She dropped the subject of family. "You ever been to the ocean before?"

"Nawp," Mollie said bluntly.

"First time I went, I was gone ten days to Wilmington. We

done more meanness than you ever seen. We left our troubles behind. Aunt Sallie got in the revolving door at Asheville and wouldn't git out, and we had to go in and push her out. She got in the line in the cafeteria and ate her food as she went down the line and come to the end and asked the lady, 'What I owe you?' and didn't have a thing on her tray but empty plates. Aunt Sallie was always short-spoken. 'What I owe you?' We got settled back down, then I turned over my iced tea and we got tickled again.

"Grandpa wouldn't sleep in the hotel room. He slept out in his truck and chewed and spit all night long. We could hear him rolling down the window on the truck to spit. I was staying with Georgia Sarles, who was so precise, so dignified. Took her plate in her lap and ate so prissy. Wrapped her false teeth up in a hanky. I scraped the wall and told her a rat had got her teeth, so she slept with them under her pillow."

Henrietta giggled again. When Mollie dropped from the conversation, Henrietta began to talk of her family, her children; she laughed and said she sent them away one by one to decide which one to keep. She would want to live her past life over, in just the same way. "I think on the past for I don't know what the future will bring." She talked of her cooking, her "one-egg cake. Dewberries, three-quarter cup milk, sugar and this, that, and t'other to make a cake." Of cooking turnips, ". . . not right till they git warmed over, the more the cat walks through them, the better." Her biscuits, ". . . squeezed them out of her fist so many times they come off even. Dropped one on the floor onc't, marked it, and cooked it anyway, then forgot and slipped and ate it. Drank onc't out of a rusty can and worried for a week." Molly sat stone-faced.

A woman walked up and put her hand on Henrietta's shoulder. "I saw Mama up here talking your ear off," she said. "Mama, it's gitting too chilly for you."

Henrietta got up and hugged her daughter. "They're too goofy over me, but that's why my arms are hung by my side."

The woman helped the old lady into a coat she had brought, a coat that hung with the looseness of old age and a shrunken body. Before Henrietta left, her arm around her daughter's waist to steady herself, she sang a little song:

"I've no wife to bother my life,
No lover to prove untrue,
I'll ne'er lie down with a tear in my eye,
And I'll paddle my own canoe."

"She's right about that," Mollie said suddenly when they were out of earshot.

"About what, Mollie?"

"That old woman talk your ear off." Mollie was looking at Ola Mae, who had started to walk up the steps to the pier. The family was gathering around the picnic table by their camper. One of the young women in the group had given Henrietta a baby to hold while she set the table. People began to collect around the tiny old woman, an army of kin to protect and care for her.

"They made me give it back," Ola Mae said, pouting as she climbed on the bench beside me.

"You had no business taking what wont yourn," Mollie said sharply.

"She give it to me. I never took it."

After a moment I realized they were talking about the shovel that Ola Mae had been playing with. They sat in silence on either side of me, a small and a slightly larger clump, their movement hardly discernible. I stood and suggested we go to the motel room where it was warmer. I would go to a take-out place and get some fish and chips for dinner.

I left Mollie and Ola Mae in front of the TV. When I got back, Mollie had not moved from the chair beside the bed. I expected some response to the room, but all she said was, "Looks like them rooms on the TV." Ola Mae sat on the bed eating fries and wearing the paper circle from the toilet seat around her neck. She asked me to read it to her, "Sanitized for your Safety"; then I had to explain what it meant:

"The government says they have to clean the toilet when new people use the room because there may be germs." Ola Mae couldn't understand that other people had lived in the room before. Mollie snapped, "No room in the world ain't been lived in before and won't be lived in again."

"I think we're the first ones," Ola Mae insisted, "because the soap is still wrapped up."

Ola Mae ran the tub deep with hot water and opened three packages of soap. Afterwards I could still see rust around her ears, though her hair was damp from the bath.

They both ate well and were ready to go to sleep by nine o'clock. Ola Mae teased Mollie because she forgot to flush the toilet, but it was as if Mollie never heard her as she rolled her stockings and threw her dress over a chair before slipping under the covers. I was surprised that I was sleepy too. I was afraid that the bed choice was going to be another crisis, but Ola Mae crawled in beside Mollie, who had her back to us and had already started to snore. I went to sleep with Ola Mae rustling her paper necklace, repeating over and over, "Shut up, Grandma. Shut up, Grandma."

We were on the beach early the next morning, walking until we left the cottages and motels behind. The light was silver across the tide pools, and the water took on the ice-yellow look of a winter ocean. We wore our coats as we walked down the sand, but soon Ola Mae was running, warming up and shedding hers over my arm. She was in the thin edge of the water with her shoes and socks on. It didn't take Ola Mae long to discover the pattern of the tiny clams that tumbled back with the surf. She dug them up, finding their hiding places by the little tail they left sifting through the moving water. She washed the sand away from their colored shells and tossed them out of reach of the protective water. The gulls and pipers dropped down and began to split the shells apart while she laughed and tried to get Mollie's attention. I was still trying to break Mollie's depression.

"Tell me the truth, Mollie. What did you think of the ocean the first time you saw it yesterday? You didn't say a word."

"I thought it was bigger than the French Broad," she said flatly, then added quickly, "Them was tasty fish. And the room you got us was real nice. I stayed in a boarding house onc't in Louisville and it wont near so nice."

"That's not what I meant, Mollie. I'm not trying to pull thanks out of you for my gesture," I said, getting a little exasperated. "I just wondered what you thought of something you'd never seen before. I remember how I felt when I first saw foreign countries and how different they were from what I was used to, that's all."

"Ain't no new left, Jean," she said strangely.

"Of course there's new left. There's new left until your dying day."

"I seen enough of this world to last me."

"What about Ola Mae? A month ago you didn't know you'd have a little girl to raise. You thought your mothering was over with your own, and now you have to do it again. Ola Mae's new, and the first girl you've ever had. That little life right out there has nobody to count on but you." I think I said too much to Mollie too fast, but I had held in my thoughts all weekend.

"No new left," she said stubbornly. "It's been there all the time with no way of my gitting to it. The Bible says that the ocean is older than Time hisself. The Judgment came to Noah with water. It could come agin and suck us off'n the world we setting on. The winds could puff up and blow us right off'n it. It's waiting all the time."

"Don't try to pull me off what we were talking about. You don't think about that Bible stuff. What about Ola Mae?"

"I'm here, I reckon. And that's 'bout it."

Ola Mae ran up to me with a tiny claw in her hand. "What's that?" she asked me.

"It's what's left of a fiddler crab. A sea gull ate him."

"Ugh!" She threw it down and stepped on it in the sand.

"Well, what did you think it was?" Mollie said angrily. "You find a foot by the side of the road and you gonna come running up and ask me what a fine thing you found? It's dead as a doorknob, et up. All of it worth eating. You see those fat white birds?" Mollie pointed at the birds that jabbered around the clams Ola Mae had tossed up. "They could git you in their mouth, they eat you up quick as that little crab."

For a moment Ola Mae looked like she might cry, but soon she grimaced and stuck out her tongue at Mollie. She laughed and ran into the birds, scattering them crying out over the water. She was too old and too big to be scared by birds.

"We better be gitting on back," Mollie started to mumble. "I want to be gitting back in time to shet up my hen house so the foxes don't gobble 'em up."

240

Mollie had lost a whole night. While she slept on the clean sheets in the motel, her hen house was open to the foxes for a whole night. This time by the ocean was no more than a short distraction from her life, which would end in Rocky Gap. I thought it would be more, but I guess I didn't know her as well as I thought I did. As we walked back to the motel to collect our things, a little boy wobbled towards us, his pants down around his knees. Ola Mae was laughing and pointing at his penis, when the child's mother caught him and pulled up his pants.

"Bird's gonna peck your worm off," she cried and hid behind me when the little boy began to cry.

\* \* \*

*I got a letter yesterday from Washington. I guess it didn't surprise me to find out my father knew what he was talking about. The Appalachian Corps program will be terminated this summer. They will help locate other projects for the workers whenever possible. The whole thing failed; I was just one small part of it. Maybe I never had a chance. But I don't feel it was a total failure; the art classes are still attended and I had designed a summer curriculum and written for speakers to come from outside. I'll have to tell them about the end of the project.*

*And Mollie. Here only since last fall, and I feel as if I've known her all my life. I know she has come to depend on me to take her places, though she doesn't need my company now. What Mollie said to me about herself and Ola Mae, "I'm here, I reckon. And that's 'bout it." She feels like a living shell with nothing inside that is worth giving the child, because the child has convinced her that she doesn't want it. All those years of experience. But the child wants the new, what she can reach out and grab. The rest is just words.*

*Last night when I cut out the lights and went to bed, I felt very tired from nothing in particular. When I was under the covers, my body felt strangely small. With my head under too, breathing the warm air my body made, I felt like the little canary bird Mollie told me they kept in the mine. If I fell off my perch, then the people would know to get out and send no one else in. Maybe I was feeling eight months' work for nothing. I counted the months; I came in September and now it was April, almost as*

*long as a school year. I never knew what it was like to work and
get nothing, not even a certificate.*

*I wasn't consciously crying, but when I turned my head side-
ways, tears came out the corners of my eyes. The sensation of the
hot tears that soon turned cold and stiff was pleasant. I remembered having to pee when I was a little girl and being afraid to
put my feet over the side because the monster would grab my
legs. Then the bed would be warm, like rolling through the sand
at the beach, and it would be a while before I woke up wet and
cold, and cried.*

\* \* \*

A sweet taste of revenge for me two days after we got back
from the ocean. When I went by Leon's cage, even though his
back was to me, I knew that he was playing with himself, an
occupation that had started to fill much of his time. He was
laughing and coughing. I looked away from him and saw the
wrappings from a package that the postmaster had given me to
deliver to Leon, a package addressed to Leon Farris, Rocky
Gap, N.C., Jailhouse. When Leon spun around on his stool, I
saw what he had gotten in the plain brown wrapper. On his
penis he wore a devil, a red devil rubber with a long tongue. He
wiggled it at me when he saw me looking, so I laughed at him,
maybe because seeing the devil wasn't as shocking as what I'd
expected. He enjoyed my laughter. His bloodshot eyes were
open so wide they appeared to have an unusual amount of
white in them. It was hard to look at any part of Leon.

Later in the afternoon, Mildred came bursting into my office,
her fat red face swollen and wet.

"What seems to be after you, Mildred?"

"That Leon," she wheezed. "That filthy Leon. I went in to
pick up the garbage he throwed on the floor. Oh, I don't want to
talk about it."

I turned back to my work. I knew that Mildred did want to
talk about it. I couldn't hide my hostile feelings towards her
and didn't want to.

"Miss Fitzgerald, he has a head on his thing," she said
finally.

"What thing, Mildred?"

She pointed towards her own fat crotch. "His thing. His dick has a head on it."

"Now, Mildred. Don't you think you're letting your imagination run away from you? It's dark in Leon's cell. Maybe you imagined you saw a head on it. Maybe you never looked closely at a thing before. What were you doing looking down there anyway?" I'd have given anything if Clara could see this.

"I'm not imagining things," she bellowed. "I have a husband, Miss Fitzgerald. I know what a dick looks like. A married woman has a right to know. Leon's dick has a head with a long tongue." Then she whispered, "I believe it was a devil head."

"Maybe you ought to bring that up in church, Mildred. Tell the preacher that you saw the devil coming out of Leon's pants."

"Oh, no. Oh, no, I couldn't tell him that. I'd be so ashamed. What would the preacher think? Seeing the devil coming out of a man's pants. Sakes alive. Oh, no." Her words were breathless now, almost incoherent, as she tried to reason aloud. She put my wastebasket down and it rocked until I steadied it with my foot. "I'll ask the Lord what to do. The devil. The Lord was speaking to me. It was a vision. The Lord is telling me that sex is the work of the devil. I seen the devil. I seen the devil."

I couldn't wait to tell Mollie. It was frustrating when something like that happened and there wasn't anyone around for me to tell. That was a sad count of my friends in Rocky Gap. If Mildred's poor husband could possibly have any desire left, I think he was about to be told to keep his devil in his pants.

When I got ready to leave, I glanced in at Leon. His devil head was on the table. He had put his penis back inside his pants, but had not zipped his fly. Mildred was gone. "Leon, you really gave old Mildred a scare."

Leon began to giggle and got strangled. His upper lip was shiny with mucus. "You did. I mean it. She came in my office and told me she had seen the devil." Leon got so hysterical he fell back on his cot. I thought maybe I had done the wrong thing, like encouraging a bad child. But it made him happy. That devil probably cost him a bottle of whiskey. I cut off his laughter as I shut the door of the building.

*   *   *

*The wind is blowing tonight, and things are banging on my roof again, sticks that go across the tin like little feet. The noise has increased, so it must have started to rain. I walked through a spider web across my door this morning. Mollie says it's bad luck to break it before sunrise, but the light had already started to come through the trees. I'm glad it was after sunrise; in the dark is when a web is scary.*

*I almost went to Clara's tonight, but I feel guilty not working through the week, even if no one cares anymore. Clara is still trying to get me to come to Hedgerow. I must admit it looks more interesting now. I think that at first she alarmed me about this place. Then I thought about it and decided we were two different people. I have never had the physical fear for my body that Clara has. She was always afraid of the sun or of doing athletic things because the thought of physical pain terrified her. I used to point my toes hard so I could get cramps in my calves. Maybe I'm a masochist. But when I pointed my toes, I was in control of my pain. I really don't think I know what pain is. Even Mollie's pain seems more like a story, like words, than reality.*

*I've been writing more lately and reading what I've written. It is a strange sensation to be thinking about no one's work but my own. That couldn't have affected the real writers; they didn't constantly need comparison because they knew what they were after. What has changed in my work is that the people I try to write about are closer to real people I know in Rocky Gap. Maybe that's a big change, from imaginary suffering to real. Even though I could never have any effect on them, I feel as if I know the people who speak on my journal pages. I'm almost afraid to admit it, but I think my work has improved. At least I have some subject matter.*

*   *   *

On Tuesday night I heard someone in my yard, someone yelling. I could see the figure in the moonlight. It was Leon. I opened the door enough to talk. "Leon, what in the world are you doing up here at night? You're getting soaking wet. Get out of here and get back into town."

He fell down in the yard as if my words had blasted him to the ground. He began to mumble, "Dragon. Got a dragon."

"You what? Leon, I said get back to town. How did you get out here? Who brought you?"

"Thumb a ride."

"Are you sure? Are you sure that your brother, Dwayne, didn't bring you? Is Dwayne with you, Leon?" I was suddenly afraid and shut the door when Leon began to giggle instead of trying to answer me. What would I have done if he'd said yes? What if Dwayne sent him to get me outside? I bolted the door and slid a chair against it. I went to the back door and dropped the floor lock, when I heard Leon banging around on the porch. When I turned on the porch light, it flashed on and out. The bulb burned out as the cold rain hit it. I could see Leon in the thin light from the window, on the floor of the porch. His clothes were dark and wet. He was tossing around and hitting the chairs, having some kind of fit. He was between me and my car. If he crawled off the porch, I would dash for my car. But soon he was quiet.

I stood behind the glass of the front window and yelled at him again, "Leon, you get out of here. You get back down to the highway and find another ride back into town." I heard my own voice loud in my house. What if he decided to break the glass? He thrashed around a while longer. I went to the kitchen to do the dishes, hoping he would leave if he thought I was ignoring him. When I went back to the window, I saw that the porch was empty. The rain had stopped. He must have waited for it to stop, then gone back down the driveway, though I wasn't sure he could walk. It hadn't been out of the thirties all day, and the rain had been mixed with sleet. Mollie told me she had seen many a frozen Easter Sunday in those hills. I walked onto the porch and felt the ice under my shoes. In the moonlight I could see the first slow-moving flakes of snow.

I wondered who would give that drunk a ride, who would let a wet, smelly drunk in his car. I had seem him that day a long way outside of town in a ditch looking for bottles. I wondered if Dwayne wasn't out there somewhere, if he was putting Leon up to this, trying to get me out of my house. I rushed back inside and bolted the door again. That afternoon when I had told

Mollie about Leon's devil, she laughed, but she told me not to make anything of him because I didn't know what went on in his head. She was right. I never would have dreamed he would come to my house.

\*   \*   \*

Leon . . .

*Old Mildred seen the devil. She wont so fat and ugly I poke my devil up in her. Wait till she sees the other one. I'm saving it. Got a dragon breathing fiar. Set a fiar in her old pussy.*

*Naw sir. Not if she give it to me. Not if she throwed up her skirts and sprattled her legs and say it was free for the taking. Not that ugly Mildred. I go see that Jean. Give her a scare. Dwayne say lean on her. All you got to do is lean on a woman. Git her so skeert she git outa town. I show her my dragon. I go up to her house and show her my dragon.*

\*   \*   \*

That night after Leon left, I watched TV until the eleven o'clock news was over, then I went to bed. It had been quiet outside for hours. I had opened the front door a crack and shined my flashlight across the yard, but I didn't see Leon. The thin snow had stopped falling, the air was clean and cold. Then I started to believe that he might have come on his own. I hoped he could get back to town. It was a nasty night, so few people would be out.

The next morning I got ready to go to work and started down the driveway, the snow already melting and falling with splashes on my car. The sky was a bright blue. Near the end of the driveway beside the highway was Leon, face down and still, his back covered with snow. I drove up on the bank and around him and stopped. I walked to him and called his name. He didn't move. I couldn't tell if he had been hit by a car. I didn't see any blood on him. I started to touch him, but I couldn't make myself. His body was too cold to melt the snow on his back. Leon had made it no further than the highway. Why did I think he could have made it back? That was so stupid. No one took care of Leon.

"Leon, I never knew that you weren't safe. I didn't know."

246

I left him and went to the small hospital on Main Street to report it. I said I didn't know his condition when I told the man who left with the pickup truck ambulance, but there was no doubt in my mind. I knew that Leon was dead and that I had let him die in the night.

Mildred was in my office with me. There was no one else left. I couldn't go to the funeral. Even the people who never had a kind word for Leon were there, because all the stores were closed. I didn't go because I had no feelings — I didn't go because I didn't know if I could cope with the feelings I had. I didn't want to listen to Mildred, but I felt cornered behind my desk as she shook my wastebasket into her canvas bag long after it was empty.

"See what I told you. Acted like Mildred Persons didn't have good sense. I told you I seen the devil on that man. The devil possessed his body and now he's gone to hell. That was a evil man, Leon Farris. People laugh at him, old drunk Leon, the funny man. The devil got his due."

I couldn't be silent. "He wasn't an evil man, Mildred. He was just a pitiful old drunk whose life must have been so unfortunate when he was younger that he gave in to alcohol. He died of exposure. It had nothing to do with the devil."

"What you know about the devil, Miss Fitzgerald? Nothing you learnt in church, I tell you. And about evil. Not evil, huh? Killing's evil, ain't it? Leon Farris killed a man, him and the rest of them." She started to leave then, just when she knew she had my interest.

"Who did he kill, Mildred?" I asked, standing up.

She rushed out the door, then cracked it and said, "Folks who come here messing in something wont none of their concern." She shut the door hard and left.

\* \* \*

Leon . . .

*Just lean on this one Dwayne say to me. Lean and push ever so easy. We got her running and keep your pants hitched up 'fore they send you off and put you where there's a lock on the door* and throw away the key. That's me he's meaning there but I made her take notice walk by so high and mighty miss too good ain't got the time of day hee hee. They betta not put no lock on my door and throw away no key. Betta watch out. Lean on her woman not like a man.

That man so dead. Dwayne never said we gonna kill him. Dwayne kill another man onc't in a fight and git off on self-defense shouldn't have started it if he couldn't finish. Can't pee git off the pot. Dwayne has a knife with a button hide it in your hand punch in the stomach mash the button dead as a doorknocker just like that. Made me cry a grown man telling me he was gonna stick my gizzard feed it to the hogs worse yet my tallywack if I drunk up his whiskey again.

Dwayne sent me up close carrying the jar of gasoline and I spilt it on my hand burn myself good but oh not so good as that man. Dwayne say you wanted one this one is yours up close and throw it in the window one side got the screen tore off 'cause Dwayne check he always think got to think for both of us he say and we hit the roof soon as we hear the busted glass and you run as hard as you can go back to the woods. It didn't go so fast up top. I run and fell down and cut my hand and it started to burning and I thought it would git me but it didn't go too fast 'cause there was a woman and three children on the porch in white clothes like angels 'fore it went woof! Just like that woof! And a yeller light come on in ever window at onc't. Lighted up the trees and it was the middle of the night like a lightning bolt didn't go out. Dwayne told me I done that and he and Hickman made me go off with them and I didn't git to watch a bit of it.

Didn't nobody come to put it out and it started into rain 'fore we was back to the road but they say that lady couldn't drive her car 'cause she went licking split out and left her keys and she went walking to another house with those children and left him there. She left him there is the reason he died but Dwayne say I could take credit for killing him if I wanted to I didn't want. Kermit on the rescue truck say he look like barbecue meat not a stitch on either burnt off or didn't sleep in nothing I don't want no credit.

Say this is Leon Farris and put his name on that statue at five *points in the space on the statue with the gun and the hat that look like a slop jar. This is Leon Farris kill more Japs than any other man in Olley County and when he goes they keep a flag on his grave. Same thing Dwayne say just as good as killing Japs killing Commies when they let them git inside the good old U. S. of A. Only he wont no Jap had yeller hair and a little girl with yeller hair look like a angel in a white dress. Dwayne always skeered I was gonna tell call me chicken Leon Farris not chicken shit. I told him I didn't tell. I did tell Sheriff Whitcomb. I made him laugh and say Leon Farris' name go right on that statue downtown but I look and it wont there. He was telling me a tale he didn't believe I did it I did it. Keep a flag on my grave . . .*

I think there have been a more than ordinary number of noises outside tonight. Probably because of the wind and because the seasons are changing. Tuesday night's snow was gone before noon. Winter is breaking finally. I turned the sound on the TV off. I watched the people, all the overacting on the commercials. You can make people look foolish by turning off the sound. I think it makes me feel good to sit back and watch other people looking foolish. With no sound and when I write by hand instead of at the typewriter, I hear noises like sticks being broken underfoot. Mollie's devil sounds, owls, and chains. Seven bangs on the roof is supposed to indicate something in particular, but I don't count them or remember what it means. There are animals out there, dogs and wild animals, but tonight I feel as if everything in the woods is crawling towards my house, that I couldn't go the distance between my front door and my car safely, like the shallow walk from the water to the shore when I was caught in the rip tide at Cape Hatteras. Sam is never coming back. I must feel like a woman whose lover left her without a note. I would rather have gotten the chance to tell him goodbye and that I love him. Anything short of seeing him dead or in pain is better than this.

I have closed all the shades so no one can watch inside, but that means I can't see out. It is completely black out there; the trees here are too thick to let the moonlight through on a cloudy night. I know I have heard car doors slam. Maybe the air is fresher tonight and sounds go farther. But I know I have heard car doors and I think I have heard car wheels spinning in the mud. There seem to have been a more than ordinary number of car sounds, as if people were coming to a meeting. Maybe a Klan meeting near here. I got a flier under my office door; I don't remember if it was to be tonight. I wouldn't go even out of curiosity anymore. I don't want any part of them.

I hear voices too. Maybe that is the TV, a little sound creeping through, though I have turned the button all the way down. I would turn it off, but it and the hum of my refrigerator would be the only noise in here, and the gurgle of the commode. I have the big fat face of Hoss Cartwright on the screen, a giant cowboy who smiles kindly and picks up people and breaks them in half. I wish I had Hoss Cartwright on my side, sitting here on the sofa with me saying, "Don't you worry none, Miss Jean. Them fellows bother you, I knock their heads together." Or Juleous would drive up in Grandfather Fitzgerald's black Cadillac and say, "Miss Jean, Mr. Fitzgerald asked that I fetch you."

But I am not being taken care of, no Hoss, no Juleous. I think if I were a man, I wouldn't be afraid right now just because I was a man. But his sex didn't save the union man. Or the snake preacher. Or Leon. Today I saw Dwayne, Leon's brother, talking to Sheriff Whitcomb when I left my office for lunch. He looked strange in a coat and tie for Leon's funeral. I hadn't spoken to him since he threatened me. I told him I was sorry about Leon. He said I should have let him in my house. He said, "Leon never hurt nobody." I felt a sting inside my chest as I turned away. You killed him, Dwayne, as much as me. You scared me.

Later I saw Dwayne walking around my car. He put a sticker on it. I read it through the glass when I got in to drive home, written in red: "You are being watched by the Knights of the Ku Klux Klan." A printed sticker with stickum on it. It is still on my car, but I plan to remove it with a razor blade, because it bothers me while I drive, bothers my vision, I mean. They must use the money they take up at the meetings to buy stickers with stickum. The printer must be on their side too. Women and children give that money too, I saw them. What is his last name, Dwayne Farris. Of course. Same as Leon. He is just one. There are hundreds of carbon copies down at the mill.

I wish it would rain on them if they're out there tonight, let

250

*the know it isn't the night to firebomb my house. I think they've all forgotten about me. After the TV goes off, there will be five hours before I can see if people are between the trees, watching my house. When you are asleep, the night doesn't seem like a long time.*

*If tomorrow comes, I'm going to Hedgerow to see Clara. I have to stay through tonight. To leave tonight, walk through that door now, would tear my brain to pieces. If I made it to my car, I would race over the border of Olley County and check into a motel. But my brain would be apart by then. I need the daylight. I've done what I used to say I liked to do, frightened myself one place so I would feel better about the secure place I returned to.*

*For a little while maybe, I'd even like to sit on the white couch in Raleigh, drinking a daiquiri, in the white sitting room, where nothing is out of place. Nothing is worn or dirty. I can touch a cold marble table, soft velvet pillow, smell the faint odor of fresh flowers from the garden. Tildie would be fixing me her special shrimp salad, making noises as she moved about the kitchen, whistling like a hen shifting her fat body around on her eggs. At dinner I could tell my father the whole story, if I could find the nerve. He would say I handled it badly, but he wouldn't blame me for Leon. Nor would Clara. Tildie doesn't approve of alcohol; she still believes her sister had been drinking when she burned herself to death. Mollie. Mollie and Ola Mae. Mollie is ruined. I have no reason to stay here. I've got to go.*

*When I'm asleep, I think that I am in another place, not here in this musty-smelling bed in a house in the woods. When I fall asleep, I will float away where no one can reach me to hurt me before the night ends.*

\* \* \*